Lenin Must Be Stopped!

Bauer pushed his chair back from the table. "You want me to kill him?"

"How else can we stop him?" Churchill demanded. "Lash him to a lamppost?"

"It's not my kind of operation."

"Nonsense, Bauer," Churchill retorted. "You've been involved in any number of operations like this. You confirmed that yourself—Cuba, Mexico, Mongolia. Don't deny it. You have every right to be proud."

"I'm not an assassin."

"You've killed men before."

"And look where it got me."

Churchill jabbed his cigar toward the American. "Don't be so bloody difficult. Lenin's our common enemy. And if he gets back to Russia, he'll be worth an entire division. Perhaps two. If Russia defects, it may cost us the war!"

Bauer drank his brandy in silence.

Churchill tilted his head forward slightly and peered at the American from under his brows. "I am offering you an opportunity few men ever get—to do something noble for your country."

"I've already done my share of noble deeds for my country. And my country told me to go to hell."

SEVEN DAYS
TO
PETROGRAD

A NOVEL BY

TOM HYMAN

BANTAM BOOKS
NEW YORK · TORONTO · LONDON · SYDNEY · AUCKLAND

SEVEN DAYS TO PETROGRAD

*A Bantam Book / published by arrangement with
Viking Penguin Inc.*

PRINTING HISTORY
Viking Penguin edition published February 1988

Bantam edition / July 1989

*Bantam Books are published by Bantam Books, a division of Bantam Doubleday
Dell Publishing Group, Inc. Its trademark, consisting of the words "Bantam
Books" and the portrayal of a rooster, is Registered in U.S. Patent and
Trademark Office and in other countries. Marca Registrada. Bantam Books,
666 Fifth Avenue, New York, New York 10103.*

PRINTED IN THE UNITED STATES OF AMERICA

O   0 9 8 7 6 5 4 3 2 1

TO CLYDE TAYLOR

AUTHOR'S NOTE

Shortly after the outbreak of World War I, the czar's government changed the name of Russia's capital city from St. Petersburg to Petrograd, on the theory that the older name sounded too German.

Changing the name officially had little immediate effect on those living outside Russia, however. During the war years almost everyone—even the Bolsheviks in exile in Switzerland—continued to refer to the city, built by Peter the Great in the early 1700s, as St. Petersburg (or simply Petersburg, or even "Peter").

For that reason, I've employed both usages, to reflect as accurately as possible the practices of the time. Any confusion this causes the reader is certainly unintentional.

Beyond the events covered by this story, the city underwent yet another name change. In 1924, the year of Lenin's death, it became Leningrad.

So far, that one has stuck.

PRINCIPAL
PARTICIPANTS

AMERICAN

Harry Bauer, American intelligence agent
Woodrow Wilson, President of the United States
Colonel Edward House, adviser to President Wilson
James C. McNally, American consul in Zurich
P. T. Berg, vice-consul, American Embassy, Stockholm

ENGLISH

Arthur J. Balfour, foreign minister
Sir Mansfield Cumming,
head of MI1c, British Secret Service
Winston Churchill, former first lord of the Admiralty
James C. Bryce, ambassador to the United States
Nigel De Grey, cryptanalyst for Room 40
Lieutenant Chase, officer at Tornio border crossing

GERMAN

Arthur Zimmermann, foreign secretary
Captain Kurt von Planetz, head of train guard detail
Lieutenant Heinz von Buhring, part of train guard detail
Parvus (Alexander Helphand), socialist entrepreneur
Baron Gisbert von Romberg, ambassador to Switzerland

LENIN'S PARTY

Lenin (Vladimir Ilyich Ulyanov), Russian political exile
Nadezhda (Nadya) Krupskaya, Lenin's wife
Karl Radek, Austrian Bolshevik
Grigory Zinoviev, Lenin's chief adviser
Zina Zinovieva, Zinoviev's wife
Ivan Morozov, Lenin's bodyguard
Fritz Platten, Swiss socialist and guide for Lenin's party
Inessa Armand, close friend of Lenin's

RUSSIAN

B. K. Nikitin, head of Russian counterintelligence
Mitya, Uzbek assassin

SWISS

Oskar Blum, Bundist revolutionary

THURSDAY
JULY 20, 1961

"How did he die?" the director asked.

Jim Adams, the CIA's public affairs officer, shrugged. "The best way. At home in bed. Of old age. He was eighty-one."

Director Dulles scratched a forefinger against his snow-white moustache thoughtfully. "Did you have any trouble with the family?"

Adams shook his head emphatically. He was a small man, and he tended to compensate for it with exaggerated gestures. "Not at all. His widow, Ingrid, was very cooperative. After I explained our concerns, she let me go through everything. She's Swedish, by the way, and much younger than he was. Still pretty good-looking, in fact."

Dulles wasn't interested in the widow. "What do you mean by everything?"

"His study. Boxes in the attic. Even a vault in the basement. He was a multimillionaire, did you know that? You ought to see the place he has up there. Huge house. Hundreds of acres." Adams cleared away the clutter from a corner of the director's desk and hefted a black leather attaché case onto it. He snapped open the lid, withdrew a thick manila envelope and handed it across to Dulles. "This is everything that seemed relevant."

The director opened the envelope and dumped the contents onto his desk—a stack of old passports, a reel of audiotape, a folded piece of stationery, and a large ringed notebook about two inches thick.

"Your instructions were a little vague," Adams added, in defense of the odd collection of items spilling from the envelope.

Dulles picked up the letter first. The stationery was browned at the edges and so brittle with age that it cracked along the folds as he opened it.

There was a single page, embossed at the top with the seal of the Imperial German Government. The text of the letter was handwritten in German. The director adjusted his wire-rimmed spectacles and struggled through it:

> Berlin, 4 April, 1917
> Dear Ulyanov,
> I presume to make the following request of you, in secret and entirely outside the channels of our agreement. I urge that you send a confidential memo to Wilson assuring him that your sympathies lie entirely with the Allied cause, and against Germany. Should you come to power, no separate peace, as is widely believed, and so forth. I trust you see the wisdom behind this. It will help allay the suspicions that will inevitably arise that you have entered into an agreement with us. I believe this will be very much to your benefit, and trust you will agree. If you choose to ignore it, however, you have my solemn promise that it will not affect our arrangement in any way.
>
> Most humbly yours,
> A. Zimmermann

Astonished, Dulles read the letter through several times. The writer was apparently Foreign Secretary Arthur Zimmermann, a top official in the kaiser's government during World War I. And the addressee was clearly Vladimir Ilyich Ulyanov—Lenin.

The director carefully refolded the document and placed it on the desk. "Can this be genuine? How in the world could Bauer have come into possession of it?"

Adams laughed. "After you've read that notebook, nothing will surprise you."

The director raised the notebook's blue cover cautiously at the corner, as if he expected something unpleasant to jump out at him. He riffled through several pages. They were covered, top to bottom, margin to margin, with a bold, precise handwriting. "They don't teach penmanship like that anymore, do they? What are your impressions of it?"

"Normally I'd be inclined not to believe a word of it."

Dulles smiled. "Why is that?"

Adams twisted uncomfortably in his chair. "Well, it's just so damned incredible, that's all. And the way it's written. It's in a loose narrative form, as if he had been trying to write a novel. No proof, no documents. Outside of that letter. A lot of the information in it would have been impossible for him to have known. At least at the time. But . . ."

Dulles waited, his watery blue eyes bearing in on his public affairs officer with that characteristic concentrated attention that so often unnerved those who worked for him.

Adams threw out his hands in a gesture of defeat. "I keep asking myself, if it didn't happen, why would he have made it up? And as improbable as it is, I doubt I could disprove one damned word of it. And I wrote my master's thesis on the Russian Revolution. I mean, I know that subject cold, and everything Bauer mentions that I know anything about is accurate. And the rest simply can't be verified. All the participants are dead, as far as I know—except for Churchill, and he's practically senile. And the governments involved must have clamped a secrecy lid on this so tight you couldn't dynamite it open. Even our government. And you can't blame them. The reasons are certainly there. It's maddening."

Dulles held up the reel of recording tape. "What's this?"

Adams blushed slightly. "Well, they told me there was quite a scene the night Harry Bauer died. All his relatives were there—he has two daughters, a son, and a bunch of grandchildren. One of them taped his final words. He jumped up in bed, his wife said, just before he died, and hollered out something. None of those who heard it could make heads or tails out of it. Anyway, she gave the tape to me, hoping we might be able to decipher it. She said it was only a few words, and she thought it might be in Spanish or Italian. I haven't listened to it."

The director slipped the tape, the passports, the notebook, and the letter back into the manila envelope. "I have to swear you to secrecy on this," he said.

Adams nodded solemnly. "Of course."

Dulles removed his glasses and wiped his eyes. "I mean complete secrecy. From everyone. Even inside the Company."

Adams gave his word and stood up to leave. "Did you know Harry Bauer, sir?"

Dulles didn't answer right away. He picked up his pipe, filled it from the humidor on his desk, then tamped the tobacco down into the bowl with his thumb. "I never met him. I was in Bern at the time, not Zurich. I heard a lot about him, though."

"He must have been something."

Dulles stuck the pipe in his mouth and patted his pocket for his lighter. "I guess he was," he replied from between clenched teeth.

Adams lingered by the office door, hoping the director might tell him more. "He once played major league baseball," he said. "Did you know that?"

Dulles's eyebrows shot up in surprise. "I didn't," he admitted.

Adams swung his right arm forward, throwing an imaginary baseball. "He pitched for the Phillies. Two seasons. Nineteen two and three. Won forty-eight games, lost nine. I looked it up. Then he blew his career. Some dumb argument with the team's owner. You ask me, I think Harry Bauer was a little crazy."

Dulles laughed gently. "He did have a reputation. Some problem with accepting authority, as I recall."

Adams slapped a hand against the doorjamb in exasperation. "The son of a bitch could have changed the entire course of modern history. I just don't understand why he did what he did. I just don't understand it at all."

MONDAY
MARCH 26, 1917

BERLIN, GERMANY

The big, gleaming black Hispano-Suiza sedan entered the imperial capital at twilight. It came in from the northeast and crossed through the city's heart at a furious rate of speed, its deep-throated exhaust echoing self-importantly through the wide boulevards. In another time its urgent haste would have drawn the stares of the curious, but by the spring of 1917, Berliners were no longer curious people.

The motorcar roared past the immense stone rectangle of the Royal Palace and the columned porticos of the Altes Museum and entered the spacious prospects of Unter den Linden. The trees of the capital's proudest avenue were still, in March, bare of leaves, and wartime shortages had dimmed its bright lights and thinned its once dense traffic to a scattering of bicycles and horse-drawn carts. The long, magnificent vista of buildings—the Arsenal, the Crown Prince's Palace, the Opera House, the Kaisergallerie—stood ghostlike and forbidding in the chilly evening air. Alfred Walterspiel's once popular Restaurant Hiller, at Number 62, was empty, and the famous Café Bauer, at the corner of the Friedrichstrasse, was closed. Only the Hotel Bristol and the Adlon, near the Brandenburg Gate, showed any activity. A small cluster of taxicabs huddled at their awnings.

Just before the Pariser Platz, the Hispano-Suiza swung left onto the Wilhelmstrasse, and passed the high, gray-walled

Renaissance fortresses that housed the wartime government
of Imperial Germany. The brass head lamps bounced pale
light along the cobblestones, illuminating small swirls of de-
bris caught up by the wind. At the Vosstrasse the automobile turned left again and braked to a halt before the massive
gate of the Reichschancellery. Two uniformed guards stepped
from the shadows, saluted smartly, and pushed open the
gate. The motorcar rumbled through into the courtyard beyond.

The vehicle crossed the yard and stopped again by a small
side entrance to the rearmost building, nearly obscured behind thick shrubbery. The chauffeur jumped out and opened
the rear door. A grossly fat man in his mid-forties stepped
down from the back seat, pressing his bowler to his head and
clutching a gold-headed walking stick out at arm's length to
maintain his balance.

The man, known by the ironic pseudonym Parvus, was an
extraordinary figure by anyone's standards. Christened Alexander Helphand in Copenhagen, Denmark, in 1875, Parvus
was a corpulent mound of conflicting passions. By turns flamboyant and secretive, assertive and withdrawn, jovial and
morose, his elephantine bulk harbored contradictions unusual
even by the confused standards of that tragic time. A Social
Democrat and brilliant Marxist intellectual, Parvus was also a
war profiteer with a thriving international black-market operation that traded in arms, medical supplies, food, and other
contraband.

From bowler to spats, his meticulously barbered and tai-
lored three hundred fifty pounds offered itself as a vulgar
parody of capitalist greed, an affront to the dignity of his
country of residence, which in the spring of 1917 was poised
on the edge of military and social collapse.

A guard opened the door for Parvus and escorted him
through a series of back corridors to a small foyer just off the
huge marble-floored diplomatic reception hall, where he was
greeted by an administrative assistant. From an interior pocket
of his Chesterfield he produced a gilt-edged calling card and
pressed it into the functionary's palm with a firm, conde-
scending flourish. "Foreign Secretary Zimmermann is expecting me," he intoned, tapping his walking stick sharply on the
floor and jutting his jaw forward to take up the slack on his
collection of double chins.

The administrative assistant bowed stiffly. "This way, Herr Helphand. The secretary will see you at once."

He escorted the Dane into a dark, high-ceilinged chamber burdened with extravagant moldings and ornate furniture. An ancient hunting tapestry covered a far wall, and a massive rug emblazoned with the red and black eagle insignia of the German Empire spanned the floor. It reminded the Dane of the ponderous anterooms he had once seen in the kaiser's three-hundred-room castle at Pless.

From behind a long mahogany desk the German foreign secretary, Arthur Zimmermann, emerged. A florid, red-haired bachelor in his mid-fifties with a luxuriant moustache and a hearty manner, he had only recently ascended to the post, and he seemed self-conscious among the trappings of his office. He bounded across the room to greet his guest. "My dear Parvus," he exclaimed, squeezing his visitor's fat fingers energetically. "I am most delighted to see you again."

Once in the presence of the foreign secretary, Parvus's demeanor underwent a subtle transformation. Despite Zimmermann's cordiality, the sheer intimidating power of his office cast a spell of servility over the Dane. "Your humble servant, Herr Secretary," he replied, his thick baritone bray hushed with deference.

"Sit down, sit down," Zimmermann commanded good-naturedly, gesturing toward a pair of overstuffed chairs across from his desk. "I have important business to discuss with you, my friend."

Parvus settled his weight into one of the chairs with a grateful sigh.

Brandy and cigars were produced, and the two men passed a few minutes exchanging pleasantries. Zimmermann had charm, Parvus reflected, listening to the lighthearted banter he was able to muster so effortlessly at the end of what must certainly have been another crisis-ridden day. That charm, in a governing aristocracy that lacked it so utterly, was both Zimmermann's strength and vulnerability. He was, if anything, too persuasive for his own good.

Zimmermann was an agile political creature—a chamelion, able to change colors to match the mood of those he sought to influence or to please. The Americans, for example. He had somehow charmed them into believing that he was a liberal, a moderating balance for the kaiser and his reactionary generals.

Parvus knew better. Zimmermann was more Hohenzollern than Wilhelm himself. How else could an untitled individual, the only important official without a "von" in front of his name, ever have risen so far among the formidable ranks of Prussian noblemen who formed Germany's ruling elite? Zimmermann held his job because the kaiser believed he was capable of fulfilling the kaiser's dreams of a *Pax Germania* better than anyone else in Germany. The moment "Der Hohe Herr" ceased to believe that, Zimmermann would be out on his dueling scar.

And His Highness already had powerful cause for doubt. Last month's Mexican telegram blunder had brutally diminished the foreign secretary's credibility. In his attempt to create a diversion to keep the United States out of the war—or at least delay its entry—he had instead outsmarted himself. Discovery of the secret telegram's contents had so enraged President Wilson that America was now certain to come in against Germany. And soon.

Zimmermann needed a brilliant coup to save his job, Parvus suspected. And that, Parvus also suspected, was why he had been so urgently summoned to this secret meeting in the Reichschancellery.

"Time is running out on Germany," Zimmermann announced, as if he meant at that very moment. "We must act boldly."

Parvus cleared his throat and looked up from his brandy glass, giving the foreign secretary his full attention.

"You remember the discussion we had in this same building two years ago?" Zimmermann asked. "When I was undersecretary?"

Parvus nodded. "Of course, Excellency."

Zimmermann rose from his chair and began pacing the room, hands clasped behind him, head tilted toward the rug. His mood was intense, preoccupied. "The spring of 1915," he said. "It seems as if decades have passed since then, but I remember our conversation well. We talked about Russia. You said you could deliver a revolution to us." Zimmermann ceased his pacing and looked squarely at Parvus. "We gave

you one million gold marks toward that aim, but you didn't
bring us a revolution. In point of fact, you brought us nothing."

Parvus's lower lip dropped open in astonishment. "But,
Herr Secretary, the revolution came just last week! The czar
is gone. I don't understand what you mean."

Zimmermann snorted. "My dear Parvus, the revolution
you couldn't bring us two years ago has now happened without your doing."

The Dane's jowls quivered with indignation. "Did you
forget the general strike? St. Petersburg, January 1916? We
paralyzed the entire capital of Russia for many days."

Zimmermann shook his head. "A few thousand workers out
on strike was not a revolution. And not worth a million
marks. I think you must agree."

Parvus drained his brandy glass. A drop dribbled onto his
chin. Irritated, he dabbed it off with his pocket-handkerchief.
This was the issue that had caused the rupture in his relations
with the kaiser's government. Perhaps he had promised too
much, but they had simply failed to understand the difficulties involved. That was the problem in dealing with the
Germans. They had tunnel vision. They never understood it
when things didn't work out exactly as they had planned
them to work out. And when their will was thwarted, they
were chronically unable to improvise their way out of the
messes they repeatedly made for themselves. When things
went wrong, the Germans simply fell to pieces. And blamed
it on someone else. You could count on it. That was what had
happened with the war. The kaiser had planned a triumphal
march through Paris for the spring of 1915, by which time,
according to the finest calculations of his generals, Germany
would certainly have won the war. Now, three years and a
million casualties later, the Prussians were a lot closer to
Götterdämmerung, than they were to *Pax Germania*.

"No, Excellency," Parvus admitted. "Perhaps not worth a
million marks. But at that time the man I was counting on
most heavily refused to cooperate. He regrets that now, I'm
sure."

"You mean Ulyanov?"

Parvus glanced sidelong at Zimmermann with a new appre-
ciation. Few people ever remembered Russian names. "Yes,
Ulyanov. Vladimir Ilyich."

"Refresh my mind about him."

Parvus held out his glass for a refill. "He's mentally tough, extraordinarily dedicated. He thinks clearly and possesses enormous powers of persuasion. His followers are a small minority, but they're militant and disciplined. And highly motivated. The talk in Petersburg is that they're rapidly growing in influence. Lenin is now the central figure in revolutionary politics."

"Lenin?" Zimmermann echoed.

Parvus nodded. "That's what he calls himself."

"Does it mean something heroic in Russian?"

"Not that I am aware. No doubt he adopted it simply to confuse the authorities. Code names and pseudonyms are a necessary part of the revolutionary game these days."

Zimmermann grinned. "Like 'Parvus'?"

The Dane blushed. He had chosen the name partly as a joke and partly as wishful thinking. In Latin "parvus" meant "thin."

"So what's become of this 'Lenin'?" Zimmermann asked.

Parvus shrugged. "He's still in exile. Stranded in Zurich."

Zimmermann's eyes widened in surprise. "It's difficult to see how his followers can be making much headway—with their leader completely removed from the scene."

Parvus started to reply, but the foreign secretary held up his palm. "If our government were secretly to offer support to one faction or another, do you still think that Ulyanov and his Bolsheviks would be our best choice?"

Parvus settled the brandy snifter on the side table by his chair and inhaled deeply to hide his elation. "Yes, Excellency. Positively."

"Would he cooperate? He refused before, you said."

"But the situation is far different now. I know he's desperate to return—before it's too late and the revolution falls into the hands of the reactionaries. But of course with the war on, all paths from Switzerland to Russia are blocked."

"We could find a way to get him back," Zimmermann said. "But would he still support a unilateral peace with Germany?"

"It's the formal position of the Bolshevik party—Russia must withdraw from the imperialists' war."

"But immediately?"

" 'Soldiers will stick their bayonets into the ground.' "

"What financial resources does he have?"

Parvus laughed, his large gut billowing inside his tightly buttoned vest like mercury in a balloon. "Pardon me, Herr Secretary. Practically speaking, he has none."

Zimmermann pressed a thumb and forefinger thoughtfully against the tips of his moustache. "Then we would have to finance him."

"Heavily," Parvus amended.

"How heavily?"

"To be certain of success, the Bolsheviks will need millions."

Zimmermann nodded solemnly. "Would Ulyanov accept money from Germany?"

"If the matter was handled discretely, I believe he would, Herr Secretary, for the reasons I have already stated. He's a stubborn man, as I have discovered to my own grief, but time is critical for him now. He knows that."

By discretely, Parvus meant that the money could be channeled secretly through his own established underground network of businessmen and banks in Denmark, Sweden, and Finland. Parvus did not have to spell that out, because he knew that Zimmermann understood it. He had used the Dane's network before. The foreign secretary also understood that Parvus would extract a substantial commission for the use of that network: 10 percent of the total.

It would be an utterly cynical arrangement on all sides, Parvus realized. But self-interest was the only reliable measure of a sound bargain. Zimmermann and the kaiser didn't care a fig who ran Russia. They were at war. All Germany wanted for Russia was chaos and collapse. If it could force a premature Russian surrender, Germany would be free to throw all its weight against France and England in a last desperate push for victory before the resources of the United States tipped the balance permanently against it.

Lenin, on the other hand, expected the kaiser's regime to be overthrown from within by the German working classes. So from his point of view, it should be only poetic justice to use that doomed government's money and assistance to hasten its own ultimate downfall.

"This project will require a code name," Zimmermann declared. He unlocked the safe behind his desk, pulled out a leather-bound folder and opened it slowly. When he found the page he wanted, the foreign secretary extracted a gold-plated pen from its holder on his desk, dipped the point in an inkwell, and carefully inscribed two words at the top of the page.

" '*Rosen Morgen*,' " he said, glancing up at Parvus. " 'Red Morning.' It strikes the right note of optimism, don't you agree?"

Parvus nodded. It sounded vaguely sinister to him.

Zimmermann rolled a blotter over the words, then closed the folder and stood up. "I'll open the file in that name, then. It'll be classified at the highest level of secrecy."

Parvus hoisted himself out of the chair with a strenuous grunt and pulled his vest back down over his belly. "I'll need a few days, Herr Secretary, to establish communications with Ulyanov. And he'll want time to consider your offer. He may have conditions, reservations. There are many difficult details to be worked out."

"I appreciate that, of course. But keep in mind, my friend, that for every day you take, another thousand German soldiers will die."

"I will work as fast as humanly possible," Parvus promised.

"One week," Zimmermann replied, his tone somber and final. "I will give you one week. No more. Germany is bleeding to death. She doesn't have much time left."

SUNDAY
APRIL 1, 1917

LONDON

By 10:00 P.M. Nigel De Grey's head began to nod. He had been working on the same cryptogram for three straight hours, and the solution still eluded him. It was an intercept of a German naval code—normally a routine matter to decipher, but for some reason he just couldn't crack it. He suspected that the transmission itself had been garbled. That often happened. And in any case, there was no rush to decipher it. Most likely it was just another U-boat captain, bragging to Berlin of the tonnage he had sunk that day off the Dogger Bank—inflated by the usual 50 percent.

He threw down his pencil, stretched his arms out, and yawned. He wasn't even supposed to be working on these low-level naval codes, he reminded himself. At thirty-one years of age, De Grey, a peacetime employee of the distinguished publishing house of Heinemann, Ltd., was an officer in the Royal Navy. His wartime service had little to do with ships or the sea, however.

He was part of a mysterious and elite entity hidden deep within the organizational charts of the Naval Intelligence Division of the British Admiralty and referred to, with classic British understatement, simply as Room 40. Its existence, known only to a handful at the highest levels of government, was the most jealously guarded secret of the Great War.

Room 40 was actually a series of rooms in the Admiralty

Old Building, protected from the outside world by drawn shutters and guarded doors. Within its cramped spaces a handpicked group of highly skilled men and women worked in shifts around the clock, deciphering the secret coded messages by which Germany communicated with its ships and its diplomatic posts around the world.

Just the previous month Room 40 had scored a spectacular intelligence coup by intercepting German Foreign Secretary Arthur Zimmermann's telegram attempting to entice Mexico into a secret alliance against the United States. To protect Room 40's work, Lloyd George's government had successfully devised a means of making the contents of the message public without revealing to the Germans that England had broken its diplomatic code.

As England had hoped, the telegram had infuriated President Wilson and the American public, and drawn the United States a giant step closer to a declaration of war against Germany.

It was Nigel De Grey, with the help of an intact code book lifted from a German diplomat's luggage in Cairo, who had deciphered Zimmermann's message. Since that remarkable performance life in Room 40 had become something of an anticlimax for De Grey. His dedication to the arcane skill of cryptanalysis remained as intense as ever, but he suspected he would never again decipher anything to match the importance of the Zimmermann telegram.

A sudden *whissh* followed by a sharp bang brought De Grey fully awake.

Welcoming the interruption, he stepped to the row of pneumatic tubes clustered by the back wall and scooped up the cylinder that had fallen into the tray below. Some days intercepts came barreling over the tubes from the post office's telegraph station with such rapidity that it sounded like an artillery barrage. But this night the tubes had been unusually quiet. De Grey plucked the wound sheet of paper from inside the cylinder and flattened it out on his desk.

His practiced eye traveled swiftly over the groups of numbers to the last cluster at the bottom right. No matter what form the code took, this last group was invariably the encoded signature of the sender. Months of breaking hundreds of these intercepts had taught De Grey to recognize the many different guises of certain important names.

And this was one he knew.

He sucked in his breath. It was the diplomatic code, 0075, and the sender was the German foreign secretary, Arthur Zimmermann.

De Grey pushed aside the naval intercept and the pages of penciled scribblings that littered his desk and began to work at once on Zimmermann's new message.

By eleven o'clock he had solved the new key. By midnight he had rammed through the superencipherment.

By 12:30 Monday morning, April 2, De Grey had successfully uncovered the entire message. He printed it out in large block letters on a clean sheet of paper and read it through several times, trying to assess its significance:

APRIL 1:

VON ROMBERG, BERN

NUMBER 1 STRICTLY SECRET

YOURSELF TO DECODE

REFERENCE RED MORNING

ACCORDING TO INFORMATION RECEIVED HERE IT IS DESIRABLE THAT TRANSIT OF RUSSIAN REVOLUTIONARIES THROUGH GERMANY TAKE PLACE AS SOON AS POSSIBLE. AS THE ENTENTE MAY HAVE ALREADY BEGUN TO WORK AGAINST THIS MOVE IN SWITZERLAND, I RECOMMEND ALL POSSIBLE SPEED IN YOUR DISCUSSIONS.

ZIMMERMANN

De Grey was still debating with himself whether or not to telephone his superior, Director of Naval Intelligence Captain Sir William Hall, at his home, and inform him of the message, when a second intercept came rattling down the pneumatic tube.

It turned out to be Ambassador Von Romberg's reply. Since the ambassador had used the same code, De Grey was able to solve it in minutes:

APRIL 2:

ZIMMERMANN, BERLIN

NUMBER 1 STRICTLY SECRET

REFERENCE RED MORNING

THROUGH INTERMEDIARY HERE LENIN HAS AGREED IN PRINCIPLE TO SAFE TRANSIT BY TRAIN ACROSS GERMANY. YOUR LIAISON NOW RETURNING BERLIN TO DELIVER HIS CONDITIONS. VON ROMBERG

De Grey checked his watch. It was 1:15 in the morning. He decided to telephone Hall. Better to risk his boss's irritation by waking him than to risk his own job by not.

Captain Hall answered on the fifth ring. His normally high-pitched voice was raspy with sleep. "Yes? Who's this?"

"De Grey, sir. Sorry to wake you."

"It's all right, my boy. What is it?"

"Another big one, I think."

"Begin with a 'Z,' does it?"

"Yes, sir."

"I'll be down straightaway."

Captain Hall arrived at 2:00 A.M., still in his dressing gown, his bald dome and big beak of a nose looking even paler than usual. His right eye, which had earned him the nickname "Blinker," was already twitching at high speed. He read the intercepts, then fixed De Grey with his birdlike gaze and nodded energetically. "You did absolutely the right thing, my boy." He reached for the telephone. "We'd better let Sir Mansfield Cumming in on this at once."

TUESDAY
APRIL 3, 1917

BERLIN

Foreign Secretary Zimmermann met Parvus in the anteroom of his Reichschancellery office early in the morning, before any of the ministry's staff had arrived for work. In the eight days that had passed since their first meeting, the secretary's normal ebullience had evaporated entirely. His eyes were ringed with fatigue, and his ruddy face wore deep creases of anxiety. His manner was abrupt. "Wilson—just hours ago— asked his Congress for a declaration of War against us," he began, ushering the Dane inside quickly. "We must move matters along at once. What are Lenin's conditions?"

"He wishes to take his closest colleagues and their families with him," Parvus replied, struggling out of his enormous tent of a topcoat.

The secretary spread his hands out impatiently. "Yes, yes, of course he can do that. How many does he want to take?"

Parvus settled into the same chair he had occupied on their earlier meeting, when Zimmermann had first asked him to approach the Bolshevik leader with an offer of German help. "Perhaps fifty, Excellency."

Zimmermann was incredulous. "He has fifty colleagues?"

"Not all colleagues. He thinks that a broad coalition of other prominent socialists and internationalists should also be included, so it doesn't appear that Germany is helping only the Bolsheviks."

"You spoke to Lenin directly?"

Parvus reddened. He had hoped not to have to explain that Lenin had refused to see him. "He's chosen a Mr. Fritz Platten to represent him in our negotiations. Platten is a prominent Swiss socialist. A wise choice, I think. Really a very charming gentleman. Completely trustworthy." Parvus fumbled hastily in his inside coat pocket, extracted a card, and placed it on the secretary's desk. "I leave you his name and address here, Excellency."

Zimmermann expelled his breath noisily through his moustache. "Fifty is a ridiculous number! We can't escort fifty people through enemy lines. You must explain that to him. We can't possibly protect such a large number."

"He doesn't want to go through the front lines. He wants to go around—through Sweden, Finland."

Zimmermann raised both hands in surprise, as if the possibility had never occurred to him. He stepped behind his desk, selected a drawstring from the half-dozen that dangled from the large map roll affixed to the wall, and pulled down a map of Europe. He traced a finger over the maze of blue lines that webbed out like the checked surface of an old porcelain vase, denoting the continent's dense network of railway lines. "It's an absurdly long trip that way," he declared, shaking his head dubiously. "From Zurich he'll have to go clear across Germany to the Baltic. He'll have to cross the Baltic by ferry and then travel damned near the entire lengths of both Sweden and Finland. It must be more than three thousand kilometers. And I need not tell you that the railroads these days are not in the best condition. God knows how many delays there'd be. It'll take him forever. And Germany cannot guarantee his safety through Sweden and Finland. He may well not make it."

"Sweden is not at war, Excellency," Parvus countered. "Their train service is as safe and efficient as Switzerland's. I've traveled on it recently myself. And Finland, after all, is under Russian rule. Once he's across the Finnish border, he's as good as home."

"But beyond our borders we cannot control events," Zimmermann persisted. "It's too damned risky."

Parvus spread his hands in a gesture of apology. "Ulyanov is quite insistent on that route, Herr Secretary. He believes that if he were to enter Russia directly from German territory, it would compromise him in the eyes of the Russian people."

Zimmermann sighed with exasperation. "He seems far more concerned with appearance than substance. What else does our revolutionary prima donna wish us to do for him?"

The Dane cleared his throat nervously. He groped for the best words to present Lenin's more difficult demands. "He wants the train—or at least the carriage which he and his party will occupy—to have extraterritorial status. And to be completely sealed off from contact with any German."

"God in Heaven!" Zimmermann exploded. "Does he fear he might catch something from us?"

"His position is difficult, Herr Secretary. He's willing to accept your help, but since Germany is at war with Russia, he can't appear to have struck any kind of bargain with you. That would be fatal to his goals. And fatal to yours as well."

Zimmermann sat rigid behind his desk, considering the situation. At last he nodded grudgingly. "Well, I suppose we can do it." The secretary glanced at the clock on his desk. "Is that it, then?"

"There is the matter of the money," Parvus reminded him.

"He will get the money later," Zimmermann snapped. "When he's in St. Petersburg."

"The Bolshevik party—" Parvus began, wiping a drop of sweat from the side of his nose. "It is in very pinched circumstances financially. There are many unpaid bills . . ."

Zimmermann cut him off. "I don't want to hear his problems. How much does he require?"

"Sixty million, Herr Secretary," the Dane blurted out, his eyes wincing involuntarily as if the German minister might strike him for his impertinence. "Sixty million marks."

An ominous silence ensued. Parvus forced his eyes to meet Zimmermann's. The secretary's ruddy cheeks had deepened to a dark, explosive purple. "*Ausgeschlossen*," he rasped. "Quite out of the question."

The Dane pulled his silk handerchief from his breast pocket and mopped the perspiration from his face. The sixty million figure was his own idea. Through Fritz Platten, Lenin had actually asked for only twenty million, but Parvus had advised Platten that to get anywhere near that amount, he had better demand a lot more. Platten had left it up to him. "Consider what he can do for Germany, Herr Secretary," Parvus coaxed.

"We'll agree to forty million marks," Zimmermann announced, his voice cold. "If the Bolsheviks prove worth it, we might invest more. Might. But I promise nothing beyond forty million. And he can't have a pfennig of it until he's in St. Petersburg."

"I will try to persuade him to accept that offer," Parvus replied, suddenly light-headed with euphoria. Lenin and Platten would be dazzled. And forty million meant four million for him.

"Does this Lenin understand exactly what his side of the bargain is?" the secretary demanded.

"I assure you he does, Excellency," Parvus cooed. "I have spelled it out exactly as you instructed."

"A separate peace," Zimmermann said, pronouncing the words slowly and emphatically, to make certain the Dane appreciated their importance. "Lenin must give us a separate peace."

"Of course," Parvus replied, anxious to reassure the secretary. "There is no doubt about that. He understands."

The foreign secretary lifted a small envelope from his desk and handed it to Parvus. It was sealed with wax and stamped with the official seal of the Reichschancellery. It was addressed to Vladimir Ulyanov. "I want you to see that Lenin gets this," Zimmermann said. "Unopened. Can I trust you to do that?"

Parvus accepted the envelope, his forehead creased with confusion.

"It's a personal message," Zimmermann explained. "Something I am asking him to do for me. A small matter, really, but one that must remain a secret between us. Merely a favor of sorts. A token expression of goodwill. He'll understand. Whether he does what I ask or how he chooses to do it will be entirely up to him. Either way it will not affect our negotiations."

Parvus nodded. "I will deliver it in person, Herr Secretary."

"Then we have no time to waste. I'll send word to Ambassador von Romberg in Bern this morning. He can work out the remaining details with Fritz Platten. How soon can Lenin be ready to depart?"

Parvus tapped his walking stick briskly on the floor. "With two days' notice, Herr Secretary."

Zimmermann accompanied Parvus to the door. "All our fortunes are riding on this," Zimmermann said, his voice betraying a sudden catch of emotion. "We must not fail. God bless Germany."

LONDON

Captain Sir Mansfield Cumming was in an uncharacteristic state of nervous tension. He wheeled around agitatedly in his office chair, causing its casters to squeak noisily across the worn floorboards, and shouted at his assistant, Margaret, to put more coal on the fire grate. Cumming was expecting an important visitor, and the warren of tiny rooms at the top of Number 2, Whitehall Court, where he both lived and worked during the week, was in its usual state of hopeless disorder. On every side, towering stacks of files, piled haphazardly and spilling their innards like victims of a bayonet charge, competed for the available flat surfaces with hordes of aging magazines, newspapers, and books, their pages bristling with thousands of tiny yellow slips of torn paper to mark long-forgotten references.

"Where's that new file clerk, Margaret? What's his name— Quigley. Quigley Something."

"Peter Quigley, sir. He quit. Friday last."

"Damn," Cumming muttered. "And we just got clearance for him."

Cumming was a short, thickset man of fifty-eight with a large, round face and a wide, humorous mouth that wriggled like a worm caught between the big rubbery protrusions of his nose and chin. Once captain of Nelson's old flagship *Victory*, Cumming was now chief of MI1c, the new designation given his Secret Service Bureau by the War Office.

To the extent that it had one, Cumming was England's spymaster. From this maze of crooked rooms and passages at the top of Whitehall Court, accessible only by a private lift, Cumming presided over a loose network of agents in all countries on the Continent. He was known simply by the first initial of his last name: "C." It lent an air of mystery and legend to an otherwise thoroughly unmysterious and unlegendary individual. Once active in the field himself, he had only the year before lost a foot in an automobile accident. Since that mishap, he had acquired a boy's two-wheel scooter to help compensate for his handicap. He could frequently be seen racing down the corridors of Whitehall, pushing along with his good leg, with the other planted on the scooter.

His abrupt manner and quick temper had earned him an undeserved reputation as a grouch. In fact, he was an extraordinarily warmhearted—even sentimental—man, who inspired great admiration and affection among those who worked for him.

A sudden rusty clank and whir in the narrow corridor outside his office alerted Cumming to the approach of the elevator car. He scooted his chair swiftly back into place behind his desk. "Here he comes," he whispered in a stage voice to his assistant. "Look busy now, damn it. I don't want him to think we're just waiting around for him."

Seconds later the lift operator pulled open the door and England's foreign minister, Arthur J. Balfour, stepped into the attic maze of rooms. Margaret made her customary apology for the untidy surroundings, and ushered Balfour into the spymaster's presence.

The two knew each other only slightly. Balfour, a graymaned, distinguished patrician who exuded an air of upperclass superiority and unruffled calm, was one of the great men of British statecraft. His lithe figure and sharp wit had been a fixture in English politics for decades. The son of Lord Salisbury, he had served in Tory administrations both as prime minister and first lord of the Admiralty, and recently had taken on the portfolio of foreign minister in Lloyd George's coalition government. Despite his durability and experience, the immense strain the war was putting on him was evident in his elderly face, now slack and pale, and his eyes, red-rimmed from lack of sleep.

Cumming stood up, bracing his bad leg against his desk, and extended his hand. Balfour shook it listlessly. Cumming gestured toward a chair. "Thank you for coming over, Minister," he said. "Margaret," he called. "Fetch our guest some tea, will you? There's a dear."

Balfour crossed his legs and looked around the room with the shrewd curiosity of an interior decorator trying to judge the occupant's taste. His eyes took in the big work table, the heavy safe, the maps and charts and seascapes on the walls, and the clutter of mechanical gadgets and odd-looking weapons for which Cumming had something of an obsession.

"My toys," Cumming explained, noticing the minister's attention. "My little escapes from reality."

Balfour nodded in sympathy. "God knows we all need escapes these days."

Cumming handed the foreign minister a folder. "From Room 40," he said. "We have a situation developing that I thought it best to discuss with you in secret."

Balfour raised an eyebrow in polite surprise and opened the folder. Within lay the intercepts of the two German secret diplomatic messages with Nigel De Grey's solutions, in both German and English.

While the minister studied the messages, Cumming wheeled his chair around to face the window, with its view of the roofs of Whitehall. A cold mist glistened on the chimney pots and shingles. A small brass clock on the fireplace mantel at the far end of the room chimed the hour of ten. Cumming glared across at the fire. Ten o'clock and a mound of ashes was all that remained in the grates. Coal, like everything else in England, was in short supply. He crossed his arms and tucked his hands under his armpits to warm them.

"Zimmermann meddling again," Balfour said, closing the folder.

The tea arrived. Cumming offered Balfour a cigarette from the box on the desk, and lit it for him with one of his gadgets, a nickel-plated tinderbox in the shape of a pistol.

"We must alert the Russian government," Balfour declared. "I'll wire Ambassador Buchanan at once."

"I suspect nothing will come of it, Minister. With the czar gone, Petersburg is a shambles. It's hard to know who's running the government from one day to the next."

"Petersburg was a worse shambles when the czar was there. What more can we do?"

Cumming rubbed his stiffened hands together to dispel the chill. "We could make Zimmermann's message public. As we did with his Mexican telegram."

Balfour shook his head firmly. "No one would understand it—except the Germans. And thickheaded as they are, they would surely tumble to the fact that we're reading their mail."

"True," Cumming admitted. He wheeled around to the fire and kicked the grate aggressively with the heel of his shoe, hoping to shake a little more warmth from it. A thin cloud of ash puffed back at him and settled onto the rug.

"Perhaps we're making too much of the matter," Balfour argued. "Suppose they do get this Lenin chap back to Russia. What's the harm? Can one more soapbox rabblerouser really make a difference there? We see a dozen in Hyde Park every day."

Cumming disagreed. "This one could. Lenin is a powerful force in the radical underground. And the Germans will probably finance him."

Balfour inhaled deeply, then allowed two thin plumes of smoke to escape from the sides of his mouth, creating the peculiar illusion that the corners of his moustache were catching fire. "I hadn't considered that," he admitted.

"German money would give the Bolsheviks a crucial advantage," Cumming added, making sure Balfour got the point.

"Suppose Lenin does seize power?" Balfour challenged. "A few heads may roll, but what can he do to hurt us?"

"Pull Russia out of the war."

"She's barely in the war now."

"She's tying down two million German and Austrian troops. If they make a separate peace, Germany'll have another dozen divisions to throw against us in France. We couldn't hold the line."

Balfour seemed offended. "What makes you so certain?"

"The French are in deplorable shape."

The foreign minister stubbed his cigarette out firmly in the ashtray on Cumming's desk. "Yes. But America will be in soon."

"It'll take them six months to mobilize. We could lose the war by then. The U-boats are decimating our supply lines."

"Germany will starve first," Balfour insisted.

Cumming shrugged. "Do we want to bet another hundred thousand English lives on it?"

Balfour raised his shaggy brows in shock.

"That was not well put, sir," Cumming apologized.

"I take your point, Captain. Where does that leave us, then?"

Cumming looked out again at the gloomy spring morning. His throat felt tight, and he swallowed to relieve the discomfort. He felt foolish for having offended the foreign minister, but English lives were the heart of the matter. The recent death of his own son had brought this home to him. And barely a family was left in all of England that had not suffered similarly. The secret casualty reports from the early battles still haunted him. Sixty thousand in one day at the Somme. An unbelievable slaughter. But more slaughters were to follow. Three years of warfare vastly more horrible and destructive than anything in mankind's entire experience had brought England to the edge of ruin.

"If there is anything we can do to influence this situation," Cumming answered, his voice betraying some passion for the first time, "then we should bloody well do it."

Balfour smiled amiably at the Secret Service chief. "You have something in mind, apparently."

Cumming straightened in his chair and tucked his monocle away in his vest pocket. "Only the obvious. Stop Lenin from reaching Russia."

Balfour batted his eyebrows again. "Really? How?"

Cumming's lips wriggled uncomfortably. "Just have someone stop him."

Balfour tilted his head back in surprise. "You don't mean kill him?"

"We're at war with Germany, Minister. Lenin plans to collaborate with them against our interests. If he succeeds, it will cost England dearly."

"And whom do you recommend we hire for this extraordinary task?"

A glow of embarrassment brightened Cumming's broad features. "I have given it some thought," he confessed. "There's a man in Zurich who could do it for us. He's an American."

Balfour's brows shot up again. "An American?"

Cumming defended himself. "Whitehall's role would have to be kept secret."

"I appreciate that, but an American?" Balfour protested.

"Why not an Arab? Or a Turk? Or a Serb? Or any of a dozen other nationalities?"

Cumming grinned boyishly. "He comes highly recommended. Roosevelt told me about him originally. He performed some delicate missions for him when he was President. And for Taft as well. He's something of a legend in the trade. You should hear Colonel House on the subject."

"Who is he?" the foreign minister demanded.

"His name is Harry Bauer."

"Is he an assassin?"

"Not especially. He's an athlete, an expert marksman, and as fearless as a tiger. And he speaks several languages fluently—German and Spanish and perhaps others, I don't recall. Roosevelt used him as a personal spy and troubleshooter. He liked to send him into difficult situations and let him solve them."

Balfour wrinkled his brow. "I'm afraid I don't follow you."

"Gather the necessary intelligence and act upon it in whatever way best suited America's interests."

"Sounds foolhardy in the extreme. Typical of Roosevelt, though, I suppose."

"He got consistently excellent results from him. Saved the United States from a major involvement in Mexico during their revolution. And he put on a brilliant show in Manchuria, I understand. During the Russo-Japanese War. I have that information directly from one of our own, Sidney Reilly. He was in Port Arthur at the same time as Bauer. Bauer's specialty is infiltration, he told me. He has a chameleon's ability to take on his enemy's colors and work from inside. Reilly credits Bauer with teaching him a great deal. And Reilly is as parsimonious with praise as a Scotsman with a tuppence."

"But for Heaven's sake, why would Bauer do this for us?"

"Because he's rather anxious for work. The Wilson administration got rid of him after his last mission—against General Huerta. Wilson detests the whole idea of secret agents and covert operations. He considered Bauer an embarrassment, apparently, even though Bauer saved the administration from an enormous headache. In any case, he's no longer in the employ of the U.S. government. He quite disappeared from view after the Huerta incident. He surfaced in Zurich only a few months ago."

"What happened with Huerta?"

"The similarities to our present situation are instructive, Minister. The Germans tried to smuggle Huerta back into Mexico, to intrigue against Carranza and stir up trouble for the United States. But the Americans caught Huerta near the border and took him into custody. He died a few weeks later, under mysterious circumstances. Officially, yellow jaundice."

"Was it?"

"No. Bauer killed him—on orders from someone very high in the U.S. administration. Huerta posed a big problem for Wilson."

"And Wilson fired Bauer for that?"

"Apparently. But that's Wilson. Principled to a fault."

Balfour rubbed a cheek thoughtfully. "So Lenin is now our Heurta, and Bauer is the cure. Is that it?"

"Multiplied by ten."

"Don't we risk offending Wilson if we take Bauer on?"

"That's possible," Cumming admitted. "I suggest Ambassador Bryce sound out Colonel House for us."

Cumming knew he was being devious here. House would support the idea because, of all those close to Wilson, he was the most eager to bring the United States into the war. House would give England the green light in Wilson's name and not even bother to inform Wilson.

"How would you establish contact with this Bauer?"

"I'd send someone to Zurich directly from here. We'd want to be certain he was properly instructed."

"I'm seeing the P.M. in an hour," Balfour said. "I'll discuss it with him. If he's amenable, let's give it a go."

For the first time in nearly a week, Cumming felt almost cheerful. "First-rate. I'll be here all day if you need my support on the matter."

Balfour smiled mysteriously, and suddenly it dawned on Cumming why. Balfour didn't need anyone's support. He knew Lloyd George would go along with it.

The Secret Service chief and the foreign minister made small talk for a few minutes, then shook hands. This time Balfour's grip was firmer. They were sealing an agreement between them. "Let's see to it that the Germans' 'Red Morning' never dawns," Balfour said.

An hour later Cumming was in his Rolls-Royce, threading his way impatiently southward through London's midday traffic. In Pimlico he turned left off Belgrave Road and a few minutes later brought the auto to a halt alongside Number 33, Eccleston Square.

A butler answered the door.

Cumming handed him a calling card and introduced himself. "I don't have an appointment, I'm afraid," he said. "But the matter is rather urgent. Is Mr. Churchill at home?"

THURSDAY
APRIL 5

ZURICH, SWITZERLAND

"Let's have a drink," Harry Bauer said.

"Here?"

"Why not here?"

"It's filthy," the Turk complained in his thickly accented English. "These people are filthy."

Harry Bauer bent his face down toward the Turk. Bauer was a big man—six feet one inch tall and nearly two hundred pounds. His hair was dark blond and thick, and he had cultivated a moustache that curled around the corners of his mouth like parentheses. His eyes were agate blue, and when they were not focused absently in the middle distance, he had a habit of fixing them on people with a bald, intimidating stare—as if he were debating whether or not to dismantle them to see what made them tick. He fixed the Turk with that look now.

The two men were standing in front of a hastily slapped-together arrangement of planks and sawhorses managed by a teenaged gypsy girl with long black hair and a crafty smile. The makeshift table was cluttered with opened, unlabeled wine bottles and a stack of glasses. Bauer thrust his hands in his pockets and studied the bottles. Finally he picked one up and examined the cloudy red contents in the sunlight. The bottle was half empty. "What's this stuff?" he asked the girl.

"French wine," she replied, flashing a dark, flirtatious smile at the tall American. *"Grand cru."* She pronounced the French words perfectly.

Bauer grinned at her. "Yeah? What does that mean?"

She ran her tongue over her top lip. "It means it's the best."

"Is that what the guy who drank the first half said?"

The girl shrugged. Her lewd smile was beginning to harden in place.

"Pour us a couple of glasses, what the hell."

"They lie, they steal," the Turk muttered, staring lustfully at the girl. "That's all they know."

The girl filled two not very clean glasses with the murky liquid. Bauer paid her and knocked back the drink as if it were a shot of bourbon. The Turk tasted his reluctantly, grimaced in revulsion, and dumped the remainder onto the grass. "Poison." He coughed, banging the empty glass back down on the plank table. "It will cause you to go blind."

Bauer took a refill, tossed it down, winked at the girl, then followed the Turk off into the crowd milling around among the hodgepodge of booths, tables, and garishly painted horse-drawn wagons that made up the fair. Dozens of gypsy cara-vans, some from as far away as Rumania and Hungary, were camped in meandering rows on the large field off the Vogelsangstrasse. Amid the pungent, garlicky smells of out-door cookfires and the squealing of infants, swarthy men with luxuriant moustaches and menacing expressions, and mysteri-ous dark women in kerchiefs and gold bracelets, operated their concessions from the backs of the big wagons that served as their mobile households. They offered the public an un-usual mixture of diversions—violin music, indigestible food, secondhand clothes and jewelry, rigged games of chance, exhibitions of belly dancing, and endless varieties of fortune telling. Part circus, part flea market, and part clip joint, the fair was an experience of the exotic and the shady that Bauer found thoroughly to his liking.

"They are ridden with disease, these people," the Turk insisted, wiping the residue of the wine from his lips with the sleeve of his thick, knobby wool suit. "Syphilis, especially, and consumption."

"It was your idea to meet here."

The Turk shrugged. His complexion was even darker than

the gypsies' around him, and although it was only two o'clock in the afternoon, he appeared in need of a shave. He was very short—barely five feet—with long arms and big feet. Bauer thought that he looked like an organ grinder's monkey—especially with the tassled red fez perched on his head. All that was lacking was a leash, a tin cup, and a little more hair on the backs of his hands. His name was Jossef Ali Ibrahim, and he held the rank of colonel in Turkish military intelligence.

"What about our offer?" Ibrahim demanded.

Bauer jammed his hands back into his pockets and hunched his shoulders up in an elaborate shrug. "I think I'll pass it up."

"What is your objection?"

Bauer grinned, showing a gap between his two front teeth, and pointed at the Turk's feet. "You've got shit on one of your boots, Colonel," he said.

The colonel jumped as if someone had pinched him. "What?"

"You stepped in some horseshit back there."

The Turk examined the bottom of his boot and discovered, to his mortification, that Bauer was right. He wiped the boot off on the grass, cursing under his breath. "Why won't you accept?" he demanded.

"I guess I just don't like Turks," the American replied. "Particularly ones with shit on their boots."

Ibrahim's face turned a mottled purple. "And I don't like Americans. What does it matter?"

"It matters to me. You're murdering Armenians, for one thing."

The colonel sneered at the accusation. "That is a dirty lie. Allied war propaganda, that's all it is. You are stupid to believe it."

"I believe what I see."

"What are you talking about?"

"Bitlis and Diyarbakir. I was there two years ago. I saw whole families hacked to pieces, babies with their heads cut off. They told me you'd already killed more than half a million."

The Turk shook his fist in the air. "That is a lie!"

"What's the truth, then?"

Ibrahim began walking again. He tried to hide his fury

beneath condescension. "You're an ignorant American. What do you know of our affairs? The Armenians are traitors."

"Even the babies?"

"They're on Russia's side," the Turk retorted. His tone was bitter. "They are trying to bring down our government."

"That'd be a shame."

The Turk refused to be goaded further. He swallowed his rage and made a strenuous effort to be ingratiating. "What do you care about politics? We are professionals, you and I. We know governments sometimes do unpleasant things. But we personally are not responsible for these acts."

"I don't work for barbarians."

Ibrahim tried sarcasm. "I suppose you have better offers."

"No, but that won't change my mind."

The Turk muttered something under his breath. He switched his attention to the large and jiggling bosom of a passing female, then bared his long yellow teeth at the American in a nasty grin. "The truth is, no one wants you anymore. You're finished."

Bauer didn't bother to reply. He paused in front of a game booth and looked it over. It offered a prize for knocking down ten wooden pins. The pins, arranged in a wedge four rows deep, were set on a small table about twenty feet back from the front of the booth. They had been crudely hand-painted to resemble soldiers. "What nationality are they?" he asked the concessionaire sitting inside, a middle-aged gypsy with a large, hairy stomach that bulged against his suspenders.

The gypsy threw out his hands and laughed. "Whatever nationality you like," he said, his voice loud. "I do not take sides."

"They look like Turks," Bauer decided. "The same tiny wooden heads."

"Then they are Turks," the gypsy agreed. "One franc for three chances."

"They say you lost your nerve," Ibrahim persisted. "They say you are too afraid now to go on secret missions. Maybe you are too old. Maybe that is the reason. Or maybe you are a coward now."

Bauer dropped a franc on the counter. The gypsy scooped it up and handed him three balls in exchange. "Who's they?" Bauer demanded.

"Certain people. Important people. They also say you've been in Zurich for months, looking for work. No one wants you."

"Why do *you* want me, then?"

The Turk's expression turned hopeful. "Information, of course. America will be in the war soon. You could tell us many things of value."

The American laughed. "For five thousand dollars? If I wanted to betray my country, I'd go to the Germans. At least they'd pay me what I'm worth."

The Turk shook his head. "You need the money. Information is all we want. All you have to do is talk. What could be easier? We can do it right here, in Zurich. Today."

The Turk was right, the little bastard. He did need the money. Desperately. He had considered taking the offer and then feeding Ibrahim bogus intelligence. There would be some satisfaction in that, but it was difficult to get away with that kind of trick. Traitors were the garbage of international espionage. Since they had proved they couldn't be trusted, they were always disposed of eventually, by one side or another. The value of their information rarely altered their fate. Once it had been separated from them, they were thrown away before they began to smell, like a chicken carcass or a grapefruit rind.

Bauer held one of the balls up under the Turk's bulbous nose. It was an old baseball, yellowed and badly scuffed, with the stitching worked loose in several places. "Look at this," he said, grinning with boyish delight. "A damn Spalding. The real thing. Horsehide. I wonder where the hell he got it?"

Ibrahim gnashed his teeth in exasperation. "I will raise our offer. To seven thousand."

Bauer gripped the baseball lovingly across the seams with the first two fingers of his right hand and flexed his wrist. "Did those certain people tell you that I used to play in the major league?"

The Turk squinted at him in confusion.

"It's true. The Philadelphia Phillies. When I was nineteen. I pitched against Christy Mathewson of the New York Giants in a game once. Beat him two to one. At the Polo Grounds." Bauer stared down wistfully at the baseball in his hand. "I only lasted two seasons. Developed a sore arm. I could have come back, but a doc in Philly gave me bad advice. I was young and didn't know what the hell I was doing. I could have had a hell of a career."

"Ten thousand dollars!" Ibrahim offered, his voice harsh.

"That's all I ever wanted to do. Play major league baseball. The pay was lousy, but it was a great life."

Bauer tossed the baseball at the wedge of soldiers. It hit the front pin and knocked down all but one in the back row.

"Damn it!" Bauer swung his fist around in frustration. "I hit those just right."

"You're a fool," the Turk said, "if you turn down that much money."

Bauer watched the gypsy set the pins up again. "Hey, that pin on the end. It's too far out."

The gypsy nodded placatingly and adjusted the pin slightly. Bauer picked up the second ball, a sphere of battered wood left over from some ancient croquet set, and threw it considerably harder. Again, it sent nine of the pins flying, but the same soldier in the back row remained standing. Bauer was certain that it had been hit by at least one of the other pins. He guessed that it was impaled on a nail protruding up through the table. Well, it was a hostile world.

"Tell you what," he said, looking down at the Turkish officer, his moustache twitching impatiently. "If I don't knock down all ten pins on this last try, I'll take your offer."

The Turk eyed him with disgust. "Why don't you stop these silly games and just say yes?"

"I like sporting propositions," Bauer said. He waited for the gypsy to set the pins back in place, then demanded the old Spalding baseball again. Begrudgingly the gypsy retrieved it from the ground and tossed it to him. Bauer paced back from the booth until he stood nearly sixty feet away from the wedge of mock wooden soldiers. He studied the pins carefully, then put his right foot forward, imagining he was stepping onto a pitching rubber.

The gypsy eyed Bauer apprehensively. "Hey, not so far back!" he complained. "You crazy?"

Gripping the ball firmly across the stitches, the American rocked forward and swung his arms down past his knees. He straightened, flung his arms up dramatically, paused with them clasped together in an arch over his head, and took a final measure of his target.

He pivoted on his right foot, kicked up his left, and reared back until his right hand almost touched the ground behind him. He uncoiled in a powerful rush, whipping his elbow and snapping his wrist to catapult the weapon toward its target at more than ninety miles an hour.

The old baseball exploded into the wedge of pins with the stuttering crack of a volley of rifle shots. The pin the gypsy had pegged to an invisible nail in the shelf split in half and shot off in separate directions.

Another pin ricocheted into the prizes on the side shelves, breaking several pottery ashtrays and a large glass figurine of the Virgin Mary. The gypsy waved his fists and bellowed like a wounded bull.

Bauer strolled back to the booth. "Where's my prize?" he demanded.

The gypsy pulled a dagger out from under the counter and held the point up under Bauer's chin. "Get out of here!" he growled.

Bauer snatched the gypsy's wrist and slammed it onto the counter with a knuckle-cracking bang. He pried the knife loose from the gypsy's fingers and held it up. "Is this my prize? Hell, you can do better than that." He spun the dagger toward a shelf at the back of the stand, where it impaled a cloth doll through the stomach.

The gypsy groaned and pulled his wrist free. Bauer scooped up several balls and began throwing them at the prizes, reducing a row of cheap vases and figurines to a shower of glass and pottery shards.

The gypsy produced a revolver from the pocket of his trousers and pointed it at the American's head. A crowd began to accumulate around the booth. "Get out of here," the gypsy warned. "Or I kill you!"

Bauer stopped. He felt his spirit suddenly crash. This was stupid. What was he doing this for? He looked around for the Turk. Nowhere in sight. He pulled a pile of franc notes from his pocket and dropped them onto the counter. "I'll take the baseball," he said. "And we'll call it even." He picked up the Spalding, pushed it into his pocket, and stalked off. No one followed him.

He wandered back to the girl with the wine concession, drank two bottles of the vile liquid in rapid succession, and tried, without success, to persuade her to go back to his hotel with him.

Drunk and miserable, he left the fairgrounds and stumbled back to the Pension Helvetia, a crumbling third-class accommodation in the old quarter of Zurich. It had been his home for the past several months.

He groped his way up the stairs to his room on the fourth floor and sat on the bed. A wave of nausea swept over him. He lay back against the mattress and waited for the feeling to subside. How come, he wondered, if he was so damned good at everything, it hadn't added up to anything? He'd been alive and healthy for thirty-eight years, and he didn't have a damned thing to show for it, except nightmares and loneliness.

The Turk had put his hairy little finger right on it. No one wanted him. Christ, he couldn't even go home anymore. His life was nothing but an endless advance into enemy territory.

He dug the baseball out of his pocket and held it up in front of him. "I beat Christy Mathewson," he murmured. "And they said he was the best there ever was." He tossed the ball into the air in front of him. It missed his hand coming down and rolled under the bed. He left it there and fell asleep.

WASHINGTON, D.C.

By three o'clock in the afternoon the large private dining room off the mezzanine of the Willard Hotel was empty, except for two guests. They were seated at a table at the far end, by a tall window that looked out over Pennsylvania Avenue. They talked in low whispers.

One of the diners, a tall, hollow-cheeked individual with a thinning crop of gray hair, was Lord James Bryce, the British ambassador to the United States. The other man—small, with a sharp nose, protruding ears, and receding chin—was Colonel Edward Mandell House. The "Colonel" was an honorary title, but House, as adviser and close confidant to President Woodrow Wilson, exercised power far beyond any military rank.

The colonel's unprecedented influence arose out of a combination of circumstances: his intimate relationship with the President, and the tide of recent world affairs. Pressure on the United States to enter the European war had so intensified by the early months of 1917 that Wilson, stubbornly determined to keep the country neutral, had shut himself up in the White House, refusing anyone's counsel but his own, and relying increasingly on House to deal with the outside world. This House was more than willing to do. Gregarious by nature, the colonel loved the play of personalities and conversations, the rhythms of political give-and-take—of stroking egos and striking deals and making compromises—all the manipulations of power that were anathema to the aloof schoolmaster Wilson.

So those who couldn't get to the President came to House instead.

House watched Lord Bryce place the strainer on his cup and pour himself more tea. The heavy silver pitcher trembled in the ambassador's grip as he tipped it over the cup. House glanced down at his own empty coffee cup and decided against a refill. It was late and he wished Bryce would get around to whatever it was that had led him to request this private lunch on such short notice.

Bryce tugged on his watch fob and peeked down across his vest to read his timepiece. "What does he do all day?" he asked. "Sitting by himself in the White House?"

House gave his luncheon companion an elaborate shrug. "He thinks long thoughts."

The ambassador smirked. "While you run the country."

The flattery was transparent, but the colonel flushed with pleasure.

"The Russian situation has gotten much worse," Bryce declared abruptly. "The Bolsheviks are persuading soldiers to defect by the thousands. The Germans are taking advantage of the chaos and flooding the country with spies and saboteurs. We're investing our own troops in as many of the border crossings as we can, to try to stem the German infiltration, but it just isn't enough. The whole eastern front is on the brink of collapse."

House listened with his customary attentiveness as Bryce went on painting his gloomy view of the situation.

Suddenly Bryce stopped. He cast a suspicious glance at the

waiters loitering by the kitchen door, as if he feared they might be eavesdropping. "I have something to show you," he whispered, turning back to House. "It's highly confidential." The ambassador reached into his inside jacket pocket and withdrew two sheets of paper. He unfolded them carefully and slid them under House's nose. "London intercepted these communications just this Tuesday and forwarded them on to me by secret cable last evening."

House read the pages, his dark eyes widening at the implications of the cryptic words. Political intrigue thrilled him in an almost sexual way, and this one appeared especially arousing. At length he folded the papers up and rested his hand on them. "Zimmermann at it again."

"Yes."

" 'Red Morning.' What's it all about?"

"There's this particular Bolshevik living in exile in Zurich. He's the 'Lenin' referred to in Von Romberg's telegram. The fellow is highly regarded in revolutionary circles. Zimmermann intends to slip him and some of his followers back into Russia and presumably finance their efforts to seize control."

House gulped audibly. "Good Lord! Do you think they can pull it off?"

"Considering the shaky state of Lvov and the provisional government, yes."

"Why is Zimmermann going to all this trouble with Lenin? There must be others already in Petersburg who would do as well."

"Because Lenin wants to take Russia out of the war—sign a separate peace."

House quivered with disgust. "I'll show these to the President right away."

Bryce held up his hand, indicating there was more. "We have a plan to stop Lenin," he whispered.

House cocked his head at an angle. "Stop him?"

"Yes. We want to send one of your chaps after him—that fellow you used to brag about all the time."

House swallowed hard. "It can't be Harry Bauer."

"That's the fellow."

The colonel felt suddenly faint. "Are you sure he's the one you mean?"

The ambassador glanced around again to make certain no

one was eavesdropping. "Of course. He's capable at this sort of thing. And it happens that he's in Zurich at this very moment."

House's brain sifted rapidly through the ramifications of what Bryce had just told him. Harry Bauer was known to him only through the stories he'd heard about his exploits in military intelligence. Stories that he in turn had used to regale listeners at Washington dinner parties for months. They provided such a welcome antidote to the dreary news of the war in Europe that he was afraid he had overused them, building Bauer into something of a superman.

"It sounds terribly risky," House said, qualifying his earlier enthusiasm. "And the Governor will not be for it. He doesn't approve of this sort of thing."

"We need your help, then, you see," Bryce argued. "Lloyd George and A.J.B. want Wilson's approval and support. Make it sort of a joint Anglo-American undertaking. Highly secret, of course."

House felt a cold trickle of anxiety. "I don't know what I can do, Ambassador," he warned. "Of course it's in our interest to keep Russia in the war, but the President just won't like it. . . ."

"We're confident you can persuade him. As you so often do."

House stared at the expanse of white linen tablecloth in front of him, his mind still scrambling to assess all the implications.

"It's settled then. I know you won't let us down."

The colonel smiled miserably. "How quickly do you need Wilson's approval?"

"Two days at the outside. Lenin may leave Zurich at any moment."

"I'll do what I can."

The purpose of the lunch finally dispensed with, it came swiftly to an end. Bryce signed the check, and the two men shook hands on the sidewalk, amid the customary effusions of diplomatic etiquette.

"I am deeply appreciative," Bryce said. The sincerity in his voice was genuine.

House nodded. He could tell by the ambassador's manner that he considered the matter already decided.

"You'll let me know, then?" Bryce asked. "As soon as possible? All I need is your word. Nothing on paper, you understand."

The colonel watched the ambassador climb into his cab, then set off himself on foot back to the White House, his heart pounding faster with each step. Of course Wilson would never go along, no matter what the advantages might be. Even though America was now in the war on the Allied side, this kind of covert plot was simply beneath the high-minded principles of the President.

So House decided that he simply wouldn't tell him about it. He would act in the President's name, as he had so often done in the past, and take the necessary precautions to make certain that the President didn't find out about it. It seemed worth the risk. Later he could always claim to the President that in the rush of events he had simply forgotten to inform him. It wouldn't be the first time he had gotten away with it. And if the plan succeeded, after all, it would make them both look good. And Wilson—despite his high-mindedness—was not above taking credit for things that his faithful Colonel House had done in his name.

But Harry Bauer? My God, why hadn't he found the courage to tell Bryce the truth? For the small tarnish it might have put on his credibility, he could have saved himself the risk of a far greater embarrassment.

House realized that he must immediately put himself in a position to control the situation—to protect the President, and to protect himself. If he could accomplish that, he would feel much better.

And the first order of business was to find someone in Zurich—someone he could trust—to find out if Bauer really was there, as Bryce claimed.

After all, the man was supposed to be dead.

BERLIN

General Klaus von Gontard, an ancient and pompous Prussian officer with a walrus moustache and a red-veined nose, sat ramrod straight in the chair facing Foreign Secretary Zimmermann's desk. It was 10:30 at night, and well past the general's bedtime. His eyes kept closing involuntarily. "If you would be so good, Herr Secretary, as to describe the nature of the mission, then I could better find the man to fit it."

Zimmermann slapped his hand on the desk. "I regret I can tell you little, General. It's really no more than a guard detail, but I need someone absolutely reliable, discreet, and competent. Those are the chief qualifications."

General von Gontard nodded stiffly. "An officer?"

"Of course."

"But you said a guard detail. . . ."

Zimmermann leaned forward. "General, it is a very *important* guard detail. I want an officer of at least the rank of captain, and I want him to be allowed to handpick several others to be placed under his command."

"We are very short of officers, Herr Secretary. . . ."

Zimmermann nodded. "I understand, General. But this takes priority. And it will only be for a few days. A week at the most. The kaiser himself has approved this."

General von Gontard stood and saluted. "I'll do what is necessary, then, Herr Secretary."

Zimmermann guided his visitor toward the door. "I appreciate it, General," he said in a hearty tone. "I appreciate it very much."

"I will have your man here by tomorrow afternoon," Von Gontard promised.

"No, General. Tonight."

The officer's sleepy eyes popped open. "Tonight?"

"Within the hour, if possible."

FRIDAY
APRIL 6

ZURICH

Harry Bauer came awake in the dark. The muscles of his throat were in spasm, and his heart was tripping furiously. He heard his own cry, or the dying echo of it, and gasped to fill his lungs. He kicked off the blankets and bunched his fists against his eyes to squeeze out the terror.

When his breathing had slowed, he huddled under the blankets, motionless, not daring to move. He felt himself still lying in the sand, his eyes closed tight against the burning sun.

The damned vultures again. They had descended straight into his sleep—shrieking, black wings beating over his head, blotting out the sunlight, greedy red eyes angry with hunger, claws scratching at his face and throat.

He twisted on his back and moaned softly, rocking his head back and forth against the pillow to expel the nightmare from his mind.

The damned vultures. Still, after more than a year. When would it end? He had wakened in the Mexican desert, to find them tugging at him with their beaks. One feeble wave of his arm had put them to flight. He had felt no fear then, only the indescribable joy of still being alive. But his unconscious had chosen to memorialize the incident, to scar his brain with it, amplifying the horror all out of proportion to what he remembered.

The events that had preceded the vultures were already fading from his memory—the pursuit across the border, Huerta's men hunting him in the desert. How many days had it lasted? Three? Four? He could no longer recall.

He gripped the side of the mattress. The familiar coarse texture of the sheet reassured him. Slowly the web of night terrors dissolved and he began to reorient himself in time and place.

He remembered the Turk, Colonel Ibrahim, and the gypsy fair and the disturbance he had caused. And the girl with the wine booth. The Turk was right. Poison. And he had consumed at least three bottles of the foul liquid. It had put him to sleep, but even good alcohol made a rotten slumber, full of pitfalls and demons. He was lucky his hangover wasn't worse. He rearranged the blankets, pulling the eiderdown quilt up tight under his chin to protect against the chill, and resigned himself to another long predawn vigil.

If the vultures hadn't wakened him, other nightmares would have. Sleepless nights had plagued him lately, and he had come to dread them. He was not normally an introspective man, but with nothing to do but lie awake in the dark, his mind kept dragging him back into his past, making him relive events that he had long since forgotten or suppressed. It was as if some force deep inside him had decided to put his entire life on trial, and were summoning him in the dead of each night for another round in an endless series of interrogations.

The same evidence, the same memories, were pushed into his consciousness again and again, the unseen prosecutor inside him demanding that he explain and justify the events and actions of a life that he was hard put to make much sense out of at all.

But even if he didn't understand his life, he was beginning at least to see its shape. He couldn't say he liked it.

There was that baseball career, for example. He had lied to the Turk. It wasn't his sore arm that had ended it. It was his sore head.

The Phillies' team manager—and owner—had a habit of putting Bauer out in left field when he wasn't pitching. Bauer felt exploited by the extra assignment and demanded more money. The owner refused and threatened to trade him if he continued to complain.

He continued to complain. And then came the Fourth of July, 1902. That day, a hot, sunny one in Philadelphia, the Phillies played a doubleheader against the visiting Boston Braves at Shibe Park.

Bauer pitched a magnificent two-hit shutout in the first game. In the second game the owner sent him out to play left field. Bauer felt he deserved a rest.

In the top of the ninth the Braves, behind by one, got the tying run on first base, with two out. The next batter hit a high fly ball directly at Bauer that should have ended the game. Instead of catching it for the final out, Bauer produced a .45 revolver he had concealed in his belt under his shirt, took careful aim, and shot at the baseball just as it reached the top of its arc.

Miraculously, the bullet hit the ball and altered its trajectory enough to send it into foul territory. After long and heated consultations, the umpires awarded the batter a ground-rule double, which tied the game. The crowd went berserk and stormed the field. Since play could not be resumed, the game was forfeited to the Braves. Bauer was arrested on the spot and taken to jail. Later he was fined five hundred dollars for a variety of offenses, including public disorderliness, reckless endangerment, and seeking to influence the outcome of a public sporting event by unlawful means. The incident made the front page of every daily newspaper in the country.

That night the owner fired him, and told him he would see to it that he never played major league baseball again. And Bauer, a celebrity of the moment, sought by every newspaper and magazine in the land, found himself blackballed by every owner in the league. Even the teams in the new American League refused to take him. He was branded a troublemaker and shut out of baseball for the rest of his life.

Why had he been willing to jeopardize so much, he wondered, for a few moments of petty revenge?

There always seemed to come a point in anything he did, he realized, where his desires and those of the people he worked for no longer coincided. And when that point came, he went his own way, no matter what the cost.

It was that same willingness to put everything on the line—to never let anyone get the better of him—that had made him such a success in covert intelligence operations.

Bauer had never backed out of a mission. Never. No matter what the odds. And he had never failed in a mission, either. Once he was fixed on his goal, he was relentless, unstoppable.

He had been like that as long as he could remember. In Germantown, Pennsylvania, where he had grown up, he had felt driven to outdo his playmates and classmates. Whatever they might risk, he would risk more.

His will to be first might have made him a leader, but he had no interest in manipulating others. Instead, his implacable competitiveness set him against everyone. It was a characteristic so deeply ingrained in his nature that he doubted he could have changed it even if he had wanted to. He had always made enemies a lot quicker than friends.

That brought him back to the vultures—and the chase across the Mexican desert.

Someone had set him up.

He had killed two of Huerta's men, and after a few days the others had given up and left him in the desert. Maybe they thought he was dead by then. He damned near was.

To save himself, he decided to play dead. He disappeared and found his way to Europe. And there he discovered that being dead had some disadvantages. No one dared hire him, for one thing. He had become a permanent fugitive.

The parallels between the Huerta affair and that Fourth of July at Shibe Park in 1902 were not lost on him. He was one man pitting himself against an establishment that he should have known could easily crush him. Why did he let it happen? He could have so easily avoided these defeats. Was he so arrogant as to believe that, even against those odds, he could somehow prevail? Did he need the hurt they could inflict on him to prove to himself how tough he was?

Bauer rolled over in bed and groaned. His father had something to do with it, he guessed.

He saw the old man's callused hands fumbling through the dog-eared copy of *Das Kapital*. His bible. He read a few pages from it every evening before dinner—when he was sober. When he was drunk, he sometimes just waved the book around, misquoting lines from it in German, throwing them out like challenges against an invisible army of tormentors, his voice hoarse with a pathetic and aimless anger. When he was in this state, he picked arguments with his wife. They yelled often, and sometimes he struck her. Harry usually hid in the cellar during these scenes, where he nursed a fear of his father that hardened, as he grew older, into a permanent estrangement.

But there were good memories mixed in with the bad. Mostly they had to do with the railroad—the yards, the signal sheds, the station houses, the locomotives. The hours he had spent as a boy with his father in the cabs of these mammoth steel-ribbed beasts still remained the most precious in his life.

It was hard to exaggerate the thrill of the experience. There were few roads and no automobiles in those days, and driving a 190,000-pound 4-6-0 engine, pulling a mile of boxcars at seventy miles an hour across Pennsylvania on a summer's night was to feel a sense of power and exalted purpose that the ordinary earthbound citizen would never know.

Ernst Bauer spent most of his life on the railroad. Thirty years of backbreaking labor—from brakeman, to fireman, and finally to the coveted right side of the cab, the engineer's seat, driving Baldwin ten-wheelers, hauling coal over the Alleghenies. The pay was bad and the working conditions hard and dangerous, but his father stuck to it, a wage slave barely able to put food on the table for his family, and with little hope of ever bettering his condition.

One winter night during a run a glass water gauge burst open barely a foot away from him, scalding his face with superheated steam and blinding him permanently in one eye.

The management of the railroad used his injury as an excuse to fire him. There were no pensions in those days, and the railroad even refused to pay his medical bills. His wife Mathilde was forced to find work as a domestic to keep the family alive.

His father had never once considered any other kind of work. The railroad was his life, and he seemed to draw an almost perverse satisfaction from his victimization at the hands of the robber barons who owned and ran the railroads. A barely literate man, he had somehow—Bauer never discovered how—become caught up in the works of Marx and Engels, and spouted on endlessly about the crimes of capitalism, the exploitation of the working class, the need to redistribute the wealth. From their texts he drew a seemingly inexhaustible supply of resentments, and Harry learned early to associate the very name of Marx with everything unpleasant in his childhood.

At fourteen, Harry Bauer ran away from home for the first time, jumping a freight train for Chicago with an older friend. He was back a week later, tired and scared, but his brief taste of the world beyond Germantown left him hungry for more. A year later his mother died of influenza, and his sister was sent to live with relatives in Ohio. Ernst Bauer rapidly deteriorated into an embittered, lonely drunk, dependent on odd jobs and relatives for his survival. When Harry turned sixteen, he left home forever.

Bauer never blamed the railroad for his father's misfortunes and the family's poverty. He figured it was his father's fault. His father and Karl Marx.

In Bauer's eyes, Marx's social theories had victimized his father far more than the railroad ever did. Karl Marx invited his father to hide from himself and from the reality around him. It was Marx who fed him the excuses he needed to explain away his miserable lot in life and to justify his not making any effort to improve it. It was all somebody else's fault—the fault of the government, the fault of the system, the fault of the ruling classes. His father was a sucker, he decided. He had let others control his life.

At sixteen, Bauer promised himself that a sucker was one thing he would never be. No man, no company, no official, no other human being, no group of human beings, would he ever allow to exploit him. He would be his own man, truly free, beholden to no one for anything.

But it hadn't worked out that way.

A distant church clock struck the quarter hour. Quarter after what? he wondered. Four? Five? Six? His pocket watch was out of reach. And he suspected that he had forgotten to wind it again, anyway.

Bauer yawned and folded the pillow up double under his neck. What a mockery he had made of those early promises to himself. He was a bigger failure than his father had been. He had nothing. No family, no work, no money, no freedom.

A sudden loud rapping on the door of his room brought him upright in the bed, his senses instantly fueled by a rush of adrenaline. He snaked his revolver out from under the mattress, cocked the hammer, and tiptoed to the door. The knock was repeated, much louder this time.

"Who is it?"

A reedy English voice answered. "Mr. Bauer?"

"Who the hell wants him?"

"His Majesty's Government."

"No kidding."

"Would you open the door, please, Mr. Bauer?"

The American took a deep breath and pulled the door open, keeping the revolver trained in front of him. In the dim glare of the electric bulb in the hallway he saw the silhouette of a tall, stick-thin figure, draped nearly from chin to ankles in a loose-hanging black greatcoat. He blinked and smiled. Another vulture, Bauer thought, sharp-eyed and cagey.

"Greyson Bruce," the vulture said in a clipped, cultured British accent. He extended his hand in greeting. It found the revolver barrel instead. The vulture gripped it in a mock handshake and chuckled, displaying a row of uneven teeth. "Better uncock it, laddie. It might go off and wake up the whole hotel."

"What the hell do you want? Who are you?"

"I intend nothing sinister, if that concerns you," Bruce replied, no hint of apology in his voice. "You *are* Harry Bauer, I hope."

Bauer nodded in resignation, uncocked the revolver, and waved Bruce inside.

"May I sit down."

"I'm not really in the mood for company, Mr. Bruce. Just tell me what you want."

Bruce reached into a pocket inside his coat and produced a calling card. "I'm here on behalf of a representative of His Britannic Majesty's Government," he said. "This is his card." He handed the embossed rectangle of pasteboard to the American.

Bauer looked down at the card. It said simply, "Clement Hosier, M.P."

The lanky Englishman grinned. "Mr. Hosier is staying at the Baur au Lac Hotel. Suite 914. He has sent me here to invite you for breakfast."

"Breakfast?"

The birdlike Bruce rubbed his hands together in a businesslike manner. "Eight o'clock this morning, if that's convenient."

Bauer glanced down at the card again, and then at the surreal apparition of this dawn intruder, so confidently dispatched to command his presence.

"Can I tell him to expect you, Mr. Bauer?"

"You can tell him to stick his breakfast up his Britannic Majesty's ass."

"Come now."

"What does he want?"

"I'm sure he'll tell you at breakfast."

"What time is it now?"

"A quarter after six," Bruce informed him, without consulting a watch.

Bauer yawned and rubbed his face to dispel the fatigue. "Tell him I like my eggs soft-boiled."

BERLIN

Captain Kurt von Planetz, cigarette cupped in his fist, surveyed his new surroundings with disbelief. He was accustomed to working in cramped and dirty quarters close to the front, amid the stink of battle and the incessant thunder of artillery. This echoing warehouse in the Pankow district seemed cathedral-like by comparison. Its buttressed brick walls towered around him, and high overhead a clerestory of skylights filtered the March afternoon sun through thousands of panes of glass, their wavy imperfections prisming the light down through a complex pattern of oak collar beams and iron turnbuckles, inundating the empty reaches of the ancient enclosure with a warm amber glow.

Tucked away in a corner alcove between two of the brick buttresses the captain spotted a cluster of furniture—several tables and chairs, an oak rolltop desk, and a filing cabinet. Another officer was already there, sitting at one of the tables. He stood up and saluted smartly as the captain walked over. "Lieutenant Heinz von Buhring, Herr Captain," he said. "Welcome to our headquarters."

Von Planetz returned his salute casually. The captain was a soft-spoken man with a decidedly unmilitary bearing. He was prematurely bald and wore wire-rimmed spectacles. His slightly stooped posture, accentuated by narrow shoulders and a thin chest, gave him the frail and preoccupied look of a university professor or a scientist. In fact, he was a career police officer in the city of Hamburg—an inspector, assigned to the city's criminal investigations division. He loved police work because he believed it had a moral worth. As a devout Lutheran and family man, it was important to him that his occupation give him not just a livelihood, but make a worthwhile contribution to society as well.

He also loved police work because he possessed an analytical mind that relished the patient brainwork required of criminal investigations—the development of clues, the following of leads, the solving of puzzles. He was dedicated and he was good. Possibly the best, if there was any way to judge such things. His reputation had preceded him into the army, and it had tried to make appropriate use of his talents by putting him in its own investigations division. His time there had been spent largely in the gloomy task of gathering evidence against desertion cases, now epidemic in the German military.

General Von Gontard had singled him out for the job of escorting Lenin and his revolutionaries through wartime Germany because of the acute shortage of front-line officers, not because of his crime-solving abilities. He was simply the most dispensable officer on hand.

Well past the age for military conscription, he had volunteered for service. The Von Planetz family was of formidable Junker stock, and the males for generations had distinguished themselves in the military. In times of crisis, it was taken for granted that a Von Planetz would uphold family honor and tradition by defending the fatherland. The captain's father had been wounded at Metz in 1870, during the Franco-Prussian War, and two of his uncles had been killed there.

And the captain's oldest son, Frederick, had died at Tannenberg, on the Russian front, during the first months of the war.

Despite his family background, Captain Von Planetz had no great love for the military. He was loyal to country and kaiser, but he saw the war as a tragic mistake that would damage Germany for generations to come. His views were not popular, so he was careful not to share them. He did his duty and kept his mouth shut.

"We won't lack for space here, will we, Lieutenant?" he said.

Von Buhring relaxed. "No, sir." He pointed to an old oak kitchen table next to his. "This is your desk, Captain. Sorry I can't do better."

The captain considered the battered tables. They were bare except for a pair of kerosene lamps with tin bases and no shades on their chimneys. "No electricity?"

"No, sir. But we're getting a telephone installed tomorrow."

"That's something."

The captain placed his briefcase on the table, pulled the hard-backed chair out, and sat down. He looked for an ashtray, found none, and reluctantly crushed his cigarette out on the floor. He gazed around the cavernous warehouse. No one else was anywhere in sight. "Just the two of us?" he asked.

The younger officer nodded.

The captain removed his cap and placed it on the desk beside him. He had been promised a staff of six. He had hoped for four.

"Better here than the front, Captain," the lieutenant said, reading his thoughts.

Von Planetz nodded. Anything was better than the front. "Have you been briefed on our detail?"

"No, sir. Only that it's top secret."

The captain looked at his assistant appraisingly. He seemed the ideal young Prussian officer: handsome, blond, excellent family, first-rate military school. According to his records, he had distinguished himself on the western front, and been decorated with both the Iron Cross and the coveted *Pour Le Merite*. He had also received a stomachful of shrapnel at the Somme last summer. Since then he had been relegated to desk work. The war didn't seem to have wounded Von Buhring's spirits, however. He still wore the eager air of an officer cadet, bent on proving himself.

He didn't seem arrogant, either, the captain noted. For those lucky enough to survive it, the front had a way of beating the arrogance out of them forever.

The captain's own military record was far more modest. He had seen the Marne, and the mud of Passchendaele, but from the rear, not from the trenches. He was too old for that. There was no glory in his duties, just a great deal of work. And that suited him fine. He was serving his country. That was all that mattered to him. He didn't give a damn about medals.

"How's your stomach?" he asked the lieutenant.

Von Buhring seemed faintly embarrassed by the captain's solicitude. "There's still pieces in there. But I can eat and go to the bathroom all right, if that's what you mean."

"Don't they cause pain?"

Von Buhring shrugged, making light of it. "They told me at the military hospital in Beelitz they would treat it after the war."

The captain nodded. Everything had to wait until after the war these days. His own wife was in critical need of surgery. But the hospitals couldn't take her. Their first priority was military. And they could barely cope with the thousands of emergency casualties that daily flooded their wards and operating rooms. So Marthe, too, would have to wait until after the war. The thought was never very far from the captain's mind that the war might outlast her.

He pulled a folder from his case and laid it out in front of him. In a very unusual departure from military protocol, he had received this file late the previous evening directly from the hands of the German foreign secretary, Arthur Zimmermann, who had personally briefed him. It still gave him a small thrill to read the legend on the cover: OFFICE OF THE REICHSCHANCELLERY: TOP SECRET.

The first item in the folder was a photograph. It showed a middle-aged male, with a pointed beard and a cloth workman's cap scowling at the camera. His cheekbones were high and prominent, and his eyes, squinting at the sunlight, had a flat, Oriental cast to them. The captain handed the photo across to the lieutenant.

"Looks like he's constipated," Von Buhring said. "Who is he?"

"A Russian revolutionary. Vladimir Lenin. He's in Zurich now. Our government has agreed to help return him to St. Petersburg. In a few days we'll escort him and a group of his followers across German territory to Sweden."

The lieutenant looked up from the photograph. "A guard detail?" he said, letting his disappointment show.

The captain felt a surge of annoyance but checked it. "Yes, a guard detail." He handed the rest of the folder across. "This will explain the conditions," he said. "Our responsibility will be to make certain that nothing happens to him while he's on German soil."

"Sounds like a holiday to me, Captain."

Von Planetz gave the younger officer a hard look. There was still some arrogance there, after all. "It may sound like it, Lieutenant, but we're going to treat it as if it were the most important assignment of our lives."

Von Buhring straightened up, clearly taken aback. The captain, despite his casual, unmilitary manner, expected to be taken seriously.

"And find me an ashtray, will you, Lieutenant?"

ZURICH

At precisely 8:00 A.M. Bauer knocked on the door of Suite 914 of Zurich's most luxurious hotel, the Baur au Lac. He was wearing his best suit, a three-piece gray tweed. It was old. A button was gone from the cuff, and the pants no longer held much of a press. He wet his thumb and forefinger and tried to squeeze up some semblance of a crease over the knee, but it was hopeless. The material just sagged back into its permanently baggy condition.

Bauer knocked again, and after a long delay a pink-faced man in a silk dressing gown and slippers opened the door and glared out at him. "What do you want?" he growled.

"Are you Mr. Hosier?"

"Suppose I am? What of it?"

"I'm Harry Bauer. I thought I was invited for breakfast."

"I was in the bath," the man replied in a peevish voice. "I wasn't expecting you to be on the dot."

"Sorry. I'm usually late."

"Eight o'clock was Bruce's idea, not mine," Hosier said. He ushered the American through the foyer and guided him to a table by the window with a panoramic view of Lake Zurich. The table was set for two. "I frankly detest the early hours," he grumbled. "Unless of course I stay up all night."

He made a sweeping gesture in the direction of the view. "Then I'll admit they possess a certain tranquil sweetness. The anticipation of sleep, no doubt, made all the keener by delay."

Bauer nodded warily.

"Bruce doesn't like me," his host continued, words flowing from him now in a rush. "But that doesn't show much discrimination on his part. At the moment I have the distinction of being the most thoroughly disliked man in England. By the way, my name is Winston Churchill, not Clement Hosier. Forgive that silly calling card. A necessary deception, my government tells me. My presence in Zurich is supposed to be a secret. Sit here, Bauer. I'll call down for breakfast."

Churchill tightened the belt on his dressing gown and padded over to a telephone stand by the sitting-room door. He inflicted several vigorous cranks on the ringer and after some shouting in a mixture of English and mangled German, he managed to place an order for Canadian bacon, Swiss rolls with butter and preserves, a pot of tea, and a basket of fresh fruit.

Bauer had heard about Churchill. His father was a duke, or something close to it. His mother was American. He had made himself an international reputation as a journalist, Bauer recalled, with newspaper articles and books about his adventures in Egypt, South Africa, and India. In English politics he was more controversial than admired. An abrasive, flamboyant public style had earned him many enemies. And his recent involvement in the disastrous Dardenelles campaign had cost him his post as first lord of the Admiralty. The Liberal Party now considered him a liability. Although he was barely into his forties, an age when most political careers were just beginning, his career seemed to be coming to an end. He and Churchill had a few things in common, Bauer decided.

From the telephone Churchill ambled over to a large, trunklike contraption and pulled down the sides to reveal a well-stocked portable bar. He poured out two snifters of Courvoisier and carried them to the table, placing one in front of his guest. "I don't normally offer brandy at this hour," he said with an impish grin, "but this is a special occasion. I hope you'll indulge me."

The American smiled. "Here's to the morning," he said, raising his glass.

"Here's to the night," Churchill countered, hefting his snifter higher than his guest's. "Cheers."

They drank.

Bauer watched his host pace fretfully about the room. His movements were awkward and graceless, and his round baby face, hunched forward over his sloping shoulders, gave him the aspect of a petulant schoolboy. But his manner was combative and forceful. Churchill struck him as someone who expected others to accommodate him as a matter of course. He was clearly comfortable with himself and didn't seem to care whether anyone else was or not. Bauer liked that.

"You once worked for President Roosevelt, I understand," Churchill said, pulling two cigars from a humidor behind his chair and offering one to Bauer. "Don't refuse it, for Pete's sake," he warned as Bauer started to raise a hand. "I'll never forgive you. It's a Cuban Corona Corona."

Bauer took the cigar. "I was in military intelligence," he admitted, tucking the fat roll of expensive tobacco leaves into his vest pocket.

Churchill grunted, clipped the end off his own cigar, and stuck it in his mouth without lighting it. "You were close to Roosevelt?"

"Hardly. I wrote him some confidential intelligence reports, that's all. He chose me to act as his eyes and ears on a number of occasions."

"What occasions?"

Bauer hesitated. Churchill pulled the cigar out of his mouth and held it suspended in front of him, waiting for a reply.

"Cuba and Mexico," Bauer replied. "And Manchuria."

The Englishman's eyes lit up. "The Russo-Japanese War?"

The American nodded.

"What do you think of him?"

Had Churchill come all the way from London to pick his brains about Teddy Roosevelt? "I don't know." He shrugged. "A great man, I guess. Isn't that the general opinion?"

The Englishman's prematurely balding pate wrinkled in disgust. "Personally I have no use for him. He was positively rude to my father. And to me, for that matter."

Bauer shrugged. "I've never met him myself."

With a look of total self-absorption, his host fired up his Cuban cigar with a silver lighter, took two puffs, and then discarded the cigar in an ashtray. "You know something about trains," he said with another sudden shift of subject.

"Something. How did you find that out?"

"I poked around in your past a bit. I'm embarrassed to admit it, but there it is." He didn't appear embarrassed in the least. He held up his hand, palm outward. "Everything between us will remain confidential. You have my solemn word."

Bauer rested his brandy snifter on the table and sat back. "My father worked on the railroad most of his life. I hung around the yards a lot when I was a kid. And he used to sneak me aboard the engines on some of his night runs."

"And you played a professional sport?"

The American's face brightened. "Baseball. I pitched and played the outfield."

"I don't know much about the game," Churchill confessed.

"I was good, but I was a hothead. Me and authority. We never hit it off."

"Odd that you should join the military, then."

"When I was shut out of baseball, I couldn't settle into a job anywhere. I tried, but it just wasn't in me to work in an office or a factory. And I didn't have the education for a profession. The military was about all that was left."

"And you did brilliantly, I understand, eventually making the rank of major."

"Only because I got into special intelligence work. I never commanded men in the field."

"That sounds very modest, Bauer. But I don't think you're a modest man."

Bauer didn't reply.

"You've had problems in the military, even so."

The American shrugged. "I always had mixed feelings about the army. It let me get away, showed me the world, taught me things. But I never liked the discipline."

Churchill turned abruptly and began rummaging among some documents next to the humidor behind him. He found the folder he was looking for and turned back to Bauer. "What happened in El Paso?" he asked.

Bauer didn't expect this. He bridled. "Why're you interrogating me?"

"I'm not. I'm interviewing you for a job."

Bauer let his breath out slowly between clenched teeth. "You probably already know what happened in El Paso."

"You killed Victoriano Huerta."

"Yes. It was sanctioned, I was told. On the highest level."

"Then what?"

"Huerta's men came after me. For revenge."

"They didn't get you, obviously."

"No."

"Why did you disappear, then?"

"Because somebody inside U.S. Intelligence tipped Huerta's men. It wasn't safe for me to go back. I was marked. So I played dead."

"You don't know who?"

"It no longer matters. I'm not interested in revenge."

Churchill scratched his cheek thoughtfully. "Well, you did the world a service. Huerta was a cruel man."

"Sure. But so were Díaz, Obregón, Villa, Carranza, and Zapata."

"You weren't against killing him, were you?"

"I had no opinion, one way or the other."

Churchill pulled his cigar from the ashtray and studied the unlit end thoughtfully. "Do you have to approve of something before you'll agree to do it?"

"It helps."

"You don't believe in unquestioned obedience—even in a military situation?"

"No."

Churchill grinned. "You must have been damned valuable—for the American military to accept those conditions from you."

"I worked outside the command structure. I was a troubleshooter. The solutions were my own, not the government's. Roosevelt and Taft accepted this. Wilson and his people wouldn't."

"So you believe they decided to get rid of you."

Bauer nodded.

"You think they tried to frame you with Huerta?"

"Frame me and hang me," Bauer replied.

"You blame President Wilson?"

"No. People under him. The military brass. I don't know who. I've collected a lot of enemies over the years."

"You don't care who?"

"Sure I care, but I can't do anything about it."

Breakfast arrived and Churchill immediately turned his attention to the food. He slurped up the tea noisily and attacked the rolls with a manic gusto, plastering enormous amounts of preserves on them and stuffing them into his mouth with a minimal display of etiquette. Bauer had no appetite. He poured milk and sugar in the tea and sipped it lethargically. He'd have preferred a hot cup of coffee.

"Are you available?" Churchill asked, his words muffled by a mouthful of Swiss roll.

"For what?"

Churchill's manner changed abruptly. He pushed aside the breakfast dishes and focused his attention on Bauer so squarely that the American felt suddenly self-conscious. "We have an important mission to offer you," he said, pronouncing the words with the solemnity of a judge passing sentence.

Bauer leaned back in the chair and waited.

"There's a man here in Zurich," the Englishman began, getting up from his chair and walking to the window. As if to emphasize the confidentiality of what he was about to say, he pulled the heavy drapes closed, shutting out the view and the bright morning light. The room darkened dramatically, and Bauer noticed for the first time that a wood fire was smoldering in the suite's small tile fireplace. He watched Churchill's back as he prodded the smoking logs with a brass poker. The fire threw off a shower of sparks, and then flamed back to life, casting shadows across the room.

Churchill replaced the poker and continued where he had left off, his voice dropping to a conspiratorial murmur. "Vladimir Ulyanov is his name, but they call him Lenin. He's a Russian. A revolutionary. He's the leader of a group of political fanatics who call themselves Bolsheviks. They're a small, radical fringe party with damned little support among the Russian masses, but they're well-disciplined and clever. Excellent organizers. And militant. Normally they would be no more than a nuisance, but in Russia's present fragile social condition they are a positive menace. The present leadership is confused and incompetent and could collapse at any moment. And with a little luck and good timing, the Bolsheviks could seize power."

Bauer felt suddenly hungry. He picked up the one uneaten roll on the plate Churchill had shoved aside and bit into it. The crust was very hard, but the insides soft and agreeably chewy. He started to tell Churchill that he had absolutely no interest in Russian politics—or any politics, for that matter—but the Englishman waved his hand, indicating that he didn't want to be interrupted.

"The Germans plan to send that little bit of luck their way. In a few days they will be laying on a special train for this Ulyanov and a sizable number of his minions. The train will return them, in secret, to St. Petersburg—or Petrograd, as they call it now. And once this gang is back, the Germans plan to finance their efforts to overthrow the provisional government."

Churchill picked up his now-cold cigar, stuck it in his mouth, and bit down hard on the end. "Lenin is an unscrupulous rascal," he continued. "He will happily climb into bed with anybody who'll help him gain his ends. And the Germans want him in power for the very good reason that he intends to take Russia out of the war. That suits the Boches perfectly, of course. If Russia lays down her arms, the kaiser will be able to throw all his weight against us in the west." Churchill pulled the cigar out of his mouth. "And if he is able to do that," he added in guttural tones so low they sounded like a growl, "he'll drive the British Expeditionary Force right into the Channel. And throw the French army in on top of us for good measure."

Agitated by his own words, Churchill rose from the chair again and paced back and forth in front of the fireplace, jabbing his fist in the air, the picture of frustrated righteousness. Bauer watched the performance with awe.

"This Mongol-eyed rabble-rouser must not be allowed to reach Russia," Churchill concluded, pointing a finger at his guest, his voice ringing with the emphatic finality of a royal edict.

Bauer was reminded of the recruiting posters he had seen last year in London, with the words "England Needs You!"

blazoned beneath the stern visage and pointing finger of Lord Kitchener. "What do you expect me to do?"

Churchill's pregnant silence gave him his answer. Bauer pushed his chair back from the table. "What's wrong with your secret service?" he demanded. "Can't they handle this?"

"They are handling it," Churchill argued. "And they've decided that you're our man."

Bauer shook his head doubtfully. "Boy. I don't know."

"What are your reservations?" Churchill demanded.

"You want me to kill him?"

"How else can we stop him? Lash him to a lamppost?"

"It's not my kind of operation."

"Nonsense, Bauer," Churchill retorted. "You've been involved in any number of operations like this. You confirmed that yourself—Cuba, Mexico, Mongolia. Don't deny it. You have every right to be proud."

"I'm not an assassin."

"You've killed men before. Huerta, for one. You just admitted it, not two minutes ago."

"And look where it got me. That's a mistake I don't intend to repeat."

Churchill jabbed his cigar toward the American. "Don't be so bloody difficult. Lenin's our common enemy. And if he gets back to Russia, he'll be worth an entire division. Perhaps two."

Bauer shrugged.

Churchill's eyes narrowed pugnaciously. "Lenin must be stopped. If Russia defects it may cost us the war!"

"There are others you could hire for this."

"No," Churchill insisted. "This is perfect for you. You're here on the spot, you know German, you know trains, and you know how to go about this sort of thing. And most important of all," he added, pausing dramatically, "you'll succeed."

Bauer drank his brandy in silence.

Churchill tilted his head forward slightly and peered at the American from under his brows. "Your country is now in this war with us. Wilson will make the official declaration today. If you fail to take our offer and Russia eventually makes a separate peace with the Germans, thousands of lives—many of them American—will be needlessly lost. I appeal to your patriotism. I am offering you an opportunity few men ever get—to do something noble for your country."

"I've already done my share of noble deeds for my country. And my country told me to go to hell."

"You fail to see what's at stake," Churchill argued, ignoring the sarcasm. "If this man and his rabble ever seize control of Russia, we in the west will find our very civilization, our democratic values, in peril of extinction. You shake your head, but I am utterly certain of what I say. This war has ravaged the social order. And in its weakened state it's prey to a virus like Bolshevism. The disease of Marxist revolution is in the air. And all over Europe men are breathing its malodorous vapors. Stopping Lenin now will be a service to posterity."

Churchill continued on in this vein for a considerable time, pacing in front of Bauer, his voice and gestures rising to theatrical heights, calling upon a range of emotion and language that only a practiced orator, in total command of his subject, could summon.

It was a moving, impassioned appeal, and while Bauer considered a lot of it to be of the same composition as the material the Turk had scraped from the bottom of his boot yesterday at the gypsy fair, he had run out of good reasons to refuse. "How much money are you offering?"

Churchill beamed at him with the look of satisfaction of someone who has just triumphed over an opponent at the poker table. "Ten thousand pounds, plus expenses."

Bauer's eyes widened in surprise. He recalculated the sum in American dollars. It came to $48,000. How could he say no?

"What's the situation?"

Churchill walked over to a desk by the window and retrieved a large rolled-up map. He returned to the table and unrolled the map across it, using the breakfast china to hold down the corners. "Lenin will board a train some time in the next few days—most likely at Zurich's central station." He jabbed a forefinger at the spot on the map. "You see that Zurich is quite close to the German frontier. Once he reaches the border," he continued, tracing the route with his finger, "he and his party will be loaded onto a special railroad car that will take them north across Germany to Sassnitz, on the Baltic. From there they'll begin a wide detour around the Russian-German front—to Sweden by ferry, north around the Gulf of Bothnia, south through Finland, and across into Russia." Churchill straightened up. "We want you to stop him when he's in Germany. That's important."

"Why?"

"So the Germans will get the blame."

"How do you know that's the route he'll take?"

"We have a reliable source."

"There's not much time to arrange anything fancy."

"I'll help you in every way I can, of course."

"Where's Lenin now?"

"That's a difficulty," Churchill admitted. "The man is rarely seen in public these days. The Bolsheviks protect him. Few people know what he looks like, and even fewer know where he lives. His movements are carefully guarded secrets."

"Is that all you know?"

Churchill shook his head. "The source I mentioned knows more. His name is Oskar Blum. He's a socialist, but he spies for us on the side. He can get you inside the radical camp. After that, it's up to you."

Bauer crossed his arms. That forty-eight thousand dollars might prove hard to get. "How much in advance?"

"Half. Just tell me your bank and I'll have the money deposited in your account immediately."

"I don't have a bank account."

"Then we'll open one for you."

"I'd rather have the cash."

"As you like. I'll have it here for you tomorrow."

The Englishman bent to the table and snatched up the two snifters of brandy. He thrust one into Bauer's hand, and raised the other in a toast. "Here's to your success," he pronounced, his voice charged with a sincerity that surprised the American. "I damn well wish I was doing this myself."

"So do I," Bauer mumbled. He felt suddenly old and alone. There was a chance here. Probably his last chance. He was going to have to take it. Forty-eight thousand dollars could buy him a good farm somewhere. A quiet life. A little independence. Make this last killing and then get out. Why not?

He smiled to himself at the two meanings of the word "killing."

He peered into the snifter. The heady caramel aroma of the Courvoisier made his nostrils itch. He tilted the glass against his lips and gulped the burning liquid down his throat.

WASHINGTON

Colonel House walked quickly along the northeast corner of the Tidal Basin. It was a sparkling spring day. The cherry trees that lined the borders of the basin were beginning to bud, showing the first hints of the color that in a day or two would explode in an extravagant fireworks of blossoms.

House felt so nervous that he was having trouble breathing. He paced along the edge of the basin, clasping and unclasping his hands, frequently glancing up in anticipation of seeing the man he had come there to meet—Brigadier General Charles Harper, chief of U.S. Army Intelligence. Despite his skill at manipulating people, House dreaded direct confrontations with anyone, even tradespeople and domestics. With someone like Harper, the thought made him physically ill. But he had no intention of avoiding it. House was a soft-spoken, almost timid man, but he was not a coward. He would confront Harper if he had to, because too much was at stake not to confront him.

He caught sight of him, finally, standing underneath one of the cherry trees at the far southern end of the basin, near the Jefferson Memorial. Harper was in mufti, but he saluted House as he approached. "Good day, Colonel."

"Good day, General," House replied, his voice flat. "Shall we walk?"

General Harper was a tall, rangy man with a genial southern drawl that disguised a tough, shrewd mind. He grinned broadly. "It's a right fine day for it, Colonel."

The two men continued along the edge of the basin, well away from the walkways, where a passerby might overhear their conversation. Harper drawled on about the weather and the opening of the 1917 baseball season.

House, the very master of small talk himself, interrupted Harper abruptly. "What about Harry Bauer, General?"

The general nodded. "Yes, sir. He's alive, sir. Just as you said."

"You told me he was dead."

House's abrupt tone put the general on guard. "Well, yes, sir. I believe I did. That's what we thought."

"He was killed by Huerta's men, you told me."

"Yes, sir, I believe that's what I told you. We had reports they'd killed him. Five of them. Across the border, out in the desert somewhere. They said they left him there. When he didn't resurface, we assumed they were telling the truth. Now it seems they weren't."

"Did Bauer actually kill Huerta?" House demanded.

"Yes, sir. He surely did."

"On your orders?"

"Yes, sir. That's correct."

"And how did Huerta's men find out?"

The general shrugged. "Does it make a difference?" he countered, his voice suddenly hard. "You wanted Huerta killed. We got him killed for you."

"And I was grateful for that, General, as I proved to you at the time," House replied, his voice soft as a breeze. "I regret to be so blunt, but please answer my question."

General Harper's big, leathery face was in turmoil, the muscles of his cheek working, his eyes blinking, his lower lip under attack from his teeth. "We have a problem there," he admitted. "It was one of our own men who tipped them off."

House pretended to be shocked. "Why would anyone do something like that?"

Harper shook his head. "Bauer was a hard man to get along with. He didn't like a lot of the things we did, and he made no secret about it. Especially after your President curtailed most of our black operations. He thought it was horseshit, if you'll pardon my language. That's what he said. He was a risk to the security of our operations. And he was insubordinate. I knew it was only a matter of time before he'd get himself—and the rest of us—in trouble. He was dangerous. A loose cannon. So one of our men saw the opportunity to get rid of him and he took it. He had it coming to him, believe me. He was a hard man."

House wrinkled his forehead mockingly. "You always spoke quite highly of him, as I recall."

Harper shook his head. His mouth was pressed closed so hard that the skin around it had turned white.

"Were you jealous of him, General?"

"I was *afraid* of him!"

"Who's the individual who betrayed him?"

"I can't tell you that, Colonel. Sorry."

The colonel smiled politely. "Did you have a hand in persuading this individual to do it?"

"No," the general retorted.

"But you took no action against him after you knew."

"No."

"Why not?"

Harper's thin coating of affability was now worn completely away. "Jesus Christ, Colonel. Bauer's death was the best thing that could have happened to the Wilson administration! We would have had to fire him anyway, with Wilson's demands that we curtail our operations. So he would have been in a position to embarrass you. Anytime he wanted to."

House stopped walking. He propped his hands on his hips and looked up at the much taller Harper. "But Bauer *is* alive, General. That's the whole point. He's alive and working for the British in a highly secret operation. When it's over, Bauer will surface again. And he *will* be able to embarrass us about the Huerta affair. More now than ever."

"Maybe he doesn't know that much."

"Then why did he disappear?"

The general shook his head. He didn't want to hear any more.

Colonel House tightened the screws. "Let me make our problem clear, General. When the war in Europe is over, the Wilson administration will play the leading role in negotiating the terms of the armistice. Europe will look to the United States for leadership in establishing world order and a lasting peace. Anything linking the Huerta affair to our President could harm his reputation fatally."

"What are you getting at?"

"It's my responsibility to protect the President."

"You're going to make me a scapegoat?"

"Frankly, I think you deserve it, General. By lying to me, you lied to the President."

Harper's face turned a dangerous hue of purple. "But,

Jesus, Colonel, it was you who ordered me to have Huerta killed!"

House motioned Harper to keep his voice down. "It was ordered for compelling reasons of national interest. And if you had not complicated things by trying to settle a score of your own, we'd have no problem today. Does anyone else know the truth of this?"

"No."

"You're absolutely certain?"

"Of course!"

House pressed a hand against his stomach to still the churning. "I will do what I can to solve this mess. For both our sakes. In the meantime, you must give me your word that you will never divulge this matter to anyone. Ever."

"Look, Colonel. . . ."

"Your word, General Harper."

"You have it!"

Colonel House nodded. "Thank you," he said. "Just leave everything to me." He turned abruptly and walked away.

BERN, SWITZERLAND

Baron Gisbert von Romberg, German ambassador to Switzerland, watched with a mixture of anxiety and irritation as the Swiss socialist, Fritz Platten, entered his office in the German Legation. It was nine o'clock, Friday evening. It had been a long day in a long week, and the baron was looking forward to a weekend in the mountains, far from the reach of the diplomats, generals, foreign ministers, journalists, and the scores of others whose sole occupation in life seemed to be to make his complicated.

Like this socialist Platten. Almost everything about the man annoyed the stodgy Prussian. Platten was secretary of the Swiss Social Democratic Party, an organization Von Romberg considered subversive. In Germany a revolutionary of Platten's stripe would be in prison, not inconveniencing the kaiser's ambassador on a Friday evening. To further irritate the baron, Platten was tall, slim, handsome, and barely past his thirtieth birthday. And unlike most radicals, he affected the dress of a *boulevardier*, favoring broad-brimmed white fedoras and bright paisley scarves, one end of which he liked to drape over a shoulder, to impart an air of sporty nonchalance.

The amount of forbearance required in a diplomat's trade sometimes gave the baron a severe headache. And Platten, as this Ulyanov's go-between, was at the moment a man to be accommodated. And how sick he was of accommodating him! He had expected that their last bargaining session, just yesterday morning, would be the last time that he would ever have to suffer the presence of this flamboyant young radical.

The baron managed a gracious smile. "Ah, Herr von Platten. You're working very late today."

There was no "von" in Platten's name, as Von Romberg well knew. He made a habit of adding it in the mistaken belief that he was appealing to the young Swiss's vanity. The truth was, he didn't quite know how to deal with this sort of man. Platten was polite, but at the same time he treated the baron in too familiar a fashion—almost a teasing condescension—as if he were a grouchy uncle to be cajoled and humored.

"I have an urgent request from Lenin," Platten declared without preamble.

Von Romberg stiffened at the word "urgent." Foreign Secretary Zimmermann had just yesterday cabled his final approval of all the arrangements that he and Platten had so painstakingly negotiated during the past week. If Lenin made new demands now, the whole project would be jeopardized. The baron's bucolic weekend at Interlaken began to fade from view. "What is it?" the ambassador demanded. "I thought he had agreed to everything? We have given him everything he asked for—extraterritorial status, guaranteed safe conduct. What more can he want?"

Platten unwound his scarf lazily. "Lenin *has* agreed to everything," he said, showing the baron a toothy smile. "You have absolutely nothing to worry about, Herr Ambassador."

"Then what does he want?"

"He merely wishes to clarify one aspect of the financial arrangement."

Von Romberg narrowed his eyes suspiciously. "What aspect?"

"The meeting we have arranged when the train reaches Berlin, Excellency," Platten answered. His expression betrayed a sudden nervous embarrassment, like someone about to tell a girl's father that he has gotten her pregnant.

"What about it?"

"Lenin requests that a portion of the funds you have promised be delivered at that meeting."

Von Romberg squeezed his fists together to fight down a murderous anger. This was outrageous. Lenin was little better than a bandit. The German government had agreed to support the Bolsheviks financially but for Lenin to ask for money to be handed over to him in cash before he had carried out even the first part of his half of the bargain was bald extortion.

"This is highly irregular," Von Romberg complained. "Why does he ask for this?"

Platten hastened to explain. "For several reasons, Excellency. The first and most important is simply that the man is destitute. He doesn't have the money to buy a decent suit of clothes. Naturally he's too proud to admit this, but I can tell you this because I know it to be the truth. And the Bolshevik party itself is desperately short of operating capital. They must have some portion of the funds you've promised as soon as possible. Lenin reasoned that if you could bring some of it to the train in Berlin, it would not only avert a crisis, it would be an important token of trust. It would reassure him about Germany's cooperation in the future."

"How much does he want?"

Platten smiled hopefully. "Ten million marks."

Von Romberg felt dizzy. "The plan was for him to leave tomorrow!" he fumed. "Saturday! I will have to telegraph Berlin. It's already the weekend. Surely he realizes that this will delay everything!"

"I'm very sorry for this complication, Excellency," Platten said. "Truly, I am."

"I will do what I can," Von Romberg declared miserably, picking up a book from his desk top and dropping it back with a heavy thud. "But there must be no more demands! Lenin must leave by Monday at the absolute latest. He must understand that. Or he can find his own way back to Mother Russia—and without any German marks to line his pockets!"

Fritz Platten nodded apologetically. "He wants it in Swiss francs, Excellency," he said.

The ambassador uttered an obscenity under his breath.

"I'm certain that he'll be most grateful for your under

standing and help," the Swiss said, rewinding his scarf carefully around his neck. "There will be no further complications,
Excellency, I promise you. We will leave on Monday, April
ninth. It will be a momentous day!"

ZURICH

Harry Bauer paced impatiently through the nearly deserted
corridors of the Swiss National Museum, a medieval-style
fortress on the Platz Promenade, north of the railway station.

He'd have preferred something better than an assassination, but he was desperate for work, after all, and Churchill's
appeal had been eloquent. And once persuaded, Bauer never
looked back. The assignment had already breathed new life
and purpose into him, and he pushed everything from his
mind to concentrate on the task before him.

First, he needed information. A lot of it. He had to locate
Lenin, discover what he looked like, where he spent his
time, something of his habits, his friends and associations,
and how much protection he had. He also needed to know
Lenin's own plans. When was he leaving? Who was traveling
with him? What arrangements had he worked out with the
Germans?

And he needed the information quickly.

At three o'clock he crossed a central courtyard, mounted a
broad flight of stairs to the museum's first floor, and found his
way to Room 50, a large hall that housed an extensive collection of armory.

He walked through an exhibit of sixteenth-century weap-
onry from the Zurich Arsenal, and near the center of the hall
he paused to examine a particular display case. The afternoon
was cloudy, and what light filtered down through the high
stained-glass windows was dim and yellow. He gazed briefly
at the items beneath the glass, then squinted at the words on
the brass plaque affixed to the wood frame at the bottom of the
case. They told him he was looking at a sword, ducal hat, and
banner presented to the Swiss Federation by Pope Julius II,
in 1512.

The room was deserted. The air felt heavy and damp,
laden with centuries of furniture polish and mildew. He
waited by the display case for almost five minutes and was

about to leave when he heard a gentle tapping on the floor behind him. The tapping came closer, then ceased.

The floor creaked and a pair of hands settled on the display case beside him. The fingers were white and thick, their backs heavily forested with red hair. Bauer turned to look at their owner. He was as tall as the American and carried a cane. Beneath his bowler hat his red-moustached face looked lumpy and coarse, as if its creator had tired of it and abandoned it unfinished. His black suit was shiny at the elbows and frayed at the cuffs.

"Have you seen Hodler's frescoes on the far wall?" Bauer inquired, following the ritual Churchill had required him to memorize.

"Yes," the man answered, his voice heavy and unsteady, as if he were catching his breath. "The Swiss retreat after the battle of Marignano."

"You're Blum?"

The man nodded. "Who're you?"

"I was told you could tell me about Lenin."

"Not so loud," Blum muttered.

Bauer chuckled. "There's no one here."

"Why do you want this information?"

"I don't think I can tell you that."

"What do you want to know about him?"

"Where does he live?"

Blum didn't reply.

Bauer pulled a Swiss five-franc note from his inside coat pocket and placed it on the display case. Blum's hand reached for it, but Bauer held it to the glass.

"Where does he live?" he repeated.

"I don't think I can tell you that," Blum replied, mimicking Bauer.

"You can't tell me, or you don't know?"

Blum shook his head. "It's a closely kept secret. He has many enemies."

Bauer sighed. "Where does he spend his time when he's not home?"

"The library at the Predigerkirche. You might find him there."

"Where is it?"

"In the Zahringerplatz, in the Old Town."

"Where else?"

"The Café Adler, in the Rosingasse. It's a hangout for the Russians."

"When did you last see him there?"

"He gave some lectures there, last year."

"Your information is useless, Blum."

Churchill's would-be informer said nothing. He kept his eyes and the tips of his fingers on the five-franc note, still held to the glass by the heel of Bauer's palm. There was no dignity in Blum's expression, only a pathetic neediness. He was a born victim, Bauer saw, a collector of resentments. A lifetime of missed chances and petty injustices had made him both fearful and treacherous.

"You'll have to do better if you want the money," Bauer warned him.

"Ulyanov is leaving soon. For Russia."

"How soon?"

"In three days."

"How do you know?"

"I was at the meeting where he announced it. Yesterday."

"Why were you there?"

"I'm on the list to go with him."

Bauer found that hard to believe. "Are you going?"

"Of course," Blum said.

"How come? It doesn't sound as if you're very close to the man."

Blum regarded Bauer contemptuously. "I'm not. He's a Bolshevik. We don't get along at all."

Bauer shook his head. "I don't get it. Why does Lenin want you, then?"

"He doesn't. But he's a realist. He knows that if he takes only his Bolsheviks with him, it'll look as if the Germans had him in their pocket. So he's broadened the party to include some other political philosophies. I'm a Bundist. So are several others. I think two are Social Democrats. But we're in the minority. Most will be Bolsheviks."

"Why bother to go, then?"

Blum seemed offended by the question. "To have my point of view heard, of course."

"How many are in the party altogether?"

"About thirty. More may be added."

"How well do you know the others?"

"Not well at all."

"None of them?"

Blum thought for a moment. "I know about twenty of them, but only by their reputation. Not personally. I don't agree with the Bolsheviks, so I've never become friends with them."

"When's the train leaving?"

"Monday. The three-ten from Central Station."

"To where?"

"Schaffhausen, on the border. Across the border they'll put us on a special German train. I don't know where or at what time."

"What's special about the train?"

"I don't know."

"No idea?"

"It probably means that it's off the regular schedule. An extra train, just for us."

"Is that all you know?"

"A lot of money is coming."

"Money? From where?"

"Germany. It'll be on the train."

"How much money?"

"Millions."

"Who told you this?"

Blum didn't answer. Bauer repeated his question.

Blum countered with one of his own: "What do you plan to do?"

"Just getting information," the American answered. "I'd like to meet Lenin."

"I've told you all I know," Blum replied. "Go see Fritz Platten, at the Café Adler. He's there every night. He's close to Ulyanov."

"Is that all?"

"Yes."

Bauer released the pressure on the five-franc note and watched Blum slide it across the glass of the display case and into the side pocket of his pants.

"I need a list of names of the people in Lenin's party. As many as you can remember. Physical descriptions, too. Everything you can recall about them. Can you write all that down for me?"

Blum shook his head. "It'll take time."

"How much time?"

"A day. Maybe more."

"I'll get it from you tomorrow. Give me an address. I'll come by and get it from you."

"It'll cost more than five francs," Blum warned. He scribbled his address on a bit of torn paper and shoved it across the glass.

Bauer nodded. "If the information's good, you'll get more."

Blum stared back. He didn't like what he was doing. Informers usually didn't. "I want a hundred."

"You're greedy."

"I'm risking my life, telling you all this."

Bauer snorted in disgust. "Don't make me feel sorry for you, Blum. Nobody'd kill you for what you're telling me. They'd send you to bed without supper."

"You don't know the Bolsheviks."

"You're supposed to be telling me about them."

"I want a hundred for the list."

"You'll get it. Any other expensive information you want to share with me?"

Blum considered the question. "Watch out for Morozov," he said finally. "I'll give you that for free."

"Who's Morozov?"

"You'll find out."

Blum walked away, his cane tapping sharply on the polished parquet. His limp was pronounced, Bauer noticed. One leg appeared to be several inches shorter than the other, causing him to list to one side every other step.

Bauer looked down again at the sword, ducal hat, and banner arranged beneath the glass, but his eyes didn't focus on them. A plan was beginning to take shape in his mind.

LONDON

Foreign Minister Arthur Balfour lingered in his Whitehall office long after most of the building's employees had left for the weekend, pondering the events of the day.

For the third or fourth time he opened the folder on his

desk marked "Top Secret" and adjusted his reading glasses. Inside lay two typewritten sheets, transcriptions of two decoded diplomatic cables received several hours earlier. The first one was from the British ambassador in Washington:

AMERICANS OKAY PLAN WITH THEIR MAN BAUER.
HAVE PERSONAL ASSURANCE FROM HOUSE. REGARDS,
BRYCE

The second was from the British consulate in Zurich:

BAUER ON BOARD. THE GAME'S AFOOT. WINSTON

Balfour replaced the sheets inside the folder and closed it. The plan was moving forward nicely. That was what was disturbing him. How good was the plan?

He moved to the window and stood there for a long time, gazing across the shadows of the Horse Guards Parade into the dark of St. James Park, his eyes following the glittering necklaces of streetlamps that defined the park walkways. The serenity of the view always made it difficult for him to believe that the centuries-old British Empire, whose sovereignty, law, customs, and language were the everyday experience of more than half the inhabitants of the planet, was tonight fighting for its very survival.

On Monday, just two days hence, the Allies would launch a major new offensive against the German lines near Arras. Casualties would doubtless be heavy, as they had been in all previous offensives. And despite the optimistic predictions of the generals, the gains that would result were highly uncertain. A conclusive victory was probably no longer possible without the help of the Americans—help which would not be felt for months.

Defeat, on the other hand, once unthinkable, now loomed as a dread possibility.

If Lenin came to power and took Russia out of the war, Germany could still win.

So much was coming to hinge on this obscure American, Harry Bauer. His success in stopping Lenin might be the single most important act of the war. Could he be depended upon to carry it out?

The foreign minister decided that there was something more that could be done. The British had troops stationed at the Haparanda-Tornio border crossing between Finland and Sweden, the route Lenin was likely to take to reach Petrograd. They could stop him there—if he got that far. On what pretext they might detain him, he could not imagine, but he decided that the border post must be alerted, in any case.

Balfour took one further step. Returning to his desk, he drafted a secret cable to Ambassador Buchanan in Petrograd. Balfour's message directed the ambassador to inform personally the Russian government of Lenin's plans, and instructed him to press the government for some indication as to whether "it intended to take any steps to counter this danger." Cumming had expressed doubts that it would do any good, but the effort had to be made nevertheless, Balfour decided. His hope, of course, was that Miliukov, president of the provisional government, would recognize the threat that Lenin posed, and if Lenin still somehow got through, he would at least have the presence of mind to have the man arrested.

Feeling marginally reassured, the foreign minister summoned a messenger to deliver his cables to the code clerk on night duty. At least there would now be three chances to stop Lenin, not just one.

But Bauer's chance was the one that counted. The next few days would decide it, he thought, switching out the light on his desk. From here on out, it was in the hands of fate.

Fate and Harry Bauer.

SATURDAY
APRIL 7

ZURICH

Calvinist Zurich went to bed early, even on Saturday night. For nearly an hour Harry Bauer wandered through the gloomy maze of empty alleys and passageways that made up Zurich's Old Town district, searching for a street called the Rosingasse. Around him the night's steadily thickening mist had wrapped the city in a damp shroud, blurring lights and obscuring shapes until it was impossible even to read a street sign. He stopped on the deserted quai along the River Limmat to decide what to do.

Had Blum invented the Café Adler, he wondered, just to get that five-franc note?

He listened to the murmuring night noises on the quai, the bumping of hulls against pilings, the lap of water against the stone embankments. A disembodied voice, or the hollow clop of a horse's hooves, filtered occasionally through the swirls of fog. He felt he was being watched. Foggy nights in old European cities could play tricks on the mind, and he shivered to dispel the sensation.

The hell with it, he decided. He'd have better luck tomorrow, in the daylight. He crossed the quai and entered the first break between buildings. He was swallowed up immediately by an inky-dark, cobblestoned alley that smelled faintly of fish and urine. It slanted up steeply from the river, and after a dozen steps he paused. A window in the wall at his left caught his attention. White gauze café curtains obscured the interior, but he could see patches of light and hear the hum of voices inside. Letters had been painted on the glass in Gothic German script, but they were so peeled and faded that he couldn't read them.

The door opened and a gust of warm air and blue smoke hit his face. Three men staggered out. The one in the middle was drunk and leaned on the others for support. They turned and headed down the alley toward the quai, talking Russian in loud, emotional voices.

He entered and stood for a moment by the door, absorbing the impact on his senses. Through the haze he saw one deep, low-ceilinged room, thick with people. A din of noise pounded his ears—raised voices, raucous laughter, chairs scraping across the bare floor. A heady aroma of tobacco, sweat, and stale beer stung his nostrils.

The Café Adler was alive and throbbing—not to music or dance or sexual flirtations, but to the raw passion of argument. Every table seemed to be the center of a heated discussion, with everyone gesticulating forcefully with fingers and fists as they shouted to be heard.

A pair of exhausted waiters were kept in constant motion delivering plates of bread and sausage and fresh mugs of beer among the dense, turbulent sea of heads and arms.

Bauer studied the customers. They were young and Slavic mostly, and poorly clothed. The men favored beards and heavy boots. The few females he could identify were drab specimens, with pale, unmade-up faces and shapeless outfits that gave them more the appearance of boys than adult women. They, too, were caught up in the passionate talk, their higher-pitched voices competing with the men's for attention.

Bauer had altered his appearance slightly by donning an eyepatch, a bowler hat, and a loud yellow necktie. This would get him noticed, of course, but that was the idea. People would remember the eyepatch and the necktie, but not the man behind them.

He tapped the arm of a departing customer. *"Sprecken zie Deutsch?"*

"Pretty good," the man replied. He was a short, skinny Slav with a round face and a mop of unruly blond hair that fanned out from a big cowlick at the top of his head. He was slightly drunk.

"I'm new here. I'm looking for Herr Fritz Platten. Do you know him?"

The Slav pointed to a big table near the center of the room. "He's the well-dressed one, with the pretentious manner," he said, weaving unsteadily on his legs. "Can't miss him."

Bauer edged through the crowd to Platten's table and introduced himself. The Swiss grinned broadly and shook his hand energetically. Platten looked even more out of place than Bauer, his slim figure resplendent in a handstitched beige suit and polished brown-and-white dress shoes.

"I haven't seen you here before, Herr Bauer," he said.

"I'm an American journalist," Bauer explained, raising his voice a little to be heard over the din. *The Saturday Evening Post.* You've probably heard of it."

"Of course I have!" the Swiss exclaimed in a way that indicated he probably had not. "An American journalist! How exciting. Please, you must join our table."

Platten hunted up an extra chair and squeezed it into the space beside him. He banged his palm on the table to silence the others and introduced his guest. Each rose to offer Bauer a listless handshake and a suspicious stare. Against the surrounding noise Bauer had not caught any of their names.

"You speak excellent German, Herr Bauer," Platten said. "I congratulate you."

"My parents were from Leipzig. They immigrated to America forty years ago."

"My parents, too, are German. But our family has lived in Switzerland for over a hundred years."

Platten seemed eager to talk, but he was constantly interrupted by visitors from other tables, all of whom he greeted effusively. His expansive manner reminded Bauer of a few politicians he had known. He affected the same air of worldly sophistication, yet bubbled over with a synthetic enthusiasm designed, like his clothes, to call attention to himself. He was naïve and narcissistic, an ambitious young man who wanted desperately to be taken seriously, but wasn't sure he would be.

The man sitting on Bauer's left nudged him. "I'm Karl Radek," he said. "A journalist, like you." He reached out and squeezed the lapel of Bauer's new topcoat between a thumb and forefinger. "But not as well paid, obviously."

Bauer changed the conversation. "Your friend is a busy fellow," he said, tipping a thumb toward Platten, now chatting with a solemn-faced young woman who kept putting her mouth near Platten's ear so he could better hear her.

Radek, a red-faced Austrian with thick glasses and a mop of curly hair, rolled his eyes comically. "Fritz does everything," he replied. "Tonight he is a travel agent. If you qualify, he'll sell you a one-way ticket to Petrograd." This caused the others at the table to laugh uproariously.

After a few more such inside jokes, Radek jumped up and moved to another part of the café. A beer arrived in front of Bauer. He sipped it, and his eyes found Radek again, entertaining another crowd several tables away.

Around 1:00 A.M. the café's frenetic pace slackened somewhat. Platten turned to Bauer. "Since the fall of the czar," he said, "this place has been pandemonium. The Russians are so hungry for news they stay up till all hours, trading the latest gossip and rumors."

"They must be anxious to return home," Bauer said, hoping to coax something more worthwhile from the Swiss.

"Some are," Platten admitted. "What newspaper did you say you worked for?"

Bauer cursed inwardly. He was triggering Platten's suspicions. "*The Saturday Evening Post*," he replied, plunging into his lie wholeheartedly. "It's a weekly magazine. I'm writing a series of articles for it on the war and the radical movement in Europe."

The Swiss seemed reassured. He smiled brightly. "What about you personally, Herr Bauer? Are you sympathetic to our cause?"

"I try to keep an open mind," the American replied blandly. "I support social change, but it's hard to sort out all the players and what they stand for."

That proved to be a good answer. Platten launched into a short lecture on the socialist movement, identifying the various camps within it and the positions they held on the major issues. Bauer pulled out a pencil and notebook and began scribbling industriously. He learned that Platten himself was secretary of something called the Swiss Social Democratic Party.

"Who are some of the emerging new leaders in the socialist movement today?" Bauer heard himself ask. "Obviously you're one yourself. But who are some other men we should be expecting to hear from in the near future?"

Platten said the socialists didn't think in terms of leaders. Bauer pressed him for names, and finally Platten mentioned several, none of whom meant anything to the American.

He pressed harder. "What about this Vladimir Lenin? Isn't that his name? How do you rate him?"

Platten reacted with surprise. "Lenin? You know of him?"

Bauer shrugged elaborately. "I've heard others mention his name." That was certainly true. Churchill, for example. And Blum.

"Ilyich is a great man," Platten declared, his tone as matter-of-fact as if he were describing the color of his hair.

"Ilyich?"

"His close friends call him that. It's his middle name."

The implication was clear that Platten considered himself to be one of those close friends.

"Maybe I should interview him," Bauer prodded.

Platten's loquaciousness withered abruptly. He sipped his stein of beer and said nothing. The others at the table fell silent as well, and several shot hostile glances in Bauer's direction. These were people who had learned the hard way to be careful in front of strangers, he realized. And in his case he had to admit their instincts were sound. He repeated his suggestion.

"That may not be possible," the Swiss said.

"Why not?"

"I'm sorry, but I really can't tell you more."

"I'd like to meet him, at least. Does he ever come in here?"

"Not anymore. Ilyich gave a few lectures here last fall. But they weren't terribly popular." The Swiss smiled sardonically at the memory. "After the first one hardly anyone showed up."

"Where does the guy live? Maybe I could just run over there and get a few quotes from him. Nothing time-consuming." Bauer sensed that he was pressing his luck.

The young Swiss socialist shook his head. "I can't share that information with you, Herr Bauer. I'm sorry. Ilyich's privacy is very important to him. And there are those who might wish him harm. We have to protect him. All I can offer is to convey your request to him personally. If he consents, then an interview might be arranged. But there really isn't much time. . . ."

Bauer waited for Platten to finish his sentence, but he never did. A woman from another table appeared at his side, leaned over, and kissed him impulsively on the ear. The young Swiss's smooth, graceful manner suddenly deserted him for a schoolboy's awkwardness. He jumped up, nearly tripping over himself, and fetched a chair for her. Bauer moved his chair over to make room. She squeezed in between them and then kissed Platten again, this time on the cheek. He blushed fiercely, and the woman laughed, amused by his discomfort.

"This is my American friend," he said, when he had recovered his equilibrium. "Henry Bauer. He's a well-known international journalist. Henry, this is Inessa Armand."

The way the Swiss was now using him to impress his friends embarrassed Bauer, especially in front of this woman. She turned toward him and held out her hand. He wasn't sure whether he was expected to kiss it or shake it. He shook it. The sensation was novel. Her fingers felt strong and warm in his palm—with a smooth resiliency that was surprisingly pleasurable. Had it been that long since he'd felt a woman's hand? Or was hers in some subtle way different?

Inessa Armand studied him boldly. Her luminous gray eyes seemed to embrace him. "Henri Bauer," she repeated, in French-accented German. "Why haven't I ever heard of you?"

The American found himself short of breath. "I'm not as well-known as I should be, I guess," he replied.

Inessa giggled. "I'm sure you are," she said teasingly. "All Fritz's friends are famous, aren't they, Fritz?"

Platten's face reddened. "I think you're a little drunk, Inessa."

Inessa ignored him. "You must know Mabel Dodge," she said to Bauer.

"I'm sorry. Who?"

"Mabel Dodge. She lives in Greenwich Village in New York City. She's *very* well-known."

Bauer shrugged helplessly. "Afraid not."

"Are you sure?" she challenged. "John Reed and Walter Lippmann know her."

"I work for *The Saturday Evening Post*," he said, astonished by his own quickness. "We're in Philadelphia, not New York."

Inessa seemed disappointed not to have made a common connection. She turned back to Platten. Bauer felt the loss of her attention keenly, as if everyone had suddenly fled the room and left him with no one to talk to. He marveled at the presence she projected, even when "a little drunk." She was as plainly dressed as her female counterparts in the café, but there was a dramatic difference in the way she carried off the revolutionary fashion. She was small but didn't seem to be. Her gestures were extravagant, like those of a stage actress, and her wide, expressive face, large eyes, unruly chestnut hair, and slightly protruding upper lip made her such a commanding figure that she seemed to take up more space than she actually did. Her voice, too, belied her size. It was unexpectedly resonant for a woman, with a slight huskiness that, coupled with her French accent, imparted an air of intimate excitement to even her most trivial pronouncements.

Bauer realized that she was talking to Platten about travel arrangements—and Lenin. He saw Platten tap her arm surreptitiously, warning her to be more discreet.

"Henry is doing an article for his magazine," Platten said. "He wants to know about our friend Ilyich."

Inessa turned and appraised Bauer with the same wary look he had received from the others at the table. "Can he be trusted?" she asked the Swiss.

Platten shrugged noncommittally. She smiled slyly. He noticed that her mouth was wide and her teeth unusually even and white.

"*Can* you be trusted?" she asked Bauer.

"Can any man?"

She laughed. "What do you want to know?"

Her eyes distracted him momentarily from his question. More than just flirting with him, she seemed to be challenging him. He couldn't shake the feeling that she could see right through him, and it unnerved him.

"Tell me about Lenin," he said.

"We're comrades." She used the Russian word *tovariches*.

He waited for her to continue. She started to say something else, but then clapped a hand over her mouth as if she had uttered something impolite.

More beer arrived. It was Munich—very fresh and cellar temperature, the way he liked it. He couldn't remember ordering it, though. And with the constant changing of tables that had been going on since his arrival, he wondered how the waiters kept the individual checks straight.

Maybe the kaiser was buying.

Someone stood up on a table, waved his stein of beer in the air, and began singing the "Marseillaise" in a loud, off-key voice. The others at his table stood and joined, and soon the whole room began to resonate with the powerful strains of the French national anthem. It petered out a minute later, in confusion over the words and melody. After some embarrassed laughter, someone at another table began the "Internationale," the theme song of the radical movement.

Everyone in the restaurant seemed to know the song by heart, and they all stood up and joined in, singing out with a bold conviction and feeling that sent shivers right down to Bauer's feet. The voices swelled until the very walls vibrated with the sad, intensely romantic melody. It was impossible not to be moved by it.

Bauer saw tears in Inessa Armand's eyes. He felt like crying himself, but he didn't know why. I'm getting drunk, too, he thought.

He was also getting nowhere. He stood up with the others and, without looking down, slipped Inessa Armand's purse off the back of her chair and under his jacket. When the song ended, he excused himself and headed for the men's room.

It was a dingy stall in the cellar, and it smelled powerfully of disinfectant. He pushed the bolt closed, sat down on the toilet, and opened the purse. The barrel of a small pistol caught his eye. He pulled it out and examined it. A snub-nosed Derringer revolver. He rolled the cylinder with the palm of his hand, peering into the five chambers as they rotated past. It was loaded. He slipped the pistol back into

the bag and pulled out a small leather address book. He
fingered quickly through the pages. Lenin was listed under
"I" for Ilyich. Next to the name a street number: 14 Spiegelgasse. No telephone. He replaced the book, shut the purse,
and unbolted the door.

A large-framed man in a black tunic and high boots was
blocking the narrow basement corridor. As Bauer edged past
him, the man dropped a hand hard on his shoulder.

"Hello, comrade. Have we met?"

"No."

"What are you doing here?"

His accent was so thick Bauer barely understood him. He
tried to pry the hand from his shoulder, but its grip only
tightened. In the dim light he could make out little of the
stranger's features, but he was enormous, looming many inches
over Bauer's six-foot frame. One side of his face and neck was
grotesquely disfigured, as if someone had applied a torch to it
and melted it like wax. His breath stank of vodka and cheap
tobacco.

"I came to take a piss. What the hell do you think I'm
doing here?"

The man muttered something in Russian. The next instant
Bauer felt his head slam against the corridor wall and his shirt
collar twist around his throat. The purse fell out from under
his jacket and clacked onto the tiles between his feet. He
tried to resist, but he was pinned helplessly against the wall.
The brute strength of the man was unbelievable. A fist slammed
twice into his stomach, and he curled up in agony, gasping
for air. Barely conscious, he was dragged by his collar across
the cellar, up a short flight of steps, and out into the street.

James McNally found himself a place in the alley were he
could sit undisturbed and still command a close view of the
front door of the Café Adler. He folded a copy of the *Neue
Zurcher Zeitung* twice and placed it carefully on the edge of
the narrow sidewalk and sat on it.

After an hour the cold damp had soaked through the
newspaper and begun to penetrate the seat of his trousers.
He got to his feet and tried leaning against the side of a
building. The clock in the Central Post Office tower struck
one. He paced up and down the length of the narrow Rosin-

gasse several times but then stopped. The alley was dark, and the fog was so thick that even from twenty feet away it was difficult to see. He returned to his spot on the sidewalk and reluctantly sat on the wet newspaper.

During the next hour the door of the Café Adler opened and closed many times. He tensed and relaxed his muscles and shook his head back and forth to fight off the growing urge to sleep. The post office clock struck two. The dampness on his rear end helped to keep him awake, but it had become a torture. He felt as if he were sitting on a block of ice. He began to fear that he had missed his man.

The sudden slamming of a door caught his attention. It wasn't the door he had been watching, but the café's service entrance, a few steps away. He stood up, tugged at his seat to separate the wet cloth of his trousers and underpants from his skin, and slid along the wall to get a better view.

A big man was pulling another man up the steps. The other one, probably drunk, staggered free. Before he could take more than a step, the big man caught him and hit him in the face, then struck him rapidly several more times, until he slipped and collapsed onto the stone pavement. The big man pulled him up by his coat collar and hit him again.

The beating continued for several minutes. The repeated smack of the fist against flesh sickened McNally. Finally the big man let his victim slide to the ground. He delivered a final kick to his head and returned inside the café.

McNally hurried over, hands clutched over his mouth, fearing what he would find.

BERLIN

Captain von Planetz and Lieutenant von Buhring had pushed together their two desks and spread a large rail map of Germany across their combined surface. Von Buhring pointed to a spot near the bottom of the map, near the Swiss-German border. "After Schaffhausen the Swiss trains come across to Singen, on our side. That's the obvious place to transfer them."

Von Planetz studied the map. "Maybe too obvious," he replied. He pointed his finger at a small dot squeezed between the town of Singen, where the major German customs post was located, and the Swiss frontier. "Gottmadingen, here to the south, is better. It's a very small station. The carriage can be parked on a siding right there and the entire area secured by the local police. It will be much easier to guard than Singen."

Lieutenant von Buhring said that he thought it was an unnecessary precaution, but the captain remained firm. The lieutenant rolled out a big sheet of drafting paper on top of the map. It contained the mechanical drawings of a rail coach, top, side and end perspectives, and a list of the specifications. "This is the carriage we're using," he said. "Winterthur A.G. is the manufacturer. These are the designer's plans."

Von Planetz studied the plans in silence for nearly five minutes, several times moving the kerosene lamp for a better view. "Whose carriage is it?" he asked.

"Prussian State Railways," Von Buhring replied.

"Where is it now?"

"In the rail yard at Mannheim."

Von Planetz looked at the telephone on top of the filing cabinet. It had arrived an hour ago, but had not yet been installed. "We'll have to telephone Mannheim," he said.

Von Buhring rolled up the drafting paper. "I'll go back to GHQ again, Captain."

"Thank you. Tell them we want the carriage at Gottmadingen no later than tomorrow midday. Don't take any excuses. Remind them that we have priority use of the tracks—even in the military zones."

The lieutenant nodded.

"And order them to add a baggage car. There are thirty-two in Lenin's party, and they're going home for good. There's certain to be a lot of luggage."

Von Buhring retied the string around the drafting paper and set it aside. "I'll go right now," he said.

"We'll go together," Von Planetz decided. "I must requisition an automobile. I want to be in Gottmadingen when those carriages arrive."

On their way into the center of Berlin, Von Planetz reviewed in his head everything they had done so far. He was not the type to leave anything to chance, especially in a matter as important as this. "Do you happen to speak any Russian, Lieutenant?" he asked.

"No, sir. Do you?"

The captain shrugged. "I grew up in East Prussia—Augustow, right near the Russian border. Our family cook was Russian, and so was our governess. Until I went off to school, my Russian was probably better than my German."

Von Buhring laughed. "It wasn't like that in Hannover. I thought everyone in the world spoke German until I was fourteen."

"Did you plan a career in the military?"

Von Buhring sighed. "Yes, but now I don't know, with this injury. . . ." He rubbed his stomach. "I'll get married and work for my father, I guess. We own a big printing business in Hannover. Two hundred employees."

"Do you have a girl?"

The lieutenant blushed. "Inge. We're engaged. She's happy I'm wounded. She thinks I'm reckless. She hated it when I was at the front. And I thought she'd be so impressed when I got my officer's rating. With women you can never win, Captain."

Von Planetz smiled. "You're not supposed to," he said. In the day they had been working together, he had developed an affection for the lieutenant. He was about the same age as Frederick, the son he and Marthe had lost at Tannenberg.

"You must bring your fiancée to dinner," he said. "After the war."

"That's kind of you, Captain. We'd enjoy that."

After the war. When Marthe would be well again. Would that day ever come? Von Planetz gazed out at the avenues of the great imperial capital flowing around them. How austerely beautiful Berlin was, even in wartime. On the broad promenade of the Sieges Allee, he pointed to the long row of statues of the Prussian rulers as they slipped past. "I once knew all their names by heart," he said.

"The guardians of our destiny," Von Buhring replied.

Was there a hint of irony in his voice? the captain wondered. A bare few months ago the talk had still been of victory. Imperial Germany, like imperial Rome in the classical age, would soon dominate the world, they said. The empire would one day stretch from the arctic tip of Norway to the jungles of equatorial Africa; from the Atlantic shores of Ireland and Portugal to the borders of Mongolia and Tibet. *Pax Germania*. It was God's will.

Now all anyone said was "After the war."

A lump formed in the captain's throat. What would life be like in a defeated Germany? Maybe it was just as well that he lacked the imagination to picture it. He hooked his thumb in his tunic belt. With his fingers he felt the raised letters of the legend on the brass buckle: *Gott Mit Uns*— "God With Us."

He wondered about that.

PETROGRAD

Colonel B.V. Nikitin, normally the most unemotional of men, felt tears of frustration well up in his eyes. The telephone on his desk didn't work. Neither did any of the telephones in any of the other offices on his floor, and there was no one in the building who knew anything about fixing them. He smashed the receiver back into its cradle, causing the black Bakelite casing, made brittle by the cold, to shatter into a hundred small shards.

Colonel Nikitin was head of counterespionage for Russia's new provisional government. Essentially, he *was* counter-intelligence for the government. Most of his predecessors, employees of the czar, had been either killed or dragged off to prison, and recruiting replacements for them had so far proved impossible.

Nikitin interpreted his franchise very simply. He was there to catch German agents. And German agents, in his mind, included Russian Bolsheviks. Especially Bolsheviks. More than any of the other radical groups, they were agitating against the war, causing desertions in the military, spreading strikes and chaos in the cities. They were doing the enemy's work, so it had to follow that they were German agents.

His alarm at the Bolshevik menace had been compounded by the extraordinary visit, just the day before, of someone from the British Embassy. A Major Alley, a personal emissary of Ambassador Buchanan himself. Alley brought news of a German plan to transport the exiled Bolshevik leader, Lenin, along with a party of his followers, through Germany to Russia.

Today, Sunday, March 25, on the Old Style Russian calendar, Nikitin had arrived at his office early, determined to have Lenin and his party arrested when they crossed into Russia. But he had found it impossible to get any help from anyone in the new government. In power for only a few weeks, they were still mired in confusion and factional infighting.

He had decided that he must act on his own. He would telephone General Lavr Kornilov, the commander of the Petrograd garrison, give him Major Alley's information, and try to persuade the general to stop Lenin.

But then the telephones refused to function. He removed his gloves—there was no heat in the building on Sunday—pulled a piece of paper from a drawer, found a usable steel-tipped pen, dipped it into the inkwell, and began to write a detailed note to the general, pleading the urgency of his case.

When he had finished it, he walked to the window and looked across Znamenskaya Street. It was snowing heavily. It would take too long to find a messenger on a Sunday. And this was too important a matter to entrust to a messenger in any case. He decided that he had better deliver the note in person.

Colonel Nikitin locked his desk and buttoned his coat. Once he had set his mind to a task, the colonel was unwavering in his determination, no matter what the odds against him.

And in the colonel's mind, Lenin was a traitor. So he must be stopped. It was as simple as that.

SUNDAY
APRIL 8

ZURICH

Bauer felt something patting his face. A wet cloth. It hurt. He reached up to stop it.

"Can you stand?" a voice asked in English. A shape loomed over him in the dark and helped him to his feet. Still disoriented, Bauer leaned against the stranger for support. His sides felt numb, and his head throbbed.

"There's some blood on your lip," the voice said, handing him the wet cloth. "Any bones broken?"

"Don't think so." Bauer pressed the cloth gingerly against his mouth. The slightest touch sent waves of pain crashing through his skull. He ran his tongue around his gums, tasting more blood. Several teeth felt loose.

"Better get you home. I've got a cab here. Come on." The stranger helped him into a horse-drawn carriage waiting a short distance away, and pushed in beside him.

"Where do you live?"

Bauer mumbled the address of the Pension Helvetia, and the stranger relayed it to the driver on top. They heard the slap of reins against the horse's rump, and the carriage bounced forward down the narrow alley.

"My name's James McNally, by the way. I'm the American consul here in Zurich."

"How did you find me?"

"I've been following you."

"How come?"

"Orders."

"Whose orders?"

"The White House. Who attacked you, do you know?"

Bauer pressed the towel to his mouth, then took it away and looked at it in the dim light of the carriage. The blood had stopped. "No idea," he muttered.

"What were you doing in there?"

Bauer glanced sidelong at the man.

McNally chuckled. "I know what you're up to," he said. "If that's what concerns you. The Lenin mission. I'm supposed to help you."

"I grabbed a woman's purse. He must have seen me."

"Why on earth did you do that?"

"I thought she might have Lenin's address in it. She did."

McNally chuckled. "I could have given you that. Fourteen Spiegelgasse. What did he look like?"

"Who?"

"The one who attacked you."

Bauer sighed. "Big as an ice truck. Disfigured face."

"Morozov," McNally said.

Bauer remembered Blum's warning. Watch out for Morozov. He should have taken him more seriously. "Who is he?"

"When he doesn't have anything else to do, he's a bodyguard for our friend Lenin. He specializes in terrorist bombings. One exploded in his face a few years ago. Unfortunately he survived. A brutal man."

They rode in silence for a while, listening to the rhythmic clop of the horse's hooves on the cobblestones. McNally produced a pipe from his coat pocket and jammed it into his mouth without lighting it. The carriage moved across the Rathaus Bridge. Through the fog Bauer could make out the gray silhouettes of several long, low buildings.

"The meat market," McNally said, pointing to the buildings with his pipe stem. He wrinkled his nose at the sickly sweet odor. "The Swiss still eat their roasts, while the rest of Europe starves."

Bauer saw the rows of empty stalls. A solitary workman was hosing down the pavement, readying the market for the next day's business.

"They say it smells like that at the front," McNally murmured, his voice heavy with disgust. "The blood and guts of the slaughterhouse. And we'll be in it soon."

Bauer said nothing. He was furious with himself. A few more kicks in the head, and Morozov would have put an end to his mission before he had even begun it. He forced his mind back to business. "You know anything about a woman named Inessa Armand?"

McNally shook his head.

"She's one of Lenin's followers. It was her purse I lifted."

"I can ask around about her for you if you like." McNally offered. "I have excellent sources in Zurich."

"It's not important. Do something else for me."

"Of course. If I can."

"I need some back doors."

"I don't follow you."

"Some escape hatches."

"Where?"

"Along Lenin's route through Germany. Three would be good. One somewhere around Stuttgart or Frankfurt, one in Berlin, and one near Sassnitz."

"You sure that's the way he's going?"

"According to the people who hired me."

"You going on the same train with him?"

"Probably."

"Know how you're going to carry it off?"

"Most of it."

Bauer fell silent. He could see that McNally wanted to hear more. But he wasn't going to get any more. The consul groped around in his pockets for matches, found some, and lit his pipe. "I can get you names and addresses in those areas," he admitted after a couple of thoughtful puffs. The smoke had a cloying cherry odor. "These will be people who could hide you for a few days, but I can't promise they'll be able to get you out of Germany."

"Hiding me is good enough."

"It'll take at least forty-eight hours to alert them," McNally warned. He dug into his pockets again, produced a small notepad and pencil, and scribbled his address on it. "Come by later today. About five o'clock. I'll have names and addresses for you by then."

"Thanks."

When they reached Bauer's pension, McNally opened the door for him and helped him out. "You sure you'll be all right?" he inquired.

"A little rest, I'll be okay."

McNally climbed back into the cab. He reached a hand out the window to shake Bauer's. "If I may say so, I think you're a great patriot for undertaking this mission."

"I'm doing it for the money," Bauer answered. "Not the flag."

McNally smiled, taking it as a joke. "Don't underestimate this Lenin," he warned.

Bauer wanted to tell McNally not to underestimate Harry Bauer, but he just nodded. Being underestimated was part of his stock-in-trade. He watched the consul's carriage until it had disappeared around the corner, then turned and hobbled up the steps of the Pension Helvetia. Tonight he was pretty certain he'd be able to sleep.

GOTTMADINGEN, GERMANY

Captain von Planetz walked the short distance from the Hotel Bahnhof across the town square to the train station, holding his breath at what he would find. Lieutenant von Buhring walked alongside.

It was just past nine o'clock in the morning. The sky was cloudless, and the sun felt warm in the crisp air. Spring had come to the small village on the Swiss border, but the town did not look up to greeting it. Although spared by its location far from the grinding apocalypse of the war zones, Gottmadingen looked forlorn and dismal. Her young men were gone, and three years of neglect showed in peeling paint and plaster, missing roof tiles and broken shutters. And no one had planted anything this year in the dozens of window flower boxes that lined the square.

Von Planetz stepped across the twin set of tracks that ran past the small station and stopped near a siding hidden in a grove of evergreens about a hundred feet from the end of the station platform. A single passenger carriage, coupled to a baggage wagon, sat on the rail, with a military guard posted around it. Both carriage and wagon, their dark green flanks gleaming from a recent scrubbing, bore the eagle and shield insignias of the Prussian State Railways.

"Where's our locomotive?" Von Planetz demanded.

"It'll be here this evening," Von Buhring answered. "It was delayed by military traffic."

"Damn it, we're supposed to have priority."

The lieutenant nodded apologetically. "I'm sorry, Captain. I did my best. They just yell back at me. They lecture me about the men dying in the trenches because they can't get replacements and ammunition to them fast enough. I just don't have the nerve to argue against that anymore."

Von Planetz understood. A new Allied offensive was imminent near Arras, on the western front, and Germany was throwing in everything it could find in preparation for it.

The captain followed his assistant up the steps at the near end of the carriage and inspected the interior. The car contained eight compartments—three second class with comfortable, padded upholstery, and five third class with bare wooden seats. A lavatory with water closet and washstand was located at each end.

"The two of us will sit in here," Von Planetz said, pointing to the last compartment in the third-class section at the end next to the baggage car. "We'll let our thirty-two passengers divide up the other seven compartments however they wish." He walked farther along the aisle. "How many doors are there?"

"I count ten, Captain," Von Buhring said. "One front, one back, and four on each side of the carriage."

"We can leave the door opposite our compartment open, but once our passengers are on board, all the other doors must be locked."

"Surely no one's going to try to escape?"

"It's not to keep them in. It's to keep everyone else out. The carriage will have extraterritorial status—like a foreign embassy. The train will be treated as a bit of Russian territory being moved across German soil. What we'll be doing, essentially, is protecting its borders until it's safely through."

Lieutenant von Buhring shook his head in wonderment.

"Most important," the captain continued, "we must obey to the letter Lenin's demand that there be absolutely no contact between his party and any German national during the trip. That includes us." The captain pulled a short stick of white chalk from the pocket of his tunic and bent down and drew a straight line across the aisle between their compartment and the next one up. "This will mark the boundary between us. They've chosen a Swiss German—Herr Fritz Platten—to be the official guide and spokesman for their party. He'll be our go-between. All communication with the travelers will have to be channeled through him."

Von Buhring nodded. "I'm not dying to get to know any of them, anyway."

After a close inspection of the track, the signals, and the railway station itself, Von Planetz was at last satisfied that everything was in order. He and the lieutenant spent the rest of the morning making telephone calls and doing paperwork. At noon they adjourned to the hotel dining room for lunch.

"A surprise for you today, gentlemen," the proprietor crowed, setting a large tray on the serving table beside them. "Real bratwurst. As delicious as prewar." He carved several generous slices onto two dishes and set them before the officers.

"Dare we ask how you managed this miracle, Herr Kunstler?" Von Planetz said.

The proprietor pressed his forefinger against his lips and shook his head in mock alarm. "The enemy may be listening," he warned in a stage whisper. "For the sake of the fatherland my lips must remain sealed."

The two officers laughed politely. To accompany the bratwurst, Kunstler produced a bowl of hard-boiled eggs, a loaf of bread, two bottles of schnapps, and left the men to themselves. They were the only guests in the hotel.

Von Buhring broke open the loaf of bread. It was gray inside. "*Ersatz*," he said, showing it to the captain. "Baked sawdust."

Von Planetz examined a piece, crumbling it between his fingers. "Be thankful for the bratwurst."

Kunstler reappeared suddenly in the doorway, gesticulating urgently. "Captain. There is a call on the telephone for you. From Berlin!"

Von Planetz went to the telephone stand in the vestibule off the dining room and took the call. He returned to the table a few minutes later, but he didn't sit down. "I'm afraid I have to go to Zurich. Immediately."

Von Buhring's jaws, busy gnashing on a slice of the sawdust bread, stopped in mid-chew.

"That was Foreign Secretary Zimmermann himself, if you can believe it. He's arranged a meeting for me. Someone in Zurich has information for us."

"About our detail?"

"I assume so. He wouldn't say any more. The train to Zurich takes about three hours. I'll be back this evening."

"At least eat some of the bratwurst before you go."

"You eat it."

Twenty minutes later Captain von Planetz was waiting on the train platform, dressed in civilian clothes. He felt a mixture of excitement and foreboding. It wasn't every day that a captain in the army got a personal call from the foreign secretary. Whatever awaited him in Switzerland, it was clear that the German High Command placed a great deal of importance on his mission. He welcomed the opportunity to prove himself worthy of it.

ZURICH

The Spiegelgasse, a steep alley of broken cobblestones a few blocks west of the Café Adler, wound up through a crooked defile of ancient buildings housing a mixture of workshops, stores, and apartments. Number 14 was on the narrowest stretch, directly opposite a sausage factory. The factory was closed on Sunday, but a lingering stench still emanated from it. Bauer caught his breath and walked over to Number 14.

The house was a dirty gray five-story structure punctuated unevenly with brown-shuttered windows. The ground floor was occupied by a shoemaker's shop. It appeared closed for the day, but behind the windows Bauer saw the cobbler sitting on a low bench, tacking nails into the sole of a boot.

The entrance to the upstairs floors was at the right of the shop, in a narrow alcove barely three feet deep. A row of four mailboxes hung by the door. Bauer squinted to read the names on them: Kraus, Kammerer, Stein, and Sverdlov. He checked them again, carefully. No Lenin or Ulyanov.

Bauer walked to the next corner, then turned around and walked back. There could be no mistake about the address. McNally had confirmed it. Lenin was either hiding behind one of those four names, or he didn't receive his mail here. Bauer looked for an inconspicuous place to stand and keep watch on the entrance. Thirty paces down the street he came to the corner and stopped. There seemed to be no place to watch Number 14 without being observed, so he did the next best thing. He just leaned against the wall and waited.

Ten minutes passed. Twenty. Half an hour. A young couple went into the building next door. An old woman in a window across the street noticed him and took to staring at him. He stared back. Two hours passed.

Bauer was about to give up for the day when he saw two men emerge from Number 14. One of them, in a broad-brimmed pearl-gray hat and white scarf, he recognized as Fritz Platten, the Swiss socialist whom he had met in the Café Adler last night.

The other man he had never seen before.

They turned in the opposite direction and walked toward the river. Bauer followed them at a distance.

Platten's companion presented a vivid contrast to the debonair Swiss. Inches shorter and many years older, he strode alongside the younger man with shoulders hunched and head jutting forward, his bearded chin protruding like the cowcatcher from the front of a locomotive. The rim of his workman's cap was pulled forward over his eyes, and he wore the hobnailed boots of a mountain climber. His pants were baggy and too long, and his coat was wrinkled and dirty. He looked like a pugnacious tramp—Charlie Chaplin with a chip on his shoulder.

He was talking to Platten in a very animated fashion, punctuating his words with frequent comic gesticulations of his arms and fists. Bauer wanted to laugh out loud. This was Lenin? The formidable revolutionary? The man the Allies feared could win the war for Germany?

The American followed them past the Romanesque eleventh-century Gross Munster, with its helmet-shaped domes and statue of Charlemagne, poised over the city with gilded crown and sword. A block past the church they came out on the Limmat quai and walked along the embankment to the Bellevue Platz, an open square by the Quai Bridge, where the river broadened into Lake Zurich, sparkling silver in the spring sunshine.

Their destination was a newsstand in the park. Bauer waited until they had purchased several newspapers and moved to sit on a bench away from the park's pedestrian traffic. The American bought his own newspaper from the same stand, and keeping out of their line of sight, circled around to a large tree behind their bench and leaned against it, pretending to read his paper. Platten was deep in conversation with Lenin. He strained to overhear their words, but caught fragments only.

"What do they expect?" Lenin asked.

". . . performance. . . ."

". . . prisoner exchange. . . ."

". . .take time. . . ."

". . .peace treaty. . . ."

". . .when we take power . . . I've always said. . . ."

Platten withdrew a fat envelope from his coat pocket and handed it to Lenin. Lenin removed some bills from it and counted them. "It's only. . . ."

". . . all I could get . . . Romberg . . . rest in Berlin . . . tomorrow or Tuesday. . . ."

"How much did the bastards . . . ?"

". . . ten million."

"Ten?"

"Yes, twelve in Swiss francs . . . at the station."

Blum's information was accurate, Bauer realized. Twelve million Swiss francs would be waiting for Lenin in Berlin. An immense amount of money. And it was only the down payment.

It was a breathtaking bargain, Bauer realized. If Russia laid down her arms, she would be putting Germany in a position to dictate the terms of the peace agreement. The Huns would strip Russia bare—take her food, her weapons, her resources, her rolling stock, her national treasury. And probably a good piece of her territory to boot. It would be an armistice indistinguishable from abject surrender. Lenin was willing for Russia to pay that price. He was prepared to sell his country—and the Allied cause—to her enemy in return for political power.

What Lenin lacked in appearance, he certainly made up for in megalomania, Bauer thought. Suddenly he felt much better about what he was going to do. It was just a shame that Churchill had insisted on his doing it in Germany. It would be a hell of a lot easier to do it right here in Zurich, today, and get it over with. But the bureaucrats, typically, couldn't settle for something so straightforward. They always wanted a little more for their money—an extra twist that nine times out of ten screwed up an operation that otherwise would have worked. The way most countries conducted their cloak and dagger operations, Bauer thought, they posed more of a threat to the initiator than to the target. Well, it was their money. If he wanted to get paid, he'd have to make it work their way.

Platten and Lenin discussed travel arrangements. Again Bauer was able to catch only snatches of the conversation, but it was enough. As Blum had told him, Lenin's party would board a train in Zurich station tomorrow afternoon, Monday, at 3:10. At the German border they would be met by a military escort to take them to the special sealed carriage that would transport them across Germany.

Lenin returned to the subject of the money several times. The matter seemed to obsess him. No doubt he had fears that Germany might renege. Or that he was stepping into some kind of trap.

Bauer's mind kept returning to the money, too. Twelve million Swiss francs was about two and a half million dollars.

The two men stood up, finally, and walked back in the direction they had come. Bauer folded his newspaper, thinking of following them, but abruptly changed his mind. He knew where Lenin was going to be tomorrow, and what time he'd be there. That was really all he needed to know.

From the train station Captain von Planetz took a taxicab directly to the police headquarters on the Werdemuhle-Platz. He spent half an hour in Room 24, renewing his acquaintance with Chief Inspector Klaus Steiner, a policeman with whom he had worked several times before the war on cases involving their two countries. He and the inspector had always gotten on well, and Von Planetz knew that Steiner, whose family had come originally from Silesia, was sympathetic to the German cause. If he needed a favor, this was someone he could count on. And he expected he might well need one.

From the police station, the captain caught the Number 8 tramway line and ten minutes later stepped off at the bottom of the Militarstrasse, the avenue that flanked the main military compound for the canton of Zurich. He walked north, alongside the vast exercise field that lay between the arsenal and the military barracks, counting the public benches that bordered the grass.

Several small marching units were out on the field, parading smartly back and forth to the shouted commands of a drill instructor. The Swiss army, the captain thought with a welling of contempt. Toy soldiers who never went to war.

At the eighteenth bench he slowed. Two benches ahead of him a man was sitting, reading a newspaper. Or pretending to read one. It was apparent from his nervous habit of peering over the top of the paper every few seconds that he was waiting for someone. The captain stopped a few paces in front of him and touched the rim of his bowler. *"Guten Tag."*

"Guten Tag," the man replied in a startled voice.

"I'm looking for a language tutor. Do you know of any?"

The man lowered the newspaper. He was supposed to say, "What language do you want?" but he just stared blankly past the captain's face.

Von Planetz touched his hat again and started to walk off. Several steps away he heard the man's voice behind him, ragged with anguish. "Please. I've forgotten my answer."

The rules told the captain to continue walking—but experience told him that this was obviously the man he was supposed to meet. He turned around. " 'What language do you want,' " he supplied, hiding his exasperation.

The man let out his breath. "Yes. That's it. I'm terribly sorry. I'm nervous and I forgot. Please sit down."

The captain sat on the bench and introduced himself.

"I'm McNally," the other man mumbled. "I'm no good at this kind of thing, and I don't pretend to be."

Von Planetz indicated that he understood. Then, for nearly a minute, the other man said nothing. The captain waited patiently, holding his curiosity in check.

Finally the American reached into his inside coat pocket and produced a photograph. He gave it to Von Planetz with a trembling hand. It showed a young couple. The man was wearing the uniform of a German naval officer.

"The girl," McNally said. "Amy. She's my daughter. They were married three years ago. They live in Berlin. Her husband, Rolfe, is stationed with Admiral von Spee." The

American took the photograph back and returned it to his pocket.

Von Planetz waited for the rest of the story.

"Now that we're at war with Germany, the authorities in Berlin have accused my son-in-law of spying. Simply because of me, because of my job here in Zurich as the American consul. They have arrested him."

"Are you in contact with them?"

"The authorities?"

"Your daughter and son-in-law."

"We've kept in touch, of course. I'm afraid that's what's aroused suspicions. Now I don't dare communicate with them at all. I'm afraid it'll make their situation worse."

Von Planetz digested this silently. The American consul seemed on the verge of tears. The captain could appreciate that McNally was in a difficult situation, but he doubted that he was telling the truth. He guessed that the man's son-in-law *had* been spying for him. Otherwise McNally would be acting outraged, not contrite and frightened. He was guilt-ridden for having gotten his son-in-law in trouble, and now he planned to risk his own career to square things.

"Rolfe faces a court-martial," McNally said. "Disgrace. The end of his career, at the least. And possibly a firing squad."

"They must have good evidence against him," Von Planetz observed.

McNally ignored the remark. "I don't know what will become of Amy."

"I'm sorry to hear about your troubles. But what do you expect from me?"

"I'm willing to do anything to help save them," McNally announced, clearing his throat.

Von Planetz shook his head regretfully. "I really don't know what I can do for you."

"I have already spoken with Zimmermann, your foreign secretary."

"So I understand."

"He told me that he would have the charges against my son-in-law dropped if the information I gave him proved accurate. It's up to you to evaluate it for him."

Von Planetz said nothing.

"The information is accurate, and I can prove it."

"What is the information?"

"There's an American here in Zurich who intends to kill Vladimir Lenin. Our governments are behind it. The British and American, that is."

The captain tried not to show the shock he felt. "Do you know the identity of this man?"

"Yes, of course. I've been assigned to watch him. I don't know much about him, however. I rescued him from the gutter outside a café in Old Town last night. He was drunk. He had gotten into a fight over a woman's purse."

"How does he plan to kill Lenin?"

"I don't know. But I know that he plans to do it while Lenin's in Germany."

"Where is he now?"

"At the Helvetia. It's a pension on the Lowenstrasse, near the station." The American consul reached into his pocket again and this time pulled out an envelope. "I've written down everything here—his name, a physical description, some past history, everything I could find that might help you."

Von Planetz took the envelope. "You said you could prove it. That he plans to do this. Where is your proof?"

McNally pointed to the envelope. "It's there, with the other documents."

Von Planetz opened the envelope and removed the contents. The top page was a photograph of a decoded secret cable, addressed to James C. McNally, at the American legation, Zurich. The cable originated from the White House, not the State Department. It informed McNally that an American, Henry Bauer, presently in Zurich, was on a secret mission against Germany, and asked McNally to keep a watch on the man and report back on his activity daily.

"It says nothing about killing Lenin."

"Of course not," McNally protested. "He told me that himself. The café I mentioned—he was there looking for Lenin's address. He found it in the purse he stole."

Von Planetz tucked the envelope inside his own coat pocket and stood up.

"Will you tell Zimmermann?" McNally demanded. "Tell him I gave you proof?"

The captain nodded. "I'll tell him."

"I believe in my country deeply," McNally blurted, suddenly angry. "This has not been easy for me—to betray it, even in this small way. If it were not for my daughter . . ."

"I understand. Good day, Consul." The captain tipped his hat and walked quickly away. At the corner of the Reitergasse he caught a motor cab and headed back to Room 24 on the Werdemuhle-Platz.

"Can't you arrest him?" the captain asked Chief Inspector Steiner.

Steiner looked pleadingly at his old friend. "Kurt. He's an American citizen. How can I? On what charge?"

"He plans to commit a murder. He must be stopped."

"How do you know? Who's he going to kill?"

Von Planetz looked down at the floor. "I can't tell you that. I'm sorry, Klaus."

The Swiss policeman eyed the captain suspiciously. "It's political, then, isn't it?"

"Just take him into custody and hold him for forty-eight hours. That's all I ask."

Steiner rubbed his hand thoughtfully over his bald head. "I suppose I could bring him in for questioning—on some matter or other. . . ."

Von Planetz handed his friend a piece of paper. "This is the man's address—and a description of him. Whatever the excuse, you must grab him. Immediately."

"He plans to do this killing tonight?"

"No. I don't think so. But. . . ."

Steiner shook his head emphatically. "It's impossible, my friend. It's Sunday. I don't have the manpower. It'll have to wait until tomorrow. I'm sorry."

The captain wanted to insist that it be done at once. There would never be a better time to neutralize Bauer than right now, before he'd even had a chance to make a move. But the captain knew he could not insist. He would have to settle for whatever Steiner was willing to risk.

"Then please," he said, "get some men there the first thing in the morning. If you don't catch him then, it'll be too late. He'll be out of the country by the afternoon."

MONDAY
APRIL 9

ZURICH

Harry Bauer woke at 5:00 A.M. and lay awake, his thoughts focused on the hours immediately ahead. This time the mental demons of the predawn hours did not ambush him. He felt charged with energy and purpose. In his mind's eye, he walked himself through each of the steps he would need to take, before the day was out, to carry out his plan.

He had survived as long as he had, he believed, by his special method of preparation. He had discovered long ago that for someone working alone, a rigidly detailed plan of attack was usually a mistake. There were always too many imponderables that would undo even the most carefully conceived and rehearsed plots, leaving the plotter off balance and vulnerable to disaster. He preferred instead simply to put himself in a situation in which the opportunity he needed would inevitably arise. And then bide his time. His superb instincts and his skill at improvising would do the rest.

Devising the right situation this time had been a bigger headache than usual, but he was confident that it would work. All that remained now was to kick the plan into gear.

Further sleep was impossible. At a little after six o'clock he rose, bathed, shaved, and dressed and left the pension to visit a gunsmith he had done business with in the past. The smith's shop was at Number 55 Barengasse, a small side street just two blocks from the Bahnhofstrasse, Zurich's main business thoroughfare.

After a prolonged consultation with the gunsmith, an old Latvian named Kolleck, Bauer went hunting for a pharmacy. He found one open on the Bahnhofstrasse. He purchased a bottle of henna rinse, a pair of hair clippers, and a new blade and strop for his straight razor.

He checked his pocket watch. Barely past 8:00 A.M. While waiting for other stores to open for the day, he bought a copy of the *Neue Zurcher Zeitung*, and ordered a breakfast of coffee and rolls at a café. The front page carried stories about the increase in Allied shipping losses to German U-boats in the Atlantic, America's entry into the war, and the situation in Russia. The account spoke of mass desertions at the front and political upheaval throughout the country.

He turned to the back pages for some news of the opening of the major league baseball season back home, knowing that of course there would be none. He wished he could somehow will a copy of the Philadelphia *Bulletin* to appear magically at the table. Or even the New York *Sun*. He'd even have settled for a week-old copy of the international *Herald Tribune*. Damn it, why didn't the world understand the importance of baseball?

He thumbed restlessly through the paper. When the news wasn't about the war, it was about the home front coping with the war. An item on page four reprinted from the *Frankfurter Zeitung*, for example, announcing new reduced rations in Germany for bread, potatoes, and meat. The article included a recipe for "blood bread" to help Germans cope with the severe food shortages. It was made by mixing pig's or ox's blood with flour, and then cooking it in boiling water. When cold, it could be cut into slices, fried in butter, and spread with jam or jelly.

He supposed the *Neue Zurcher Zeitung* reprinted items like that to demonstrate how smart the Swiss were to stay neutral. Certainly nobody in Switzerland was going to be saving that recipe.

Bauer folded the newspaper and closed his eyes. The Giants were a shoo-in in the National League this year, he decided. Their pitching was solid, and with bats like Robertson, Zimmerman, Burns, and Kauff, they looked even tougher than last year. The Cardinals might give them a run, especially since they'd switched Hornsby to short, and the Reds had Edd Roush, but he was betting on the Giants. In the American, it was between the White Sox and the Red Sox. He'd give it to Chicago. Boston had traded Speaker to the Indians, and Carrigan had resigned. They were still a strong club, but the White Sox looked overpowering, with a lineup that included the likes of Eddie Cicotte, Red Faber, Eddie Collins, and Joe Jackson—not to mention Chick Gandil and Happy Felsh. A Giants—White Sox World Series in 1917. By God, he'd like to see that.

Bauer shook himself from his reverie, finished his rolls and coffee, and went off to complete his errands.

After successive stops at a shoe store, luggage shop, haberdashery, men's clothing store, and cobbler's shop, he returned to the Pension Helvetia, arms laden with packages.

A subtle change in atmosphere, like the drop of a barometer before a storm, caught his attention as he crossed through the small lobby. The desk clerk's behavior was abnormal. He actually smiled when he handed Bauer his room key. The Pension Helvetia was run with a level of frostiness toward its guests that was high even by Swiss standards. So the smile was suspect. But the clerk also avoided making eye contact. That was alarming.

Bauer took the key and walked toward the back stairs, whistling "Take Me Out to the Ball Game." On his way he passed the open door to the dining room. He glanced inside. Two burly, red-faced strangers were sitting at a table near the door. One was smoking. Neither of them was eating breakfast.

The American paused at the top of the first landing and listened. He heard two chairs scrape the floor below.

The door to a bedroom on his right was ajar, the chambermaid's cleaning cart parked in front of it. He ducked inside. The maid gaped at him, startled. He grinned reassuringly and pressed a finger to his lips.

Heavy steps pounded up the stairs, paused briefly on the landing, and then continued upward. Still carrying his bundles, Bauer dashed back out into the corridor and down the stairs. He caught the clerk returning from the dining room to his desk. He dropped his packages on the desk and grabbed the clerk by the front of his shirt and slammed him against

the wall. He twisted the collar around his throat, cutting off
his wind. "Don't make a sound, understand?"

The clerk pressed his chin against the American's fist in a
tiny nod. His face was stiff with terror. Bauer relaxed his
grip. "They after me?"

"*Ja.*"

"Who are they?"

"Police."

"What do they want?"

"Don't know."

Bauer let him go. "Sorry. I didn't mean to scare you," he
said.

The clerk straightened his collar, his fingers trembling
visibly.

"Go get them," Bauer ordered. "I'll wait here."

The clerk hesitated, uncertain what to do.

"Hurry up," Bauer commanded. "You're not going to let
them walk all the way to the fourth floor for nothing are
you?"

The clerk hurried toward the stairs. As soon as he was out
of sight, the American picked up his packages and walked out
of the hotel, blessing his luck.

But why the hell were the Swiss police after him?

Half an hour later Bauer arrived with his packages at the
front door of a small white cottage on the Mittelstrasse, a
street in a working-class quarter on the southeast edge of the
city.

He knocked and waited. No answer. He knocked again.

He tried pounding on the door with the bottom of his fist.
Still no reply. The house was so small that Blum would have
to hear him. A fresh bottle of milk, delivered that morning,
sat untouched on the stoop.

Blum appeared, finally, in a tattered bathrobe. He was
unshaven, his eyes still puffy with sleep. "What do you
want?" he growled.

Bauer picked the bottle of milk up from the stoop and
handed it to the Swiss. "Good morning, Blum. I want to
come in."

Blum started to shut the door.

Bauer pushed it open against Blum's weight and stepped in
beside him. The front room was a small, poorly furnished

parlor cluttered with books, magazines, and stray articles of clothing. A bedroom, even smaller and more densely cluttered, adjoined the parlor. All the cottage's shades were drawn, casting the interior in a gloomy twilight. Bauer pushed aside a stack of books from the top of a chest of drawers to make way for his packages. The volumes were old and dogeared—and oddly familiar. He remembered why. They were like the books his father had collected. Hundreds of pages of alternating boredom and invective; cloth-covered little volumes of grievance and outrage against the social order.

Blum retreated with the bottle of milk into the kitchen. Bauer followed him. A cramped shedlike addition at the back of the house, the kitchen had its own clutter—dirty pans and dishes, empty bottles, several opened tins of food, and a three-foot-high stack of yellowed newspapers. The smell of sour milk hung in the air—beneath it lurked more profound odors: poverty, failure, despair.

"Please go away," Blum said. "I have no more to tell you. And I have a very busy day."

Bauer grinned. "Not as busy as you think."

"What?"

"You're not going on that train today."

Blum was still holding the milk. He looked at Bauer with a mixture of paranoid suspicion and confusion. "What? Why not?"

"Because I'm going in your place."

BERLIN

"I hurried here the instant I received your summons," Parvus said, his enormous bulk heaving breathlessly as he bustled through the door into Foreign Secretary Zimmermann's office. He was carrying a large Swiss ham wrapped in waxed butcher's paper, which he deposited on the surface of the secretary's desk, smack on top of a stack of urgent diplomatic messages. "For you, Excellency," he murmured.

It was a crude, insensitive gesture, Zimmermann thought, with the German population reduced to a 1000-calorie-per-day ration. The secretary himself had not seen a ham in more than a year. He felt the urge to toss the damned bundle back in the fat Dane's face but controlled himself. He would have his revenge soon enough. He thanked Parvus for the gift and invited him to sit down.

"The Entente has launched a major offensive against us in France this morning," he said. "Matters are extremely hectic here today, so I hope you will take no offense if I come straight to the point."

Parvus parked himself in the high-backed chair facing Zimmermann's desk and caught his breath. "Most assuredly not, Herr Secretary."

Zimmermann clasped his hands behind him and cleared his throat loudly. "Are you aware, Herr Parvus, that Lenin has made another demand of us?"

The Dane's eyes widened in startled innocence. "I was not aware," he confessed.

Zimmermann's expression remained tight-lipped. He picked up a telegraph dispatch from his desk and thrust it at Parvus. "This came in late Friday from Baron von Romberg, in Bern. According to Lenin's representative, Herr Platten, your revolutionary prima donna expects ten million marks in advance, delivered to the train when it reaches Berlin!"

Parvus read the telegram, his face mottling with embarrassment. "A difficult demand, Excellency," he admitted, his baritone voice taking on the lugubrious tones of an undertaker. "But not impossible to satisfy. Surely, at this crucial moment, you don't intend to let all our meticulously laid plans come undone?"

Zimmermann fought to contain his annoyance. "You're quite right about that, Herr Parvus. He leaves us no choice."

The Dane replaced the telegram on the secretary's desk with elaborate care, as if it were breakable china.

Zimmermann began pacing the office. "The train will arrive in Berlin this Wednesday. Less than forty-eight hours from now. And when it does, I intend to pay Lenin a personal visit."

The folds of flesh over Parvus's eyes quivered in dismay. "But Herr Secretary, I doubt that Lenin will meet you. Remember the terms of the agreement. He's consented to travel through Germany only on the understanding that there be absolutely no contact between the members of his party and any German national. This is regrettable, but his reasons are sound. He's concerned that this would compromise him politically in Russia."

"No one need ever know," Zimmermann replied. "We'll move the train to a remote siding in the Potsdam yard and meet him in his carriage after dark. That should satisfy everyone's need for secrecy."

Parvus grunted. "He still may refuse you. He's a stubborn man, Herr Secretary. And he's highly suspicious of Germany's intentions.

Zimmermann shook a fist at Parvus. "If Lenin wants his money, he'll see me."

"Excuse me for my stupidity, Excellency, but why do you insist on meeting him?"

"Because there must be no further disagreements or misunderstandings. This mission has become critical to us. The Americans are in the war now. They have unlimited resources and they can mobilize rapidly. In six months the balance will begin to shift against us. In a year the American presence could prove decisive. That gives Lenin less than a year to take power and negotiate Russia's withdrawal." Zimmermann stopped pacing and turned toward his visitor. "I've decided that I must make a direct appeal to him, personally, while he is still inside German territory—while we still hold his destiny in our hands. I want him to hasten his revolutionary timetable. As an inducement, I intend to offer him further financial support."

"Beyond the forty million marks?"

"Yes. I'm prepared to go to sixty million."

Parvus beamed. Zimmermann supposed he was calculating his increased commission.

"I want you to accompany me to the train, Herr Parvus," the foreign secretary continued. "If there are any difficulties, I will need you to smooth the way."

Parvus looked glum. Obviously he didn't relish the prospect. "It would be a privilege, Herr Secretary," he muttered.

"Good. Then the matter is settled."

Zimmermann paced the office in silence for nearly a minute. Parvus wiped a nervous hand on his trouser leg and followed him with his eyes.

The secretary stopped in front of the Dane and stared down at him. "This money we are taking to the train—he wants it in a neutral currency. So that he can take it into Russia without raising embarrassing questions. I am agreeable to this, but I need your help."

"I am at your service."

"He wants Swiss francs. And I want you to provide them. It's very difficult for our government to get together this much in a foreign currency quickly and secretly. But I understand you have sufficient funds on deposit in Swiss banks to make up the sum."

Parvus raised his chubby hands as if to fend off Zimmermann's words. "But Excellency, that is unfair! I have already taken many risks, incurred many expenses. . . ."

Zimmermann laughed. "You needn't be so distressed, Herr Parvus. Germany will repay you in due course. And you'll still get your percentages. We'll need your network later, after all—to transfer money from Berlin to the Bolsheviks in Petersburg."

In truth, the foreign secretary had searched for an alternative way to transfer the money, so that he could cut the devious Dane out of the picture altogether. But Parvus was the only sensible choice available. He had the experience, he knew the players on both sides, and he had the network in place, through his international business dealings, to make this kind of dirty game possible. And he was willing to take the risks involved.

Beads of sweat broke out on Parvus's forehead. "But this is such a large sum of money. Why do you impose this burden on me?"

"The burden will give you additional motivation to see that Lenin fulfills his part of our bargain."

Parvus swallowed and licked his lips. "I don't need the motivation, but naturally I will do as you ask, Herr Secretary."

"Good. You must have the money here by Wednesday afternoon. Secrecy is essential at every step. Bring it alone, in person. Don't let anyone know the reasons that you're making such a large withdrawal. When you have it here, we'll count it, and then we'll take your motorcar to the train station. Plan to make yourself available for the entire day. The meeting with Lenin will have to take place after dark, and if the train is at all delayed, that might be quite late." Zimmermann walked back behind his desk and surveyed the formidable mound of paperwork that awaited his attention. "You must excuse me now," he said.

They shook hands and the Dane lumbered out. Zimmermann watched the broad back as it barely cleared the doorjambs. The secretary had to admit to himself that the crafty Parvus had proved his worth again. He felt a brief twinge of regret for having treated him so roughly. But he had done the right thing, he assured himself. Showing Parvus that he didn't entirely trust him would help keep him honest. And with ten million marks of his own money riding on Lenin's mission, the greedy entrepreneur was certain to let nothing interfere with its success.

ZURICH

"You can't stop me from going," Oskar Blum protested, shaking his fist at Bauer. He limped agitatedly back and forth across his tiny front parlor, like a wounded animal not certain whether to defend itself or run for it.

The American removed a crumpled sweater from a chair and sat down. "It has to be this way, Blum. Get used to it."

"I'll go to the police," Blum threatened.

"No you won't."

"And why won't I?"

"Because I'll spread the word among the Bolsheviks that you've been snitching on them to the British. They won't like that. Especially Morozov."

Blum didn't answer. Bauer removed a stack of franc notes from his wallet and placed the bills on the threadbare cushion of the footstool in front of the chair. Blum stopped pacing and stared at the pile of paper money suspiciously. "What's that?"

"Compensation."

"Why do you have to go in *my* place?" he demanded.

"Because it's the only way I can see to do it."

"I don't understand. Do what? What are you going to do?"

"It's crucial I be with that party on that train," Bauer answered, trying to blunt Blum's outrage. "That's all I can tell you."

"I'll go to the police," Blum repeated. His attention was still on the pile of money. He seemed to be circling it, as if he half expected it to jump up and disappear if he didn't keep his eyes on it.

"It's a thousand francs," Bauer said. "If you're wondering."

"This trip is the most important event in my life," Blum protested, his tone slackening from anger to self-pity.

"Mine, too," Bauer retorted. He pulled another thousand francs from his pocket, threw those on top of the others, and stood up. "I'll tell you something. A few days from now you'll be glad you stayed home. Take my word for it."

Blum snatched up the money angrily and counted it. "How can you go in my place? You're American. You don't look like me. You'll be recognized as an imposter immediately."

"You said none of the other travelers knows you."

"But they've seen me. I've met them."

Bauer picked up one of his packages and began unwrapping it. "Then I don't expect any problem."

While Blum sulked in the background, Bauer began transforming himself into a passable likeness of the Swiss. He shaved the hair from the front and top of his head to conform to Blum's baldness pattern, trimmed his moustache to match, and then dyed his hair red, from head and eyebrows to chest and arms.

Blum was of roughly the same height and build, and Bauer had considered wearing his clothes, but he finally decided against it. The idea depressed him. He opened the packages from the haberdashery and the men's store, stripped down nude, and outfitted himself with new underwear, socks, garter belts, shirt, collar, tie, brown wool suit with vest, suspenders, spats, and bowler hat—all of European manufacture. He studied the effect in the mirror.

Was it Blum in his Sunday best, ready for the most important event of his life? The disguise would hardly fool an old friend, but fortunately the Swiss didn't seem to have any. It would do.

Blum's limp presented the most interesting challenge. His crippled left leg was about two inches shorter than the right, and he wore a special shoe on that side with a built-up sole and heel to compensate for the difference.

Bauer couldn't shorten his own leg, but he could create the illusion. That morning he had purchased a new pair of shoes and taken them to a cobbler. Following his instructions, the cobbler had built up the sole and heel on the left shoe by two inches.

He removed the altered shoes from their box and tried them on. The effect was precisely what he had anticipated. The extra inches on the left shoe forced him to walk with a limp. Anyone who looked carefully enough to notice that one shoe was thicker than the other would likely conclude that it was to help correct his condition, not cause it. And walking with a limp fit Bauer's philosophy of disguise—it was something that called attention to itself. People would remember the limp, not the man.

Bauer limped into the kitchen, where Blum was making a halfhearted attempt to clean some of the accumulation of dirty pots and dishes. "I'll need your passport," he said. "And a few other documents."

Blum turned off the water faucet and dried his hands with a rag hanging from a hook by the sink. "No," he said.

Bauer sighed.

Blum's passport, a couple of old photographs, a membership card in the Swiss Socialist Party, and a library pass cost the American another thousand francs. "For a socialist, you make a hell of a good capitalist," he muttered, counting out ten more one-hundred-franc notes.

Blum recounted the bills himself and then tucked them into his bathrobe pocket, where he had put the other two thousand francs. "If I was a good capitalist, I wouldn't be in this position."

"What position is that?"

Blum jammed his hands in the robe's pockets. Bauer could hear the bills crackling in the grip of his fingers. "The position of having to sell my life—everything I stand for—to a murderer for a few thousand francs."

Bauer laughed. "A murderer? What makes you think I'm a murderer?"

"You're going to kill Lenin, aren't you? You're a murderer, then."

Blum had touched a raw nerve. Words rushed to Bauer's mouth to defend himself against the accusation, but Blum was right, after all. He slipped the Swiss's documents into his billfold. "Blame it on the war, Blum," he replied. "Every dead soldier and every dead civilian was killed by somebody.

Start with Lloyd George and the kaiser and work your way on down through the arms makers, the diplomats, the hate mongers, and the war profiteers to the soldier who squeezes the trigger. The war has made murderers out of millions of us."

Blum shook his head. "There's a difference, Herr Bauer. The others don't kill for hire."

The American shrugged. "You have a point, Blum. I'll tell you, though. If I had to choose between killing for hire or, like you, squealing on your comrades for it, I'd pick killing every time."

Blum looked stricken. He didn't reply. Bauer checked himself in the mirror one last time, picked up his suitcase, and started for the door.

The Swiss roused himself from his depression. "Aren't you forgetting something?" he said, the sarcasm in his voice heavy as lead.

Bauer glanced back. "Am I? What?"

"This." Blum held up his cane, his mouth twisted in a petty smile.

The American laughed, then waved his hand. "You keep it. I'm getting one of my own." He limped out the door on his built-up shoe. "*Auf baldiges Wiedersehen*, Blum. See you after the war."

By 2:15 Bauer was back at the gunsmith's shop on the Barengasse. The proprietor, Kolleck, gave Bauer's disguise a cursory, disinterested glance and then beckoned for the American to follow him into the back room.

"Just finished," he said in his laconic manner. He handed Bauer a polished walnut walking stick with a squared-off, leather-covered grip.

Bauer examined the cane carefully, passing it from hand to hand to test its grip and feel its heft. "It's a beauty," he said. "How does it work?"

Kolleck took the cane back. "Watch," he said. He tipped the cane up to expose the bottom and then pulled off the rubber tip to reveal, hidden in the hollowed-out wood shaft of the cane, the business end of a rifle barrel. "Steel," he said, running his forefinger around the end of the barrel. "And rifled, not smooth bore."

"What about that rubber tip? Do I have to remove it?"

"No. It's thin at the center. Shoot right through it."

He twisted the carved nickel ferrule that joined the leather-covered handle to the cane's shaft. A small metal trigger popped out at the inside of the handle's elbow. "Cocked and loaded," he said.

The gunsmith held the cane up to his eye and pointed it at a straw-filled target propped against the far wall. Resting the shaft against his forearm, he took aim and squeezed off a round. A sharp bang and a slight smell of cordite, and a new hole appeared near the center of the target. Kolleck picked up a bullet from his workbench and held it out for Bauer to see. "Six millimeter caliber," he said. He twisted the handle of the cane half a turn to the right and removed it from the shaft. "Bayonet mount." He loaded the single bullet into the handle, twisted it back into place on the shaft, and handed it to Bauer. "You try."

The American twisted the ferrule as he had seen Kolleck do, and felt the trigger spring out into place against his finger. Gripping the handle firmly, he raised the cane toward the straw target, as casually as if he were merely directing someone's attention toward the back wall. He squeezed the trigger and hit the target dead center.

"I like it," he said.

Kolleck scratched his chin thoughtfully.

Bauer took several more practice shots, loaded the cane, and pushed the rubber tip back into place over the muzzle. He stowed six extra bullets in the built-up heel of his left shoe, which the cobbler had hollowed out for him, and fished out his wallet.

"How much?"

"Three thousand francs."

Bauer counted it out and placed it on the workbench.

"Good luck," Kolleck said. One professional to another.

"Yeah. Thanks."

Bauer glanced at his pocket watch. A quarter to three. He was cutting it close. He picked up his suitcase, gripped the cane in his right hand, and limped out the door, headed for Zurich's Central Station.

PETROGRAD

Colonel Nikitin stared at the inkwell on his desk in disbelief. Overnight the temperature in his office had dropped so low that the ink in the glass well had actually frozen, breaking the container and leaving a large black stain on the desk corner where the ink had separated and later thawed.

He sent his assistant, Smerdyakov, to find some unfrozen ink, but his hopes were not high. If it had frozen in his office, it stood to reason that it had also frozen in all the other offices in the building.

His assistant had replaced the telephone he had smashed, but the line remained dead. Indeed, it had been nearly a week since it had last functioned. He considered walking over to General Kornilov's office again, but he knew it would be a waste of time. Sunday Kornilov had given him a polite brush-off, implying that he had more important things to do than hunt down some Bolshevik who might or might not be returning to Russia.

"I'll do what I can," was all Kornilov had promised. Nikitin knew that that meant he would do nothing, and Nikitin had no power to make him do more.

A less determined man might have given up, but not Nikitin. If Kornilov and the provisional government refused to act to protect Russia, then he would have to act himself.

He stepped into the outer office and beckoned to his assistant. He was sitting hunched at his small desk, his coat collar pulled up over his neck and chin, his hands jammed into the side pockets.

"No ink, Colonel," Smerdyakov said, retracting his scrawny neck farther down inside his collar.

Nikitin thought he looked like a turtle. "Forget the ink. I have another assignment for you. Come inside."

Smerdyakov followed Nikitin into his office. "We'll have some heat tomorrow, Colonel. The new custodian promised."

"The new custodian is a nitwit," the colonel replied calmly. "Forget the heat. We have more important matters to concern us."

Smerdyakov nodded docilely. Nikitin was afraid that his assistant was also something of a nitwit, but at the moment he didn't have the time or the means to look for a better man.

"Find a motorcar for us," he said. "With enough gasoline to take us to the military prison on Sadovaya Prospect and back. We must get there this afternoon."

Smerdyakov was perplexed. "I beg the colonel's pardon . . ." he managed, stuttering over the word "pardon."

"What troubles you, Smerdyakov?"

"Well. . . . Why are we going there?"

Nikitin appraised his assistant suspiciously. Was he spying on him for someone? And if so what difference did it make? He must not become sidetracked. "We're going there to hire an assassin," he said.

ZURICH

In the guise of Oskar Blum, Harry Bauer limped into the main waiting room of Zurich's Central Station at 2:55, new cane in one hand, new leather suitcase in the other. The shoe with the raised sole and heel was pinching him unmercifully. He glanced around to find the main ticket counter. Blum had told him that everyone was to purchase his own ticket from Zurich to the German border. Once in Germany, tickets for the entire group would be purchased by Fritz Platten, whom Lenin had designated to manage the trip.

Bauer bought a ticket north to Singen, the first stop on the German side of the border, and made his way through the cavernous waiting room to the long row of gates outside that fed onto the train platforms. There were two trains to Singen, departing within ten minutes of one another—the first via Eglisau from Gate 4 at 3:10, the second via Winterthur from Gate 6 at 3:20. The one he wanted was at Gate 4.

On the other side of the gate, a boisterous throng more than a hundred strong had packed the platform alongside the waiting train, many waving hand-painted posters.

The Zurich police had set up a barricade at the gate and were checking everyone who went through. Were they looking for him? Since he had eluded them at his hotel, it was natural they would check all departing trains. Who the hell had put the police onto him? And why? If it had anything to do with the Lenin mission, then he was already in trouble.

He took a deep breath and started toward the barricade. A policeman with a wispy blond moustache and pink cheeks demanded to see identity papers. Bauer handed Blum's passport across, and distracted the Swiss officer with a blustery protest in his most arrogant German. The policeman glanced at the document briefly, handed it back, and waved Bauer through with a contemptuous frown.

The American edged his way slowly through the crowd on the platform. The mood around him was electric, the air almost snapping with tension and impatience. Lenin and his party had not yet arrived.

The train that would carry the "Internationalists" out of Switzerland was a short one—three carriages and a mail car coupled to a locomotive and tender. The engine was a powerful two-cylinder compound with an oversize boiler and superheater, the sort of sturdy workhorse needed to negotiate Switzerland's long, steep grades. The carriages were green, with a heavy mantle of black coal dust deposited on them by their many trips through Switzerland's multitude of tunnels.

The steam pressure was up, and the big iron locomotive hissed and shuddered like a live beast, drawing its breath for the hard haul ahead.

Bauer stepped up into a doorway on the rear carriage and looked around. It was an overcast day, and a chill breeze was blowing in off the river. Men in the crowd ducked their heads into their collars and turned their backs from the gusts. Drab and anonymous in their black coats and hats, they looked to the American like a gathering of village priests.

A sudden commotion from inside the station caught his attention. A large group had begun filing through the gate onto the platform. The crowd parted to let them pass, then closed in behind them. Four women led the way, their long gray skirts swirling around their ankle boots. Three wore kerchiefs, the fourth sported a broad-brimmed white hat with a floral arrangement on top. With the women came two young boys, clinging to their mothers' skirts, and behind them, the men.

Bauer recognized some of them from the Café Adler. There was Radek, swinging a walking stick like a baton; and Zinoviev, with his wife; and Kharitonov. Everyone was laden with luggage, from trim leather suitcases to carpetbags, to baskets and packages tied together with rope. Some carried pillows and blankets. Their mood was cautious, even fearful. A few of the men glared defiantly at the onlookers, but most marched hurriedly through the crowd, their attention fixed narrowly on the open doors of the train.

It was an oddly moving sight, Bauer thought. A ragtag collection of social misfits, their modest possessions clutched to their sides, were returning home to an uncertain future. They looked like a band of war refugees, but in fact they were something quite extraordinary. They were the core survivors of a movement whose existence was dedicated to the notion of discarding the existing social order of civilized man. To that end, they were openly conspiring to overthrow every political regime on earth—democratic, monarchic, and despotic alike.

Most had spent years in hiding, prison, or exile for promoting their cause, and all had suffered privation. But they had survived to see this day—and along with their radical ideology and their preposterous ambitions, they now carried hope.

Bauer cast his eyes around the sea of black shapes in vain for some sign of the distinctive figure with the squinting Mongol eyes, hobnailed boots, and goatee. Had he gone aboard the train earlier?

A sudden chorus of hoots and jeers went up from the back of the crowd. Bauer stretched on tiptoe to see the cause and found Lenin, his cloth cap barely visible in the middle of a knot of people just coming through the gate. Morozov walked in front, his deformed visage glowering out at the throng, daring those in his path to obstruct his way. Lenin, nearly a foot shorter, was almost completely hidden behind him. He walked with his arm linked through that of a stout, fish-eyed woman Bauer supposed was his wife, Nadya Krupskaya. Fritz Platten, in snappy fedora and flowing white scarf, brought up the rear, keeping step with the others.

In company with Platten was the woman Bauer had met in the café, Inessa Armand. She wore a long gray skirt and a big hat that hid her face from view. She gave the impression of striving to blend in with the others, but was instead setting herself apart with an expensive-looking bag draped nonchalantly over her shoulder, and the slightly provocative manner in which she thrust her hips out when she walked. A bluebird among crows, Bauer thought. And she couldn't change her feathers no matter how much she desired it.

Since the encounter at the café, she had never been far from his thoughts. And now the sudden restricted glimpse of her, beneath her big hat and ankle-length skirt, caused a warm hurt to tighten across his heart.

His preoccupation with the woman mystified him. What was it about her? She wasn't particularly young or especially beautiful. Why couldn't he get her out of his head?

With Lenin's appearance, the crowd on the platform deteriorated almost instantly into a mob. Some few had come to wish him and his fellow radicals *bon voyage*, but most were there to taunt. They pressed forward, fists and voices raised in angry gesticulations and shouts. Bauer didn't understand the Russian, but he heard the words "swine" and "traitor" in German, and that gave him the gist.

The women began climbing into the first carriage. Someone threw an egg. It broke near the open door and ran down the side of the car. A scuffle broke out on the platform, and Bauer was astonished to see the sophisticated Fritz Platten trading blows with someone in the crowd. Platten's attacker seemed almost deranged, so furiously did he flail at the young Swiss. Platten struggled to keep from being knocked down.

Morozov rescued him, finally. The hulking Russian chopped the protester on the back of the neck with the edge of his open palm. The man dropped to the platform like a pole-axed steer and lay there, unmoving. The Swiss police watched the melee from behind the gate, but made no move to intervene. They seemed to be enjoying it.

Morozov helped Platten onto the train. The rest of Lenin's party was already aboard. Some pushed down windows and from the relative safety of their seats inside the carriage they began trading insults with the crowd. Another fight erupted when some outnumbered well-wishers tried to yank down a protester's placard.

Two uniformed conductors moved nervously along the carriages and began slamming the doors shut. The Swiss Federal Railway was punctual to the point of fanaticism, and it was clear it did not intend to let this unruly confrontation disrupt its timetable. Bauer walked forward into the carriage where Lenin's party had concentrated. He hesitated at the doorway a moment, fixing in his mind who he was supposed to be, and then, his suitcase clutched resolutely in hand, he pushed his way up the aisle. The trains in Switzerland were of the center aisle type—open rows of seats instead of compartments—so the whole interior of the carriage was visible.

No one had yet settled into a seat. Anxiety about the trip and curiosity about what was happening outside kept the travelers in an agitated state. They bustled up and down the aisle, talking nervously. In the chatter and confusion "Oskar Blum" was totally ignored.

Bauer's eyes moved quickly from face to face. He found Inessa Armand near the middle of the car, at a window seat across from Fritz Platten. She was watching the demonstration on the platform, but suddenly she turned, as if she had felt his gaze, and looked directly at him. The irrelevant notion popped into his head that this was the first time he had seen her in the daylight. She radiated the same warm energy, but those big, intense eyes and that wide mouth wore a subdued expression.

Bauer spoke to Platten. "I'm Blum," he said.

The young Swiss looked up at him and then back down at an open notebook in his lap. Pencil in hand, he ran down a neatly hand-lettered list of names and made a small check-mark near one at the bottom. "Oskar Blum?"

"Yes."

Platten showed his big, slightly crooked teeth. "We were worried that you hadn't made it. Is everything in order, Herr Blum?"

"Yes. I'm fine, thank you."

"You're a Swiss national, aren't you?"

"Yes."

"Do you have your visa?"

Bauer hesitated, thrown by the question. He felt Inessa's eyes still on him. Did she notice something? Was he acting out of character?

Platten furrowed his brows impatiently. "Well, do you?"

"I'm afraid I've lost it," Bauer said, hoping Platten would enlighten him.

The Swiss slapped his forehead and groaned melodramatically. "My God, Blum, they won't let you into Russia without a visa. You were told that at the meeting. All foreign nationals must have visas."

"I know. I'm sorry. It was careless of me." Jesus, Bauer thought, since he wasn't planning on staying even through Germany, the visa problem had never occurred to him. And Blum had no doubt been happy not to tell him about it.

"You'll have some time in Stockholm," Platten said, reassuring him. "Report the loss to the Russian consulate there. They should give you another."

"Thank you, Herr Platten. I'll do exactly as you suggest."

Platten patted Bauer on the arm consolingly. "Good luck," he said. "I'd hate to see a fellow countryman left stranded at the Finnish border."

Bauer nodded, then tipped his hat at Inessa Armand, allowing her a brief glimpse of the red-fringed dome beneath. She turned away, utterly incurious. The success of his disguise was reassuring, but her sudden lack of interest disappointed him. He moved quickly away from their seat.

Where was Lenin? He glanced up and down the rows on both sides, and finally spotted him, at the far front end of the car, seated with his wife. He, too, seemed unusually subdued. This surprised Bauer. When he had followed him to the park in Zurich, he had been struck by the extraordinary level of energy the man projected. But now his eyes looked tired and his movements phlegmatic—as if he had been drugged. It struck Bauer as odd, considering the occasion. But then, he knew little about this man. The other members of the party, perhaps in deference to his somber mood, were keeping their distance.

At precisely 3:10 the engineer sounded a couple of long, high-pitched blasts from his whistle. The carriages shuddered and the train inched into motion. Bauer retreated down the aisle and took a seat near the rear door, just past the area where most of Lenin's entourage had concentrated. He leaned out the window for a last look at the platform. Several protesters had turned their placards upside down and were using the poles to beat against the sides of the carriage. The racket they made was nearly loud enough to drown out the deep-throated chugs of the locomotive as it gathered force.

The train eased out of the station yard, rumbled across the trestle bridge over the River Sihl, and to the cadenced puffs of its engine, let the city of Zurich slip slowly from view.

According to the timetable, they would reach the German

frontier in about an hour and a half, Bauer reflected. Meanwhile, there was nothing to do but sit and wait. He watched the Swiss landscape roll past. Snow-melt from the mountains roared in the brooks, and the bare fields were showing pale hints of green.

Ten minutes out of Zurich, the train slowed to a stop in the tiny village of Oerlikon. Bauer felt a large figure looming beside his seat. He looked up. It was Morozov. The Russian stared hard at him, his mouth twisting up on the unscarred side of his face into an ugly grin. For a terrible moment Bauer feared that he recognized him. Then Morozov's eyes shifted away, and he walked on past.

The American exhaled slowly. At some point, he suspected, he was going to have to deal with Morozov. He didn't look forward to it.

He considered the situation immediately ahead. Schaffhausen, on the Swiss border, would be the next danger point. Swiss customs always examined everybody thoroughly, determined to see to it that no one compromised Switzerland's neutral status. And after his narrow escape from the police in Zurich, he had to assume they might be looking for him at the frontier.

Past Schaffhausen, there would be German customs. They might be looking for him also.

But Blum's identity would hold up, he assured himself. It would have to.

GOTTMADINGEN, GERMANY

"Telephone for you, Captain." It was the proprietor of the Hotel Bahnhof. Von Planetz walked into the hotel's lobby to take the call. He heard a few clicks, a long dead pause, and then a distant voice. Since the beginning of the war, telephone connections between countries had frequently been bad.

"This is Steiner. Can you hear me?"

"A little echo, but yes."

"I'm calling from my office. Do you understand?"

"Yes." It was widely assumed that most government and embassy telephones were tapped by the enemy.

"Your friend was at the hotel. But he left."

"I see."

"We did not see him at the station, either."

"Did you see him at all?"

"No." There was a long pause before the Swiss police inspector spoke again. "We have one more try."

"Yes." Von Planetz guessed he meant Swiss customs at Schaffhausen. "Good luck, then."

"I don't have the same authority there. You understand."

"I understand."

"But I'll do my best." Steiner didn't sound optimistic.

"Thank you."

"*Auf weidersehen*."

The captain walked down to the station, where Lieutenant von Buhring was supervising preparations for the arrival of the Swiss train. "They didn't find him," he said. "He was staying at a pension in Zurich. They verified that. But they got there too late."

"What do you think?"

"He might have taken an earlier train. Or even driven to the border."

"Then our own customs should catch him."

The captain shook his head. "He's no doubt figured a way around that."

"Do you think the American consul could have made the story up about the plot on Lenin?" Von Buhring asked. "Just to have something to trade for his son-in-law?"

"It's occurred to me, but I think he was telling the truth."

"What do you want to do, then, Captain?"

"The only thing we can do. Assume the plot is real and that Bauer is headed our way. What time did their train leave Zurich?"

"You know the Swiss. Three-ten, on the nose."

The captain looked down the platform of the tiny Gottmadingen station at the row of soldiers lounging on the benches. "How many men do we have?"

"Twenty. All Home Guard. Plus the three customs agents inside."

"Can we get more?"

"It won't be easy."

"We have priority. Call the commandant of the Singen barracks. Tell him we want another twenty men immediately.

When the train arrives, I'll go aboard before anyone is allowed off and explain the circumstances to them." The captain paced off the distance from the edge of the platform to the station door. "With forty men," he said, "we can set up a solid double phalanx, from the train door to the station door. We'll herd Lenin's party right through it into the third-class waiting room and post a guard. That way, we can make certain that this Bauer can't get near them."

Von Planetz pointed toward the special train, waiting in the trees just south of the station, its engine boiler fired and waiting. "As soon as it gets dark, we'll load them aboard the special train the same way, using the soldiers as a shield. Once we have them aboard, we can move them to Singen and post a heavy guard around the carriage for the night." The captain scratched his chin. "Have I left anything out?"

"I don't think so" Von Buhring replied. "Anyway, Captain, we have one big advantage over this Bauer."

"What's that?"

"He doesn't know we're looking for him."

The older man smiled challengingly. "What makes you so certain, Lieutenant?"

"Well, how could he?"

"I don't know. But experience tells me it's better to assume that he does."

"We'll catch him, don't worry."

The captain nodded. "Maybe. But that's not our real job. We're here to protect Lenin. If we're successful, Bauer may never surface at all."

The lieutenant got up. "I'll go call Singen," he said.

The captain watched his assistant as he loped across the town's main square toward the hotel telephone. If we're successful, he thought. And if we're not . . .

Well, there was really no point in pondering the consequences.

SWISS-GERMAN BORDER

Bauer kept his face at the window, to avoid conversation with the other passengers. The sun was low in the west, and in the deepening shadows he watched several stations slip quietly by—Oberglatt, Bulach, Eglisau. The countryside seemed im-

possibly clean and picturesque, a fairy-tale-like idyll of serenity that seemed almost threatening in its perfection.

Between Bulach and Eglisau the train crossed a high via-
duct bridge spanning the Rhine. Below, a series of dramatic
cascades called the Rheinfall dropped the level of the river
several hundred feet.

Bauer glanced around the carriage. The mood was somber
and tense. Some of the men in Lenin's party were still
nervously pacing the aisle near the front of the car, as they
had been since the train departed Zurich. Most sat quietly,
some talked in low voices. The confrontation at the Zurich
station had clearly left the travelers in a black humor. Everyone seemed to be holding his breath, waiting for the fateful
moment when the train would cross into Germany.

"Ilyich is clever," Bauer heard someone in the seat ahead
of him whisper to a companion. "He knows how to protect
himself."

"But so much subterfuge," his companion answered. "I think
it's excessive."

"With the kaiser every precaution is necessary. I sympa-
thize with Ilyich's fears. I'm nervous myself."

The other one laughed. "You're German. They won't shoot
you."

"What'll happen when we get to Russia? They *are* shooting
Germans there."

Past Neuhausen the train threaded through a tunnel and
emerged on the other side in Schaffhausen, their last stop
inside Switzerland. As they slowed toward the station, a
conductor appeared at the head of the car and instructed all
the passengers in Lenin's party to congregate at Platform 3,
to the immediate left of the train.

The travelers gathered their suitcases, baskets, and string
bags and filed out of the carriage. No one spoke above a
whisper. Bauer let the other passengers off ahead of him and
found himself behind Grigory Zinoviev; his wife, Zina; and
their nine-year-old child, Stepan. Zinoviev, he had learned,
was Lenin's closest friend and adviser, the number-two man
in the Bolshevik party.

The boy, Stepan, complained about needing the bathroom.
His mother hushed him with a gentle cuff on the back of the
neck. Immediately ahead of the Zinovievs Bauer saw Fritz

Platten and Inessa Armand. The Swiss had his arm around her, his hand resting loosely on her shoulder. Bauer was surprised to find that this annoyed him.

A wall of portable metal barricades divided the platform down the middle. Swiss customs agents were stationed at a row of tables at the far end. Bauer counted six of them. They looked unusually grim, even for customs officials.

To the American's surprise, the inspectors set about opening every single bag, box, and suitcase presented to them, a time-consuming task that would inevitably be repeated all over again by German customs across the border.

Zina Zinovieva deposited her two big baskets in front of one of the agents, and opened them so he could see their contents. "Only food," she said, smiling sweetly.

The inspector, a fat-faced young man with watery blue eyes and a rosebud mouth, pawed through the baskets roughly, then pushed them to the side. "You will not be allowed to take any food with you into Germany," he declared, averting his gaze.

"But this is all we have to eat," Zina protested. "We will be traveling for days!"

The agent shook his head. "No food can leave Switzerland. Sorry."

Bauer noticed that the other agents were also confiscating the women's baskets. He heard Inessa Armand's voice, sharp and commanding. "There is no law against it!" she cried. "Let us take our food."

Zina's husband, Grigory Zinoviev, came over and continued the argument. Soon similar complaints and arguments had broken out at all six stations, and the entire inspection process came to a halt.

Fritz Platten was the most visibly outraged. As a Swiss, and as the group's official guide, he felt responsible. He had also personally distributed to the travelers the chocolate bars and sugar his fellow countrymen were now confiscating. He argued strenuously, taking the names of all the customs officials and threatening to take action against them when he returned to Switzerland.

None of this made much impression on the Swiss officials. If the travelers refused to part with their food, the senior official in charge informed him, then they would not be allowed to leave Switzerland. "Let the Germans feed you," he said, barely disguising the contempt in his voice.

"It is so like them," Bauer heard Zina complain to Inessa, tears streaming down her face. "They are horrible people, the Swiss!"

Inessa nodded in agreement, but she seemed more resigned than angry. It was mean-spirited to confiscate their food, Bauer thought, but the Swiss were fanatic about their neutrality. The agents must have orders not to collaborate with the Germans in this controversial event in any way. And they were following orders to the letter.

Platten and Zinoviev huddled with Lenin and several other members of the party at the edge of the platform. After several minutes of intense debate, they decided they had no choice but to let the Swiss confiscate their food.

Morozov, who for some reason was carrying a dozen cans of stewed tomatoes with him, calmly pried the lids off each of them with a can opener, dumped the contents out onto the inspection counter, and repacked the empty cans in his luggage. The customs officials were furious, but none of them dared confront him.

Nearly an hour passed before the party was cleared through Swiss customs. Bauer watched Inessa Armand, who, like him, had hung back so that she would be among the last to go through. She smiled seductively at her inspector, the senior one in charge, and distracted him with questions about himself. Mumbling embarrassed replies, he still opened her bags, but they had already delayed the party so long that he barely took time to look inside. Bauer wondered where she had hidden the Derringer he had found in her purse at the café. Strapped to the back of her thigh, perhaps?

Bauer's inspector was excruciatingly thorough, but after failing to turn up any contraband items in the American's suitcase, he gave his passport only a cursory glance. Bauer's cane didn't interest him in the slightest.

The inspection finally over, Lenin's party boarded the same carriage that had brought them from Zurich for the short trip across the frontier. Their mood was desolate. If the Swiss could cause them this much trouble, what would the Germans do to them?

A conductor closed the doors and the train chugged north

out of Schaffhausen and creaked slowly toward the border, its
carriages bumping against each other in a swaying, mournful
rhythm. The small village of Thaingen, the last town on Swiss
soil, slid past them on their right, and then they were in
Germany.

A steep, wooded hill materialized on the left, and spreading out apronlike down the side of it was the village of
Gottmadingen, the first settlement on the German side of the
frontier.

Bauer opened the window by his seat and craned his head
forward to see as far down the line as he could. The carriage
creaked around a corner, and he caught a glimpse of something in the thick woods bordering the track. It took him a
second to recognize that it was another train, parked on a
siding parallel to the main track. He identified a locomotive
and tender, one carriage and a baggage van. The window
shades of the carriage were drawn tight, and a heavy guard
was posted around it.

Soon a narrow three-story hotel rolled into view, followed
by the station itself, a squat gingerbread building with a
single platform, protected by a low shed roof.

Two German officers were waiting on the platform. Their
eyes scanned the carriage windows, their expressions nervous, expectant. Behind them, standing at attention by the
station wall, was an armed detachment of several dozen soldiers.

With a final exhalation of steam, the train shuddered to a
stop. Someone blew a whistle, and the soldiers, their rifles at
the ready, moved across the platform and spread out quickly
around the track, to surround the train. The Swiss conductor
opened one of the exit doors and stood there, waiting for
instructions from outside.

One of the officers shouted a command, and Bauer saw the
soldiers form into a double file, five feet apart, extending
from the carriage door all the way across the platform to the
station entrance. At another command, the soldiers in the
two lines turned to face outward, and brought their rifles
from their shoulders into firing position. There was now a
snaking passageway, between solid walls of armed men, from
train door to station door, through which Lenin's party could
pass.

A long, tense silence ensued. One of the Swiss train conductors came up the aisle and stopped by the American. "What's going on out there?" Bauer asked him.

The conductor wagged a finger of warning. "It's something political," he muttered. "We stay out of these things."

How true, Bauer thought.

"I'm a socialist, myself," the conductor whispered, surprising Bauer. "Good luck to you people."

Bauer smiled.

After several more minutes' delay one of the officers stepped up into the train. He was a tall young lieutenant, resplendent in belted green-olive tunic and polished black riding boots. He saluted smartly and requested the passengers to follow him outside. Wordlessly, the thirty-two revolutionaries began filing out, one at a time, through the gauntlet of armed men.

Bauer cursed quietly to himself as he started through the line. This kind of security could make things tough. In their characteristically heavy-handed way, the Germans almost seemed to be expecting him.

Once inside the station, the party was led into the third-class waiting room. Another officer, a Captain von Planetz, stood at the doorway and counted them as they passed through. When all thirty-two were accounted for, the big double door was slammed shut and a guard posted outside.

The unexpected transfer to a waiting room instead of the train left the party stunned and frightened. It was an ominous beginning. Instead of welcoming the travelers, the Germans were herding them around like prisoners of war. A pall descended on the room. No one seemed to have the courage to speak.

Zina Zinovieva, standing near Bauer, pulled her son Stepan tight against her skirt. She stared at Bauer accusingly. "What are they doing to us?" she demanded.

"It'll be all right," he assured her.

"The damned Boches," the woman muttered. Someone hushed her.

The waiting room was a cold, dingy chamber with a single row of dirty windows near the ceiling. There were several benches, but no one was in a mood to sit on them. Bauer watched Zina's husband, Grigory Zinoviev, and Fritz Platten. They had moved to a corner and were talking in low voices with another man whose identity he didn't know. Several other men bent their heads close, listening. The tension in the air was palpable.

Karl Radek, normally the irrepressible clown, materialized alongside Bauer, his composure in shreds. "The bastards," he swore, his voice trembling. "They're up to something." His face was tight with fear. "The bastards," he repeated, nearly choking on the words.

"What're you so worried about?"

"I'm a deserter," he whispered. "From the Austrian army. They could shoot me."

The big doors opened suddenly, and the German captain appeared. "Herr Platten, *bitte?*" he called.

The young Swiss separated from the group of men and stepped up to the officer. "What are you doing?" Platten demanded. "We are supposed to be escorted to our special train!"

The officer nodded placatingly. "You are Herr Platten?" he inquired.

"Yes, I am Herr Platten."

"I am Captain von Planetz." Despite his evident weariness, he snapped his fingers against the visor of his cap in a crisp salute. "You and your party will be officially my responsibility during your transit through Germany. I am at your service."

Bauer edged his way closer to the two men, to hear their conversation better.

Platten repeated his complaint. The officer just nodded. "Could you please summon Herr Lenin?" he asked.

"Herr Lenin will not speak with any German," Platten retorted, his voice firm. "As you must know, it is a condition of our passage through your country that none in our party, myself excepted, speak with any German national. Anything you wish to convey to Herr Lenin you'll have to convey through me."

Von Planetz clasped his hands behind him and swayed back and forth on the balls of his feet, considering Platten's statement. Finally he nodded. "I understand. But since it is my responsibility to get him safely across Germany, I must at least know which of your passengers is Lenin. Will you please point him out to me?"

Platten hesitated, suspicious of the German's intentions, then gestured toward the back of the room. There, on a bench, sat a small man with a worker's cap and a goatee. Next to him, her hands clasped tightly to the handle of a carpetbag, was Lenin's wife, Nadya Krupskaya. Her bulging eyes confronted those of the captain with unintimidated hostility.

The German officer regarded the slouching figure on the bench for a long time. Uncertainty clouded his face. He turned to Platten again. "Could you ask him to come forward, please?"

Platten tilted his chin back and folded his arms across his chest. "Begging your pardon, Captain. But it is not part of our agreement."

The German's face deepened with fatigue. He looked slowly around the room, taking in each of the thirty-two travelers separately. His eyes found Bauer and lingered on him briefly, without a hint of suspicion. There was no way the German could know he was here, Bauer thought. Absolutely no way. But he sure as hell seemed to be looking for somebody.

Fritz Platten reached into his coat pocket, withdrew a bulky envelope, and held it out to Von Planetz. "This is payment for our passage, in German marks. Lenin has insisted, and you have agreed, that we pay our own way. It is exactly the correct amount for thirty-two tickets, second-class, from Singen to Sassnitz."

The German officer pushed the envelope back against Platten's chest. "I'm not the fare collector," he said, insulted. "Your tickets will be issued on the train."

Platten swallowed his pride and returned the envelope to his pocket. The captain gestured for him to follow him out of the room. Through the doorway Bauer could see them, standing in the middle of the station lobby, gesticulating back and forth in animated conversation. The exchange took several minutes, and when it was over, Platten returned looking remarkably subdued. Bauer expected him to march over to Lenin to deliver whatever message the captain had given him, but he did not.

Von Planetz reappeared at the doorway with the other officer. "This is Lieutenant von Buhring," he announced. He looked across at Platten, keeping to the letter of their agreement by addressing him only, but raising his voice so that everyone in the room could hear. "Tell your party that he will escort you all to the customs area, on the other side of

this station. When you have completed that formality, you'll
be taken aboard the special carriage provided for you as a
humanitarian gesture by His Royal Highness, Wilhelm the
Second, Emperor of Germany. Through his generosity you
will be allowed to transit our country on your way back to
your homeland. During the trip the doors of your carriage
will be locked. No one will be allowed in or out. This is in
keeping with the agreement you have made with us, but I
stress that it is also for your security."

From across the room Platten tossed the trailing end of his
scarf over his shoulder with a defiant flourish. "We will abide
by the agreement—and expect you to do the same."

Captain von Planetz nodded wearily. "Today your train will
take you only as far as Singen. There it will be shunted onto a
siding for the night. You will be fed and have any other of
your needs attended to. I wish you a safe journey. Good
day."

Von Planetz gestured to Lieutenant von Buhring to take
over in his place, made a perfunctory salute, and strode out.

The German customs inspection, which Bauer had feared
would be the most dangerous ordeal of all, went quickly and
without a hitch. The passports were collected and the names
in each of them written down. That was all. No bags were
opened, no questions were asked.

The inspection formalities complete, Lieutenant von Buhring
led the party across to the special train, waiting on the siding
to the south of the Gottmadingen station. Everyone crowded
eagerly into the carriage, and after some debate and confusion, the single men settled into the third-class compartments, with their hard wooden seats; the women and couples
took the more comfortable second-class ones. Lenin comman-
deered the compartment at the front of the carriage for
himself and his wife. Bauer saw Inessa Armand go into the
one two doors down, with Olga Ravich, Karl Radek, George
Safarov, and his wife, Valentina.

Platten, together with Von Buhring, supervised the loading
of the traveler's luggage into the baggage wagon. That done,
all the doors to the carriage were locked, to "seal" its occupants, as Lenin had insisted, from Germany and the Germans, during the transit of their territory.

The two German officers—"the 'von' brothers," he heard

Radek call them—took the compartment at the far rear end of the carriage, behind the white chalk line. Bauer settled into the next compartment up, with five other men.

At 7:20 Monday evening the train rumbled off the siding and onto the main trunk line north, and got up steam for the short run to Singen.

In the carriage the mood of the revolutionaries lifted dramatically. For the first time since the beginning of the journey, they sensed that they were really on the way at last.

Someone in the compartment immediately in front of Bauer's started singing "The Marseillaise," and soon the entire carriage took it up, bawling it out, amid tears and laughter, as the train rolled through the southern forests of the German Empire.

THE TRAIN

Captain von Planetz stared out at the twilight beyond his window. Despite his efforts to keep his mind on Lenin and the threat from the American, thoughts of his wife, Marthe, kept intruding. For the first time since her illness, an entire day had passed without his seeing her. His sister had promised to look in on her regularly, and he supposed he was worrying unnecessarily, but the thought that he might not be there when she needed him most upset him. He would telephone her as soon as the train reached Singen, he decided.

Lieutenant von Buhring, sitting opposite him, stretched his legs out across the wooden bench. "Remind me never to travel third class after the war, Captain," he said. "These seats are harder than Bismarck's ass."

Von Planetz nodded without really hearing him. "When we get to Singen, I'm going to request a guard detail from the local barracks. We'll be parked on that siding all night. We're vulnerable."

"How many?" von Buhring asked.

"Six men in two shifts."

The lieutenant whistled softly. "Do we need *that* many?"

"The Swiss failed to catch him at the border. And so did we. We can hardly afford to relax now."

Von Buhring adjusted his position to get more comfortable. "I don't think he's coming, Captain."

Von Planetz scratched his chin and considered it. Maybe the lieutenant was right. He hoped so, but he didn't think so. "He has to be clever, this Bauer," he said. "The Allies wouldn't send a moron on such an important mission."

"We're more clever than he is," the lieutenant answered.

The captain frowned. "No one can outsmart a German? Is that what you mean?"

"We have to have self-confidence," the lieutenant replied defensively.

"That's complacence, not self-confidence."

Von Buhring looked unhappy. "I'm sorry, Captain. I didn't intend to offend you. But you worry too much. Honestly, you do."

The captain grinned in spite of himself. Von Buhring wasn't the first to tell him that. "Well, if you're such a clever German, Herr Lieutenant, how would *you* kill Lenin if you were sent to do it?"

"That's easy. I'd have gunned him down in the streets of Zurich days ago."

"That's pretty crude."

"So what? It would've worked. Isn't that how most assassinations are carried out? In broad daylight? With a bomb or a gun?"

"I suppose so," the captain admitted. "But I think Bauer may be under orders to accomplish something more. Not just to kill Lenin, but to kill him inside Germany, for example."

"What difference does it make?"

"He'd do more damage to us that way. The Allies'd be rid of Lenin, and Germany'd get the blame."

The lieutenant thought about it. "Yeah, that's probably right," he admitted.

"Well?" the captain prodded. "How would you do it? With Lenin locked on the train all the way to the ferry at Sassnitz?"

"I'd have tried to get him at Gottmadingen, then. When he changed trains."

"Think you could have?"

Von Buhring shrugged. "It would've been tough, with that guard we posted. Maybe we stopped Bauer there and just didn't realize it."

"Suppose we did. Won't he try again?"

Von Buhring began to fidget impatiently. Inference and

deduction were not his forte. "Then he'll be waiting at the ferry, in Sassnitz. That's the only other possibility. But frankly, Captain, I don't even see how he can do that. He can't be certain that's our destination. And even if he was, how can he get there ahead of us?"

"I don't know," the captain admitted. The conversation ended, and Von Planetz returned to gazing out the window. Darkness had fallen. The moon would be rising in a few hours, but at the moment all he saw was an inky blackness, broken occasionally by the dim glow of a light in a window somewhere beyond the tracks. In the compartments beyond the chalk line the mood had become festive. The Russians were laughing and singing boisterously, a great change from their earlier sullenness. He had warned their guide, Fritz Platten, that Lenin's life might be in danger, but the young man did not seem to take the matter very seriously. Lenin's life is always in danger, he had replied.

More arrogance. At least Lenin himself seemed to treat the threat seriously. While the other travelers talked and visited in the corridor, their leader kept well out of sight.

The captain lit a cigarette and watched the blue smoke curl toward the ceiling of the compartment. He asked himself the same question he had asked the lieutenant. How would he do it if he were the assassin?

He tried to assemble the scant information he possessed about the man into a rough character portrait. Tall, sturdily built, and about thirty-eight years of age. Experienced. Very experienced. And American. What did that mean? That he was a gambler perhaps? Someone prone to take chances. And impatient? Americans were notorious for their impatience. What else? A loner, most likely. The captain thought of the former American President, Teddy Roosevelt. Like him, Bauer was perhaps a rugged individualist, a man of action and instinct. A man accustomed to improvising.

Suppose the assassin was all those things? What did that tell him? Not much. Except that Bauer's plan would likely be a simple one. Not just simple like the lieutenant's ideas, but clever as well, capable of variation under changing or unknown circumstances. A plan with a high probability of success, no matter what went wrong.

If he could only put his mind more firmly in Bauer's frame

of reference, he thought, he might get a glimmer of what that plan might be.

He struggled to picture himself in the American's place, stalking Lenin in Zurich, sizing him up, looking for the best way to carry out his mission. What would be his main considerations?

The captain extinguished his cigarette in the ashtray beneath the window, rubbed his eyes and yawned. His questions were just spawning more questions. He needed a rest. In a few minutes they would reach Singen. Pray God he would be able to sleep there for a few hours. The next few days threatened to raise hell with his peace of mind.

At the village of Singen, the sealed train was backed onto a siding for the night. The German officers in the rear compartment arranged for food and drink and passed them across the white chalk line—sliced dark bread, trays of cold meats, milk, coffee, and beer.

The Germans were no doubt eager to make up for what the Swiss had done at the border by confiscating the party's food. Bauer was particularly grateful for the beer.

The meal stretched on far into the evening, the travelers too excited to settle down. Amid the endless clatter and visiting back and forth between compartments, Bauer noticed that a sorting out had occurred. The hard core of Lenin's followers—the old friends and Bolsheviks—were bunched together in the front compartments. Most of the rest—the outsiders, the ballast with which Lenin had inflated his entourage to make it appear broad-based and "international" in character—were sitting with Bauer in the last compartment. None of his five traveling companions were either Russian or Bolshevik. Most were Jews from Germany, and like him—or like Blum, the man he was pretending to be—they were Bundists.

Rosenblum, Abramovitch, and Scheinessohn sat on the front bench, opposite him. On his left was Gobermann; on his right, Aisenbud. The situation struck him as comical. Not only did none of them know the real Oskar Blum, they were all strangers to each other as well. Obviously Lenin had taken care that no united opposition might develop among the non-Bolsheviks that could challenge his authority.

Several doors down, Bauer could hear the Austrian, Karl

Radek, convulsing the others in his compartment with a nonstop patter of imitations and jokes. His clowning seemed to have reduced one female in the group to helpless hysterics. Her high-pitched squeals echoed gratingly through the carriage.

After his third bottle of beer, Bauer got up to use the toilet. There were two lavatories in the carriage—one at the back of third class, on the German side of the chalk line, the other all the way at the front, in second class. In order to stay on their side of the line, all thirty-two of Lenin's party were forced to use the front one.

Bauer pushed through the swinging door that separated the third- and second-class sections and found himself at the end of a long line waiting for that one lavatory.

Earlier, Lenin had sent word down that smoking would be allowed only in the lavatory. This made the carriage air marginally more breatheable, but created an intolerable traffic jam. Several loud arguments had erupted between smokers and nonsmokers. Lenin had solved this problem by having Fritz Platten issue passes that gave the nonsmokers first priority. This quelled the arguments, but didn't diminish the length of the line in front of the lavatory.

Karl Radek jumped out from his compartment and started dancing up and down alongside the line, one hand holding an unlit cigarette, the other pressed urgently against his crotch. He looked plaintively in the direction of Lenin's closed compartment at the front. "What if you have to smoke and piss at the same time?" he yelled.

The entire carriage erupted in laughter. An irritated voice, apparently Lenin's, shouted at him to shut up.

When Bauer finally got back to his compartment, Gobermann, sitting beside him, became talkative. He was an excitable little man who chewed on his fingers compulsively. "I've never been to Petrograd," he said. "Have you?"

"No."

"I'm a Jew, too, you know."

Bauer nodded. He didn't know what to say. He supposed Blum was Jewish, but he'd never asked him. Better not admit anything.

"They don't let Jews into Russia," Gobermann continued.

"That was under the czar," Bauer said.

Gobermann shook his head. "The provisional government will be no different."

Bauer shrugged.

"How's your Russian?" Gobermann asked.

"Nonexistent."

"They might arrest us all, you know. At the Russian border."

"Why?"

"As traitors."

It occurred to Bauer that Gobermann was quietly going to pieces under the stress of the trip. "Russians, maybe," he admitted, trying to reassure him. "Not us. At worst, they might send us back. Just as you said." Bauer didn't mention the remark he'd overheard earlier—that the Russians were shooting Germans.

"The Russian prisons are the worst in the world," Gobermann declared, opening his eyes wide with childish amazement. "The Ohkrana are experts at torture."

"The czar's gone."

"But not the Ohkrana. They'll still be there."

"Lenin will fix all that," Bauer assured him, hoping he sounded sincere. He rested his head against the wooden seat back and tipped his bowler over his eyes, indicating that he didn't want to talk anymore. Claustrophobia was beginning to take hold of him. The thought of spending many more hours in this cramped space with these men didn't appeal to him at all. If only he could do the job right now. Get it over with.

Later tonight, maybe. When everyone had finally gone to sleep.

BERLIN

By midnight the dining room of the Hotel Adlon was deserted save for one last couple—the fat Dane, Parvus, and a female companion—a fleshy blond woman wearing a white bare-shouldered silk gown and a feather boa. The orchestra had gone home, and the ruins of an eight-course dinner had long since been swept away. An open bottle of champagne— their sixth of the evening—sat in an ice bucket by the table. Parvus and his companion were both quite drunk.

The Dane fumbled another cigar loose from the case on the table and tried to summon the waiter with a snap of his fingers, but was unable to click thumb and middle finger together. The waiter appeared anyway, lit the Dane's cigar, refilled the glasses, and retreated to his station by the kitchen door.

Despite the gluttonous indulgence, Parvus still felt morose. Even the gallon of sparkling wine bubbling through his guts failed to extinguish the angst that had been building inside him all day long.

Much of the day he had spent on the telephone with Furstenberg, his business associate in Stockholm; and with banks in several countries.

By borrowing heavily against collateral from a number of sources in Zurich and Stockholm, and by quickly switching some already heavily leveraged stocks and bonds through a series of blind accounts, he could scrape the twelve and a half million francs together. But he simply couldn't get the money into Germany. Swiss and Swedish neutrality laws forbade it, and doing it illegally would take too much time.

Tomorrow he would have to face Foreign Secretary Zimmermann and admit the truth—that he would not have the money in hand in time to meet Lenin's train Wednesday night.

Zimmermann's fury would be apocalyptic. He knew nothing about the complicated world of international finance, and he would not want to hear excuses, no matter how persuasive. Too much was at stake.

But Zimmermann's expected rage was only a small part of his worry. It was the possibility that the whole painstakingly orchestrated German deal with Lenin would fall through that caused waves of terror to quake through Parvus's elephantine hulk. If that happened, it would almost certainly cost Zimmermann his post in the kaiser's government. And Lenin's grand scheme to seize control of the revolution in Russia would be aborted.

And Parvus himself would be ruined.

His position as the financial intermediary between Germany and the Bolsheviks would evaporate, and with it the money he expected from Germany as his percentage of the arrangement—money against which he had already borrowed heavily—to buy new black-market shipments of hospital supplies, food, and arms.

Desperation crept over the Dane's broad folds of flesh like a malarial chill, bathing him in sweat. No amount of champagne would staunch it.

He saw only one possible solution. Somehow he would have to persuade Zimmermann, and then Zimmermann would have to persuade Lenin, to accept the delivery of the money in Stockholm instead of Berlin. And in Swedish krona instead of Swiss francs. It was merely a matter of waiting another day or so. Parvus was certain that Furstenberg could easily get the money together for him in Stockholm.

But of course Zimmermann wouldn't like it. The foreign secretary didn't trust him, especially after all the money the Germans gave him for the fiasco he had produced in 1905. Zimmermann would want to see the Swiss francs tomorrow, and would probably want to count them, as well.

And even in the unlikely event that Zimmermann bought the idea, would Lenin? Lenin trusted the German government even less than it trusted Parvus. He would assume they were trying to cheat him. He would probably refuse further cooperation. He might even refuse to continue the trip. It would be in character.

Parvus squeezed his eyes shut in dismay. He began to feel queasy. There was no easy way out.

He tugged his watch from his vest pocket and strained to bring his eyes to focus on the dial. Past midnight. It was still not too late to visit the Chausseestrasse, the "street of little girls." Despite the frequency with which the Dane appeared in public with women on his arms, Parvus was utterly impotent. All his sexual pleasures were derived as a spectator. And Berlin, for those who could afford it, offered spectacles to suit the most depraved tastes. Tonight, to escape his cares, he would need something especially exciting. He wanted to see blood, hear screams, witness erotic atrocities so shocking that his own problems would dissolve into insignificance. He would go to 119 Tauentzienstrasse, where he and his *frauline* could sit and sip champagne and watch Mistress Beate, the Amazon with her whips and restraints, torture her slaves.

Parvus burped mightily and felt a giant surge, an acidic tide of liquid welling upward from his stomach. His blond *frauline* stared at him, alarmed. "You look very ill, Alexander," she said.

Parvus clapped a hand to his mouth and pushed back his chair. "I am," he replied, his words muffled behind his fingers. "Very ill."

TUESDAY
APRIL 10

THE TRAIN

Captain von Planetz awoke with a start. The carriage lights had been dimmed and for several seconds he couldn't remember where he was. He pushed himself up into a sitting position and massaged his shoulder, stiff from lying on the hard wooden bench. He was shivering violently, although the compartment felt warm. Lieutenant von Buhring lay on the seat across from him, stretched out on his back, snoring gently, his tunic folded under his head for a pillow.

The captain tipped the face of his watch to catch the thin shaft of light leaking from the corridor in under the compartment's shade: 3:30 in the morning. Muted voices and an occasional low laugh filtered through from the compartments up front. He rubbed his face with his hands to help wake himself up, then tiptoed out into the corridor and back to the carriage's rear exit. He unlocked it and stepped outside to check that the guards were doing their job. He counted three soldiers—two circling the perimeter of the train in opposite directions, and the third sitting on the roof of the carriage, his rifle across his knees.

He returned inside, carefully locking the door behind him. He was still shivering. He slapped his hands together against his sides to stimulate his circulation.

For nearly a minute he paused at the chalk line that divided the carriage into German and Russian territory and listened to the restless late-night murmurings of the thirty-two passengers in his charge.

It came back to him then, what it was that had awakened him. Not some external noise, as he had at first supposed, but a subconscious alarm. Even in sleep, his brain must have continued to work at the problem of the American assassin, because now he saw the answer that had so thoroughly eluded him just a few hours before.

He went back into the compartment and shook the lieutenant awake. "I know where he is," he whispered.

Von Buhring pushed himself up on one elbow and yawned powerfully. "What are you talking about, Captain?"

"Bauer. The American. I know where he is."

The lieutenant struggled to a sitting position and looked around, still dazed with sleep. "Where?"

"He's on this train."

Von Buhring blinked his eyes in confused alarm. "Did you see him?"

"Of course not. But I know he's here."

"How do you know?"

The captain held a finger up to his lips, warning the lieutenant to keep his voice down. "He's in Lenin's party. He's one of the passengers."

Von Buhring scratched his belly. His confusion was complete. "Begging your pardon, Captain, but how the hell do you arrive at that?"

Too agitated to sit, Von Planetz lit a cigarette and began pacing back and forth in the restricted confines of the compartment, two steps left, two steps right. "It came to me in my sleep," he admitted. "But it's clear as spring water. This must be exactly what the American has done. It solves all his problems. He easily eludes the customs checks, all our security precautions, everything—because of course we're looking everywhere but in the right place. And it puts him close to Lenin. Not just for a few minutes or a few hours, but for several days. He can pick his best opportunity to strike at his leisure. It's simple and it's clever. It's perfect, by God."

Von Buhring found a comb in his tunic and began pulling it slowly through his hair to work out the night's accumulation of snarls. "Can I play devil's advocate, Captain?"

Von Planetz slowed his pacing. "Of course."

"If he were hiding in Lenin's party, it seems to me the others would know it instantly."

The captain squinted at the glowing end of his cigarette. "No," he said. "Not necessarily. It's a mixed group. There's a hard core of Bolsheviks—they all know each other, of course—but at least a dozen of the rest are relative strangers—to each other and to Lenin's people. Bauer must be traveling in place of one of them."

Von Buhring reached over and turned on the electric lamp by the window. "But, Captain, we know—at least roughly—what he looks like from the description we have. Hell, you've seen all the passengers. None of them bears any resemblance to him. At least I don't see any."

The captain picked his officer's cap off the hook by the door and put it on. He always felt better with his bald head covered. "He's disguised himself," he said.

The lieutenant shook his head in doubt. "He's an American. Even with a disguise, he'd stick out."

"As a Russian, perhaps. But not as a German Swiss. According to the American consul, he speaks German, and his family was German. He could pass easily."

"But why would any of them give up his place for him?"

"There could be many reasons. But it's not important."

Von Buhring thought about it. Finally he just nodded sleepily.

Von Planetz put out his cigarette and pulled his briefcase down from the overhead rack. "If I'm right, we have a hell of a problem on our hands. He's already inside our defenses. Our only chance now is to identify him and neutralize him before he strikes. No more sleep tonight. We'd better get to work at once."

He sat down next to his assistant, retrieved from his pocket a pencil and the list of the thirty-two travelers that the Swiss, Fritz Platten, had given him. He unfolded the list, a piece of hotel stationery, and spread it out flat on top of his briefcase. The names were scrawled hastily in two columns but were clear enough to decipher without strain:

V. Lenin	G. Brillant
Frau Lenin	M. Kharitonov
Georg Safarov	D. Rosenblum
Valentina Safarov-Mostitchkine	A. Abramovitch

Gregor Ussijevitch	S. Scheinessohn
Helene Kon	Tskhakaya
Inessa Armand	M. Gobermann
Nikolai Boitzow	A. Linde
F. Grebelsky	M. Aisenbud
D. Slussareff	O. Blum
A. Konstantinowitch	Pripevsky (Radek)
E. Mirinhoff	Souliachvili
M. Mirinhoff	O. Ravitch
A. Skowno	I. Morozov
G. Zinoviev	B. Eltchaninov
Z. Zinovieva (und Sohn)	F. Platten

Von Planetz drew a pencil line through the names of Lenin and his wife, through all the other married couples, through all the women's names, through all the obviously Russian or Slavic names, and through those, like F. Platten, whose identity he knew. That left eight names. Von Planetz copied them neatly in a separate column alongside Platten's original list:

A. Skowno

G. Brillant

D. Rosenblum

S. Scheinessohn

M. Gobermann

A. Linde

M. Aisenbud

O. Blum

"Most likely he's one of these," he said.

Von Buhring peered down at the remaining eight names. "Let's call them back and start questioning them."

"We can't."

"Why not?"

"The agreement between Zimmermann and Lenin, remember? We're not allowed to talk to them. We can't even examine their passports."

The lieutenant threw up his hands in resignation.

The captain tapped his pencil impatiently against the side of the briefcase. "We'll have to wait and talk to Platten."

It was an absurd difficulty, but there it was. They could not cross the chalk line, and they could not speak with any of the other passengers. And the only way he could summon the Swiss intermediary was to shout his name down the corridor. At four o'clock in the morning he was unwilling to do that.

Von Planetz folded the list up and returned it to his pocket. "He'll check with us at eight o'clock. That's our agreement. We'll just have to wait until then."

The other five occupants of Bauer's compartment fell silent around midnight and began the search for a position compatible with sleep—no easy task in such a confined space.

Four of them ended up with their heads propped in the corners where the seat backs and the walls met. The fifth, Gobermann, sprawled out on his stomach on the narrow floor space between the benches. Bauer himself sat rigid in the middle of the forward bench, his hands resting on his cane, listening to the voices from the other compartments. Every outside door and window in the carriage was shut tight, and the air had become stale and unbreatheable. Drowsiness crept up on him, and his head began dropping to his chest. He needed fresh air more than sleep, he decided.

He stepped carefully over the prostrate form of Gobermann and retreated to the corridor. It was deserted. He draped the crook of his cane over the horizontal safety bar that ran beneath the corridor windows, unlatched one of the windows and slid it partway down. A bracing, cool breeze flowed against his face. He rested his chin on the top edge of the glass, and gazed out at the night.

"Can I have some, too?"

The voice was female. He turned, and in the faint light of the corridor's dimmed lamps, he saw the silhouette of a sizable mane of hair. "Good evening, ma'am," he replied, touching the brim of his hat. "Have what?"

"Some of your fresh air. I think we've used up all the oxygen in here."

Bauer made room for her beside him. She wasn't very tall, so he pulled the window farther down.

"Thank you," she whispered. "It's a difficult night to sleep, isn't it?"

"Yes."

"You're German, aren't you?"

"Swiss. I'm Oskar Blum."

"Inessa Armand."

They shook hands, awkwardly. He remembered their previous handshake in the café. Her palm felt cooler this time, he thought, more tentative. Was she nervous about something? The trip? At least she showed no sign of recognizing him. But of course the light was bad.

Inessa pushed her chin just over the edge of the glass and drew a deep breath. "When I was growing up, my mother never let me sleep with the window open, no matter how hot it got." Her tone was intimate and unselfconscious. "She was convinced the night air carried all manner of diseases. *Courants de l'air*. We French seem to have a phobia about it."

"When I was in Mexico I slept outdoors most nights," Bauer replied. "Under the stars. Never made me sick. In fact I got to like it."

"Really? I've never done that—slept outside. I'd worry that it would rain. Or that some creature would bite me. Did you like Mexico?"

Bauer shrugged.

"Why were you there?"

Bauer hadn't had the time to prepare a detailed biography to go with his disguise. He hadn't anticipated that he would need one. But Mexico seemed like a pretty safe subject. There were European socialists like Blum crawling all over the country when he was there. "It had to do with the revolution," he answered, honestly enough.

"I wish I'd been there," Inessa said, her voice wistful. "I read some of what the Americans John Reed and Lincoln Steffens wrote about it. It must have been exciting."

"It was depressing."

"Why?"

"Cruelty, hardship, injustice. A lot of people dying for nothing."

Inessa shook her head firmly. "They died so their children would know a better life. That's not for nothing."

Bauer didn't answer her. No use telling her that the Mexican revolution was just an illusion—a daydream destroyed by guns and men on horseback.

She sensed his reluctance. "What are you thinking?"

"You French have an expression," he said. "The more things change, the more they remain the same."

Inessa laughed. "What an odd revolutionary you make," she said.

"Any more odd that you?" he countered.

She seemed surprised. "What do you mean?"

He looked away from her, at the darkness beyond the window. "You're refined. You probably come from a rich family."

"My father was in the theater. Vaudeville, at that. I suppose we qualified as middle-class French. And it's the bourgeoisie that feeds revolution, isn't it? I've often wondered why. Ilyich himself comes from a very respectable middle-class family. I think those who are the most oppressed don't believe change is even possible."

"Are you married?"

"I *was* married. I have five children."

Bauer studied her out of the corners of his eyes, trying to see her better in the poor light. She looked about twenty-seven or twenty-eight, with the restless energy of a teenager. Her chestnut hair framed her face seductively. Her skin was smooth, unblemished. "You can't be old enough."

"I'm thirty-eight." She said it with no trace of coyness, as if the subject didn't interest her.

"Tell me about your husband."

"Alex? Well, he's half Russian and half French. The Armand family owns a big textile factory in Pushkino, outside Moscow. After my father died, I was sent there to live with an aunt. She was a tutor for his family, so that's how we met. I was nineteen. We were married ten years. I left him after the birth of Andrei. That was in 1903." She paused and shook her head in wonderment. "My God," she whispered, "it does seem a lifetime ago."

"Don't you miss it at all?"

"Sometimes. I miss the children most, and some of my friends." She paused. "And I miss trivial things, too. We went to such beautiful parties, Alex and I."

Inessa closed her eyes and dropped her voice to a whisper. "Once we went to the Winter Palace in St. Petersburg. I danced with Czar Nicholas himself. He was a handsome man, wonderfully charming. And what a beautiful dancer he was! I remember one moment especially. The orchestra was playing a Strauss waltz, and as we twirled across the huge ballroom, I suddenly felt giddy—euphoric beyond anything I had ever experienced. It was the champagne, I suppose, and the music, and dancing with the czar amid that glittering throng of royalty. The stuff of a young girl's daydreams. But there was something more. I was overwhelmed by an intuition so intense and perfect that it took my breath away. I felt a sudden connection with everyone in that enormous place, as if we were all part of the same exalted being. All of us on that ballroom floor were moving together, hearing the same glorious music, feeling the same joy, being swept up together in a sense of oneness and harmony, all part of a larger, common consciousness—all experiencing a moment of shared ecstasy." Inessa stopped, embarrassed by her confession. "It was decadent, I know. . . ."

She looked up into Bauer's eyes, then turned her gaze back to the window. "Later I thought how few people on earth could ever hope for such an experience, for just one such moment in their lives. This realization caused me great anguish. It made me begin to think, finally, about people other than myself. For the first time I began to see the basic evil of a society where not just material riches, but almost all the experiences that make life meaningful and pleasurable, are limited to an extraordinarily lucky handful. Once I understood this, I could no longer justify my life."

"And that's why you left it all behind?"

Inessa laughed self-deprecatingly. "That's what I like to think. But sometimes I think I'm hopelessly self-indulgent and just fooling myself. I didn't want to spend the rest of my life as a Moscow matron. It was suffocating. We saw the same people week after week, year after year . . ." She reeled off the names in a tone of comic boredom: ". . . the Khludovs, the Prokhorovs, the Guchkovs, the Ryabushinskys, the Abrikosovs, the Katuarmamis—all the elite families of the 'White Stone City.' That's what the Muscovites called the *nouveaux riches*, because they imagined we all lived in white stone houses. And Moscow is very provincial. There was little to do except have children, have affairs, and gossip with the other wives. We didn't even travel very much. It wasn't enough for me. I wanted to be part of something more worthwhile. So I became involved in things—temperance campaigns, fighting prostitution, the suffragette movement. I even led a campaign to improve the working conditions in the Armand family mills."

"That's still a long way from becoming a Bolshevik."

Inessa twisted her fingers in her hair and sighed. "You're right. It all seems so tame now, my little agitations with the wives and petty local officials. And my husband always there to bail me out of trouble. Since then I've earned my stripes as a revolutionary."

Bauer thought she was boasting a bit. "How?"

"I joined the SRs in Moscow," she said. "The first time I was arrested—on Bloody Sunday—it scared the devil out of me. In Czarist Russia serious political convictions require serious courage. But I learned. In a few years I had a long record of arrests. The last time, I was sent to a work camp in Siberia—Arkhangelsk Guberniya. It was a frightful place, and I knew I wouldn't live long if I didn't get away. I escaped to Switzerland. That was in 1908. I moved to Paris in 1910. I met Lenin that same year. I'd read his book, *What Is to Be Done?*, and I knew that I had found my life work. Bolshevism showed me what I had been looking for ever since that night at the Winter Palace—some way to bring people together in a common cause, a shared sense of oneness and happiness." She laughed apologetically. "I'm sorry. That sounds like a speech, but you asked me."

If he had been there as himself, Harry Bauer would have felt intimidated. He had never met a woman with her kinds of experience, and she made him feel uneasy. But tonight he was Blum, speaking Blum's language, and that liberated him from himself. "What will become of you?" he asked.

Inessa chided him. "You men. You never think a woman can take care of herself. What will become of *you*, Herr Blum?

Bauer laughed. "I don't know. Someday when I'm looking the wrong way, something will get me."

Inessa regarded him with somber eyes. "You sound like you don't care. Don't you?"

"I care. But if I've learned anything from life, it's that a man doesn't have as much control over it as he'd like to."

"Yes, he does!" Inessa cried. Her protest was passionate. "He makes his life what it is."

Bauer shrugged. "Well, mine's been a lot different from yours. No revelations in the ballroom of the Winter Palace."

"Now you're making fun of me."

"Maybe I'm jealous."

"I don't believe it. Were *you* ever married?"

He nodded. He wanted to tell her about it, but if he started in on his autobiography, he would soon be punching big holes right through that flimsy facade of Oskar Blum, Swiss Bundist. "It's hard to talk about it."

She looked disappointed.

"Some other night."

"Sometimes there aren't other nights," she said.

He had no answer for that. They stood silently for a while, hands on top of the opened window, watching the dark beyond the train. A thousand desires crowded his thoughts, and he wondered if she could feel them, emanating from him like invisible pulses of a telegraph. The longer he stood there beside her, the greater the risk that he would reveal himself.

"I haven't seen much of Lenin," he said, breaking the tension between them.

"He's very nervous," Inessa said. "He doesn't want to see anybody. He's paranoid about the Germans. He's worried they'll double-cross him."

"Still, he could come out and talk to us," Bauer tried.

"I know. I think he's resentful that the whole party couldn't be exclusively Russian and Bolshevik."

Bauer wanted to pursue the matter, but was prevented by the appearance of a German guard outside the window. The soldier pointed his rifle directly at them. "Close the window!" he commanded. Bauer stuck his head out the window and looked down at him. The guard stepped toward him. Bauer wanted to tell him to go to hell, but Inessa prevented it.

"Don't talk to him," she whispered. She tugged at his collar and pulled his head back inside. "Do as he says."

The guard repeated his demand.

Bauer muttered a frustrated curse and slid the window back up into place.

"I hate the Germans," Inessa muttered, her voice fierce. "They killed my brother at the Marne."

Bauer touched her shoulder consolingly. He could feel the anger vibrating inside her. She stood facing him, barely inches away, her eyes searching his face. He put an arm around her shoulder tentatively. She rested her head lightly against his chest. Her hair brushed his chin. A subtle fragrance of roses tickled his nose. They remained like that for a moment, barely moving.

"I'm afraid," she whispered. "I tell myself that I shouldn't be, but I am. For the first time in my life, I feel really afraid."

"Of what?"

"The future. About what's going to happen."

Bauer could think of no reply. Inessa lifted her head and pressed her hand briefly against his cheek. Then she walked away. He watched her retreat down the corridor and disappear through the door into the second-class section.

He was afraid himself, he thought. Afraid of Inessa Armand.

Near five o'clock Tuesday morning the sealed carriage was jolted slightly as a locomotive of the Baden State Railway backed against it. A few minutes later, coupled to its new engine, the train rumbled from the siding onto the main line north, into the heart of Germany.

Barely thirty kilometers from Singen the train stopped to switch engines again, this time to the Württemberg State Railway, and begin a slight eastward detour toward Stuttgart, to avoid the military traffic choking the lines west and south through Karlsruhe and Offenburg.

At seven o'clock the sealed train passed through the medieval town of Rottweil, with its fortresslike brick walls and cathedral spires, then wound through a long tunnel to emerge onto a broad valley alongside the River Neckar.

At eight o'clock the ancient stone watch tower of the village of Horb loomed into view and then was gone as the train rushed downhill through a narrow pass and out into the flat, open farmland of Baden-Württemberg.

Captain von Planetz glanced at his wristwatch again, only to find that its hands had not advanced more than half a minute from his last look.

Finally, at four and a half minutes past eight, the Swiss intermediary, Fritz Platten, appeared at the compartment doorway, looking well-rested and cheerful. His face was freshly shaved, and his clothes—although like everyone else he must have slept in them—were remarkably free of wrinkles. He greeted the two German officers with a hearty good morning and a tip of his pearl-gray fedora. "You must do something about breakfast," he complained. "My people have nothing to eat, except those stale rolls from yesterday."

"We plan to have a restaurant car put on in Frankfurt," the captain assured him. "Meanwhile, I'm afraid we'll have to rely on what we can find at the stations. We'll be in Stuttgart later this morning. We'll buy food there for everybody."

"I'll tell the others," Platten said, and turned to go.

The captain jumped up and caught the Swiss by the elbow as he headed through the door. "Please sit down, Herr Platten. I have a serious matter to discuss."

Von Planetz explained why he thought the American assassin was with them on the train. The Swiss listened with a mixture of inattentiveness and annoyance. "But you have no proof of any of this whatsoever," he objected. "None."

The captain admitted that was so. "If we wait for proof, Lenin may be killed."

Platten stood up to leave. "It's your responsibility to prevent that, Captain. Not mine. Back at the station in Gottmadingen you raised this same alarm. An assassin was after Lenin, you said. We gave you the benefit of the doubt. Ilyich has taken pains to remain out of sight. Now you tell me that this killer is actually among us on this train—in disguise. Really, Herr Captain, I think you're having delusions."

Platten's attitude was galling, but Von Planetz was careful to remain polite. "All I ask of you, Herr Platten, is to consider the possibility. I have narrowed down the likely suspects to eight. If you would only question them for me . . ."

The Swiss raised a hand to cut him off. "No. Absolutely not. You're trying to shift the blame to us in case anything goes wrong."

The captain rose from his seat and bore in on the Swiss with determination. "Herr Platten. I'm trying to carry out my duties to the best of my capabilities—and without violating the agreement between Lenin and our government. You're making that very difficult. Why?"

Platten became defensive. "It's not my intention to make things difficult, Captain. But you're being unreasonable."

"I admit my case is weak, but you give me no chance to prove it. Your attitude is cavalier—and dangerous. If anything goes wrong because of your failure to cooperate with me, you *will* be to blame. Are you prepared to accept that responsibility?"

The Swiss took a deep breath. "All right," he snapped. "What do you want me to do?"

"Just take a close look at these eight men. That's all I ask of you. Just talk with each of them long enough to collect an impression. You needn't interrogate anyone. I'll trust your instincts and your perceptions. If none of these men raises any doubts in your mind, then I'll accept that I'm wrong and apologize for putting you to this extra trouble."

Platten still resisted. "Do you seriously suppose, Captain, that one of our group would have permitted an assassin to take his place?"

"He may have been pressured into it. Blackmailed. Paid off. Murdered. There are many ways it might've been done."

"But the identity of the passengers on this train has been kept absolutely secret. You and I and Lenin have the only lists."

"Doesn't it occur to you that you could have had a spy in your midst?"

Platten's young face registered shock at the idea. "I still think our suspicions are absurd."

"I'll ask you again. Are you willing to risk ignoring me and finding out too late that I was right?"

Platten sighed extravagantly. "Good Lord, Captain. If it will put your overworked imagination to rest, I'll do it. Who are these eight suspects of yours?"

Von Planetz copied the names onto a separate slip of paper and handed it to the Swiss. Platten ran his eyes over the list, then shook his head. "Well, your killer is not Aisenbud or Gobermann. Or Rosenblum. I know all three of them personally. And I've spoken to them since Singen. And it's obviously not Brillant. That's an alias."

The captain raised his eyebrows in surprise. "An alias?"

"I can't supply you with the man's real name, Captain. I'm sorry. He's wanted by the police in several countries. But I can vouch that he's not this American assassin."

The captain made small X's with his pencil by the four

names on his copy of the list. "You see, Herr Platten, you've been very helpful already. We've halved the list in barely a minute. Now if you'll just check these remaining four for me—Skowno, Blum, Scheinessohn, and Linde."

Platten nodded and shoved the list hastily into his pocket.

"This Bauer is tall and sturdily built. Around a hundred ninety centimeters and ninety kilos. Height and weight are hard to disguise. Keep that in mind when you talk to these men."

"I'll keep it in mind."

"You must not delay," Von Planetz warned. "Please talk to them within the next few hours."

Platten adjusted his fedora, twisting the brim down to a more rakish angle with his forehead. "Is that all, Captain?"

"No. I was very troubled this morning. I was not able to communicate with you for several hours. This one-way system must end. Since you're the only member of the party we're allowed to speak to, you must make yourself more available."

"What do you propose?"

"That you sit in the compartment adjacent to ours. If anything arises, we can be in instant voice contact."

"Really, Captain . . ."

"I insist, Herr Platten. It's not an unreasonable demand."

Platten obviously thought it was, but he couldn't very well refuse. He left the compartment in considerably worse cheer than he had entered it.

The captain turned to his lieutenant, sitting silently by the window. "A spoiled child," he said, letting his anger show. "He doesn't want to be bothered. He thinks he's on a holiday and he doesn't want anything to interfere with it."

Von Buhring nodded but said nothing. The captain suspected that his lieutenant secretly agreed with the Swiss.

But the captain trusted his instincts. They had seldom failed him. He glanced out the train window and saw another small station slipping past. The platform was deserted. All the stations they had passed so far this morning had been empty.

"Where are we? Do you know?"

"Herrenberg," the lieutenant replied. "We should make Stuttgart in two hours."

The captain picked up the passenger list again and studied

the four remaining names, half hoping they might yield some further clue that would help him. If Platten didn't find something when he talked to the four—and the odds were that he wouldn't try very hard—then Von Planetz didn't know what else he could do.

The train arrived at Stuttgart station about midday. Food—mostly beer, bread, and cheese—was brought aboard and turned over to Fritz Platten, who oversaw its distribution.

The arrival of the food brought a crowd from the compartments out into the corridor, and Bauer took the opportunity to use the lavatory at the head of the carriage.

The door to Lenin's compartment at the front was open as he passed it. He slowed and glanced inside. There were four occupants. Lenin's wife, Krupskaya, was knitting by the window. The shade was raised just high enough to allow some daylight to spill onto her lap. Morozov's menacing hulk slouched at the other end of the same seat, his deformed face hidden from view behind the half-open door. Opposite sat Lenin and another man Bauer didn't know. Lenin seemed to be sleeping. The other man, short and middle-aged with a clean-shaven chin and squinty Mongol eyes like Lenin's, was reading a newspaper.

Bauer stepped into the lavatory, latched the door, and set quickly to work shaving away the day's worth of hair growth to keep the top of his head bald, and touched up the remaining fringe and moustache with henna rinse. Finished, he opened the door and limped out past the front compartment again. A woman—someone called her Olga—was bringing the occupants their share of the food in a wicker basket.

The man seated next to Lenin caught Bauer's eye as he passed. Bauer nodded a greeting, but the man just glared back at him. Another bodyguard, he guessed. Lenin was certainly protecting himself.

Back in his own compartment, Bauer joined the others eating the cheese and bread. The bread was of the poorest quality, laced heavily with sawdust and almost impossible to chew. The cheese was goat and reasonably fresh. The beer was warm but good. Bauer drank his bottle and Gobermann's, who turned out to be a teetotaler.

At 2:00 P.M. the sealed train slipped out of Stuttgart and

into the Württemberg countryside. Barely an hour later it stopped at the town of Bretten to switch engines again, this time back to the Baden State line. Bauer sat silently by the window, gazing out at the unpopulated brown fields and bare trees, trying to solve the problem of how to get to Lenin.

At the Karlsruhe station they were held up again—this time to make way for military traffic. Several long supply trains thundered by, headed toward Offenburg and the front.

A hospital train, moving far more slowly, rumbled through the station in the other direction.

"They usually come through at night now," Aisenbud said. "So no one will see them."

"It's just creeping along," Linde added. "Some of those soldiers must need emergency attention."

Bauer shook his head. "It's not a real hospital train," he said.

The others looked at him. "What is it, then?" Linde demanded.

"It's a hearse. They're bringing back the dead."

The compartment watched in silence as the shuttered carriages, big red crosses painted on their sides, clacked by with a funeral cadence. Bauer counted twenty cars.

From Karlsruhe, the sealed train moved out onto a long stretch of desolate flatland and gathered speed toward Mannheim.

At Mannheim the Baden State Railway engine was uncoupled and a locomotive of the Prussian-Hessian State Railway attached.

"It's maddening, all these engine switches," Gobermann complained.

"We'll nationalize the railroads," Bauer joked. "As soon as we come to power."

Gobermann stared at him thoughtfully. "A good idea," he said.

Back out on the Württemberg plains, the train hastened north toward Frankfurt.

The compartment door slid open and Fritz Platten appeared. He glanced around the carriage, and his eyes settled on Bauer. He smiled. "I'd like to exchange seats with you for a while, if you don't mind." He jerked a thumb toward the wall beyond him. "Our little German High Command needs me close by, you see."

Bauer stood up, bracing himself heavily against the cane, and moved to let Platten take his place.

"I've been sitting up front in second-class—first compartment just the other side of the swinging door," the Swiss told him. "You can go there if you like."

The American tipped his hat in thanks and started out.

"You're Blum, aren't you?" Platten said, settling onto the hard wooden bench.

Bauer paused and turned. "That's right. Oskar Blum. From Zurich, *mein Herr*."

"The one who forgot his visa. Am I correct?"

Bauer felt Platten's eyes appraising him. They lingered a long time on his shoes. Had he done something to arouse suspicion? "I'm the one," he admitted, laughing apologetically.

"Yes. Another mistake. Just like that time at the Predigerkirche, Blum. Remember?"

Bauer swallowed. A trap. There was no mistaking it. Platten was trying to flush him from his cover. It was amateurish because it was so obvious, but that didn't mean it wouldn't work. His first thought was to ask Platten to repeat the question, but he rejected it. That, too, would be obvious—a simple stalling for time. Better to chance a quick, vague answer. If caught, he could claim that he had misunderstood the question.

Which way to jump? Blum had insisted that he didn't know Platten. Bauer would have to go with that. "I beg your pardon, Herr Platten. To what do you refer?"

"The Predigerkirche. You know it, don't you?"

"In Zurich. Yes, of course."

Platten sighed and shook his head. "Nothing. Never mind. It was someone else."

Bauer headed toward the first compartment on the other side of the swinging door, weak with relief. He had fended the Swiss off easily, but the warning flags were up. They were looking for him. And they were getting close.

He must get this business done with, he told himself. Tonight, no later. Every hour he stayed on the train, he was increasing his risk. Tonight, then. With the noise of the running train to mute the deed. He touched his hat politely and took the empty space by the window. "Excuse me," he said, "I've been asked to change seats."

When he raised his head, he found himself opposite Inessa Armand. She seemed very happy to see him. She smiled brightly, then leaned forward and touched his knee in that restless manner of hers. "I'll introduce you to the others."

The others were George Safarov and his wife, Valentina; Olga Ravich, the woman he'd seen bringing food to Lenin's compartment, and the noisy Austrian deserter, Karl Radek.

Fritz Platten returned to the German officers' compartment late in the afternoon. He tipped his hat with his usual ostentatious flourish and dropped onto the bench opposite Von Planetz.

"You're smiling," the captain said. "Does that indicate some kind of good news?"

"With you, Captain, I'm not sure," the Swiss replied. "In any case, I've done as you requested. I've taken a good close look at your four remaining suspects."

"And . . . ?"

Platten pulled out the list Von Planetz had given him and unfolded it with great deliberation, enjoying the suspense he was creating. "Well, two of them are far too short to be Bauer. Linde is around a hundred seventy centimeters, and Scheinessohn is barely a hundred fifty-five. Skowno is tall enough—about a hundred eighty-five—but thinner than prison soup."

"What about Blum?"

"He's a hundred ninety centimeters and stocky."

Von Planetz caught his breath and leaned forward intently. "So it's him, then!"

Platten shook his head. "No, it's not. Blum also happens to be a cripple. One foot is shorter than the other. He walks with a pronounced limp, and supports himself with a cane."

"Are you certain? He could be faking."

The Swiss propped an ankle across his knee and tapped the bottom of his shoe. "I doubt it. His footwear is specially made. The sole and heel of one shoe is considerably built up—at least five centimeters."

The captain slumped back against the bench. "Well . . . thank you, Herr Platten," he muttered.

"Don't be so depressed," the Swiss said. "Now that we know he's not on the train with us, we can all relax. That includes you." He stood up to leave. "I hope you'll have better food for us at Frankfurt."

Von Planetz nodded weakly.

"Do you believe him?" Lieutenant von Buhring asked when Platten had left.

"What choice do I have?"

Von Buhring twisted uncomfortably in his seat. "Perhaps you were wrong after all, Captain."

Von Planetz wondered. He lit a cigarette and exhaled the smoke noisily against the window to relieve his frustration. Could Bauer have simply lost his nerve and backed out? No. Of course not. He was just smarter than the captain had thought. And meanwhile, he was making an ass out of Hamburg's best police inspector. *Damn you, Bauer, where are you?*

Karl Radek was a compulsive talker. The wiry-haired Austrian dominated the conversation in the compartment completely, concocting glib monologues and diatribes around an endless variety of subjects. He was often funny, occasionally profound, and invariably caustic. His favorite target was the Germans. He ridiculed them at great length, capping his tirade with a burlesque of the kaiser, strutting around his castle at Pless, repeatedly stuffing his withered hand back between the buttons of his tunic, à la Napoleon, while bellowing nonsensical orders to his generals.

Safarov, bored with the chatter, escaped to another compartment, leaving Radek with Bauer and the three women—Valentina, Olga, and Inessa. They listened politely. Valentina nodded, Olga giggled appreciatively, Inessa stared out the window.

Bauer tried to tune Radek out and concentrate on preparing himself for what he had to do. Ever since Singen he had been thwarted by a seemingly unsolvable problem: how to get Lenin alone. The Bolshevik leader rarely left his compartment, and when he did, it was always in the company of others—usually Morozov.

But finally Bauer had solved it. There was one place where Lenin would have to be by himself. One, and only one. The rest of the plan was simplicity itself. A wait of undetermined duration, then the bullet in the back of the neck. Then another wait until it was safe to jump the train. Bauer was not a patient man, and the two long waits the plan required didn't please him. They would be hard on the nerves.

"When Ilyich comes to power," Radek was saying, "I, for one, want to be a thousand kilometers away. No, make that five thousand kilometers."

"Why?" Valentina demanded.

Radek leaned near her, opened his eyes wide, and chopped his hand against the back of his neck. "When Ilyich has the power," he whispered, his tone ominous, "heads will be separated from shoulders all over Russia—from Archangel to Sevastopol, from Minsk to Magadan. Mine will go first. You know why? Because Ilyich can't stand it when anyone disagrees with him. Let me illustrate: I tell him Russia should keep the old-style calendar. But he wants the new style. But I say, 'Look, Comrade Lenin, according to our fine old-style Russian calendar, today is Tuesday, April tenth. If you adopt the new-style calendar, tomorrow will have to become Monday, April twenty-third. The Russian people will lose thirteen days! They'll never forgive you. "Give us back our thirteen days!" they'll cry.' 'The old calendar was corrupt!' Ilyich retorts. 'The people must accept the sacrifice.' 'But the Russian people are deeply religious,' I reply. "God created the world in seven days," they'll say. "And now Lenin has stolen thirteen!" ' 'Those reactionaries and obstructionists who stand in the path of our revolutionary calendar reform will be crushed,' Lenin says. 'Annihilated. And that includes you, Radek, you Jewish Austrian revisionist sodomite. To the guillotine.' " Radek repeated his neck-chopping gesture, opening his mouth and adding a theatrical gurgling sound to make it more graphic.

Olga shrieked with delight.

"That's scandalous," Valentina declared primly.

Radek grinned, enormously pleased with himself. He pointed at Bauer. "I'm right! Ask him. Ilyich will cut his head off, too. Twice, in fact. Why? Because as a good Russian, Ilyich despises Jews. As a good Bolshevik, he despises Bundists. So when Lenin comes to power, our friend Blum here better catch the first train out of Petrograd. And I'll be in the seat behind him!"

Inessa turned from the window. "Shut up, Karl," she said.

To Bauer's surprise, Radek did shut up. Or, more accurately, he wound down. After a few grumbling comments to the effect that revolutionaries possessed no sense of humor, he polished his glasses with his shirttail and buried his head behind the copy of an old newspaper that he had been reading earlier. Olga and Valentina fell to discussing domestic matters, wondering aloud what the food and housing situation would be like in Petrograd.

Inessa smiled knowingly at Bauer. Clearly she felt they had established a bond from their meeting last night at the corridor window. He thought so, too. He wanted to talk to her, but casual conversation with her was dangerous. Sooner or later he'd give himself away.

"Do you mind if I do this?" Inessa asked. She slid down in her seat and put her legs up on the edge of Bauer's seat so that her black-stockinged feet rested between his legs. "I didn't get any sleep at all last night," she said, pressing her fingers over a wide yawn.

"I don't mind." It was an extraordinarily intimate gesture, he thought. She closed her eyes and seemed to drift off almost at once. Her feet were small and she had crossed them at the ankles, bringing her toes to within inches of his crotch. Her stockings looked to be silk, although he was no expert in such matters. It was an arousing sight.

He looked out the window to force his attention elsewhere. The train seemed to be creeping along, making no better than twenty-five miles an hour, he guessed, and halting frequently—sometimes to let a military train pass, sometimes for no apparent reason at all. He had expected the Germans would haul this fugitive caravan across their territory in record time, but instead, their progress had been agonizingly slow. It was now a full day since they had left Zurich. They ought to be near Sassnitz, on the Baltic, not still plodding like a milk wagon through southern Germany.

But the slow pace was a break for him. It had taken him the full day just to settle on the details of his plan. And it was going to take at least another half day to carry it out.

The gentle swaying motion of the train brought Inessa's

toes bumping softly against his thigh. He placed a hand carefully on her ankles to steady them. She stirred and smiled faintly, but didn't open her eyes. The feeling of the warm silk against his palms made his mouth dry. As surreptitiously as possible he adjusted his pants to make room for a now raging erection, and turned back to the window.

The train crossed a small dirt road out in the countryside. A solitary horse-drawn cart waited at the grade crossing. Bauer noticed a signpost on the road, pointing the way to Darmstadt. It was somewhere around here, he realized, that his father had been born. Just a few miles from Darmstadt. A little village called Reinheim. Maybe this was the village. "Everybody knew the Bauers," he could hear his father saying. "We were the biggest family in town."

What would his father think, he wondered, if he could see his homeland now, crushed by the worst war in its history? One thing he knew for certain. His father would have approved wholeheartedly of Lenin.

Bauer dozed off for nearly an hour, sleeping fitfully against the noise and lurches of the carriage on the trackbed. He saw his father in a dream, holding a pistol to the back of Inessa's head. She was crying. Then his father became Lenin. He laughed and pulled the trigger and Inessa toppled forward. Bauer woke with a start and cried out.

He straightened up and rubbed his eyes. Inessa was still sitting across from him, but she had withdrawn her feet from the space between his legs. She was staring at him oddly.

"Bad dream," he explained, grinning sheepishly.

She nodded.

They reached Frankfurt during the evening rush hour. For the first time since Zurich they saw something resembling a crowd. The mood was palpably grim. People rushed past on the platforms around them, sullen and withdrawn, their heads down, eyes focused immediately ahead. Most surprising, Bauer thought, was the silence. Except for the locomotives, hissing steam and squealing brakes, the only noise was the muffled tromp of shoes and boots. No shouts, no laughs, no conversations.

After a short wait a new locomotive pulled their carriage and baggage car onto a siding away from the station platforms. Awhile later a dining car was attached, and for the first time the revolutionaries were treated to something like a sit-down meal. Amid groans and protests, Fritz Platten told everyone that there was a further delay. They would have to remain parked at the Frankfurt station for the rest of the night. "We'll leave early in the morning and be in Berlin at midday tomorrow," he promised. "And in Sassnitz in time for the evening ferry."

This last announcement was greeted with cheers. Someone in the dining car started singing "The Marseillaise" again, but was quickly hushed. After an earlier complaint by Von Planetz that the singing was provoking anger among the Germans who overheard it, Lenin had decreed that no revolutionary songs could be sung during the station stops.

It'll have to be done here, tonight, Bauer decided. He had hoped for a moving train, to hide the noise of the shot, but he would have to risk it while the carriage was in the Frankfurt yard.

It was just past seven o'clock. At least another five hours to wait. He grabbed his cane from the seat beside him and went out into the corridor. He hooked the cane on the railing under the window and stared out into the night.

The siding was at the edge of the train yard, and from the window Bauer had a good view of one of Frankfurt's wide, tree-lined avenues. Only every fourth street lamp was burning, creating a long row of dim, isolated pools of light in a surrounding blanket of murk. The bare tree branches rustled in a strong wind. There were no pedestrians and no motor traffic. One horse-drawn wagon plodded along the cobblestones.

He never did get those names the American consul, James McNally, had promised him in Zurich, he recalled. So he had no escape hatch waiting for him in Frankfurt—or anywhere else in Germany—if he had to go to ground.

He was on his own. But that was the way he liked it.

WASHINGTON

Colonel House walked down the narrow vestibule off the West Sitting Hall and rapped lightly on the door at the far end.

A voice answered immediately: "Come in, Eddie."

House pushed the door open carefully and stepped inside.

The President was in the room alone, sitting at his small desk by the window. He was hunched over his famous battered typewriter, hitting the keys with the concentrated attention that he seemed to apply to everything he did. He typed another line or two, then stopped and looked across at his longtime friend and closest adviser. "Please sit, Eddie," he said.

House took a seat across from the desk. "It's a beautiful day, Mr. President," he said.

Wilson nodded absently. He wasn't interested in the weather. Both windows in the cramped study were closed, and the shades were drawn partway down, cutting out much of the light and all the view of the South Lawn.

The President had converted the space, a small dressing room adjacent to his bedroom on the southwest corner of the White House, into an office about two years earlier. Originally he had used it only for working in the evenings, after the secretaries and staff that populated the West Wing had gone home for the day. But now he spent most of his time here, putting in appearances at the Oval Office only when absolutely necessary.

The President's stomach pump, an evil-looking steel and rubber contraption, was out of its case and resting on a table by the doorway. House gagged every time he saw it. Wilson normally kept it hidden in the bathroom. Its presence meant that he had probably used it recently. The President's intestinal problems—his "troubles in Central America" he called them—were a closely kept medical secret, as was the bizarre fact that he had taught himself to use a stomach pump on himself to relieve them.

Wilson came directly to the point. He picked up a manila folder from his desk and handed it across. "This came over yesterday evening from the secretary of the army," he said, his tone stern. "Can you explain it to me?"

The colonel opened the folder, curious to know what it could contain that would cause the President to summon him on such short notice. The top sheet gave him the answer, and his heart sank.

It was a memo from the secretary to the President asking for a routine confirmation of House's request to forward the military record of Major Henry Bauer, U.S. Army Intelligence, to the British Embassy. The other pages were carbons of Bauer's military record. House closed the folder with a sweaty palm and placed it back on the President's desk. He had made that request by telephone. He had forgotten about the written confirmation, and it had slipped by him.

"Well, what's it all about?" Wilson demanded.

"It turns out Major Bauer is alive, Mr. President. In Zurich. The British were interested in his services. That's all."

"His services? To do what?"

House knew his boss well enough to know that his only alternative was to divulge everything and hope for the best. He explained the plan, and his involvement in it, coloring it, as he habitually did with the President, with subtle flattery. The colonel had long ago discovered that Wilson, despite his fierce objectivity of mind, was highly susceptible to praise, no matter how disingenuous. "Of course I didn't intentionally keep this from you, Mr. President. I was merely seeking to relieve you of some of the burden of your office, which I appreciate has been enormous of late."

Wilson removed his spectacles and rubbed his temples with his fingers, a look of exquisite pain distorting his gaunt features. House wondered if his expression indicated his distress with his old friend or that he simply had another headache. "Assassinate Lenin, indeed," he muttered in an extremely irritated tone. "To gain what advantage?"

"Germany plans to use Lenin to undermine Russia. It'll be a terrible blow to the Allied war effort if they succeed. And our own boys will be over there soon—facing those German guns."

"I am totally opposed to it," Wilson pronounced. "It's an expediency, and it's utterly immoral."

House bit his lip and nodded.

Wilson rummaged in a stack of documents by his typewriter, pulled out a document and handed it to House. "Read this," the President said. "It's from our legation in Bern. It came in last night."

House placed the decoded copy of the secret diplomatic cable in his lap.

APRIL 9, 1917. 2100 HOURS P.O.T.U.S. TOP SECRET AND
PERSONAL. WE RECEIVED THE FOLLOWING LETTER TODAY
FROM VLADIMIR LENIN IN ZURICH. CONTENTS FOLLOW: DEAR
PRESIDENT WILSON: TODAY I EMBARK ON A JOURNEY THAT
WILL RETURN ME, ALONG WITH A PARTY OF OTHER INTERNA-
TIONALISTS, TO MY HOMELAND, RUSSIA. I DO SO WITH THE
HOPE OF PLAYING A CONSTRUCTIVE ROLE IN MY COUNTRY'S
STRUGGLE TO ESTABLISH A DEMOCRATIC GOVERNMENT THAT
WILL BE RESPONSIVE TO THE NEEDS OF THE MASSES. YOUR
IDEALS HAVE LONG INSPIRED ME IN MY OWN QUEST TO SERVE
MY COUNTRY IN THIS TIME OF HER GREATEST CRISIS. I HOPE
THAT YOU WILL SUSPEND JUDGMENT ON WHAT YOU MAY READ
IN THE INTERNATIONAL PRESS AND HEAR FROM VARIOUS GOV-
ERNMENTS AND INDIVIDUALS IN THE DAYS IMMEDIATELY
AHEAD.
I ASSURE YOU MR. PRESIDENT THAT OUR BOLSHEVIK PARTY
SUPPORTS THE ALLIED CAUSE AGAINST GERMANY AND WILL
CONTINUE TO SUPPORT IT. SINCERE GOOD WISHES, V.I. LE-
NIN. END OF LETTER. ORIGINAL COPY OF
THIS WILL BE SENT IN NEXT DIPLOMATIC POUCH.
SINCERE REGARDS, DULLES. BERN LEGATION

House looked up. "Do you believe him, Mr. President?
He has publicly condemned Russia's participation in the war
many times."

Wilson pressed his fingers together in a tent and held them
against his mouth. "I've given it some thought. The only
conclusion I can come to is that it would not be fair for me to
disbelieve him. Men can change their minds. Let his deeds
speak for themselves. We'll have to wait and see. And of
course he may play no role in Russia's future at all. It's too
early to tell."

"I think he's trying to neutralize you."

"Why would he want to do that?"

"Possibly to head off the very thing we're discussing—his
untimely demise."

Wilson dropped his spectacles on the desk and stepped to
the window. He raised the shade and stared out across the
South Lawn. "Good Lord, Eddie. We're talking about com-
plicity in murder. No matter what the political justifications

might be, that's what it is. It was a murder that started this insane war. Archduke Ferdinand in Sarajevo. Has England forgotten that already? I appreciate your efforts to spare me work, but if something like this is allowed to happen, it can only reflect badly on the United States in the eyes of the world. What claim can we have to moral authority if we're party to such an act?"

There was nothing to be gained by argument, House saw. When the Governor saw an issue in moral terms, he could never be budged. The colonel knew he would just have to swallow this one, even though he was going to choke in the process. A heavy cloud of depression settled over him. What a mess this was going to be. "Of course I see your point, Mr. President," he muttered.

"You must tell Ambassador Bryce immediately that I disapprove of this business," Wilson insisted. "Disapprove of it completely. If you need me to communicate my feelings personally to the ambassador, I will. Otherwise, I shall rely on you to see to it that England understands our view."

"Bryce said Lloyd George was very enthusiastic," House countered falteringly.

Wilson made a face. "That's disgraceful. You'd think that if anybody would appreciate the rule of law, it would be an Englishman."

"Lenin's train has already left Zurich. He's somewhere in Germany now. Bauer may already have acted."

Wilson sat back down. He pinched his nose thoughtfully between his thumb and forefinger and then replaced his spectacles.

House began formulating in his head what he would tell Ambassador Bryce. Since Bryce believed that House had secured Wilson's permission, House would have to tell him that the President had changed his mind. The English would just have to go it alone. Results were all that mattered, in this instance.

The President shattered House's thinking. "I want it stopped. We'll have to turn the English around on this. It's a terrible mistake. Make that clear to Bryce. Use leverage if you have to. They need us now, in the war effort. A few strong hints that we might develop a degree of reluctance if this business goes forward ought to be enough to change their minds. Do whatever it takes. But I want this Bauer stopped."

House fought to hide his alarm. "But how? He must already be in Germany."

Wilson leaned forward in his chair. "Then we haven't a moment to lose. We have friends in Germany. Use them. If it's too late to stop him in Germany, then use the Swedes. Wire a request to Stockholm to arrest him. We'll file extradition papers with their embassy here tomorrow. If the Swedes drag their heels, then there's still the English. They have soldiers at the Finnish border. They can certainly stop him there."

House clasped his hands together nervously. "What if he's already acted?"

"Then there can be no question but to arrest him. The government of the United States cannot encourage, share in, or acquiese in the commission of a crime—especially this sort of crime." Wilson shook his head. "It's just another of Zimmermann's demented schemes. Like the Mexican telegram. It won't work. Lenin has probably told him what he wanted to hear, just to get back home. How can he promise to take Russia out of the war? He's in no position to do so and most likely will never be in such a position. And there just isn't any reason for him to do it if he could. It would be abject surrender. Lenin is too proud a man for that. And he is Russian, after all. Why would he betray his own country? Zimmermann is both arrogant and naive to imagine that he would."

House just nodded.

"And we're not going to be party to an assassination," Wilson concluded. "If it's in our power to stop it, then we must stop it. That's all I have to say on the matter."

House got up to leave. He felt his legs trembling.

The President turned back to his typewriter, then looked up as the colonel was halfway through the door. "I'm sorry, Eddie. I know this puts you in trouble with the English. When you talk to Ambassador Bryce, blame it all on me. I'm unreasonable, stubborn, out of touch with reality, and so forth and so on." Wilson cracked a rare smile. "All those things they say about me in the press."

House managed a shallow grin. He wished his "dear Governor" a pleasant day, and closed the door softly behind him.

BERLIN

Zimmermann's reaction to the news was even worse than Parvus had feared. He had expected something vintage Prussian—a ranting, desk-pounding, chair-kicking performance —but that was not the foreign secretary's style. The normally easygoing official listened to Parvus's explanation about the money in frigid silence. Only when the Dane had finished, offering his alternative solution of delivering the money in Swedish krona in Stockholm instead of Swiss francs in Berlin, did Zimmermann finally speak.

"You have put yourself in the way of Germany's destiny," he said ominously. "I could have you shot."

Parvus shook visibly at the words. There was no bottom to German arrogance. "That will not solve our problem," he answered, hunching his shoulders submissively and looking at the floor.

"No," Zimmermann admitted, maintaining his arctic calm. "But the satisfaction would be enormous."

"Excellency, if there had been a way—any way at all—I would have found it. There is no way. The movement of currency across international boundaries during times of war . . ."

Zimmermann raised a hand to cut him off. "I don't want to hear explanations. They're useless now. You've put me in a situation where I have no choice but to wait for you to get the money in Stockholm. God help us if Lenin won't go along."

The relief leaked out of Parvus in a long, grateful exhalation. "You won't regret this, Herr Secretary. . . ."

Again Zimmermann held up his hand. "You're to leave Berlin for Stockholm at once," he ordered. "I'm going to assign a military escort to you to make certain that you do as I say. When you have collected the money in Stockholm, you are to take it to our embassy there. Together with our ambassador you will deliver it to Lenin on the train. I will wire him instructions today."

"An excellent plan," Parvus agreed, eager to ingratiate himself again.

Zimmermann glared at him scornfully. "If you don't get the money this time, Herr Parvus, I really will have you shot."

PETROGRAD

Colonel B. V. Nikitin opened the spigot on the battered brass samovar in the corner of his office and filled two cups halfway with tea. The charcoal in the pipe had already died and the tea was barely lukewarm. He uncorked the bottle of vodka tucked in behind the samovar and splashed a generous amount into both cups.

"How old are you, Mitya?" he asked, handing one of the cups across to his guest.

Mitya frowned in concentration for several seconds, his callused hands squeezing the cup in his lap as if it might produce the answer. "Twenty-four?" he replied, posing it as a guess.

"You're not sure?"

Mitya shook his head. "No records."

Nikitin frowned. Mitya was an Uzbek, from near Kungrad, on the Aral Sea. He was completely illiterate, even in his own tongue, and his spoken Russian was so poor that Nikitin had a difficult time communicating with him.

He was a fierce warrior, however. His military record, which Nikitin had acquired through General Brussilov's office, was both impressive and regrettable. He had fought on the Austrian front and later distinguished himself in Brussilov's offensive against the Germans last June in Poland. "Distinguished" was not quite the right word, Nikitin thought. Mitya was not intelligent enough to distinguish himself. What was unusual about him was his bravery. Under the nightmare conditions of the front lines he had managed to maintain an utter lack of concern for his own life. His superior officers had repeatedly sent him to his death, and each time he had come back in one piece, eager to be sent out again.

The regrettable aspect of his record was his tendency toward savagery. Appropriating the possessions of killed enemy soldiers, taking liberties with the enemy's women—these were considered acceptable behavior in the Russian military. Venerable Cossack customs. Mitya, however, had gone well beyond the bounds of ordinary rape and pillage. His record indicated that he had on several occasions, outside battle conditions, killed and dismembered a number of Polish women. And bragged about it afterward.

None of this surprised Nikitin. War brought out the barbarian in many people. Mitya's bravery and his brutality both sprang in some degree from his circumstances. His Muslim religion taught him that if he was killed in battle he would die a martyr's death and go straight to Heaven. And what his religion didn't do, hashish did. The colonel saw the ravages of the drug in his underweight body and his eyes, gleaming feverishly from gray, sleep-starved sockets.

Nikitin picked up the photograph of Lenin from his desk and handed it to the Uzbek. Mitya drank the tea and vodka in one gulp and set the empty cup on the floor before taking the photo in his hand. He studied the picture in slack-jawed fascination, repeatedly turning it over in apparent expectation of seeing Lenin's backside.

Nikitin lifted a heavy revolver from his desk. "This is the man you must kill," he said, pressing the revolver's barrel against the photograph and pulling the trigger. "Do you understand?"

Mitya grinned and nodded. "I understand," he replied.

"Good." The colonel gathered up the pistol, a box of bullets, and the tickets and papers his assassin would need in his travels, dropped them into a worn cloth satchel and handed it across to him. Then, with the aid of a map, Nikitin guided Mitya laboriously over the route he must take to intercept Lenin at Tornio, on the Swedish border. "When you have accomplished your mission," he said, rolling up the map, "you must dispose of the weapon. Drop it into a lake somewhere."

"What about my money? You promised me money."

The colonel unlocked the bottom drawer in his desk and pulled out a pile of rubles he had stashed there. He counted out a few and handed them across to his assassin. It wasn't a very large sum. With the terrible inflation that had hit Petrograd since the beginning of the war it would buy only a good pair of felt-lined boots, or a decent room in the Grand Hotel d' Europe on the Nevski Prospect for about two nights. Perhaps not even that.

Assassination just didn't command a very high price in Russia at the moment. If he had shopped around, the colonel could probably have found someone willing to do it for nothing, but he needed Mitya's fearlessness.

God knows he had little enough faith that even this half-crazed Muslim killing machine would see the job through. But the colonel knew that he must try. If he tried enough times, sooner or later he must succeed.

Nikitin, watching Mitya count the bills, wondered if he could read their denominations. When he was done, the colonel showed him to the door, admonishing him strenuously. "This is a sacred mission I am sending you on, Mitya. Russia's future is at stake. Your future. Mine. If you fail, those rubles I just gave you will soon be worth hardly a kopek."

The Uzbek offered him a shrug and a grin and left. The colonel closed the door and walked to the window. It was getting dark. Large snowflakes were falling, gently as feathers, through the twilight. In the depths of the Petrograd winter the snowflakes were small and hard and fell so thickly together you sometimes could not see five feet ahead of you. But these were spring snowflakes, big and lazy and short-lived.

Spring. Colonel Nikitin felt his spirits lift momentarily at the thought of it. It was one event he always looked forward to seeing. Mother Russia's ceaseless renewal. Her triumph of life over death.

Spring would come to Petrograd in about three weeks, and it would come suddenly and violently, as it always did. He rubbed his hands together to warm them. That was the way everything happened in Russia these days. Suddenly and violently.

THE TRAIN

Inessa Armand appeared at Bauer's side by the corridor window. She was flushed and a little out of breath. "I tried to leave the train," she said. "I thought I'd just go for a walk. I'm getting claustrophobia, cooped up in this damned carriage. It feels like prison."

"What happened?"

She pushed her hair back. "The guards outside. They stopped me."

"I'm surprised you got that far. Aren't the doors all locked?"

"No. The exit at the back is left open. Of course the German officers can see you from their compartment. But they weren't there tonight. They went into town. I felt like such a fool."

"How many guards did you see?"

"I don't know. Two, I think."

Bauer nodded. That was worth knowing.

Inessa slipped her arm inside his. "Let's try it again, together," she whispered. "I've been watching them. If you time it right, you can sneak past them. Let's try it."

He looked at her. Her expression was hard to read. Maybe there was nothing to read. She just wanted a break from the boredom and tension. "We're not supposed to leave the train. Why stir up trouble?"

Inessa poked him playfully in the side with her elbow. "Don't be such a disgustingly law-abiding Swiss. What harm is there? Ten minutes of fresh air. We won't talk to anybody. What are they going to do? Shoot us?"

"Maybe later." The crazy notion crossed his mind to take her with him, after he'd killed Lenin. Then she'd get all the fresh air and excitement she could stand.

"Is it your leg?"

"What do you mean?"

"Are you worried about getting around?"

"I do all right on it. Running around in the dark in a train yard ducking armed guards might be a little tough, though."

"What happened to it?" Her tone seemed more annoyed than solicitous, as if it were something he'd purposely done to himself just so he couldn't accompany her on the walk.

"Infantile paralysis. When I was a kid."

"Really?" She lifted his cane gently from the railing in front of him and held it between thumb and forefinger, as if judging its weight. Bauer watched her hand closely.

"You don't believe me?"

She laughed. It was soft, apologetic. "Of course I believe you. It's just ironic. I expected to hear that you'd wounded it in a battle with the police. Or that they'd broken it, torturing you in prison. Most men I know would have made up some brave tale. Male revolutionaries seem to wear their injuries like badges of courage. Like the Germans and their silly dueling scars."

"It never occurred to me to lie about it," he replied, deadpan.

"What *would* you lie about, Herr Blum?" Her tone was playful, even mocking.

"A matter of life and death."

"So I suppose you don't lie often."

"That's right."

"You're a mysterious person," she pronounced. "I've never met anyone like you."

Bauer said nothing.

"You see. You never say anything about yourself."

"Not much to say."

Inessa let the cane drop back onto the railing with a small clack. "I'm sure there is," she said. "I'm sure there's a great deal."

"What'll you do when you get to Russia?" Bauer asked, getting off the defensive.

"Help the revolution, of course."

"How?"

"Any way I can."

"Even fighting?"

"You think I can't?"

Bauer smiled at her bravado. "I think you can probably do any damned thing you set your mind to."

Inessa blushed with pleasure. "That's an extravagant compliment, coming from you, Herr Blum."

"Why?"

"You've not yet said anything nice to me."

"Men compliment you a lot?"

Inessa shrugged. "I've had my share of flattery."

"How about Lenin? Does he flatter you?" He wasn't sure why he'd asked that question, but the answer proved interesting.

"No. He's not one to compliment people. Everyone seems to disappoint him—sooner or later."

"Including you?"

"Yes. In a way."

She didn't elaborate, and he didn't press her. Several other passengers squeezed past them in the narrow corridor. A line was forming to get into the front lavatory again, and the talk and banter grew louder near the front of the coach.

Inessa took back the initiative. "How did you get into radical politics?"

"That's a hell of a boring thing to talk about."

She tugged his arm in a coaxing gesture. "I'm interested even so."

Bauer was ready for it. He described his father, and his father's passion for Marxism, and simply changed the locale of his story from America to Germany. It was remarkable how well everything fit.

"Your father converted you?"

"More or less."

"Odd," she mused.

"Odd? Why?"

"All those I know became Marxists long after they were adults. You're the first one I've ever met who grew up that way."

Were they having an intimate little talk, he wondered, or was she interrogating him? Three or four times now she had challenged something he had said.

"Maybe that's why I'm not very dedicated," he said.

"You're not? What do you mean?"

"I wouldn't give my life for a cause."

Inessa's lips parted in shock. "Why not?"

"It's not worth it."

"If you're not willing to die for something, then you don't really believe in it."

"If someone holds a gun to my head and demands I recant my belief that the world is round, I'll humor him. Because the world will remain round, no matter what I say. And I'll still be alive to enjoy it."

"That's a false argument. The shape of the world is a matter of scientific fact, not belief."

"Would you die for Bolshevism?"

"Yes."

Bauer was startled by the conviction in her voice.

"What would you die for?" she challenged. "There must be something."

"My country."

Inessa laughed.

Bauer reddened in anger. "You think that's funny?"

"I'm sorry. It's just that the idea of someone giving his life for Switzerland seems—I don't know—irrelevant, I guess."

Bauer gritted his teeth. He forgot he was supposed to be Swiss. "You wouldn't die for France?"

"Of course not."

"Or Russia?"

"No."

"Just Bolshevism?"

"I'd also die for someone I loved."

Bauer didn't reply. Inessa looked at him. "Wouldn't you?" she demanded.

He shook his head. "It's easy to say yes, but you really don't know what you'll do until you're faced with the situation. I'm pretty sure I'd *risk* my life. God knows I've done it often enough for other reasons. Whether I'd go so far as to sacrifice it on purpose is another question."

Inessa brushed aside a thick strand of hair that had fallen across her face. "You seem to qualify everything. How can you enjoy life that way?"

Bauer laughed. "I don't enjoy life. Do you?"

"Not all the time. But I try."

He wanted to change the subject. The strain of this kind of conversation—and the possibility of tripping himself up—was wearing on him. "Well, I gave up trying."

"That's sad."

"Not if you don't worry about it, it isn't."

Inessa fell silent and turned her head away.

The urge to rip away the facade of Oskar Blum was becoming hard to resist. He didn't like Blum, and he hated playing him. He wanted to tell her who he really was, tell her everything about his life. Even tell her what he'd come here to do. She would only despise him for it—and he would only get himself killed—but the desire to confess to her was powerful. He wanted her to understand him.

"There's talk about a plot against Ilyich," Inessa said, turning back to him. "Have you heard?"

"No."

"Our German captain claims that the Allies have sent someone to kill him."

Inessa's words exploded around him like artillery shells. He quickly cushioned the shock behind a counterbarrage of questions. "Does he have proof?"

"I don't know."

"Does he know who the man is?"

"He has a description and a name. I think that's all."

"That's terrible" Bauer said. He looked straight into her eyes. "Who told you this?"

"Fritz Platten."

"How did the Allies find out? I thought this mission was a secret?"

Inessa tilted her cheek coyly against her shoulder. "They have spies everywhere," she said. "It probably wasn't that difficult."

"I guess that's right."

She tossed her hair dismissively. "Well, the German captain seems quite paranoid about it. I suppose he sees his career on the line if anything goes wrong. Fritz said that he even believed that the assassin was on the train—disguised as one of us. Isn't that extraordinary?"

That accounted for the questions and odd looks the Swiss had given him in the third-class compartment earlier. *Jesus*. They were practically stepping on his heels and he hadn't even noticed. This German captain must be part bloodhound. "Pretty crazy," Bauer agreed.

"Fritz persuaded him that we were all genuine," Inessa said. "And anyway, Ilyich is used to this sort of thing. He's had death threats before. He knows what to do."

Bauer wanted to follow up on her remark, but the way she had said it made him hesitate.

Inessa changed the subject again. "I like you, Blum," she whispered.

Bauer held his breath.

"I don't know why. We don't seem to have much in common. Maybe it's because you're a mystery to me."

Bauer fidgeted with the handle of the cane.

"Do I interest you?" she probed. "At all?"

He nodded.

"I'm making you uncomfortable, aren't I?"

"A little."

"You're full of secrets."

"No."

Inessa rested her palm against his chest and leaned gently against him. He felt her warm thigh against his knee. "Why won't you talk to me?"

Bauer put his hand on her arm, not knowing whether to pull her to him or push her away. "I will. After the war."

Inessa moved away and leaned against the window rail. She folded her arms in front of her and gazed out across the dark train yard. "You smell of danger and death," she said, her mood suddenly grim. "You excite me and repel me both. You confuse me." She turned her face toward him. Her expression was hurt and accusing.

"I guess I'd better go back to third class," he said. "You and the other women should have the compartment to yourselves for the night."

She looked away.

"Good night," he said.

She didn't reply.

He pushed back through the swinging doors into the third-class side of the carriage and leaned against the wall to collect himself. His heart was pounding. He felt weak, almost sick. He examined his cane in the dim light, absently twisting the ferrule to reassure himself that something was still in working order.

Was she really attracted to him, or was something else going on? He had never been that popular with women, after all. He never made a good first impression. Most women were turned away long before they saw anything worthwhile behind the rough edges. Why should she be different? Especially since, as Blum, he had added baldness and a pronounced limp to an already overstocked arsenal of shortcomings? She had beauty, charm, culture, intelligence. She could have any man. Why him? And why now?

He must put her out of his mind.

He tugged out his pocket watch. Just past ten o'clock. He could hear voices from several of the compartments, and the slamming of doors as the passengers went to and from the lavatory at the front end of the coach.

He'd wait another hour, he decided. And he would wait out here in the corridor, so he wouldn't disturb anyone in the compartments.

With a little American luck he would soon be off this damned train forever.

Sleep would not come. For what seemed like the ten-thousandth time Captain von Planetz heard the crunch of the sentry's boots on the gravel outside the compartment window, as the young soldier plodded his nocturnal circuit of the carriage and baggage car. The captain shifted his position on the hard wooden bench and readjusted the folded blanket under his head.

He had made a fool of himself. He didn't mind that. He often made a fool of himself, because he operated in his profession without guile, without concern for appearances. Which no doubt explained how the man considered by those who knew him well as among the best criminal detectives in Germany had never advanced beyond the rank of inspector in civilian life, and captain in the military. And at forty-seven, it was far too late in his life to change. Not that he would have, anyway. He thought of himself as a scientist of sorts, whose first loyalty was to the discipline of the profession. He left the lesser disciplines—politics and the arts of persuasion and influence—to others. The hell with what people thought. He had his job to do. And that job, begun as a simple military guard exercise, had now grown into a deadly manhunt.

The complacency around him worried him. No one else, including even Lieutenant von Buhring, took his fears about the American seriously anymore. He was like the boy who had cried "Wolf!" once too often. Unless he could produce some better evidence—or actually locate the assassin—he wasn't going to get much more cooperation from the others on the train.

He forced all the details through his mind yet one more time, from the meeting in Zurich with the American consul, James McNally, to Platten's dramatic elimination of the last four suspects just this morning past.

Damn it, Von Planetz thought. What had he missed? He had been so certain that the American had hidden himself among the other passengers. It fit so well. The assassin's ability to elude all the customs checkpoints and the heavy military surveillance meant almost certainly that he was in disguise. And what other disguise would he possibly choose, other than that of someone in Lenin's party? It was the only plausible way to get close to his target. The theory still seemed solid, but it hadn't yielded any results.

What could he do that he hadn't done already? Perhaps another look at the list of passengers. Maybe some detail had escaped his attention. But he doubted it. He had looked at the list so many times that he knew it by heart.

Another hospital train rolled past on the adjacent track, its windows dark. He thought of his son, Frederick. He came home on one of those trains, two weeks after he had died. God, poor Marthe, she had never recovered from it. And now the war was depriving her of medical help. And proper food. Damn the war to hell. Every day it continued, the odds against his wife's making it through would grow. And if she died, he didn't know what he would do.

He felt guilty being away from her for so long. He had talked to her for a few minutes on the telephone from the Frankfurt post office that afternoon, but the connection had been bad. He'd call her again when they reached Berlin.

Another day and he'd be home again. Thank God for that, at least. He fumbled under the bench for his glasses, slipped them on, and got up. He slid back the compartment door as quietly as he could and stepped out into the corridor.

Bauer passed the hour staring out the window and counting the number of times he thought he heard the lavatory door up front in second class click open or closed. Bauer had stationed himself as inconspicuously and as far to the rear as he could—by the last window before the chalk line. The third-class compartments opened and shut at regular intervals as the men made their last trip up front to the lavatory and then came back to settle in for the night.

A late-setting moon still shone in the western sky, casting a pale illumination over the Frankfurt rail yard. A few dim lights from lanterns glowed here and there—in the switching tower, the station office, and at several work sheds in the yard.

The door to the rearmost compartment slid open and one of the German officers emerged. He was the senior officer in charge, Captain von Planetz. Bauer looked him over. The man was slightly built and balding, with spectacles. He nod-

ded at Bauer. Bauer nodded back. How had he learned about
me? he wondered. Had he just guessed it? It seemed unlikely. But who could have told him? The only human being
who knew that he was on the train in disguise was Blum
himself. And if Blum had told anyone, they'd obviously know
just whom to go after. But they didn't.

Bauer almost laughed out loud at the irony of it. Here was
that clever German captain, the only one who was convinced
that Bauer was on the train, standing eight feet away and
nodding good evening to him.

Someone had told him. Not Blum, but someone. The
secret wasn't that closely held, after all. Churchill knew, and
his aide, and God knows how many others back in London.
And Washington as well. He remembered the arrest he had
barely avoided at the pension in Zurich. Some government
bureaucrat—British or American—had probably shopped him
for personal advantage. It could have been McNally, the
American consul. It was beginning to look like the Huerta
affair all over again.

He checked his watch again: 11:25.

The door separating third and second class swung open,
and a man with a broad face and receding hairline strode
briskly down the corridor toward him. It was Grigory Zinoviev, Lenin's chief lieutenant.

"Herr Blum?" The Russian seemed disturbed about something.

"Yes?"

"Could you come with me, please." His German was precise and almost without accent.

"What's wrong?"

Zinoviev smiled, but his eyes were cold. "There is something I must discuss with you. Do you mind?"

Bauer lifted the cane from the window railing. He god-
damn well did mind, but he was not in a position to refuse.
"No. Of course not."

Bauer limped slowly up the corridor toward second class,
his mind whirring frantically. Zinoviev crowded him from
behind. Twice he felt the Russian's fingers push against his
back. The shoves were slight, but they told him that Zino-
view was in a hurry, and that he wanted Bauer to know it.

"Here," the Russian said. He reached in front of the American to slide a door to one of the compartments open. Bauer stepped in.

Someone else was already there.

"You know Comrade Morozov," Zinoviev said. He pulled the door shut and flipped the latch into the locked position.

Morozov sat by the window, finishing a snack. A square of butcher's paper rested on his lap, with a small, bitten end of sausage left in it. He rolled the paper up around it and stuffed the package into a pocket. In the subdued light the terrorist's disfigured face looked stiff and lifeless, like a mask. He wiped some grease from his mouth with the edge of his shirtsleeve and nodded.

"We haven't met," Bauer said, tipping his bowler in Morozov's direction. He recalled the night the Russian had pounded him insensible outside the Café Adler. He still had the bruises. "Not formally, at least."

On the seat beside Morozov Bauer was astonished to see the dozen empty tomato cans. In place of the stewed tomatoes left behind with the Swiss customs officials, Morozov was inserting a brown putty-like substance that Bauer recognized as gelignite, a pliable compound of dynamite, potassium nitrate, and wood pulp. It was used by military sappers to blow up bridges. Among the tin cans and the gelignite there was also a coil of fuse cord and a pile of detonator caps.

Morozov was making bombs.

The transformation of one can appeared complete. The terrorist had run a short length of fuse cord from the detonator buried in the explosive out through a hole punched in the lid, then bent the lid back down into place over the opening and pressed it into the gelignite to hold it closed. Bauer guessed the can would pack at least the equivalent explosive force of a hand grenade—enough to blow several of the carriage's compartments apart and kill everyone in them.

The other ingredients had been easier for Morozov to get through Swiss customs than the tomato cans, Bauer reflected. The gelignite he appeared to have disguised as modeling clay, the fuse cord he had probably tied around his waist as a belt, and the detonator caps he could have hidden in any of a dozen places.

Zinoviev dropped onto the cushion beside Morozov and motioned to the seat facing them. "Please sit," he ordered.

Bauer sat, doing his best to convey innocent puzzlement. He steeled himself for the worst.

He propped his cane on the floor in front of him, resting one hand on the curved grip and the other on the shaft just beneath, so that his fingers rested on the ferrule as inconspicuously as possible. He twisted the ferrule a half-turn to the left, disguising the motion with an elaborate display of settling himself comfortably on the cushion. He felt the trigger click out and into place against the inside of his forefinger, cocking the firing pin.

The small chamber carried only one bullet. Morozov would get it. He would swing the cane up swiftly and press the tip directly against the terrorist's chest and fire. Half a second was all it would take. Six millimeters point-blank against the heart would kill him instantly.

Then Zinoviev. One swift whirling strike to the Adam's apple with the edge of his hand would crush his windpipe. Then another to the back of the neck for good measure. Call it two seconds altogether.

Then what?

He had to assume that the door that opened from the compartment directly to the outside was locked. So he would have to flip up the latch on the door into the corridor, retreat back through the carriage and out the door behind the Germans' compartment. It was left unlocked, Inessa had said. If she was wrong, he'd go out one of the corridor windows instead.

The shot would wake the entire carriage. People would crowd into the corridor in a matter of seconds. And if he made it through that gauntlet, there'd be the German officers at the back of the carriage to contend with, and immediately outside, an armed guard of one, possibly two, men.

If he could get past the outside guard, he had a chance. He could lose himself quickly in the dark streets of Frankfurt.

But he would have to be fast—and lucky. And even then, his mission would end in utter failure.

Zinoviev lit a cigarette, in defiance of Lenin's prohibition against smoking in the compartments. He extinguished the match with a phlegmatic shake of his hand, snapped it in two, and dropped it into the ashtray built into the armrest at the side of the bench. "We have good evidence that you've been informing on us," he said.

Bauer's mouth fell open. "Informing? Is that what you said?"

"That's what I said." Zinoviev sucked in the smoke in a deep gasp, then let it trickle out lazily through his nostrils as he waited for an answer to his accusation.

Luckier than he deserved, Bauer thought, his spirit soaring. They still believed he was Blum! But ironically, they had somehow found out about Blum's informing. That put him in a bizarre position. If he wanted to stick it out, he was going to have to take the heat—and possibly the punishment—for Blum's transgressions.

"Is this true, Herr Blum?" Zinoviev demanded.

"Absolutely not," Bauer replied.

"You didn't tell the English important details about this trip?"

Bauer shook his head vehemently. "Of course not! I'm shocked by this accusation. Who told you this?"

The Russian glanced over at Morozov, then back at the American. "We don't have any room on this train for traitors," he said.

"I haven't told the English anything!" Bauer insisted. If they had any proof, he decided, they wouldn't have bothered with questions and answers.

"You Jews are cowards and traitors," Morozov muttered, uttering his first words since Bauer had entered the compartment. "You'll do anything for money."

Zinoviev gestured to Morozov to shut up, then turned to Bauer. "You're going to have to tell us what you've done," he warned. "Everything. Make up your mind about that right now."

"I've done nothing!" Bauer protested, waxing histrionic. "I resent these accusations. I demand to know who has spoken against me!" If he could tough this out, and do it convincingly, then his identity as Blum would be more solid than ever.

Zinoviev glared at him, the muscles in his broad-cheeked face tight with contempt. He nodded to Morozov. The half of the terrorist's face that was still mobile broke into a grin.

Bauer groaned inwardly. Ten to one this sideshow freak

was about to pound the stuffing out of him again. Could he stand to let him do it?

Morozov pushed himself leisurely to his feet and loomed over Bauer, hands on his hips. How much of an effort should he make to protect himself, Bauer wondered. Blum himself would no doubt have gone to pieces quickly and confessed anything. But that didn't mean he had to. But any demonstration of skill in defending himself would be suspect. He was simply going to have to hunker down and take whatever they decided to dish out, no matter how humiliating. Or painful.

Morozov reached down suddenly and snatched the cane out from beneath Bauer's hands. Christ, the trigger, Bauer thought, he'll see it.

Gripping the cane from the bottom end, Morozov swung it out of Bauer's reach, then brought it back swiftly against the side of the American's neck. The weight and rigidity of the hidden metal barrel inside amplified the force of the blow. Bauer gasped and sank back against the cushion, his hand on his neck.

"Tell us what you know about the English plan to stop Lenin," Zinoviev demanded.

"I don't know anything about it. I swear." Morozov brought the cane down on him again. The American raised his arms to fend off the blow, but the barrel landed on the space between his neck and shoulder with stunning power. Again he gasped. The effort to suppress a cry of pain brought tears to his eyes. Zinoviev calmly repeated his question.

"Please! I don't know anything!" It galled Bauer to beg like this. He looked up at Morozov, sliding the shaft of the cane back and forth across the palm of his hand, ready to deliver the next blow. It was a miracle that he hadn't tripped the trigger and discharged the bullet.

"What did you reveal to the British, Blum?"

"Nothing, I've told you. Nothing! What evidence do you have against me?"

Zinoviev leaned back against the cushion, disappointed. He nodded to Morozov. The terrorist swung the cane at Bauer's head. This time the American caught the hook of the cane and held on. Enraged, Morozov hauled back with both hands, pulling Bauer right out of his seat, and twisted the cane from his grip. He shoved him back onto the seat and fell against him, jamming the shaft of the cane across his throat.

Bauer tried desperately to push the cane away, but Morozov's strength and weight were overwhelming. The cane crushed steadily into his windpipe, cutting off his breath. Deprived of air, his lungs began to burn, his chest to tremble. He felt his strength ebbing.

His vision began to blur and darken. He closed his eyes and began to spiral down toward unconsciousness.

Abruptly the weight against his throat lifted. He opened his eyes. He gulped for air and felt searing pain as the oxygen rushed past his injured windpipe and into his starved lungs. His eyes watered heavily, drowning his sight. He wiped them with his sleeve, then rubbed his bruised throat to work out the raw hurt.

Morozov stood over him still. Grasping the cane by the grip now, he pressed the end against Bauer's chest and pushed the American back against the seat. Bauer watched with terror as the Russian's fingers closed on the wood under the curve of the grip, just millimeters from the sliver of steel trigger.

Zinoviev leaned forward from across the compartment, shaking his finger at the American like a schoolteacher delivering a reprimand. "We've been suspicious of your behavior for some time, Blum. We have good reason to believe that you've sold information to the English in the past. Because of that, we seriously considered denying you permission to come on this trip."

"It's not true," Bauer replied, barely able to get out the words. His eyes remained fixed on Morozov's broad, spatulate fingers, praying they wouldn't move.

"I'll ask you one more time," Zinoviev said. "If you have anything to tell us, now is your last chance. We will not punish you for it, if you confess the truth. We will leave you in Stockholm. From there you can return to Zurich on your own. But if you lie to us now, we are certain to discover it later. And then we will kill you. Do you know anything of a plan to assassinate Lenin?"

"No."

"You swear it?"

"I swear it. Yes."

Zinoviev stubbed out his cigarette in the ashtray. "Let the Bundist bastard go," he said.

Reluctantly Morozov removed the tip of the cane from Bauer's chest.

"Stockholm, Blum," Zinoviev warned. "That's as far as you go. We'll be watching you."

Bauer pushed himself to his feet, snatched the cane out of Morozov's hand, and with as much dignity as possible, walked out of the compartment.

Back in third class, he leaned heavily against the corridor wall for support and gasped to fight off a wave of dizziness. He ached profoundly in the neck, shoulders, and arms, and the effort to swallow caused a raw spasm of pain to shoot down his throat.

He twisted the grip on the cane counterclockwise against the shaft to uncock the firing pin and free the trigger to be pushed back into its groove under the curve of the grip. He held the cane up to the corridor light and sighted along the shaft. Despite the bashing by Morozov, the barrel still looked straight.

He should get Lenin now—tonight, he thought. It might be his last chance. But the plan required strength, patience, and quickness. He was out of all three.

He opened the door into his compartment. Both benches were full of sleeping bodies. He staggered in, collapsed on the floor among the tangle of legs, and passed out.

WEDNESDAY
APRIL 11

THE TRAIN

At dawn an engine was coupled onto the sealed carriage and its baggage car in the Frankfurt yard, and the train began the run across the low hills and farmland of Hesse and Thuringia toward Berlin.

Captain von Planetz sat up and hooked his glasses over his ears. He felt enormously fatigued. Another night with too little sleep. He yawned and pushed up the window shade to look outside. The morning was gloomy and wet. Swirls of rain splattered against the glass, blurring the view of the countryside.

If there were no more delays, the train would reach Berlin, 450 kilometers distant, by midday, and Sassnitz, another 180 kilometers to the north, by late afternoon. By nightfall Lenin's party would be on the ferry to Sweden. And there—at the water's edge—the captain's jurisdiction would end.

Whatever happened to this Bolshevik and his ragtag collection of social misfits once they left German soil would no longer be his concern.

But the next twelve hours were. Was he going to be forced to spend them just waiting impotently, praying that the American assassin would not strike?

He pulled the list of thirty-two passengers from his leather case and held the now dog-eared sheets of paper up to the gray light seeping in the window. Suppose the American consul, McNally, had been wrong about Bauer's height and weight? That would bring several of the Bundists back into the realm of suspicion. But could he prevail on the impatient Fritz Platten to investigate them for him again?

He threw the list down on the bench in exasperation. This was impossible, he thought. He was being asked to protect Lenin with his hands and feet tied and a blindfold over his eyes.

Lieutenant von Buhring came awake with an audible, jaw-stretching yawn.

"Good morning."

"Good morning, Captain. We're moving already?"

"Yes. Since dawn."

"Didn't you sleep?"

"A little."

The captain lit a cigarette and pulled in a deep lungful of smoke.

"You're really addicted to those things," Von Buhring said.

"They relax me."

The lieutenant frowned. "They're bad for the health. They clog your lungs. My father smoked. He died of emphysema."

"Is this your way of cheering me up, Lieutenant?"

Von Buhring sat up and tried to smooth the wrinkles from his trousers. "I'm sorry, Captain."

"We'll be at the Sassnitz barracks tonight," Von Planetz said. "Sleep in a real bed again."

The lieutenant bent down and pulled his boots from beneath the bench. "If we don't get stuck in Berlin."

The captain watched his aide slip his feet into the boots and pull them up. "How old are those boots?" he asked.

Von Buhring looked up. "These? About two years. Why?"

"They look new. You have them resoled recently?"

"Yes. Just before this trip, in fact. The uppers were still good, and I'm not entitled to a reissue yet. They've really gotten tight about that. Shortage of leather. Like everything else."

The captain wasn't listening. He picked up one of his own boots, dug out his pocketknife, and pried off the heel. "Pull off your right boot and give it to me," he said.

The lieutenant removed the boot and handed it across. Captain von Planetz placed his pried-off heel underneath the one on Von Buhring's boot, pressed the nails in far enough to hold it in place, and then banged the boot hard on the floor, driving the second heel up tight against the first. He handed the boot back to Von Buhring. "Put it on now," he said. "And walk across the compartment."

The lieutenant squinted at the captain in disbelief.

"Go ahead, just do it."

Von Buhring shook his head incredulously, but pulled on the boot with its two thicknesses of heel and stood up.

"Now walk," the captain directed. "Just as you would normally."

Von Buhring stepped across the compartment—a bare three paces—and then turned around and hobbled back.

"You're limping," the captain observed.

"Impossible not to."

The captain smiled.

The lieutenant sat down, looked at the boots, then back at the captain. "God in heaven," he murmured, the realization dawning on him at last. "The one with the cane—what's his name?—Blum. You think it's him, don't you?"

"I'm sure of it."

Bauer awoke sometime before dawn. He shifted his position on the floor several times, trying to find a comfortable angle among the tangle of loose shoes and boots and stockinged feet dangling down from the benches on either side of him. No one seemed to have changed his socks since Zurich, and at floor level the odor was breath-catching. Bauer rested on his back and stared up at the brown varnished wood of the compartment ceiling, the wavy lines of its grain just beginning to materialize in the early light.

His own shoes, even with the laces undone, pinched and chafed him unmercifully, but he wasn't about to remove them, under any circumstances.

His neck was swollen and stiff, and the rocking of the carriage over the rails beat a steady pulse of pain through his head. His throat, against which Morozov had crushed the cane with his full weight, troubled him the most. It felt both raw and numb, as if he had just had his tonsils removed. The simple act of swallowing took careful preparation. Everything considered, he was thankful that he was still able to function.

He thought of Inessa Armand, her intense eyes gazing up

into his in the corridor. "I like you, Blum," she had said. Images of her past life floated through his head—dancing with the czar at the Winter Palace, escaping from Siberia, living as an exile in Paris. Why did her life seem so romantic to him, and his so grim? Maybe it was just the way you looked at things. He had had his adventures, too, after all.

Port Arthur, for instance.

More testimony for that nocturnal judge and jury, he thought, still sitting in judgment somewhere deep inside him.

How long ago was it? Thirteen years? Fourteen? He was only twenty-four then, a lieutenant in the United States Army Intelligence Corps. His superior officer rated his performance there as satisfactory, even though he was drunk much of the time, and was twice reprimanded for insubordination.

Port Arthur did that to you. He could still summon up a picture of that traders' metropolis of the Far East in his mind's eye: the fingernail on the crooked finger of the Dairen Peninsula, jabbed obscenely into the Yellow Sea. The dense conflict of ships and boats in the harbor, the stink of the open sewers in the slums, the smoky, clangorous din of the outdoor market, the confused and clashing sprawl of narrow streets and ramshackle buildings spreading back up into the hills like a mold advancing across decayed meat.

A kingdom of warlords and beggars, prostitutes and starving children—and by 1904 the killing ground in a territorial conflict between Russia and Japan, neither of which had any right to be there.

Harry Bauer didn't have much right to be there, either. President Roosevelt wanted an observer in the area, and the commander of his company, no doubt anxious to be rid of him, had recommended him for the job. It was the beginning of his career in military intelligence.

And the beginning of some tough lessons in survival. The Cossacks captured him. They bound him hand and foot, and then the captain of the band, a Mongol with a long black moustache and a toothless grin, tied him to the pommel of his saddle and dragged him, at a gallop, through the streets.

Someone shot the Cossack off his horse right in the middle of the market square.

A woman rescued him. Elizabeth. He couldn't remember her last name. Maybe he never knew it.

She took him to her house outside the city, found him a doctor, then nursed him back to health herself. The cuts and abrasions mended fast, the broken bones and sepsis took longer. After a week the delirium and fever abated, and in three weeks he felt strong enough to leave. He never saw her after that.

Elizabeth. She was the wife of a prominent Russian, a nobleman and friend of the czar. Must have been in the Russian legation. A diplomat. Vice-consul, maybe. She spoke English. She told him she knew the man who had shot the Cossack. An act of conscience, she called it. She was much concerned with moral and political issues.

She smiled like Inessa and possessed the same bold eyes, the same intensity. How he had ached for her, this impossible, beautiful woman married to another man. She had shown him a little attention and care, and that was all it took, in those days, to win his love.

Today was Wednesday, he remembered. Their last full day in German territory. By tomorrow morning the train would reach Sassnitz, on the Baltic Sea. Tonight would be his last chance at Lenin.

A stray foot swung out near his face, the toes tickling the skin of his sore neck. He pushed it out of the way, causing its owner to come awake with a startled snort. Bauer clenched his teeth and squeezed his eyes shut. It was going to be a hard day.

WASHINGTON

Colonel House sat up in bed, his back propped against two big pillows, working out the solution to his current problem in his customary manner.

A portable writing desk, laden with several lined pads of paper and a large inkwell, straddled his lap. Many pages had been torn from the pads, crumpled up, and tossed on the floor. The wooden shaft of a steel-tipped pen, already heavily dented with teeth marks inflicted by the colonel during his long hours of concentration, was clenched between his teeth.

On the night table by the bed, an uncorked bottle of port wine sat half empty.

The grandfather clock in the downstairs hallway chimed the hour of 2:00 A.M. House pulled the pen from his mouth, scratched out several lines from the sheet of paper he had been writing on, and then ripped the sheet from the pad.

On a clean sheet of paper he copied several lines from the old sheet, added a new line, and read them over carefully, as if committing them to memory.

He stuck the pen in its holder, reached for the bottle of port, tipped the neck to his mouth, and took a long drink. It was a peculiar private habit of his—to drink wine straight from the bottle when he was home alone. He did it for two reasons: it gave him a bit of a feeling of swagger—something utterly missing from his life in the Wilson administration; and he didn't wish to leave a telltale dirty glass for the house-keeper to find in the morning. The reasons were in obvious conflict with each other, but the solution was the same—drink from the bottle. A classic Colonel House compromise.

He removed the desk from his lap, slipped out of bed, and went to the fireplace. He piled all the pages on the cold hearth, lit them with a kitchen match, and as he watched them burn, he reviewed the distillation of his efforts in his head one last time.

The British wanted Bauer to kill Lenin. Wilson wanted Bauer stopped. House wanted both.

The needs of all parties could be met only one way: Bauer must be given time to kill Lenin.

And then Bauer can be stopped.

He had already told Ambassador Bryce yesterday, Tuesday, that Wilson was opposed to Bauer's mission and wanted it ended. But he had done it in such a low-keyed way, with a little wink here and a little nudge there, that he knew he could depend on the British to drag their heels with Wilson long enough to give Bauer time to act.

Lenin was two days into his trip. Bauer had probably already killed him. Wilson would be furious, of course. But he would get over it. Meanwhile the British would be happy that he, House, had kept Wilson off their necks. The Allied war effort would be greatly served, and House could repair any damage done with the President by seeing to it that Bauer was never heard from again.

If Bauer came back, the Wilson administration would be vulnerable to a scandal so severe that its role in the postwar world would be severely damaged. And Wilson's place in history permanently tarnished. House could not let that happen. He would have to get Bauer out of the way.

He thought he knew how he could do it. Ironically, it was General Harper who had given him the idea. Once Bauer had killed Lenin, all House would have to do was see to it that the Bolsheviks got the chance to get back at him. They could be counted on to do a better job than Huerta's men had done.

The colonel deeply regretted the idea of betraying Bauer, but he believed it would be necessary for the sake of the future of the country and the world. Somewhere in the back of his head, of course, he knew that Bauer's death would also protect his own career and good name from possible harm, but he saw his own person inextricably entwined with that of the administration and the nation. By protecting himself, he believed, he was protecting President Wilson and the country.

So when the time came, he'd give Bauer to the Bolsheviks. It could be done. The apparatus of the United States government could reach out to anyone, anywhere in the world, and alter that individual's fate for good or ill forever. Colonel House had become a master at manipulating that apparatus.

The exercise of such power was an awe-inspiring and terrible thing, House thought, taking a last drink from the bottle of port. And, he had to admit to himself, tremendously thrilling as well.

LONDON

Foreign Minister Arthur Balfour stalked to the fireplace mantel and turned to face the other two men in his office—MI1c Chief Mansfield Cumming, and Winston Churchill, just back from Zurich.

The foreign minister, Cumming noticed, was having a hard time keeping his temper. "We have no choice, Winston," he said, his voice beginning to show an edge. "It's really that simple. None of us likes it, obviously, but the P.M. wants it this way, so there's really not much we can do about it. So I would be terribly grateful if you would not persist in prolonging our agony."

Churchill sat slouched in a Queen Anne chair by Balfour's desk, shaking his head throughout Balfour's words. "The P.M. must be persuaded to change his mind," he replied. "And I didn't think that the aim of our war policy was to avoid discomfiting the P.M."

Balfour thrust his hands into his pants pockets and made fists of them. "Really, Winston, I think you're being childish about this."

"If it's childish to object to a craven retreat on a matter of national peril, then yes, Arthur, I am being childish."

"It is *not* a matter of national peril. The situation in Petrograd has improved markedly in recent days. Ambassador Buchanan reports that Miliukov and Lvov have consolidated their position. And the sentiment to continue the war against Germany is apparently very strong in Russia. Stronger than we thought."

Churchill sat up. "It's a shambles over there, and our ambassador knows it." He craned his head around toward Cumming, who sat silently on the sofa behind him. "Sir Mansfield. Is this a matter of national peril or not?"

Cumming cleared his throat to stall for time to think. "I would have to say it is not a *serious* matter of national peril," he replied, embarrassed with his words even as he spoke them.

Churchill slapped the cloth-covered armrest of the chair with a resounding thud, raising a cloud of dust. "Good God, Cumming, you sound like the Archbishop of Canterbury. If we don't stop Lenin now, gentlemen, we'll regret it all our lives. I swear we will. With Germany's connivance, that shovel-bearded little fanatic will have Russia out of the war before the first snowfall, and Germany will overrun us in France. To hell with President Wilson. It's not his country that's bleeding to death—"

Balfour cut Churchill off. "We've gone over this ground repeatedly, Winston. Bauer is an American. We can't offend Wilson, especially now. We need America's assistance and cooperation, and we need it desperately. That's worth more than a hundred Lenins."

"You're tragically wrong," Churchill snapped. "America

already *is* in the war. She can't change her mind about that. We'll have her cooperation because Wilson can't deny it to us any longer. We must let Bauer proceed. Wilson will send a few stiff notes of protest, call in Bryce and give him a stern lecture on the morality of government, and that will be that. In a month's time it will be forgotten."

"The P.M. disagrees," Balfour replied, his tone abrupt. He could never best Churchill in an argument, so he took refuge behind authority.

"We're setting an abominable precedent for our relationship with the United States," Churchill thundered. "If we let Wilson shove us around so easily on this first issue between us, it'll only encourage him to shove us around some more. If we stand up to him now, he'll be more reasonable in the future."

Balfour shook his head, refusing to be drawn into any further verbal sparring.

"And what about Bauer?" Churchill persisted, turning toward Cumming in hope of support. "What happens to him? We've put him in harm's way. He trusts us, at the very least, not to betray him."

"We'll intercept him at Tornio," Balfour pronounced with an air of finality. "And we'll tell him thank you very much, you can go home now. Then we'll send him packing. That will hardly betray him."

"I suppose you'll ask him for our money back as well?" Churchill retorted.

Cumming broke in. "He will almost certainly have killed Lenin by then."

Balfour strode back toward his desk, indicating that the meeting was at an end. "Well, we can't stop him before Tornio," he said. "But if he's killed Lenin, we'll have to detain him."

"Detain him?" Churchill protested. "Yesterday you'd have pinned the Victoria Cross on him!"

This stung the foreign minister deeply. "You're not reconsidering your cabinet appointment, are you, Winston?"

Churchill blanched and shook his head vehemently. On his return from Zurich, Lloyd George had awarded him a minor post in the coalition government—minister of Munitions.

Churchill had accepted it eagerly. "I don't intend to make our disagreement public, if that's your concern."

"I'm relieved to hear it. I'm sure the P.M. will be, also."

"What becomes of Bauer if we arrest him?"

"I assume we'll have to turn him over to the Americans."

Churchill grunted in disgust. He turned again to Cumming. "Do you support this, Sir Mansfield?" he demanded.

Cumming fiddled with his monocle for a moment before replying. For all his cleverness with words, Cumming thought, Churchill seemed remarkably obtuse sometimes. He just didn't possess the subtlety of mind necessary for a good diplomat or statesman. "If you consider the probable course of events," he said. "I think you will, too, Winston. If Bauer does the job as you've instructed him—and he has several days in Germany to do it, after all—then he'll have no reason to stay on the train all the way to Tornio. Quite the contrary, I would assume. It's unlikely, then, that we'll have to arrest him."

"Exactly," Balfour chimed in. "By the time the Bolsheviks get to the Finnish border, Bauer will have already done his work and disappeared. That's what we expect. That's what we hope. Privately. Publicly, to please the Americans, we must show that we're doing everything in our power to stop Bauer. So if Lenin is still alive at Tornio, we'll call it off. That means that if Bauer tries to follow him across, we'll have to detain him. What the Americans do with him is none of our concern."

Churchill pushed himself up out of the overstuffed chair and headed toward the door, his jaw jutting forward pugnaciously. "I find the government's management of this affair pusillanimous, hypocritical, and shabby," he growled. "Good day to you both."

THE TRAIN

All Wednesday morning the sealed train sped northeast across Germany. Civilian and military traffic on the line ahead of it was rerouted or delayed to clear the tracks for its passage. It paused briefly at Halle, to change engines from the Saxony to the Prussian State Railway, and then resumed its journey, pulled by a big four-cylinder Berliner Maschinenbau locomotive, straining under a full head of steam toward Berlin's Potsdam Station.

It reached the capital late in the afternoon, approaching through the western suburbs. The travelers crowded at the windows of the carriage, eager for their first look at the enemy's wartime capital. Allied air raids, frequent in recent months, had pockmarked the city with destruction. A long row of warehouses near the track had been gutted by fire. Holes gaped in the roofs of other buildings. A row of blackened brick chimneys, standing like abstract works of sculpture in a rubble-strewn field, was all that remained of one entire block of houses.

Gobermann, the Bundist who bit his fingernails, pointed out the devastation to Bauer. "It's unbelievable," he said, his voice vibrating with anger. "The Allies drop these terrible bombs right in the middle of a city—right on innocent civilians. What kind of warfare is that?"

Bauer didn't share Gobermann's outrage. "The same kind that lets the Germans shoot hostages," he said.

Gobermann smacked a fist into his palm. "It's capitalism that promotes this kind of barbarism," he said, his voice strangled to a whisper. "These governments—the whole system—they must be destroyed."

"Without hurting any innocent civilians, of course."

Just before the station, the train slowed to a crawl around a curve in the tracks, and the windows of the carriage dipped down close to street level. A banner hung across the street, announcing a drive to collect blankets and bandages for soldiers at the front. Under the banner a military band was stationed, its bright brass horns blaring out martial music in front of a small gathering of onlookers, mostly children and old women.

Bauer cracked the window open and let the strains of the music filter into the carriage. They were playing a shaky rendition of a march that he recognized as Erdl's "Grand Masters of the Teutonic Order." His father used to play it on the gramophone. The band leader, a fat middle-aged man with a red-faced grin and a jolly Saint Nicholas bounce in his step, was working hard to raise the patriotic fervor of the crowd, but if anything, he seemed to be making his listeners unhappy. Bauer noticed one old women weeping openly.

As the band rolled out of sight, Bauer felt oddly moved. This was the land of his parents and his grandparents. The home of his ancestors. The familiar music reminded him of his kinship.

The platform at Berlin's Potsdam Station—actually a wide row of platforms running underneath an enormous open iron-and-glass shed—was ringed with a ten-foot-high fence of barbed wire. Guards with Alsatian dogs patrolled the perimeter.

"Like a prison," Gobermann said.

Bauer rotated his neck slowly back and forth, trying to ease the still-throbbing pain.

"What the devil happened to you?" Gobermann inquired. "Your neck's red as fire."

Bauer grunted. "Somebody must have stepped on it when I was asleep."

The sealed train, now two full days into its journey, no sooner reached Potsdam Station than it was shunted onto a siding away from the station platforms. Captain von Planetz had been told that someone from the Reichschancellery was coming to meet the train in secret. He had not been told the reason, but he had pieced together, from bits of conversation that he and Lieutenant von Buhring had overheard during the past two days, that it involved the transfer of a substantial sum of money. The matter didn't interest him. His mind was wholly focused on the assassin, Bauer.

He summoned Fritz Platten to the rear compartment. "I regret that I must raise this issue with you again, Herr Platten," he said. "But I have excellent reason to believe that the man I've been looking for is disguised as the Bundist, Oskar Blum. If you examine him carefully, I believe you'll discover that his limp is not genuine."

Platten made no attempt to hide his contempt for the captain's suggestion. "I thought we had settled this matter once and for all," he complained, his voice rising.

The captain nodded placatingly. "Yes, yes, I know. It all seems very foolish on my part. Please just indulge me. In a few hours you'll be on the ferry and free of me forever." And good riddance to you, at that, the captain thought.

"Is Blum the only one you suspect?" Platten asked, an amused edge in his tone.

"Yes," the captain admitted.

The young Swiss socialist sat down, placing his pearlcolored fedora on the seat beside him. "Good," he said. "Now then, Captain, I shall put your mind to rest about this matter for good."

BERLIN

The special military telephone on the desk of Foreign Secretary Arthur Zimmermann's chief aide jangled briskly. The assistant, expecting the call, snatched up the earpiece from its hook and shouted a greeting down the line.

He listened for a few seconds, then slammed the earpiece back into the cradle, jumped from his desk, and headed across the reception area to the foreign secretary's office. "The train is here, Excellency," he said, flinging open the secretary's door. "Potsdam Station."

Zimmermann looked up from the stack of papers on his desk. "What time is it?"

"Just after five o'clock."

Zimmermann nodded. "Alert the motor pool. I want an auto and driver reserved for me at eight o'clock."

"Will you be going alone, sir?"

"Yes."

THE TRAIN

Early Wednesday evening, dinner was served to the revolutionaries from the new restaurant car, attached to the train at Frankfurt. Waiters brought trays up through the baggage car and handed them silently across the chalk line to the women, who had volunteered to distribute them. The meal was a surprisingly lavish offering of veal cutlets, boiled potatoes, peas, and milk.

After dinner Fritz Platten appeared in Captain von Planetz's compartment. He was agitated. "Why is there no word from the Reichschancellery?" he demanded.

The young Swiss had already had a busy afternoon meeting with two other delegations—a group of German Social Democrats who wanted to meet Lenin and had to be refused; and the long-awaited staff officer from the Wilhelmstrasse, who to Platten's distress came not with the promised money for

Lenin, but only to check on the travelers' well-being. The officer had informed both Platten and Captain von Planetz to expect a second—and very important—delegation from the Reichschancellery later that evening.

"Nothing yet," the captain replied. "Lieutenant von Buhring is at the stationmaster's now, calling the foreign office. He'll be back shortly."

The Swiss gritted his teeth. "We're losing so damned much time," he complained. "We'll miss the last ferry from Sassnitz."

The captain nodded. That meant more hours for him to worry about Lenin's safety. Platten had told him about Zinoviev's and Morozov's brutal interrogation of Blum, but he wasn't convinced that it meant anything. Except that if Blum was Bauer, his imposture was now more secure—and more dangerous—than ever.

Lieutenant von Buhring burst into the compartment, his face flushed with excitement. "The delegation's on its way," he said, catching his breath.

"Who's coming?" Platten demanded. "Did you find that out?"

Von Buhring nodded vigorously. "Yes. Foreign Secretary Zimmermann himself!"

Von Planetz was as stunned as Platten. "Are you sure, Lieutenant?"

"Yes. I talked directly to his aide. He's coming alone."

Fritz Platten slapped his forehead with the heel of his palm. "God save us! I hope he doesn't expect to see Lenin."

About an hour after the dinner trays had been collected, Bauer decided the time had come. He grabbed his cane, walked to the lavatory at the front of the carriage, found it unoccupied, and slipped inside. He bolted the door, urinated, pulled the flush chain on the water closet, then dropped the wooden seat rim back over the bowl, and stepped up on top of it.

On the ceiling above his head was a metal grille, about two feet square, held in place by a single screw in each corner. The grille ventilated the lavatory through the ceiling and out through the continuous row of vents that ran like a backbone along the centerline of the carriage roof.

Bauer had loosened the four screws on previous visits, so it took him only seconds to remove them, put them in his pocket, and slide the panel back inside the ceiling and out of the way.

He pushed the cane up inside the opening, grabbed the edges, flexed his knees, and propelled himself upward with all the force he could muster. He got his elbows through, and rested them for a few seconds on the edges of the opening, his legs and torso suspended in midair over the toilet below.

He grabbed a support brace with one hand, took a deep breath, then scrambled the rest of the way up through the opening. The space between the carriage roof and the ceiling was dusty and dark, and obstructed at intervals by iron braces. He squirmed around until his head and upper chest were positioned over the opening. There was just enough clearance for him to raise his head about twelve inches.

He lowered his cane through the opening and with the rubber-tipped bottom nudged the bolt on the door back into the unlocked position. He retracted the cane swiftly, slid the panel back into place over the opening, and rested his cheek on it, to catch his breath and let his pulse slow to normal.

Barely a minute passed before someone came in. Bauer brought an eye up against the grille. It was the woman who giggled a lot, Olga Ravich. She locked the door, pulled up her voluminous skirts, struggled for several moments with her undergarments, then parked herself on the toilet seat with a sigh of satisfaction. Bauer closed his eyes to give her the benefit of some privacy.

After Olga's departure Bauer twisted the silver ferrule under the crook of the handle to expose the trigger and cock the firing pin.

The tip of the cane's shaft just barely fit through the openings in the grille. He slid the cane about a foot down through the narrow slit. Not far enough. He slid it farther. Nearly two feet of the shaft had to be pushed through before he could maneuver the cane sufficiently to aim it and pull the trigger.

He had expected the moment of truth to come when the train was in motion, counting on the chuffing of the locomotive and the clacking of the wheels on the rail to hide any noise he might make sliding the cane into position. And of course to muffle the sound of the shot itself. But now he realized that his target might arrive at any moment, while the train was still parked on the siding.

And there was the problem of escape. He had thought hard about it. Presumably the lavatory door would be locked, so even if the shot drew an immediate response, he should still have time to let himself down out of the ceiling, unlatch the lavatory window, and scramble out.

If the train was still in the station, the escape through the window would be quick and easy, with only the guards outside to worry about. If the train was moving, he would have to risk a jump into the dark.

Now came the waiting. It might be hours, he realized. It would be hard on the nerves. But he knew he'd see his prey sooner or later. Because the call of nature would inevitably bring Vladimir Ilyich Lenin to that lavatory.

BERLIN

At eight o'clock that evening Foreign Secretary Arthur Zimmermann left the Reichschancellery building on the corner of the Wilhelmstrasse and the Vosstrasse, and rode the short distance to Potsdam Station. For the first time since he had initiated the plan to return the Bolshevik leader to Russia, he felt real anxiety.

Despite the hourly crises that routinely engulfed the German foreign office, the secretary had found time to ponder what he would say to Lenin—and how he would say it.

He would be totally honest and businesslike. There was no sense pretending that he had any admiration for this radical, or expecting Lenin to exhibit any for him. It was a business dealing, that was all, an arrangement in the best interests of both parties. So he would be businesslike. Correct, polite, even gracious. But above all, businesslike.

He would begin with an explanation of why he was not bringing the promised twelve million Swiss francs. It would be an honest explanation, but not an apology. There could be no hint of that. He would not allow himself to become defensive. That was very important when dealing with a predatory individual like Lenin, a man who would smell out your weaknesses and pounce on them without mercy. Lenin's sudden demand for such a large sum of cash, in a foreign currency, had been both unreasonable and late, and Zimmermann intended to make that clear to Lenin. He would make a very strong point of this. Germany had tried its damnedest to comply, but the demand was simply unreasonable.

When he had forced Lenin to appreciate the difficulties, he would then turn magnanimous: Nevertheless, despite these problems, et cetera, et cetera, Germany still intended to live up to its part of the bargain. The twelve million Swiss francs would be delivered in Stockholm, instead. In Swedish krona, an equally reliable neutral currency. So it was only a matter of Lenin's waiting a few hours more.

Lenin would probably complain bitterly and hurl insults. That was his style, according to Parvus. He would accuse Germany of trying to trick him, and so forth and so on. Zimmermann was prepared to put up with that. Lenin could exhaust himself with complaint and invective if he wished. As long as the result was positive, Zimmermann would tolerate his tantrums.

Eventually Lenin would accept. How could he not? What choice did he have? Would he refuse to continue the journey, only hours from his goal? Not likely. He had as much, if not more, to lose than Germany if he backed out.

Lenin would threaten and bluff, Zimmermann calculated, and make further demands. And then he would take what was offered.

And Zimmermann would be ready for him. The foreign secretary would then make his offer to increase the total amount of money promised the Bolshevik party from forty to sixty million marks. But he would make Lenin fight for it, allow him to think that he had beaten it out of him.

And then Zimmermann would extract his own concession in return. With the added funds from Germany as the bait, he would persuade Lenin to advance his timetable for seizing power.

Six months, he decided. That would be the outer limit. The Bolsheviks must be in power within six months. Before the brunt of America's entry into the war hit Germany in the west. That meant by the end of October. If the Bolsheviks then called for an immediate cease-fire on the eastern front, Germany and Russia could negotiate a peace treaty in a matter of days. Zimmermann had already put a team of military experts and diplomats to work drafting the terms of the treaty.

The end of October, then. If Lenin was not in power by that time, Germany would cut off all money and support.

Lenin would agree, Zimmermann thought. Not just in words, but in actions. Because behind the radical posturing he would be realist enough to see that without Germany— and without Germany's money—he had no chance of success.

The driver applied the brakes to the wheels of the heavy limousine, bringing it to a bouncing stop directly in front of the porticos of the tall neoclassical stone facade of Potsdam Station. A small delegation of Army officers and foreign office staffers were waiting on the steps for him, alongside one of the barricaded machine gun emplacements that now bracketed all the station's entrances.

Could the converse be true also, Zimmermann wondered, as the driver opened the door for him: Without Lenin, did Germany have a chance?

THE TRAIN

The lavatory was a busy place, Bauer discovered. The women, particularly, made use of it, frequently coming in for no other reason than to comb their hair and powder their faces.

The men, he noticed—at least the Russian men—often didn't bother to bolt the door. This began to worry him. If Lenin left the door unlocked, anyone could open it after the shot. For the length of time it took him to scramble down from the ceiling and bolt the door himself, Bauer's escape would be jeopardized. Fifteen seconds, he estimated. Perhaps less.

Bauer rolled over on his side and pulled his watch from his pocket. He held the face up close to the grille and tilted it to catch the light coming up from below. Quarter of nine. He had been up in the ceiling for more than an hour.

Why hadn't the train left Berlin yet? he wondered. It was only a matter of a few hours to Sassnitz, and the last ferry to Sweden wasn't until midnight. They could easily make it. Why weren't they trying?

Zina Zinovieva came into the toilet with her husband,

Grigory Zinoviev. He bolted the door and whispered urgently to his wife in Russian. She giggled, then bent over the toilet, bracing herself with her hands on the rim. Zinoviev pulled up the back of her ankle-length skirts, bunched the material over her shoulders, grasped her bloomers and slid them down.

Quickly he dropped his own pants, pushed himself into her, and pistoned his hips against her rear with a loud slapping motion. Bauer watched in annoyance. If he'd had an extra bullet, he would have been tempted to shoot Zinoviev in the ass with it.

The coupling lasted less than a minute. Without a word, Zinoviev pulled up his pants, buttoned them, unbolted the door and left. Zina lingered to rearrange her undergarments and skirts and powder her face. Then she, too, departed.

Bauer caught himself drifting off to sleep. The air was stale and the cramped space in which he had jammed himself allowed him almost no movement. He massaged the muscles in his legs and arms, rubbed his face briskly, then took out his watch again: 9:05. He yawned so hard he felt his jawbone crack. The accumulated stress was beginning to exhaust him.

Captain von Planetz and Lieutenant von Buhring stood outside the carriage and watched as the stationmaster, several railroad officials, and a large crew of workmen from the train yard escorted Foreign Secretary Zimmermann across the obstacle course of tracks and signals and switching equipment to the now-darkened siding where the sealed train sat waiting. The workmen carried lanterns to light the way. From across the yard all the captain could see was a mass of walking legs, like some giant centipede sidling toward them in the gloom.

When the party reached the carriage, Zimmermann stepped forward. The two officers, their uniforms badly wrinkled after two and a half days on the train, did their best to stand smartly at attention and snap off a pair of crisp salutes.

Zimmermann stepped briskly up into the carriage and allowed Von Planetz to usher him into the officers' compartment at the rear.

Fritz Platten was waiting inside. He removed his hat, and shook the secretary's hand solemnly. "Good evening, Herr Secretary," the Swiss said, eager to impress himself on this important official. "I greet you on behalf of Vladimir Ilyich Lenin and the party of Internationalists on route to Petrograd."

The secretary harrumphed pompously. "I hope you and your party have found everything to your satisfaction so far?"

"The accommodations and service have been quite adequate," Platen declared. "We are most grateful, Herr Secretary. And we are of course flattered that you have taken the time to pay us this personal visit. Won't you please have a seat?"

Zimmermann declined impatiently. "I have come to meet personally with Herr Lenin," he announced.

Fritz Platten drew in a deep breath. "Begging your pardon, Herr Secretary, but I don't think that will be possible."

Zimmermann wagged his hand to dismiss the expected objection. "I realize that this is a technical violation of our agreement, but the matter is urgent. I insist that we meet. It will be unofficial and completely confidential. Lenin will not regret it."

"If it concerns the money, Herr Secretary, Lenin has empowered me to receive it in his name."

Zimmermann locked eyes with the younger man and stared him down. "It concerns the money, and other matters as well. I must see him."

The Swiss averted his eyes and nodded glumly. "I will take your request to him, Herr Secretary."

Platten opened the compartment door and hurried toward the front of the carriage. Zimmermann folded his arms and stood in the center of the compartment, nervously shifting his weight from one foot to another. No one dared speak.

Platten returned shortly. "He refuses, Herr Secretary," the Swiss said, his voice contrite. "I'm sorry."

Zimmermann continued to stand between the seats, arms folded and feet apart, not moving. In the bad light of the compartment, his face looked bone pale, and the rings under his eyes were as dark as bruises. Beads of perspiration had broken out along his hairline. Captain von Planetz, standing a few paces away, could feel the anger radiating from him.

"He must allow me to see him," Zimmermann declared, enunciating the words in a measured, menacing fashion. "It is late at night and we are at a guarded siding at the Berlin Station. No one, other than those in this compartment and the driver with me tonight, know of my presence here. And it will remain a secret. Forever. But I will not tolerate Lenin toying with me. You will remind him that despite the extraterritorial status of this train, it is a German train, inside the borders of the German Empire. You travel at Germany's pleasure. I am sorry that I must resort to coercion, but he leaves me no alternative. Tell Herr Lenin that this train will not leave Berlin until after we have met."

Bauer pulled out his watch again and held it up to the opening: 9:45. The damned train had not yet moved from the siding. It was too late now to make the last ferry at Sassnitz. Most likely they would remain here until morning.

That meant escaping into Berlin. The capital was big enough to offer a thousand places to hide. But the train yard itself was guarded like a fortress, with fences and machine gun emplacements.

He heard raised voices coming from the compartment nearest the lavatory—Lenin's compartment. He held his breath and strained to catch the words. Two men were conversing in Russian. Then a third man spoke, in German. Bauer recognized the voice as Fritz Platten's.

"I'm sorry, I don't know what to tell him. He demands to see you."

"We made an agreement. Tell the bastard I expect him to honor it."

Lenin's voice, Bauer guessed.

"He won't let the train go until you see him, Ilyich."

This remark was followed by a long silence. Some high German official, Bauer guessed, had come to visit. Who else was in a position to hold up the train? Low voices in Russian now. Lenin conferring with others.

Then Lenin spoke to Platten.

"Did he tell you why it was so God-damned important to see me?"

"A serious matter to discuss. That's all he'll say."

"Did he bring the money?"

"I don't know. He's not carrying anything."

"Go find out. Tell him I want to see the money first."

Bauer heard the compartment door slide closed and Platten's steps retreating down the corridor. The men in the

compartment continued to talk, but in Russian. The voice
levels rose and fell and then rose again. An argument was in
progress.

Platten returned.

"He wants to discuss the money. He wants to improve the
offer. That's what he wants to discuss, he said."

Lenin didn't answer Platten directly, but instead shouted
something in Russian at one of the other men in the compartment. The door slid shut again, and Bauer heard no more.

The next time he looked at his watch it was 11:10. He
guessed that he had seen almost everyone else in the lavatory
but Lenin. Did he possess some special kind of revolutionary
bladder that never needed to be emptied? Where the hell
was he?

Bauer massaged his legs and arms again. He was yawning
steadily and fighting to keep his eyelids from closing. He bit
the back of his fingers, using the pain to keep himself awake.

Occasionally he caught more voices from below. The compartment door opened and shut several more times. He
guessed that Lenin had finally consented to see whoever it
was demanding to meet him.

He felt a moment of panic. If Lenin had gone down to the
other end of the carriage to meet this party, he might also
have used the lavatory there—the one reserved for the German officers.

No, he wouldn't do that, he decided. His instincts were
petty and legalistic. He would stick to the letter of an arrangement, no matter how trivial. He would use this toilet.

Gradually the carriage settled down. The arguments and
raised voices and footsteps and banging doors diminished and
then ceased altogether. It became very quiet.

At five minutes before midnight the door to the lavatory
opened. Lenin stepped in. He turned and locked the door
behind him.

BERLIN

Back in his motorcar again, Arthur Zimmermann collapsed
against the seat cushions. His driver turned for instructions.
"Take me home," he muttered.

The chauffeur shifted the heavy vehicle into gear and drove

off from the station into the darkened streets of Berlin. An unsettling mixture of fury and satisfaction churned in Zimmermann's stomach.

He had finally been admitted into Lenin's compartment. The meeting had been humiliating. He had not expected to find the Russian especially likable, but neither had he expected the boorish little monster he found there. Never had the foreign secretary been treated with such rudeness and hostility. By anyone. A man of his rank and status was entitled to deference and courtesy. He expected it as his due, and he was prepared to offer the same to others of similar importance. But this particular individual—this strident, impudent, arrogant martinet—had interrupted him, contradicted him, accused him of lying, assaulted him with insults, called him names. It was a shameful, inexcusable performance, an indulgence of base emotions more fit for a waterfront saloon than for international diplomacy.

It had required all the steel in his Teutonic soul for Zimmermann not to retaliate, not to walk out and leave this ingrate in the lurch. It galled him to think about it, and he knew that it would be many hours before he could put the confrontation out of his mind.

But on the other hand, he had accomplished everything he had set out to accomplish. Lenin—once he had vented his spleen on the foreign secretary, the kaiser, and the German government—accepted his terms completely—the money to be delivered in Stockholm, the six-month timetable, everything.

And that was really what mattered, of course, Zimmermann assured himself. Getting his terms. The unfortunate fact that Lenin had agreed to them with such bad grace was hardly important in the long run.

But it rankled still. If the circumstances had been private, he would have unhesitatingly challenged the man to a duel.

Bauer concentrated on steadying his nerves and blanking from his mind everything but the immediate task before him. He watched Lenin from the top of the grille with the perfect stillness of a cat focused on its prey. Nothing moved but his eyelids.

The Russian examined himself briefly in the mirror over

the tiny sink, stroked his goatee a few times, and then stood against the toilet bowl and began unbuttoning his fly.

Bauer flattened his left hand on the ventilator grille, then rested the tip of the cane on the back of his index finger, so he could use it to guide the shaft through silently, without scraping the metal of the grille. He tipped the cane up into position, and started it through the hole, letting it slide until nearly two feet of its length was through the grille. The motions made him think of lining up a cue stick for a difficult banking shot in billiards.

Lenin bent his head forward, intent on the toilet bowl. The cane's tip now protruded down to within inches of the exposed patch of his neck between the bottom of his hairline and the top of his collar. Bauer stared at the spot, mesmerized. So white and vulnerable. Such an easy target. It would be a classic Russian execution: The bullet in the back of the neck.

Lenin's head snapped up suddenly, his neck almost hitting the tip of the cane. Bauer barely managed to pull it back out of the way in time.

Had he seen the reflection of the cane in the mirror? Bauer had considered this possibility earlier and decided that the angle of view from the toilet made it unlikely. He steadied the tip of the cane again, and snaked it back down to the same spot, a hand's width from the nape of Lenin's neck.

The American's mouth felt dry. Time to pull the trigger. He hesitated. Why? Lenin's worth an entire division, Churchill had said. Perhaps two. You'll save more human lives by this single act than any other man in history. Hard to believe that now. The man beneath him, so self-absorbed and unsuspecting, seemed hardly to merit the violent end he was about to meet.

Two divisions, Bauer thought.

He closed his finger on the curved sliver of steel protruding beneath the handle of the cane. It felt cold to his touch.

He let his breath out slowly and pressed his finger firmly against the trigger.

Two divisions.

He squeezed his finger tighter against the metal. The firing mechanism was sensitive and needed only the gentlest of pressure to trip it.

He felt the trigger give way against the pressure of his finger, then heard the tiny click as it slipped past its escapement and struck the firing pin.

And that was all he heard.

He relaxed his finger, felt the trigger still riding against it, and pulled it back again. Another harmless click.

Nothing happened.

A spasm of panic gripped his gut. He had made no provision for this.

One more time.

Still nothing.

Bauer's arms and fingers felt heavy, paralyzed. He was unable to move, to breathe. Nothing more he could do.

Lenin was buttoning his fly.

Bauer recovered his senses and quickly retracted the cane back up through the grille. He gripped it in both hands, afraid to put it down.

Lenin pulled the chain on the toilet, then moved to the wash basin. He opened the faucet, let the trickle of cold water splash over his hands, pulled down a clean section of towel from the roller dispenser, dried his hands, unlatched the door, and walked out.

Bauer moaned inaudibly, turning slowly onto his side to ease himself out of the cramped position he had maintained for so long, and squeezed his eyes shut, as if in pain.

For five minutes he lay there, oblivious to everything, not wanting to move or to think or to feel.

He finally roused himself, crawled down out of the ceiling, bolted the door again, and slid the ventilator grille back into place.

He dropped the rim on the toilet bowl and sat down on it to collect his thoughts. He held the cane in his hands and gazed at it for a long time, his mind unable to register anything except how stupid and frivolous the damned thing looked to him.

But it had worked before. Worked perfectly. He had tested it.

The beating by Morozov. That must have broken it. He thought there had been no damage, but he had not been able to test-fire it again. Lethargically, he unscrewed the handle and examined the breech and the firing mechanism.

The shiny, brass-jacketed six-millimeter slug was still in place. He withdrew it and held it up to the light. Was it a dud?

He looked closely at the base of the shell. The center, where the firing pin should have struck, showed no evidence of impact.

He looked at the cane's firing mechanism. It was a fragile device, hand-made to operate in the very restricted space of the cane's handle.

The firing pin was missing.

At first he thought that it must have somehow broken off. But it could not have fallen out of the breech until the breech was opened. He was sure it hadn't spilled out, but he checked carefully around the floor to make certain.

There was no sign of it—in the breech or on the floor.

Someone had removed it.

THURSDAY
APRIL 12

TORNIO, FINLAND

Private Alfie Cooper rubbed his mitten on the guardhouse window until he had cleared a circle about six inches wide, then peered out, his nose pressed to the glass. The view was to the west, across the frozen river that marked the frontier between Finland and Sweden. A crude wooden plank footbridge spanned the river, and at its far end, 450 feet away in neutral Sweden, was another guard post, even smaller than his. Around it were scattered a few sledges loaded with goods destined for Petrograd. Nothing else met his eye but miles of snow-covered evergreen forest and open tundra, tinted a feeble bone yellow in the weak slanting rays of the afternoon sun. Cooper had been stationed at the Russian border post for only a week, but already he felt nearly crazy from the cold, the boredom, and the loneliness.

Lieutenant Chase kept telling him that it was an important assignment. The Russians were too busy retreating from the Germans and fighting among themselves to bother protecting their borders. So the Huns were taking advantage of the situation, sneaking thousands of saboteurs and spies across to foment more discord and violence.

At least that's what Chase had told him. So far neither he nor the lieutenant had seen any of these spies or saboteurs. In fact, they hadn't seen much of anything, except each other and occasionally, when they chose to show up, a drunken Russian frontier guard or two.

Cooper exhaled against the window, watched it fog up, then wiped it clear again. The glass squeaked under the friction of his mitten. "When's that bleedin' party coming through, lef'tenant?"

Chase, absorbed in trimming his moustache in front of a small mirror on the rear wall, paused to examine his progress. "Tomorrow. Or the day after. Who the hell knows? Headquarters doesn't tell me anything."

Suddenly Cooper stopped his wiping. Some movement outside caught his eye. He cleared a bigger circle and looked out again. "Bugger all," he said. "There's someone out on the bridge, sir. Coming from our side."

Lieutenant Chase ambled over to have a look. "Another Laplander," he said. He returned to the mirror, disappointed.

"The next train's not for three hours," the private said. "Where the bleedin' hell did he come from?"

The lieutenant adjusted the angle of his cap in the mirror. "He probably has a reindeer flock around here somewhere."

"Herd, sir."

"What?"

"They call it a reindeer herd. Not a flock. That's for birds."

Chase held up a finger in an indecent gesture. "Jump on this bird, private."

"Want us to give him a once-over, sir?"

Chase shook his head. "Let the Swedes across the river do it. We check them coming the other way."

"Hell, they never check anybody," Cooper complained. "Too bleedin' drunk all the time."

Chase chuckled. "You'd be bloody drunk all the time too, Cooper, if you had to live up here."

Cooper watched the heavily clad figure approach the customs house, a dirty canvas knapsack slung over his shoulder.

"He's carrying a big grip, sir. Maybe we ought to have a peek inside."

"Suit yourself. If he's got any vodka, confiscate it."

Cooper sniffed and rubbed the end of his nose on his sleeve. "Too bleedin' right, I will," he muttered. He watched the figure until he was within a few yards of the customs house, then put on his cap, straightened his tunic, and walked out into the cold to confront him.

The man stopped in his tracks the instant Cooper stepped outside.

"Right this way, mate," Cooper said. He made a sweeping gesture with his mittened hand toward the guardhouse door. "There's a good lad."

The stranger just stood there and stared, like a threatened animal, as if uncertain whether to fight or flee. Cooper thought his complexion and his eyes were too dark for him to be either a Finn or a Slav.

"We don't have all day, mate," the private warned, stepping toward the figure and pointing more emphatically toward the door. "Let's move your bleedin' ass inside. It's freezing out here."

The stranger reached into the side pocket of his greatcoat, drew out a pistol, and fired it twice at Private Cooper.

The English soldier clutched his chest in astonishment, then pitched over sideways into the snow without making a sound.

The stranger picked up his bag and ran onto the bridge.

Hearing the shots, Lieutenant Chase jumped to the door and flung it open. The man shot at him on the run and missed. Chase stumbled back out of sight, retrieved his own firearm, and stationed himself behind the door, ready to ambush the man if he tried to come inside.

Nothing happened. After a few minutes Chase crept to the window, his heart still pounding with fright, wiped a spot clean, and looked out. Nothing. He stepped outside, pistol at the ready, and made a circuit of the customs house. The man was gone. He followed his tracks and saw that he had crossed the bridge into Sweden.

Chase thought of trying to warn the Swedish customs house by telephone, but he remembered that it took anywhere from several hours to several days to get through. The Finns routed the calls down through their capital at Helsingfors, over through Stockholm, and then up to Haparanda. He could run over there himself in two minutes.

But the Swedes usually left their customs house unoccupied between the twice-daily arrival of the trains. He was pretty sure it was unoccupied now.

The hell with it, he decided. He'd better worry about Cooper. He walked over to the soldier, kneeled down, and searched for a pulse. There was none.

THE TRAIN

A cold front from the north settled over Berlin on Thursday morning, dropping a damp steel-gray blanket of overcast onto the already depressed atmosphere of the wartime capital.

At 11:00 A.M. the sealed carriage was finally rescued from the siding where it had spent the night and was pulled by a small locomotive through a complicated series of track junctions and switchbacks through the center of the city, moving it from Potsdam Station at the southern end to Stettin Station at the north end. All the carriage window shades were tightly drawn to preserve the secrecy of the train's occupants—and to shield the revolutionaries from a closer look at Berlin.

At Stettin the train acquired a new locomotive and was shunted onto the main trunk line north for the last leg of its run across Germany—the 300 kilometers to Sassnitz, on the Baltic Sea.

Harry Bauer had returned to the third-class compartment near the back just before dawn and slept for a few hours on the floor. No one had expressed any curiosity about his absence. Or his appearance. His clothes were now thoroughly wrinkled and dirty from the hours spent in the crawl space over the toilet. The others in the compartment appeared equally disheveled, he noticed. Everyone was saving one clean change of clothes for the grand entrance into Petrograd.

He folded his hands over the handle of his cane, and tried to work out the mystery of its missing firing pin. Only once had the cane been out of his possession: when Morozov was beating him with it. He knew that Morozov hadn't tampered with the pin, because he would have seen it. But someone had. How?

While he was sleeping?

Had the German captain finally puzzled out which one of the thirty-two travelers he was? But why hadn't he arrested him? Or killed him? Why just dismantle his weapon? And how would he have discovered that the cane was a weapon in the first place?

The train would reach Sassnitz by the early evening. There'd be another customs inspection, and then the party of revolutionaries would board the ferry and leave Germany forever.

The cane was useless without the firing pin, and he had no immediate means of obtaining another weapon.

What were his choices? Quit now? Surrender to failure when it mattered most for him to succeed?

He had never failed on a mission. It wasn't much to hang the meaning of his life on, but it was all he had working for him. If he fell short here, nothing that had gone before would be worth anything.

What could he do but continue on? If he couldn't get Lenin in Germany, then he'd just have to get him in Sweden. It wouldn't be exactly what the English had wanted. Churchill had told him to kill him in Germany. But killing him was the important thing.

In some ways it would be easier. They'd be in a neutral nation. Lenin would no longer have the protection of the sealed train and the German guards. Or that dangerously persistent German captain.

In other ways it would be riskier. Whoever had dismantled his cane might still be with the party.

SASSNITZ, GERMANY

The sealed train reached its final destination in Germany at a little after four o'clock Thursday afternoon. It hissed and clanked to a stop alongside the Sassnitz terminal, a long shed-covered platform at the water's edge. Directly across the platform, its two bays jutting out into the harbor in the shape of the letter E, stood a large ferry slip. Waiting in one of the bays was the Swedish ship *Queen Victoria*, scheduled to depart in twenty minutes.

The thirty-two members in Lenin's party rushed from the carriage, collected their belongings from the baggage car, and crossed the platform to the ferry gate. It was their first moment off the train in three days, and they stood in the gray drizzle of the late afternoon looking dazed and unsteady, like sailors long at sea, feeling the novel sensation of *terra firma* beneath their feet again.

Formalities were brief. The German authorities collected

the revolutionaries' tickets as they left the train, and the Swedish authorities took down their names as they trudged up the ramp and onto the ferry.

Captain von Planetz and Lieutenant von Buhring stood together on the platform and watched them as they boarded.

"It was better duty than the trenches," Von Buhring said. "But a bed and a bath will feel damned good tonight."

The captain didn't respond. He was watching the passengers as they walked up the ramp.

"I guess now we'll never know," the lieutenant said, reading the captain's thoughts.

"We'll know," Von Planetz replied. "He'll have a much better opportunity now, without us and the confines of the sealed carriage to inhibit him. Lenin will be dead within a day."

"Well, you've warned them."

"They don't believe me."

Blum came into view and started up the ramp, leaning heavily on his cane. The two officers studied his progress closely.

"At least nothing happened on our watch," the lieutenant declared.

The captain pressed a finger against the bridge of his glasses. "If Lenin doesn't make it to St. Petersburg, our efforts will have been for nothing."

"Not your responsibility anymore, Captain. Time to put the whole business out of your head."

"You don't believe me either, do you?" Von Planetz said, turning toward his assistant.

Von Buhring scratched his chin, embarrassed to disagree with the captain. "If what you say is true—about the disguise, the phony limp, and everything else—then why hasn't he tried to kill him by now? If he wasn't going to kill him in Germany, why did he go to all that trouble to get himself on the same train?"

The captain kicked at a small stone lying near his boot. "I don't know why. I'm sure there's a reason, but I just don't know what it is."

Lenin appeared last, in company with his wife and four others. The raised collar on his greatcoat, caught by the cold blasts of wind coming in off the Baltic, flapped comically against his cheek.

"Hard to accept that we've gone to all this trouble for that disheveled runt," Von Buhring said.

As soon as the last of Lenin's party was aboard, the ramp connecting the dock to the ferry was pulled up and the gate on the ferry's fantail closed and secured. Dockmen freed the lines, and the big boat trembled in the water as the pilot engaged her twin screws.

With a mournful blast from her foghorn, the *Queen Victoria* slipped from the dock and in a wake of foaming water began the crossing to Sweden.

Captain von Planetz excused himself and went inside the Sassnitz terminal. He found the stationmaster in his office and showed him his military identification card. "I would like to use your telephone, if you please. In private."

The stationmaster quickly agreed and left the captain alone. Von Planetz put a call through to his commanding officer, General von Gontard, in Berlin. The connections were faulty, and it took a long time. Eventually he heard the general's gruff voice on the other end.

"The boat has left the dock, Herr General, with Morning Star on board."

"Good, good!" Von Gontard shouted. "Well done, Captain!" Like many men who had grown up before the invention of the telephone, he had a tendency to shout into the mouthpiece at the top of his voice, convinced that his words would otherwise not make it all the way to the other end.

"But I must report, Herr General, my belief that Morning Star is now in graver danger than ever." Von Planetz repeated to the general his belief that Bauer was traveling with the party in disguise.

"You're sure of this?" Von Gontard demanded. "Your evidence is entirely circumstantial."

"I'm sure, Herr General. Our vigilance on the sealed train must have prevented him from acting. In Sweden he'll have a much easier time of it."

"Have you warned Morning Star of this danger?"

"Yes, Herr General, but he and his men refuse to take the matter seriously."

For a long time Von Gontard was silent. The captain waited,

the receiver to his ear, listening to the hollow hums and echoing vibrations that routinely plagued long-distance connections. He began to wonder if the general was still on the line.

Suddenly his voice boomed at him again, vibrating the receiver's diaphragm painfully against his ear. "Call me again at this number in one hour, Captain. I'll have new instructions for you then."

The line went dead.

Captain von Planetz wanted to call his wife, but decided he'd better wait until he had his new orders. He spent a nervous sixty minutes pacing the station waiting room, smoking one cigarette after another. He placed the call to Berlin headquarters exactly an hour later.

The general came on the line immediately. "I've given your report to the Reichschancellery, Captain. They want you to continue on."

"What do you mean, sir?"

"Morning Star will have to stop overnight in Malmo or Stockholm. Take the next ferry. Catch up to him."

"I have no authority. . . ."

"Sweden is neutral but pro-German. You'll have no problems traveling in uniform. The success of Red Morning is vital to Germany's future. We're counting on you."

"What do you want me to do?"

The general turned away from the phone for several minutes. Von Planetz could hear a muted conversation in the background but couldn't catch any of the words.

"Captain von Planetz?"

"Yes, sir."

"You must see to it that the American is killed. Quickly. Do it yourself if necessary. As quickly as possible."

The captain felt his chest constrict.

"Did you hear me, Captain?"

"Yes, Herr General."

"We are at war with America now. It will be in the line of duty. Do you understand?"

"Yes, sir."

"The Fatherland will be grateful. We know your wife is ill. As soon as you report the completion of this assignment, we'll get her the treatment she needs. Immediately. That's been authorized by the highest authority."

"Yes, sir. Thank you, sir."

"Good luck, then. Captain. *Gott Mit Uns!*"

THE BALTIC

The sky was purple and the sea rough. A maddened crowd of whitecaps from horizon to horizon, it pummeled the hull of the *Queen Victoria* from all sides, causing her to pitch and roll through the turbulent waters like a sailor on a drunken binge.

Harry Bauer leaned on the railing on the port side of the deck, watching the ocean crash and seethe below him. Most of the other passengers had retreated to safety below, but a hardy group remained near the bow, bawling out chants and songs into the howling elements.

He saw Inessa, clinging to the rail by the bridge. The wind whipped her coat up like a cloak around her.

He worked his way closer, moving sideways along the railing, careful not to lose his footing on the slippery deck. "Got caught in a typhoon once!" he yelled. "In the Yellow Sea. Makes this look like Sunday on the lake!"

Inessa slipped an arm under his elbow for support and moved her face close so they could hear each other. "What were you doing in the Yellow Sea?"

"Headed for Port Arthur. That was a long time ago. During the war there." He probably shouldn't have said that much, but what difference could it make now?

Inessa squeezed his arm and smiled up at him. Her chestnut hair was damp with sea spray. Curled strands clung to her forehead and her neck, and her face was filmed with a fine mist. "You've been to many exotic places," she observed. "I thought the Swiss hated to travel."

Was she mocking him? Bauer changed the subject. "They seem in a good mood." He motioned with his head toward the group at the bow.

"Of course! We're all in a good mood. We made it through Germany. We're practically home now."

"What are they singing?"

Inessa listened, trying to catch the sounds over the howling of the wind. "It's one of Ilyich's favorites," she replied. " 'Don't cry over the bodies of fallen comrades.' "

Bauer laughed. "I'll bet that has some catchy lyrics."

"What did you say?"

A big wave struck the ship, sending the deck into a steep roll. Inessa slipped. She struggled to regain her footing and lost her grip on the handrail. Bauer was thrown off balance, and as he tried to steady himself, he heard her gasp and then felt her arm slide out from beneath his elbow.

He held tight to the rail, letting his stomach bear his weight as the roll deepened. He saw Inessa's legs disappearing beneath the bottom railing.

He dropped a hand from the rail and managed to catch her arm. The roll grew worse and she continued to slide. He squeezed, but her arm kept slipping through his grip. In a matter of a moment she was completely through the railing. He fell to the deck, one hand clasped on the wet wood of the rail, the other on her arm. He tightened his fingers with all the strength he could muster.

She screamed, her voice lost in the tumult of wind and water.

The ferry reached the steepest part of its roll and seemed to stall there, its deck tilted at a nearly forty-five-degree angle with the boiling sea.

Inessa hung suspended in midair, the wind tugging at her drenched garments. For an eternal few seconds Bauer took her entire weight in his one hand and willed himself to hold on. Still, her arm continued to slip through his grasp.

The temperature of the Baltic in April was too cold for anyone to survive for more than a minute or two, and the ferry would not be able to maneuver for a rescue attempt. He had to hold on.

At her wrist he was able to improve his grip. He squeezed his fingers around the slender stem of flesh, knowing that he couldn't let it slip any farther.

He managed to hook one leg around the lower railing, hoping that he could somehow free his other hand to get a better grip on her, but even the tentative loosening of his fingers from the upper railing told him that it would cost him his balance and take both of them overboard.

Finally, agonizingly, the ship shuddered through the trough

of the wave and began to right itself as the steep slope of the next wave swelled under its hull. The moment the deck's tilt approached the horizontal, Bauer grabbed Inessa with both hands and yanked her swiftly back through the railing.

They ended up sprawled on the deck in a twisted, spray-soaked bundle, Bauer still clutching Inessa's wrist. He reached an arm around her waist and pulled her to him. Her teeth were chattering with shock. She clutched him around the neck and held on, shivering violently.

TRELLEBORG, SWEDEN

P.T. Berg, Esq., the vice-consul at the U.S. Embassy in Stockholm, stood on the ferry dock, training a pair of Zeiss military binoculars south across the Baltic. Out of the swirls of rain and mist he spotted the squat black shape of the ferry, wallowing in the heavy seas, the smoke from her twin stacks rolling out horizontally and whipping away in the wind, like kite tails.

It was the *Queen Victoria*, the last of the day's five scheduled ferries from Germany.

Berg had been at the ferry dock to meet every single run for the past two days. He was becoming worried. His continued absence from Stockholm was getting hard to explain to the ambassador. And Colonel House had been adamant that he was to inform no one of what he was doing.

Berg tucked the binoculars out of sight beneath his coat and walked down to the disembarcation point.

Fifteen minutes later the ferry maneuvered into her berth, the rough waters bumping her hard against the wooden pilings. The deckhands struggled to secure her lines, then lowered the ramp onto the dock and opened the gates.

Berg dug from his overcoat pocket two crumpled photographs—one of Vladimir Lenin, the other of Harry Bauer—studied them for a few moments, then returned them to his pocket and focused his attention on the passengers coming down the ramp.

He felt a sudden rush of adrenaline. It was Lenin's party. The line of Slavic faces with their furtive glances and disheveled dress left little doubt.

His eyes settled immediately on the fourth passenger back. Beneath his workman's cloth cap he fit Lenin's description perfectly—short, wiry, with a spade-shaped goatee and Mongol eyes. And still very much alive.

No one in the line resembled Harry Bauer.

Berg moved over to the customs shed and took up a position behind one of the barricades. He studied the revolutionaries from a discreet distance while Swedish customs officers checked them through.

When the last arrival had been let through the gates, Berg approached the customs chief, an easygoing bureaucrat with whom he had established a friendship over the past few days. "Vladimir Ilyich?" he asked.

The Swede glanced around surreptitiously to make sure no one was watching them. Then he nodded curtly.

"Bauer?"

The Swede shook his head, slowly and emphatically.

"Any Americans?"

The Swede shook his head again.

"Thanks."

Berg strode off. Bauer might be in disguise, he thought. But even allowing that, he had seen no one with even a close physical resemblance. Colonel House wouldn't like it, but that was his problem.

The young vice-consul was secretly relieved that Bauer hadn't shown up. Now maybe he could drop this whole business. If the ambassador, or Secretary of State Lansing, ever discovered that he was doing covert work for Colonel House behind their backs, he'd have some hard explaining to do.

LONDON

Secret Service Chief Mansfield Cumming handed the decoded cable across to Foreign Minister Arthur Balfour without explanation. Balfour held it out at arm's length and read it:

URGENT TOP SECRET
TO BE DECODED AT ONCE
DO NOT DISTRIBUTE
DELIVER IMMEDIATELY TO COLONEL HOUSE
MESSAGE AS FOLLOWS:
LENIN ARRIVED TRELLEBORG INTACT THURSDAY EVENING.
STILL NO SIGN OF BAUER. BERG
END OF TRANSMISSION

Balfour looked across at Cumming with pained embarrassment, as if he had noticed that his fly was unbuttoned. "My God, how long have we been intercepting American messages?"

"We just got onto them. Room 40 worked them out through the 'Swedish roundabout' the Germans were using. Serves the Yankees right for trusting the Germans."

"Or us, for that matter," Balfour replied tartly. "We'd better be careful."

Cumming's elastic mouth drooped into a frown. "Of course, Minister."

Balfour tossed the cable onto his desk and sank into his chair with a profound sigh. "This is damned bleak news about Lenin."

"I'm sorry, Minister," Cumming muttered.

"You're not to blame, for Heaven's sake," Balfour replied. "You had every reason to believe that Bauer was the right choice. I believed he was, and so did the P.M. Perhaps Churchill gave him confusing orders. At the moment it needn't concern us. What we have to worry about is that Lenin is still alive, Bauer is still unaccounted for, and the Americans are breathing down our neck. What do we do?"

Cumming pulled his monocle from his vest pocket by the chain and absently spun it in his fingers. "Let's wait it out for a bit longer. Bauer has time yet. If Lenin's still alive, then Bauer's still in the hunt. I'm sure of it."

The foreign minister smacked his fist into the palm of his hand. "Well, what in the name of Christianity is he waiting for?"

"We agreed to leave him in until the Finnish border," Cumming reminded Balfour. "And Lenin won't reach there for another day, at least. We've got to hold on until then."

Balfour rose from his desk and paced the room restlessly. He stopped in front of the window. The trees around the Horse Parade had just begun to leaf out. The branches, bare for so long, were thickening with a bright pale green that glowed optimistically even through the dense brown fog that was beginning to settle on the city. "You're right, of course. We're due some luck."

"There's another worry, though," Cumming said.

Balfour turned to face him. "What is it?"

"Colonel House and the Americans are up to something. They might decide to warn Lenin."

"I don't follow you."

"Thanks to their Mr. Berg, Washington now knows what we know—that Lenin is alive in Sweden and that Bauer is still unaccounted for. Wilson may well direct his embassy in Sweden—or Berg himself—to warn Lenin of the danger. Why else would House have gone to the trouble to post Berg by the ferry docks?"

"Not much we can do about it."

Cumming tucked his monocle into place beneath the fold of flesh over his eye. "Perhaps we can," he said. "Suppose we tell their ambassador here that we have a report that Bauer was captured in Germany. Perfectly plausible. And worth it, if it'll give Bauer another day. After the fact, we can simply inform Washington the report was in error. Terribly sorry and all that. Happens all the time."

A wide grin stretched slowly across Balfour's face. "That's quite good, Sir Mansfield," he said. "Really quite good."

FRIDAY
APRIL 13

BERLIN

By the time Zimmermann had finished composing his urgent message to the German ambassador in Stockholm, it was two o'clock Friday morning. He handed it to the night duty officer, who took it downstairs to the locked and guarded cipher room, where a team of clerks set to work at once encoding the document in preparation for telegraphing it to Stockholm.

The telegram read as follows:

> 13046
> 0200 HOURS 13 APRIL.
> VON SCHEER, STOCKHOLM
> NUMBER ONE STRICTLY SECRET. YOURSELF TO DECIPHER.
> SUBJECT RED MORNING. LENIN TRAIN ARRIVES STOCKHOLM
> EARLY MORNING FRIDAY APRIL 13. URGENT REPEAT URGENT
> YOU WARN HIM IN PERSON OF PRESENCE OF AMERICAN
> ASSASSIN HARRY BAUER IN HIS PARTY. BAUER TRAVELING AS
> GERMAN BUNDIST OSKAR BLUM. INTENDS TO KILL LENIN.
> SUGGEST HE TAKE STRONGEST ACTION IMMEDIATELY. DO
> NOT REPEAT NOT INVOLVE SWEDISH AUTHORITIES.
> ACKNOWLEDGE RECEIPT.
> ZIMMERMANN. END OF DISPATCH

The purpose of the telegram was simple. If Von Planetz failed to reach Bauer in time, at least Lenin might finally be roused to protect himself.

As he left the Reichschancellery building for home, Zimmermann reflected on the events of the evening. He had strong misgivings about letting General von Gontard send Von Planetz on after the American. Pitting a middle-aged desk man against a ruthless professional assassin was hardly fair to Von Planetz, but there was no choice. Von Planetz was on the scene, and he was motivated. If Lenin wouldn't protect himself, then Von Planetz was simply Germany's best last chance.

Why Captain von Planetz himself had failed to make clear to Lenin the menace he faced was a mystery. Perhaps he wasn't as competent as Von Gontard had claimed when he first recommended him.

It would serve Lenin right if he was assassinated, Zimmermann thought. In any other circumstances he would have welcomed it. But Red Morning must not be allowed to fail. Far more than his career was on the line. That was becoming more apparent with every passing day, as the casualties from the western front continued to mount and the food available to feed the German population continued to dwindle. Germany could not sustain another year of war. Either the kaiser's government would fall, or Germany would simply run out of able bodies to send to the front lines.

Lenin must make it to St. Petersburg. At all costs.

LONDON

In Whitehall's Room 40 cryptographer Nigel De Grey wiped the sleep from his eyes and stared down at the fresh page of numbers he had just pulled out of the pneumatic tube. He glanced at the first group of digits at the top of the page—13046—and recognized it as a sub group under the German diplomatic code, 0075.

This one, he saw with mounting excitement, was also from Germany's foreign secretary, Arthur Zimmermann. He shook himself awake and started to work. Half an hour later he had the full text of the message deciphered.

He checked his watch. Ten after four o'clock, Friday morning. He carried the message over to the Reverend William Montgomery, another of Captain William "Blinker" Hall's civilians whom he had recruited into the arcane cryptographic world of Room 40.

"Another torpedo from Zimmermann," he said. "Have a look at this."

They discussed the telegram for several minutes, and then Montgomery cranked the telephone to waken their boss from the middle of another night's sleep.

Half an hour later Hall was on the telephone to his opposite number at MI1c, Captain Sir Mansfield Cumming. The secret service chief, his voice clotted with sleep, picked up the receiver after many rings.

"Hall here. Terribly sorry to disturb you, Sir Mansfield. We have something you must see immediately. Shall I bring it over?"

Foreign Minister Balfour read the intercepted telegram through several times, then dropped it on his desk with a groan of anger. It was six o'clock in the morning, and he felt only half awake. Cumming, to his annoyance, looked positively alert and glowing. But then Cumming had been up since four. He could smell the scent of lime aftershave on the secret service chief's jowls.

"How do you suppose the Germans got onto him?"

Cumming fiddled with his monocle and grimaced, causing his thin lips to stretch seemingly the entire width of his face. "I've been puzzling over that very question myself, Minister, ever since Hall showed it to me, barely two hours ago. Even *we* didn't know he was traveling in the place of this Oskar Blum."

Balfour ran his fingers through his hair. "It seems absolutely foolhardy, disguising himself as one of Lenin's own people. Obviously someone on the train must have recognized that he was an imposter."

"I suppose so, but why didn't they do something on the spot? It seems odd that the warning to Lenin should come all the way from Berlin."

Balfour propped his hands under his chin and stared sleepily at the far wall. "It's useless to speculate further. At least we know Bauer is still on the job."

"He may not know the danger he's in."

The foreign minister raised an eyebrow. "Meaning?"

"Well—we should try to warn him."

Balfour leaned back in his chair, put a hand to his mouth, and yawned. "How can we do that?"

"Send someone from our embassy to meet the train."

"No," Balfour replied, his tone emphatic. "If we warn him, we run the risk of implicating ourselves." He tapped a forefinger forcefully several times on his desk, to drive home his argument. "Worse, if we show our hand in this fashion to the Germans, they might well suspect we're reading their diplomatic messages. You know we can't risk that. And there's still opportunity for Bauer to get to Lenin before they get to him. The only course of action for us, Sir Mansfield, is to let the situation ride. Hold tight. You told me that only yesterday, as I recall. Bauer knows the risks of this kind of thing. He'll take precautions. He has a sporting chance. He can't expect more."

Cumming cleared his throat, his mouth twitching nervously. "I disagree, Minister. Sorry. The situation has changed considerably since yesterday. As soon as Lenin knows, Bauer's as good as dead, I'm afraid. He's resourceful, of course, but how can they fail to catch him?"

Balfour gazed sleepily at the clock on the fireplace mantel. Too late to go home and back to bed. Today would be an unbearably long one. "I understand your concern for a fellow agent out in the field, Sir Mansfield. Really, I do. But you know we can't jeopardize Room 40 just to give him better odds. We'll stick with yesterday's plan. If he makes it to the Finnish border, we can pull him out of the water there. But until Tornio he's on his own."

STOCKHOLM

Through the hours of Thursday night and Friday morning, the train transporting Lenin and his party from Malmo to Stockholm—an "Atlantic" 4-4-2 express locomotive pulling eight carriages and two baggage cars—sped through the flat southern forests of the Scandanavian countryside. It arrived in Stockholm's Central Bangard precisely on schedule, at nine o'clock Friday morning.

The scene at the station contrasted dramatically with their departure from Zurich four days earlier. It was a cool, windy day, but the sun was shining, and instead of Zurich's jeering mob of hecklers, a far more enthusiastic and friendly group awaited, including the mayor of the city, a handful of prominent socialists, and several dozen reporters and photographers.

The news of Lenin's journey was spreading.

Waiting on the platform also was the German ambassador, Horst von Scheer, stiffly dressed in dark suit and Chesterfield, high collar and derby, Zimmermann's secret telegram burning a hole in his pocket. Next to him, impatiently shifting his ponderous weight from leg to leg, was the Dane, Parvus, one hand clutching his walking stick, the other clasped tightly to the handle of a bulky leather case, its two thick straps secured by small padlocks.

The travelers opened the windows and leaned out, a little awed by the friendly crowd and the journalists and photographers who pressed around them, firing questions and clicking cameras. Karl Radek handed a written statement from Lenin to the members of the press.

"Where's Lenin?" someone yelled.

"Everything is in the statement, gentlemen," Radek said. "Lenin does not wish to meet the press at this time. Thank you." Radek offered his audience a coy grin and wave of the hand, and then disappeared back into the train.

Parvus and Ambassador von Scheer, who had been totally ignored, stepped to the carriage and started up the steps. Morozov blocked the door with his broad shoulders and refused to allow them on.

Parvus found Fritz Platten out on the platform and grabbed his arm. "For God's sake!" he panted. "We must see Lenin immediately!" He jabbed a finger in the direction of the portly, goateed gentleman waiting impatiently beside his uniformed chauffeur a few paces away. "I have the German ambassador with me. He has an urgent message from Berlin!"

Platten glanced over at the ambassador, then back at Parvus. "Do you have the money?"

Parvus slapped the leather case with his hand. "Of course."

Platten nodded. "Wait here. I'll talk to Lenin."

"I don't want to stand here another damned minute!" Parvus howled.

Platten held out his hands placatingly. "I'll be right back."

It was nearly five minutes before the Swiss returned.

Morozov accompanied him. "Lenin won't see either of you," he told Parvus. "I'm sorry."

"He must see us!" Parvus wailed.

The German ambassador, not accustomed to such public humiliation, looked as if he were about to pass out.

Platten took Parvus aside. "Lenin can't see the German ambassador in public!" he rasped, pulling on Parvus's shoulder so that the fat man's ear was only inches from his mouth. "Doesn't Zimmermann understand anything? Tell the ambassador that I'll deliver the message to Lenin for him."

Parvus, in his turn, took Von Scheer aside and flustered his way through an explanation of the situation. The ambassador was finally persuaded to agree that the important thing was that Lenin got his message, not that he deliver it in person.

Von Scheer handed the telegram, neatly sealed in an envelope with a wax stamp, to Parvus. Parvus immediately turned it over to Platten. The ambassador whirled around, beckoned to his chauffeur, and without having uttered a word, stalked off.

"Now what about me?" the Dane demanded. "Why can't he see me?"

Platten spread his hands out in a gesture of helplessness. "I'm afraid Ilyich considers you a lackey of the Germans, Herr Parvus. He doesn't want you in his presence. That's the brutal truth. I'm sorry. Give Morozov the money. He'll take it in to him."

Parvus, his face a simmering stew of hurt pride and indignation, continued to protest, but when he saw that he was attracting the attention of several newsmen and photographers, he abruptly shut up. He shoved the leather case, stuffed with the twelve million Swedish krona, into Morozov's big hands, banged the tip of his walking stick on the wooden platform, and like the ambassador before him, stormed off.

By 9:30 the hubbub on the platform outside had died away, and the Swedish conductors ejected Lenin's party from the train so that it could continue on. Fritz Platten gave each of the travelers Lenin's instructions for the day. The overnight train to Haparanda, on the Finnish border, would leave the Central Bangard at 6:30, so everyone was to report back to the station by six, to get their compartment assignments for the twenty-four hour, six-hundred-mile journey.

Until then, Platten said, they were free to enjoy the city of Stockholm. To make their stopover a little more enjoyable, Platten handed each traveler a small stack of folded banknotes. He offered no explanation as to their source.

Bauer received his with an embarrassed nod. He unfolded the bills and counted them: one hundred Swedish krona.

Karl Radek, hauling his scuffed pressboard suitcase along the corridor, stopped alongside Bauer. His bespectacled face was drawn in a rare frown. He held out his hand.

Bauer shook it. "Where are you going?"

"Nowhere," Radek replied, resting the suitcase on the floor. "That's the problem. I'm Austrian. The damned Russians won't let me through. I'm staying in Stockholm."

"That's too bad."

Radek shrugged. "Maybe it is, maybe it isn't. I've warned Ilyich they'll probably arrest everybody at Tornio."

"You think so?"

"They must already know the Germans've let us through. And when they find all those Swedish krona Ilyich is carrying, they'll have an open-and-shut case for treason." Radek made a cutting motion across his throat with the edge of his palm. "More martyrs for the *Narodnaya Volna.*"

Bauer looked down at the krona banknotes in his hand. "How much is he carrying?"

"Christ, I don't know. A lot. Millions." Radek shouldn't have told him, but at the moment the Austrian didn't seem to care what he said.

"Why?"

Radek threw out his hands. "He demanded the Germans prove their good faith. I told him to leave the cash here in Stockholm. Get it in a bank account. The Russians'll steal it from him. Zinoviev is still in there trying to persuade him. But Ilyich wants it with him. It's tangible power—something he's never felt before. It's the ticket to a Bolshevik triumph. He wants to look at it, smell it, taste it, feel it, tell himself that he stole it out of the kaiser's vaults. Maybe he'll wipe his ass with some of it, I don't know."

The Austrian picked up his suitcase and started toward the exit again. "It'll give him an edge over the opposition, no

doubt about that. If he gets it through. But the hell with him.
I'm going to get drunk."

Bauer tucked the bills into his inside coat pocket and
followed Radek out onto the platform. Some of those krona,
he decided, were about to be invested in a cause quite
different from what either Lenin or the kaiser intended.

WASHINGTON

URGENT TOP SECRET
TO BE DECODED AT ONCE
DO NOT DISTRIBUTE
DELIVER IMMEDIATELY TO COLONEL HOUSE
MESSAGE AS FOLLOWS:
BAUER NOT CAPTURED BY GERMANS AS BRITISH CLAIM. IS
TRAVELING WITH LENIN PARTY DISGUISED AS SWISS BUNDIST
OSKAR BLUM.
MCNALLY ZURICH
END OF MESSAGE

URGENT TOP SECRET
P.T. BERG STOCKHOLM EMBASSY
MESSAGE AS FOLLOWS:
HARRY BAUER WITH LENIN PARTY DISGUISED AS SWISS OSKAR
BLUM. PROCEED WITH ASSIGNMENT IMMEDIATELY.
HOUSE.
END OF MESSAGE

STOCKHOLM

It took some searching, but Bauer finally located a gunsmith
in a small street just around the corner from the posh shops
of the Drottning Gatan. The smith was an ancient, white-
haired Swede with a hunchback's stoop and a hearing problem.

"You speak English?" Bauer yelled.

The old man nodded patiently. "Yes, yes. What can I do
for you?"

Bauer diassembled his cane and showed the old man the
breech and the disabled firing mechanism. "I need a new
firing pin," he said. "Can you make one for me?"

The old man took up the cane and examined it with great
interest. "Nice piece of work," he cried, looking Bauer over
with crafty admiration. "Needs a firing pin, though."

Bauer smiled. "Can you make one?" he yelled.

"Of course I can make one."

"*Will* you make one?"

"That depends. How soon do you need it?"

Bauer held up his hand with three raised fingers. "In three hours."

"Three days? That doesn't give me much time, son."

"Three hours!"

The old man scratched his grizzled chin and after some thought shook his head.

Bauer pulled out the roll of krona banknotes and counted off fifty of them. "Three hours!" he repeated.

"What's the hurry?"

"I've got to kill somebody with it. Tonight!"

The old man cackled. He eyed the pile of banknotes, then examined the cane again, scratching his chin harder than ever. "You come back in two hours," he said. "I'll have it fixed."

Back out on the Drottning Gatan, Bauer felt his confidence returning. He could still do it, he thought. He checked his watch. Just 11:30. Seven hours to work out a new plan.

He felt a hand press lightly against his back. Startled, he whirled around, primed to defend himself.

"My, you're jumpy," Inessa said, falling into step with him. A large shopping bag swung from her side. "Like my new hat?"

Her face was partially hidden beneath a white wide-brimmed straw *chapeau*. She rested a hand on her hip, patted the crown of the hat, and smiled flirtatiously.

Bauer grinned. "Very pretty," he said. "What's in the bag?"

"Presents. Sunday is Easter, you know."

"I'd forgotten."

"And today is Good Friday. I saw a beautiful church back a few blocks. Let's go there."

He hesitated.

Inessa noticed his reluctance. "Are you Jewish? I didn't mean to offend you about Good Friday."

Bauer nodded. "But I'm not religious, anyway."

Inessa flashed him a stern look. "We Bolsheviks are supposed to be atheists, but I'm still a Catholic," she said. "What happened to your cane?"

He could hardly tell her he was getting it outfitted with a new firing pin. "The ferrule," he muttered, groping to think of something. "It worked loose. I found a shop that would repair it."

"Can you walk without it?"

Was she mocking him again? "I can manage," he replied.

The church was a narrow, dark stone edifice with a tall, graceful steeple that towered over the surrounding buildings. Inside, it was cool and dim. They stood at the back and waited for their eyes to grow accustomed to the dark. A few candles flickered near the altar. The rows of wooden pews on each side of the aisle were empty, their black hymnals lined up neatly in their racks. It suddenly struck him how military the arrangement looked—the perfect rank and file of pews and hymnals. *Onward, Christian soldiers . . .*

The last time he had been in a church was in Monterrey, Mexico, at a funeral mass for Francisco Madero. None of Madero's men had come, fearful of being identified by the Federales. Bauer remembered only a young priest and many woman in black, their lives crowded with enough grief for a hundred funerals.

Inessa knelt and crossed herself and then slipped into the back pew. Bauer, feeling awkward, removed his hat and slid in beside her. They sat in silence, letting the shadowy recesses of the church absorb their thoughts.

His main sensation, he realized, was fear. His mother had been religious. A Lutheran. She had taken him to church with her often when he was a child. His father, true to his Marxist convictions, scoffed even at the notion of a God.

Snatches of old hymns from that church in Germantown echoed faintly in his consciousness, stirring a deep sadness. Like most men, he never thought about God much. He didn't figure in his daily life, except in curse words and rare moments of extreme peril. The truth was religion made him uncomfortable. Church had been important to his mother, but what his mother had embraced he somehow feared. Maybe it was the hypocrisy that bothered him. What could a sinner like himself pray for that wasn't utter hypocrisy?

Please, God, grant me a good line of fire and a reliable weapon so that I may dispatch the atheist Lenin to his grave

*and shorten the war. Just a slight edge over my opponents,
God, that's all I ask. I can handle it from there. Amen.*

The truth was he just never had much respect for the
Supreme Being. From what he had seen of life on earth, it
was hard for him not to come to the conclusion that if God
did exist, He just didn't know what the hell He was doing.

There it was. His problem with authority again.

Inessa was on her knees, hands clasped together, forehead
resting on the back of the pew in front of her. What was she
praying for? he wondered. The success of the Bolshevik cause?

Inessa sat back against the bench and hid her face in her
hands.

"You all right?" he whispered.

She took her hands down and nodded. He thought he saw
tears on her cheeks, but in the dim light it was hard to be
sure. She picked up her purse and stood up. Bauer moved
his knees aside to let her slip past, then got up to follow her.

She retreated rapidly down the aisle, and he increased his
pace to keep up with her, stumbling along noisily on the
built-up shoe. She turned right at a break in the rows of pews
and strode hastily along the cross aisle. At the far side she
paused and glanced around the gloomy interior. Bauer caught
up with her. A large statue of the Virgin Mary loomed over
them from a high pedestal, her eyes cast down, her arms
open in a welcoming gesture.

Inessa's behavior puzzled him. "What's the matter?"

She shook her head and walked away again. A short distance along the side wall she paused by a closed door, then
opened it and stepped through. Bauer followed her. Instead
of an exit the door led into the vestry. Dozens of purple-and-
white choir robes hung from a long wooden clothespole across
one side of the narrow room. The other side was occupied by
a large, ornately carved chest. Inessa moved quickly across
the small room to another door at the far end. She grabbed
the heavy wrought-iron handle and pushed down. It was
locked. She yanked on the handle a few more times and then
dropped her arms to her sides in defeat.

Bauer stood in the middle of the vestry, waiting for her to
turn around. She didn't seem to want to. "Is it something I
said?" he tried.

She turned and confronted him. Anger distorted the soft

features of her face. She replied in English. "It's not what you said, Harry Bauer. It's what you are."

He flinched, as if struck. Beyond shock, he felt an almost tangible sense of grief.

He felt little additional surprise to see that she was pointing that small pistol of hers—the one he had examined in her pocketbook that night in the Café Adler—directly at his chest.

Captain von Planetz arrived in Stockholm on the 2:15 from Trelleborg. He had been violently seasick on the ferry crossing, and the contemplation of the ugly mission ahead of him left him nervous and hungry.

He hurried into the station, found a telephone kiosk, and put through a call to the German ambassador, Von Scheer. He explained to the ambassador why he was in Sweden, and the ambassador, in turn, told him that Lenin and his party were still in Stockholm, scheduled to leave for Haparanda on the 6:30 train. Von Scheer didn't know Lenin's present whereabouts and made it clear that he hoped never to hear of the man again. The ambassador then read Zimmermann's telegram to Von Planetz—the one instructing him to warn Lenin personally about the American assassin traveling in his party.

"He refused to see me," the ambassador complained. "But I delivered the message. I hope that it helps."

"Thank you, Excellency."

"Good luck, Captain."

Von Planetz placed another call—to Germany.

"Marthe? It's Kurt. Are you all right? . . . That's good. Yes, I know. I'm sorry, but I'll be home soon. Two days at the most. I can't tell you anything more now, but I should have very good news for you. Yes, very good news. . . . Just keep yourself well. That's the important thing. Give my love to Katrina. I love you and miss you very much. . . ."

Captain von Planetz purchased a ticket on the 6:30 train to Haparanda, and then, with four hours to wait before the train departed, he left the station to find a restaurant.

Inessa advanced toward Bauer. The pistol trembled uncertainly in her hand, but he didn't doubt she knew how to use it.

She gestured toward the chest. "Sit down, Harry. We have some things to talk about."

He pushed himself back onto the chest's marble top, folded his arms together, and watched her.

"You aren't even surprised?" Inessa demanded. She was still speaking in English. Her French accent was strong, but her command of the language was excellent.

"For what it's worth, I'm surprised as hell."

Inessa kept the barrel of the small derringer pointed dead at him, her index finger resting firmly on the trigger. "You said your cane was being fixed. Did you discover that I had disarmed it?"

"I never guessed it was you. When did you do it?"

"When you were asleep. After Zinoviev let you go. Did you try to use it?"

"Of course. That's how I found out it didn't work."

"Why are you doing this?" she demanded.

Bauer shrugged. "I'm being paid to do it."

"Vous êtes bête!" She spat the words at him.

Bauer looked down at his feet, dangling over the edge of the chest. The built-up shoe on his right foot looked suddenly ridiculous, like part of a clown costume he had forgotten to remove. "How did you get onto me?"

"The German ambassador in Stockholm gave Ilyich the information this morning—your real name, your disguise as Blum, your intentions, everything. How the ambassador knew, I cannot say. But it was decided to have you killed immediately."

"Who decided?"

"Ilyich. And Zinoviev. They wanted Morozov to do it. But I persuaded them to let me."

Bauer's eyes popped open. "You persuaded them?"

"Because I hate you. And the people behind you. I hate what you're doing. You're the enemy of everything I believe in. Why did you save my life on the ferry?"

"You need an answer to that?"

Inessa pressed her lips together, fighting to hold her emotions in check. "But you're the enemy!" she insisted.

There was probably some way to explain it, Bauer thought. But he doubted he knew the right words. "The war's the enemy," he said. "Not me."

Inessa took a step toward him. In the gloomy light her face

looked stricken. He was sure at that moment that she was going to shoot him, yet he felt powerless to defend himself. Even to move. He squeezed his arms tighter to his chest and waited. Instead of fear, he felt despair. His mission was in ruins, and so was he.

She hit him in the face with the pistol. The edge of the steel barrel caught his cheek and opened a gash. He pushed her away, but she came at him again, striking out wildly with both fists. He fended off most of the blows with his hands, but a few landed. For good measure she kicked him several times in the shins.

Her attack quickly spent itself, and gasping in rage and exhaustion, she threw the pistol onto the marble-topped chest and sank onto a pile of linen in the corner, next to the line of hanging choir robes. Bauer glanced sidelong at the pistol, just a few feet from him, but made no move toward it.

Inessa raised her head from the linen. "I don't have the cold nerve it takes to kill you," she said, her voice choked with self-loathing. "Why don't you kill me instead? Show me how you brave men do it."

Bauer picked up the derringer, popped open the cylinder, and let the bullets drop out. They clattered noisily onto the marble and rolled off in five different directions. Two fell onto the floor. "Why did you volunteer, then?"

"Haven't you guessed? Because I wanted you to have a chance to get away. Now that they know who you are and what you plan to do, you'll have no choice. I'll tell Ilyich I tried to kill you, but we struggled, and you escaped. He'll believe that." Inessa brushed her hair out of her eyes. "And then we'll be even, you and I."

"Even?"

"You saved my life. I saved yours. Even. I'll owe you nothing."

"You said Lenin just found out about me this morning?"

Inessa nodded.

"But you sabotaged my cane at least two days ago."

Inessa sat up. She plucked distractedly at the pile of clothes beneath her. "I didn't know what you were then," she said. "I was suspicious of you, that was all. And the closer I looked, the more suspect you became. You just didn't act like the others. You had no enthusiasm for our cause. You never wanted to discuss politics, or the future. And you wouldn't talk about yourself. Once I began to look for them, I saw clues everywhere. Your German was good, but you didn't act like a German. I can't explain it. But now that I know you're an American, it all fits. There's a certain careless nonchalance about you. A sort of arrogant fatalism. Germans are more rigid. And boastful. I thought that cane of yours might be a weapon, so I contrived to get a closer look at it."

"I thought all the attention meant you liked me. By God, a man can never be humble enough, can he?"

She slapped at the linen as if she were slapping him. "I *did* like you. I hoped that even if it turned out that you were sent to kill Ilyich I could stop you without exposing you. It was my idea that Zinoviev interrogate you. I told him I had reason to suspect that Blum had been spying on us. I thought that if you were an imposter, that would scare you off. But it didn't. So I had no proof that you were planning anything so dreadful. Even the cane rifle could have been innocent. I have a pistol myself, after all." She squeezed her hands together in her lap and looked down at them. "But this morning the German ambassador removed all doubt. . . ."

She began to sob violently. The tears welled out of her in a sudden flood of passionate sorrow. He slid off the chest and knelt at her side, feeling stupid and helpless. "Look," he said, "it's an act of war. Lenin is in league with the Germans. The Allies have good reason to stop him. You have to understand that. It's not personal. It's the war."

"Why did you save me?" she wailed. "It would have been better if I'd drowned. Then I'd never have to be grateful to you. Or care about you. My God, how I hate you!"

Bauer sat back on the floor. "I'm the one who ought to be doing the hating. You've sabotaged my last chance."

Inessa pressed her face into the linen.

"What's so great about this Lenin?" he demanded. "What do you all see in him?"

Inessa wiped her eyes with one of the choir robes. "You couldn't begin to understand."

"You mean you can't explain it."

"He has a vision of a society where men are truly equal. A world without injustice. And he knows what has to be done to achieve it. I believe in him. I believe we Bolsheviks can make a better world."

"The Russian people just threw out the czar. Why can't Lenin and the rest of you Bolsheviks just go back and help the new government?"

Inessa laughed scornfully. "They're corrupt."

"Who isn't these days?"

"You don't understand Europe. You don't see the evil of the present system."

"I see evil everywhere I look. I see it in Germany, in England, and in my own country. And I see it in Lenin as well. He's an absolutist, a fanatic—convinced that he's right and the world's wrong. That kind of man should never govern anything."

"That's slanderous and idiotic! What do you know about suffering? About abuse of power?"

"Quite a lot. I've seen it firsthand. In Mexico, among other places. I saw it in the dictator Díaz. He was a tyrant. Corrupt, brutal. The people finally got up the courage to throw him out. But nothing changed. No reforms, no end to injustice. No improvement in the lives of the people. Just an endless merry-go-round of plunder and death. That's what Lenin will bring to Russia. Fanatics believe only in themselves."

"Ilyich is not some illiterate peasant on horseback."

"He's all the more dangerous then."

Inessa sat up and pushed her hair back with a violent shove. "You know nothing about him. Everything you say is ignorant presumption, a pathetic attempt to justify what you came here to do."

Bauer shrugged. "Didn't you tell me he decided to have me killed?"

"He's entitled to defend himself!"

Bauer pushed himself up from the floor and sat down on the top of the chest again. "Are you that close to him?"

She sighed. A faint amber light from the small stained glass window behind the chest fell across her face. "We were lovers," she said.

Bauer's mouth dropped open. The idea of the two of them together—that ugly little egomaniac and this beautiful French woman—seemed so improbable. But she was right. He knew nothing about the man. And not much more about her. Ignorant presumption.

"We're not lovers anymore, but we're still close. He depends on me for various things. Our relationship is complicated."

"Why did you stop being lovers?"

Inessa didn't answer for a moment. "I suppose I gradually just lost interest in him that way. I love him differently now."

"You don't sleep with him anymore?"

"No."

"Why?"

"Because I don't love him like that anymore. But don't misunderstand. I'd give my life for him."

"Does he still want you? As a lover?"

Inessa was silent.

"I guess it's none of my business."

"He does. Yes."

"What about his wife?"

"Nadya? She suffers. Ilyich is a difficult man to live with, and their circumstances have been very bad. He's frequently in a rage. But she's patient and giving. Very self-sacrificing. She suffers in silence and sticks by him. I'm very fond of her."

"Isn't she jealous of you?"

"No. We're good friends."

Bauer touched the spot where Inessa had struck him with the pistol. He felt a warm stickiness.

Inessa raised herself from the pile of linen and stepped over beside him to examine the wound. "You've bled a little," she said. "I'm sorry I hit you."

He pushed her hand away.

She stepped back and looked at him. "You're the one who's jealous, aren't you?"

"Of what?"

"Of Ilyich. Because we were lovers."

"That's ridiculous."

Inessa smiled. "You're acting jealous."

"I don't like it, but I'm not jealous. We aren't lovers."

"We might have been."

"Why? You hate everything I stand for, remember?"

"I hate what you're doing," she replied. She slipped her

arms around Bauer's waist and leaned against him. "I don't know what you stand for. Tell me."

Bauer stiffened. "I don't stand for anything. I'm who I am, that's all."

"And who is that? Until a few minutes ago you were pretending to be a Swiss named Oskar Blum."

Why did the question seem to threaten him so? Who he was was something he took for granted. He didn't have to stand for anything, believe in anything, or explain anything.

"What do you love?" Inessa persisted. "Your work? Your country? What?"

She waited. He could feel the warmth of her arm, still around his waist. He studied the floor.

"You're thinking of something. Tell me what it is."

"You'll laugh."

"No. I promise."

"Baseball."

Inessa frowned in confusion. "What in the world is that?"

"A sport. A game. I used to play it. When I was a kid in my twenties, I played professionally. In the major leagues. Got paid for it. Not much, but I'd have done it for nothing, come to that."

Inessa broke her promise and laughed. "I can't believe you. Sports are for schoolboys. Why did you like this 'baseball' so much?"

"Because I was good at it. And because it was something a man could do in his life that didn't hurt somebody else. It was innocent and it was fun. People paid to come see you play, and they cheered you on. It made you feel good, knowing that you were able to do something that lifted their spirits. And there was that feeling of being part of a team that played well. Maybe it was a little like your ball at the Winter Palace."

Bauer paused. He felt suddenly hollowed out inside. Christ, he thought, that was the truth. That was all there was in his life that he could speak of with pride and fondness. It astonished him and frightened him at the same time. "Not much to stand for," he muttered. "But it's all I can think of."

"Were you a great star?"

Bauer braced his hands on the edge of the chest's marble top and leaned forward. "I could have been. But I only got to play two seasons. I gave the owner of my team a hard time, so he fired me. I was a dumb, hotheaded kid. I pushed too hard to get more money out of him, and when I didn't get it, I started raising hell—on the field and off. I was my own worst enemy. I couldn't get a job in professional baseball after that. The owners blackballed me."

"Sounds to me as if the owner exploited you for his own profit, then callously discarded you when it suited him. You were a victim of capitalist greed."

"I guess it could seem that way. But it was his team. I could have started my own team if I'd had the money."

Bauer turned his head slightly, so he could see Inessa's face. She placed her hands gently on his cheeks. "You're quite a different person when you talk about your sport. Do you know that?"

"It was all a long time ago," he said, feeling suddenly foolish for having confided so much. "It doesn't mean anything anymore."

He felt Inessa's fingers tighten in his hair. She pulled herself closer, squeezing between his legs. "I'm sorry," she whispered, her mouth next to his ear.

"Why?"

"Because you didn't get to do what would have made you happy."

Bauer's mouth was dry. He swallowed and licked his lips. The pressure of her hips against the inside of his thighs inflamed him to the point of making him slightly dizzy.

"Here?" he said. "In church?"

"It's the only chance we'll ever have."

Her hands stroked his neck and behind his ears with gentle caresses. His face was burning. He felt like a bumbling adolescent. He grabbed her wrists to hold her hands still.

She looked disappointed. "You don't want to?"

"I want to, but . . . you're not the kind of woman I'm used to," he mumbled.

"Nor are you the kind of man."

She kissed the cut on his cheek, then moved to his lips and pressed herself against him. Bauer wrapped his arms around her and kissed her back. He realized that he had spent his life making love to girls. Even his wife. They had both been so young and inexperienced. But Inessa was a woman. He wasn't sure he had ever made love to a woman before.

They fell onto the pile of linen, Bauer tugging roughly at her clothes, like an anxious teenager afraid of being caught. Inessa coaxed him to slow down.

"Somebody'll come in," he whispered.

"Then lock the door."

"There's no lock on the damn thing."

"Then what do we care?"

He let out a ragged breath and then laughed. Of course, she was right.

At the height of her passion, Inessa bit his shoulder and raked her nails down his back hard enough to draw blood. So intense was his own pleasure that he only noticed later, when they were lying beside each other. He rubbed his shoulder tentatively. "First you point a gun at me," he said, "then hit me in the face with it, and now this. . . ."

"So you'll remember me," she said, helping him slip his shirt back on.

Bauer rose unsteadily to his feet and struggled back into his pants. "I need a drink."

He tried the doors of the cabinet in the corner and found a collection of silver goblets and a decanter of red wine used for communion. He took the decanter and two goblets, filled them, and knelt down beside Inessa again.

"What do we drink to?" he asked, handing her a goblet.

"To Good Friday. Our Good Friday."

They touched the rims of the goblets together and tasted the wine.

"You make a toast," Inessa said.

"I'm no good at it."

"Try. Whatever comes into your head."

"Okay. Here's to baseball in the summertime. And grand balls in the wintertime."

"I like that."

They drank and Inessa kissed him. He thought of another toast. "Here's to our short love affair."

"And to our long memories," she added.

Bauer placed the decanter on the chest above him. They looked at each other in silence for a long time. "I'm not a romantic," he confessed. "I'd rather see you grow old."

Inessa laughed. "You are a romantic. You expect the impossible."

"You're the one who wants to change the world. I just want to get by in it more or less the way it is."

Inessa slipped her undergarments over her legs and knelt to pull them back over her thighs. He picked up her derringer and gathered together the scattered shells while she straightened her garments. He looked at the revolver and the five bullets and then at Inessa. He loaded four of them back into the cylinder, closed it, spun it, and handed the loaded revolver back to her. Inessa replaced it in her bag without a word.

"I'll keep this one," he said, holding up the fifth bullet. "As a souvenir."

She pointed to her eye. "Hit me here. So it'll show."

"Why?"

"We struggled. You hit me. You got away."

"I can't do it."

"You must."

Bauer pulled her to him and kissed her fiercely, biting her lip and drawing blood. Inessa cried out and clapped a hand to her wounded mouth.

"Tell them I hit you there."

Inessa nodded, tears in her eyes, and wiped some of the blood on her blouse.

"I'm sorry if it hurt. . . ."

Inessa smiled. "That'll be my souvenir. You'd better go."

Bauer didn't argue. "I'll find you," he promised. "After the war."

HAPARANDA, SWEDEN

Mitya woke up and pushed himself to a sitting position. It took him several minutes to remember where he was. Gradually, through his drug-clogged brain, some details wavered into focus. He was across the border. In Sweden. He remembered killing a guard on the Finnish side. Maybe it had been two guards.

He was fully dressed. He usually slept that way. Sometimes he took off his boots.

He staggered to his feet and swept aside the length of

hopsacking that covered the attic window and peered outside. Daylight. A wide street. Black buildings. White snow. Endless white snow. A yellow-and-pink horizon. Blue sky.

The clock tower on a nearby church was just visible near the corner of the window. The hands were at three o'clock.

Hours yet.

He felt inside his tunic for the pistol, pulled it out, and placed it on the bedding beside him. From another pocket he removed the photograph of Lenin that Colonel Nikitin had given him. He smoothed out the accumulation of wrinkles it had collected, wiped off a smudge with his sleeve, and stared at it for a long time. He picked up the pistol, pointed the barrel at Lenin's head, made a "Pow! Pow!" sound with his mouth, and laughed out loud.

Later he returned the pistol and the photo to his pockets and went downstairs to the bar. He bought a bottle of vodka, brought it back to his room, and drank it. The next time he looked at the clock across the street it was dark and the hands were at eight o'clock. He flopped out flat across the bed, lit his opium pipe, and smoked it quietly.

Hours yet.

STOCKHOLM

Bauer found himself back out on the Drottning Gatan. It was midafternoon, and the sidewalk was crowded with pedestrians leaving work early for the long Easter weekend. The sun was bright, and a brisk wind tugged at hats and coats. Trolleys squealed in their tracks, motorcars honked horns and dodged past plodding horse carts and bicycles. Like Zurich, Stockholm was untouched by the war.

He found a bench in front of a cigar store and dropped down on it, to contemplate his predicament.

He'd had five days to kill Lenin, and he hadn't done it. What he'd done instead was disgrace himself. He had been twice beaten up by Lenin's bodyguard, had his cover blown and his cleverly concealed cane-rifle disabled by Lenin's former lover. And if she hadn't taken pity on him, she would have capped his misadventure by shooting him.

And to complete the circus of unfortunate events, he was

in love with the damned woman. Even though he would almost certainly never see her again.

It was easily the most wretched performance of his career.

Good Friday, hell, he thought miserably. It was Friday the thirteenth, 1917. Another unlucky day in an unlucky life.

He considered the prospects of trying to continue the mission. Without a cover, without a plan, and with Lenin and his party fully alerted and ready to kill him on sight, it seemed hopeless.

On the other hand, he was still free, conscious, and able to put one foot in front of the other.

That reminded him. He glanced down at the built-up shoe that he had been stumbling around on for the past five days. The uneven gate it had forced on him had made the thigh and calf muscles of his right leg sore. He propped the shoe on his knee, pried off the heel with his pocketknife, and threw it out into the street.

The heel bounced against the side of a trolley track and rolled back across the cobblestones toward Bauer, coming to rest in the gutter. A horse stepped on it and flattened it out.

He tested the shoes. They still felt uncomfortable. He pulled the heel off the other shoe to even them up, but that made him feel like he was walking uphill. He'd have to invest in a new pair.

He found a shoe store a block away and purchased a pair of cheap black work shoes. Coming out of the shop, he caught sight of one of the Russians in Lenin's party. He was standing in front of a clothing store across the street, with his hands in his coat pocket and his black derby pulled low over his forehead. Bauer couldn't recall his name. Was he following him? The whole crowd was loose in Stockholm for the afternoon, so seeing one of them wasn't in itself a cause for suspicion.

But of course the man was following him. Why should Lenin entrust the job of getting rid of him solely to Inessa? He was a thorough man. He'd send out backups.

Bauer checked his pocket watch: 2:45. He suddenly felt as if he hadn't eaten in days. He found a smorgasbord restaurant a short distance away, ate a big plate of sliced ham and mutton with potato salad and beets, washed it down with three bottles of beer, and returned to the gunsmith's.

"You come back too early!" the old man hollered. "Not ready yet!"

Bauer laughed. He was sure that at least a year had passed since this morning. "Never mind the cane," he said.

It took several minutes to make the old man understand that he had changed his mind. "You keep the damned thing," he hollered, touching the cane, still locked in a vise on the old man's workbench. "It's a gift. Me to you."

Bauer went to the front of the shop and picked out a Model 1910 Mauser automatic pistol from one of the display cases. It was small, lightweight, and flat—easy to conceal. What it gave up to a revolver in accuracy it compensated for with its ten-round magazine.

He bought the pistol and a box of shells with the remaining fifty krona Platten had given him.

The old man grinned at him, showing a mouthful of yellowed teeth. "You not limping anymore."

"No." Bauer broke open the box of bullets and filled the clip. He slid the magazine into the Mauser's walnut-covered grip, jacked a round into the chamber, checked that the safety was on, and slipped the weapon into a side pocket. "Thanks," he said.

Outside, the Russian in the black derby was still with him. He was standing with his back to him, pretending to study the displays in a store window across the street. He had positioned himself so that he could watch Bauer in the reflection of the store's glass.

The Russian followed him back to the railroad station, and watched from a distance as Bauer bought a ticket and boarded a four o'clock train headed back south the way he had come—to Malmo, Trelleborg, and the ferry to Germany.

Captain von Planetz returned to Stockholm's central station at 6:15, found the 6:30 train to Haparanda and boarded it. Lenin's party, he discovered, was already on board. He caught Fritz Platten emerging from a first-class compartment near the front of the train. The young Swiss was astonished to see him.

"What on earth are you doing here, Captain?"

"Good evening. The German ambassador has warned you about Blum?"

Platten sighed extravagantly. "Yes. If you want me to admit

that you were right about Blum and I was wrong, then I freely admit it, Captain. You've been a veritable Sherlock Holmes. Blum was an imposter after all. And we have taken matters into our own hands, thank you."

The captain tilted his head questioningly. "Your own hands? What do you mean?"

"Blum—or Bauer—no longer poses a threat to Ilyich."

"Why?"

"Because he is no longer with us."

"Where is he?"

Platten offered the captain another of his irritatingly coy smiles. "He's gone. Vanished. I don't know where. But he's no longer on the train. You can check that for yourself, of course. I assume that's why you're here. You are a remarkably persistent individual, Captain."

"Do you mind if I ask you how you know Bauer is no longer a threat?"

"We drove him away ourselves," Platten bragged, tapping his own chest immodestly. "We sent Inessa Armand to kill him. She failed, but she scared him away. He knows that we're onto him now. Boitzow followed him through Stockholm all day. He saw him take the train south to Malmo several hours ago."

"I see."

Platten touched the rim of his fedora to dismiss himself from the German's presence. "So you can relax, Herr Police Inspector, and just enjoy the trip to Haparanda. Or better yet, get off now and return to where you came from. Berlin, wasn't it?"

The captain nodded wordlessly and watched the Swiss walk away from him toward the front of the carriage. If what Platten had just told him was true, he thought, it was a great relief. He walked back to second class, opened a compartment door, and settled onto a seat next to an elderly missionary priest and a grizzled fur trader who reeked of beer.

If it was true.

Vice-Consul P.T. Berg stood just inside the platform gate, clutching a small overnight bag and watching the passengers as they filed through to board the several coaches and sleepers that made up the Haparanda train.

At 6:25 he heard the bell announcing the final call for boarding. He waited a few minutes longer, his eyes searching the emptying platform. Finally, satisfied that he was the last one to board, he climbed up the steps of the rear coach and took a seat in the first compartment up.

He had memorized the physical description of Harry Bauer that House had provided him, and he was certain that the man had not boarded the train.

That left Berg no choice but to stay with Lenin. If Bauer still intended to kill him, he'd have to show himself sometime, somewhere. And Berg intended to be there when he did.

At precisely 6:30 the train pulled out of Stockholm's Central Bangard and began the long overnight run up along the western shore of the Gulf of Bothnia. In twenty-four hours it would reach its terminus at Haparanda, on the Tornio River, which marked Sweden's frontier with the Russian Grand Duchy of Finland.

SATURDAY
APRIL 14

HAPARANDA

A fat man ambled into the saloon, paused inside the door and looked around. Conversation stopped as every eye turned to inspect him. He wore a thick Russian fur cap and an expensive sable fur coat that reached to the ankle tops of an equally luxurious pair of boots. His gloved hand gripped a gold-headed walking stick.

He purchased a bottle of brandy at the bar, picked up two glasses, and waddled directly toward a table at the back. Another patron, a British Army lieutenant, was already seated there, nursing a mug of beer. He was pale-faced and skinny, with sharp cheekbones and a pointed nose. His dark eyes were sullen, and his lips, pressed tight together under his neatly trimmed toothbrush moustache, suggested that he thought a good deal of himself.

"*Guten abend*, Lieutenant Chase," the fat man said. "My name is Alexander Helphand." He settled the bottle and the glasses onto the table. "But my friends and associates call me Parvus. Please call me Parvus."

Lieutenant Chase rotated the mug of beer between his fingers. A man of gross appetites and the money to satisfy them, he guessed. And many miles from home. "Sit down, then, Mr. Parvus."

Parvus straddled the chair and lowered his bulk cautiously onto the seat. Puffing hard from the exertion of his walk, he removed his fur cap and placed it on the table next to his walking stick. He shrugged out of the sable coat and hung it over the back of the chair. Several feet of it dragged on the dirty sawdust floor, but he didn't seem to care. His suit testified to the same extravagant taste as the sable.

Parvus uncorked the brandy, filled both glasses, and pushed one toward Chase. The lieutenant was still taking in his visitor. The fat man's hair was sparse and brushed straight back across a white dome. His eyes were ice blue and gazed out at the world from under bulging sockets of flesh. His bloated hands sported several rings, and his fingernails were manicured.

Chase had expected someone more like a Liverpool pickpocket—lean, small-minded, and scruffy. Parvus's opulent presence was intimidating.

"*Skoal*," the Dane said, and drank the brandy off without waiting for Chase to join him. He lowered his glass onto the table with a heavy thud. "What a long and tedious journey I have just endured. I never guessed the end of the earth was quite this far away."

Chase picked up the bottle Parvus had brought and tilted the label toward the light. "Courvoisier. Good brandy."

"I can afford good brandy, Lieutenant. I am a rich man."

Chase laughed. "What the bloody hell are you doing up here, then?"

Parvus smiled indulgently. "I came here to make you a rich man, too, Lieutenant."

The English officer shook his head in confusion. He waited for Parvus to elaborate.

The Dane adjusted his weight on the narrow saloon chair. It squeaked sharply under the stress. "An important party of Russians will be crossing the border here tonight."

"I know all about that, Mr. Parvus."

"Ah? And what precisely do you know?"

"London has sent me orders."

"And what orders are those?"

"I can't tell you."

Parvus sighed deeply. "I expected we could establish a working relationship, Lieutenant. Mutual trust. I'm frankly very disappointed by your attitude."

"We're on the lookout for an American," the lieutenant replied, almost apologetically.

"Why?"

"We're supposed to detain him. That's all I know."

Parvus wagged his hand back and forth, as if to brush the subject from the table. "There will be no American. It's of no importance." He leaned forward and spoke in an intense whisper. "This party will be carrying a great sum of money with them. That's what's important. Twelve million Swedish krona. I know this because I personally gave them this money in Stockholm yesterday."

The lieutenant was utterly dumbfounded by this revelation. "Why did you do that?" he asked.

"I was acting as an intermediary between their leader, Mr. Lenin, and the German government. I put up that money myself, you see. It's mine."

"Germany will be paying you back, then?"

Parvus pulled a handkerchief from his lapel pocket and dabbed at the perspiration accumulating on his brow. "I don't trust the Germans anymore."

The English officer tilted his head in a sly grin. "So you're hoping we'll confiscate it for you at customs."

Parvus folded the handkerchief carefully and tucked it back into his pocket. "That is precisely what I hope, Lieutenant. And for that service I am prepared to offer you a finder's fee of ten percent. That's one million, two hundred thousand krona. A hundred thousand English pounds. An enormous sum, you'll agree."

Chase affected not to be impressed. "What's to prevent me from taking it all?"

"Your British sense of fair play." Parvus flashed his gold teeth. "And your fear of the consequences if I report you to the appropriate authorities."

Chase scratched his nose, thinking it over. "You know where the money will be?"

"No. Only that it'll be well hidden."

"Nobody can sneak twelve million krona past us."

The Dane rubbed his palms together in a washing motion and looked around the room for possible eavesdroppers. "Lenin and his traveling companions are very practiced smugglers, Lieutenant. With the help of certain businessmen in

Stockholm, the Bolsheviks have been using the Haparanda-Tornio crossing for years. They smuggle everything—correspondence, printed propaganda, money. And in both directions. They're experienced. And they're successful."

Chase wondered if Parvus himself wasn't one of these businessmen. It fit. The man looked like a living advertisement for illegal profiteering.

Parvus drank more brandy. He had the unattractive habit of rinsing the liquid around the inside of his mouth, as if it were a mouthwash. Waiting for him to continue, Chase half expected him to spit it out on the floor.

"Lenin knows that when they reach the border, they'll all be searched," Parvus said. "He knows that the Russian guards often strip the men naked, but not the women. The guards are reluctant to strip-search a woman—unless perhaps she is alone, in which case they do more than just remove her clothes." Parvus chuckled. "This has happened. But in the presence of others, they don't take liberties with the women. Lenin counts on this. He's been using women as couriers for years. In his party tonight there are at least five women. He will probably divide up the money among them on the train, and tell them to hide it in their undergarments. If you don't find it elsewhere, that's where you must be certain to look. You must confiscate it all."

"I don't know," Chase said, losing some of his earlier bravado. "It sounds risky. Too many people will know about it. I don't think I can do it."

The Dane leaned forward, pressing his stomach against the edge of the table. "Look, my friend. I'm taking risks too. I'm a resident of Germany, and I'm defying the German government. If I'm discovered, I'll be shot. But I'm willing to take that risk because I must get back this money. For you, it's a windfall. You have nothing to lose by rescuing my money. You're obligated to confiscate it, in fact, to uphold the law. And you have everything to gain. Everything! Think what you could do with all that money. You'll be rich! You'll be able to own houses and motorcars. To travel. Entertain and impress beautiful women. After the war you'll never have to work for anyone, again, ever. You'll never get another opportunity like this. This is your one chance to step out of your class. To become someone important, someone substantial. Don't you see that?"

"I need time to consider it," Chase said.

The Dane threw out his hands. "Of course. How long would you like? An hour?"

Chase shrugged. "Well . . ."

"I'll give you two. I plan to take the train back to Stockholm at nine."

"Where will I reach you?"

"I'll be right here. Until nine."

The officer drained the brandy from his glass and got up to leave. The Dane laid his big paw on the Englishman's arm as he walked past. "Don't think of double-crossing me, Mr. Chase. I have many more friends in this part of the world than you do. And I can afford to pay them to do almost anything for me. Do you understand?"

The lieutenant understood.

THE TRAIN

Captain von Planetz leaned on the window railing in the corridor just outside Inessa Armand's compartment and waited patiently. It was late Saturday morning, nearly sixteen hours north from Stockholm, and the greening fields of southern Sweden were giving way to vast and gloomy stretches of evergreen forest, still buried deep in snow.

The captain waited two hours. Finally, around noon, Inessa Armand emerged, on her way to the dining car.

He removed his officer's cap and made a courtly bow. Inessa paused and glanced at him questioningly. He cleared his throat. "I'm Captain Kurt von Planetz, madam. I'm sorry to intrude on you, but I would be grateful if I could speak to you in private."

Inessa smiled. "Aren't you the captain who protected us through Germany?" She gave the word "protected" an ironic little spin.

The captain blushed. "Yes, madam."

"What in the world are doing on this train?"

"I will explain that, madam, if I might take the liberty of asking you a few questions."

Inessa measured him with her eyes. "What about?"

"Herr Bauer, madam."

Inessa hesitated, then nodded. "Of course."

"Thank you, madam. There's an empty compartment in the next coach back. If you'd be so kind . . ."

Inessa let the captain escort her back. "It's third class, madam," he said, gesturing her to a seat on the bare wooden bench. "I apologize. . . ."

"Oh, for Heaven's sake, Captain, stop being so polite. And stop calling me 'madam.' I'm Miss Armand."

The captain bowed. "I'm sorry. Miss Armand." He had always been such an awkward fool in the presence of attractive women. He never really understood why Marthe, a woman of surpassing charm and beauty, had ever consented to marry him. It was one of those rare gifts in his life for which he was endlessly grateful. "I'll come directly to the point," he said. "I was told by Fritz Platten that you met with Herr Bauer in Stockholm."

"Yes. When the German ambassador delivered Zimmermann's note, we decided we must act at once, before he got to Ilyich. I volunteered because I thought it would be easiest for me to get close to him. He wouldn't suspect me."

"What did you intend to do?"

"Kill him, of course."

Von Planetz blanched. On the lips of such a refined woman, the words seemed jarring. "May I inquire how you were going to do it?"

Inessa opened her purse and withdrew her derringer. "With this," she said, pointing it playfully at the captain. "I lured him into the vestry of a church. I tried to kill him there, but he was faster and stronger than I realized. I fired a shot, but it missed him. We struggled, he hit me and then ran off." Inessa pointed to her lip. "He knocked me down."

The captain bent forward to look more closely at the red marks just below her lip. He could smell her perfume, and it made his heart race. "Did you let him know that you were aware of what he was up to?"

"Yes. I'm afraid that's what gave him the time he needed to hit me and get away." Inessa crossed her legs and casually rocked the top one back and forth, the quintessence of calm self-possession. "I was quite nervous, of course."

"Of course. May I examine your revolver?"

Inessa handed the derringer to the captain. He snapped the revolving cylinder out and noted that one of the six chambers was empty. He held the barrel up to his eye and sighted through it. Satisfied, he clicked the cylinder into place again and handed the derringer back. He rubbed his chin thoughtfully. He wanted a cigarette but resisted the impulse.

"Is that all, then, Captain?"

"Herr Bauer saved your life on the ferry, I understand."

Inessa stopped her leg rocking. "Well, he caught my arm once when I slipped on the ship's deck. I wouldn't say he actually saved my life."

"Did you spend a lot of time with him?"

A hint of hostility crept into her tone. "What do you mean."

"Pardon me for pressing the issue, but during the trip I believe you were often seen talking to him."

She laughed dismissively. "Well, of course. I told you. I was suspicious of him. Something about his accent, and the way he behaved. He was very clever, Captain. He never slipped up. Even when I confronted him with the truth in the church, he didn't admit anything."

"I see."

"Why are you interrogating me like this, Captain?" Inessa asked. Her voice was sweet and chiding, betraying no evidence of guilt.

"Again I apologize, Miss Armand. I must make a report of the matter to my government."

"Of course."

"Do you have any idea where Bauer might have gone when he ran out of the church?"

"No. Absolutely none, I'm afraid."

"You're quite sure?"

"Of course. Wouldn't I tell you if I did?"

"I retract the question, Miss Armand."

Inessa smiled. "At least he's gone, thank God. He no longer poses a threat to Ilyich, that's the main thing. So I don't feel that I failed entirely. I'm really glad I didn't kill him. It would have been a terrible thing to do, don't you agree? And in a church? On Good Friday?"

"A terrible thing indeed." The captain stood up and bowed.

"You've been most kind, Miss Armand. And helpful. Again, I'm sorry for this intrusion." He opened the door and escorted her out into the corridor.

Inessa lifted his hand from her arm. "I can find my way back, Captain. Thank you."

Von Planetz returned to the compartment, sat down heavily, and immediately lit a cigarette. She had lied to him. Cleverly and convincingly, but years of interrogating suspects had given him a sixth sense about lies. And it wasn't just subtle clues in her manner that had given her away.

The cut on her lip was from a bite, not a blow. An odd way for Bauer to attack her. And despite the empty chamber in her revolver, it had obviously not been fired recently. And she must have known that Bauer had taken the train to Malmo. He had learned from Platten that their colleague, Boitzow, had seen him and reported the matter to the others. So she must know it. Why didn't she repeat it to him?

For some reason she was protecting the American.

The captain propped his chin in a palm and gazed out the window. The forests had thinned and disappeared, replaced by barren, snow-blanketed tundra, blinding to look at in the midday sun. A beautiful sight, he thought. Pure and empty. Empty of people. Empty of events. Empty of sin. He drew the shade partway down to reduce the glare.

In about six hours they would arrive at Haparanda. He had had ample time to think about Bauer, and he felt pretty certain he had worked out the American's plan.

Bauer had taken the train to Malmo to convince Lenin's party that he was abandoning his mission. They had believed it. But Von Planetz did not.

He pulled out a Swedish train schedule he had picked up in Stockholm, and checked it one more time. If Bauer had taken the four o'clock to Malmo, as Boitzow claimed, he could have gotten off at the first stop, Elfsjo, fifteen minutes later. There he could have purchased a new ticket and boarded a 4:20 train north that would arrive in Haparanda two hours ahead of Lenin.

No longer able to travel in disguise with the party, Bauer was doing the next best thing: going on ahead and setting up an ambush. Lenin's train would reach Haparanda after dark.

And Bauer would be there, waiting, his vantage point chosen, his field of fire measured.

The captain dug his service revolver out of his bag and examined it, nervously rotating the cylinder with its six 9-millimeter bullets. The American loomed in his thoughts like something from a child's nightmare—an invisible menace, relentless and unstoppable.

"But I will stop you," the captain swore. "This time, by God, I will stop you."

HAPARANDA

Harry Bauer stepped off the train, inhaled the frigid air, and looked around him. In twenty-four hours he had traveled into another season and another world.

About half a mile to the east of the station house he could see a sprawling cluster of one- and two-story buildings, thin blue plumes of smoke leaking from their chimneys. He buttoned his coat and followed a well-worn footpath that zigzagged through the snowdrifts toward the town.

Haparanda reminded him of the American West, a rough frontier settlement with rows of weathered wooden stores and shops facing each other across a truncated hunk of street that didn't go anywhere or come from anywhere. Behind the stores a few houses huddled—many no more than one- or two-room cabins—up to their windowsills in the accumulated snows of the long northern winter.

Bauer exchanged some of Churchill's advance money from Swiss francs to Swedish krona in a saloon, and went to find a clothing goods store. He bought a woolen shirt, twill trousers, and a heavy corduroy tunic. At a fur-trading post two doors away, he purchased a secondhand fur coat, new fur hat, and fur-lined reindeer-skin gloves. At a shoemaker's across the street, he traded in his black work shoes for a pair of high leather boots with felt liners.

Back at the saloon, he ate a not very fresh fish and drank a glass of aquavit.

Thus fortified, he walked from the saloon down to the edge of the frozen Torniojoki River, for a look at the border crossing. The sun had gone, and in the waning daylight the temperature had begun to drop. He pulled the collar of his newly acquired fur coat up tight around his neck.

A long plank footbridge spanned the mouth of the river, just before it widened into the Gulf of Bothnia. The pressure of the ice had caused its high, stiltlike pilings to tilt at crazy angles. At the near end of the bridge a small cabin stood imprisoned behind a high rail fence with a sliding gate. A flag on a short pole near the hut snapped briskly in the chill wind.

Swedish customs, he guessed. At the bridge's far end, he could see another cabin with a fence around it. Finland.

The footbridge was lit at sparse intervals with electric light fixtures suspended from steel poles like city streetlamps. The yards around the customs houses at both ends were lit as well. Bauer could hear the big flywheel on the gasoline-powered generator that supplied the power thumping rhythmically somewhere in the distance, like a giant beating heart.

The footsteps of a solitary guard crunched the snow on the Swedish side of the bridge. A short distance away, dozens of pallets, stacked high with wooden crates, sat waiting to be transported across the river.

Bauer checked his pocket watch. Ten after six. Lenin's train was due in twenty minutes. He took a last careful look at the border crossing and then walked back to the railroad station, on the other side of town.

He wondered how Lenin and his party would get across the border. The Haparanda station was at least half a mile from the Swedish end of the footbridge, and on the Finland side the Tornio station might be even farther. And traversing the long, precariously tilting footbridge at night in the cold and snow would be difficult and dangerous.

The answer was at the station. Eight horse-drawn sledges— low, flat wood frames mounted on pairs of metal runners, like an overgrown version of a child's sled—were parked in a ragged line alongside the duckboard platform, waiting for the train. The horses shook their bridles and pawed the ground restively. The drivers leaned against the station wall, smoking and talking in low voices.

Bauer noticed somebody else waiting. He looked faintly Arab, with dark skin and a thick black cossack-style moustache. His fur hat sat askew on his head, and his big sheepskin coat was unbuttoned. He paced back and forth alongside the track, his boots crunching noisily in the snow. Once he slipped and fell. Drunk, Bauer guessed. Almost everybody he had seen since his arrival was drunk. It was the only way the town got through the winter, someone in the saloon had told him.

Looking for a place to hide, Bauer stepped into the shadows around the corner of the station house and found a stack of firewood for the station's big potbellied stove piled against the side wall. The pile was about five feet high and extended out from the side of the building a distance of four feet. Enough to hide him from the platform.

He crouched down and carefully jiggled loose a single log from the middle of the pile. Through the small opening this created, he had a narrow but adequate view of the platform directly in front of the station.

He sat down, dug the pistol from his inside coat pocket, checked the clip, and practiced steadying the weapon in the aperture between the logs. It worked well. He could grip the pistol with both hands, steady it by resting the butt on a log, and still have sufficient space left to see through the hole to aim the weapon.

Thirty feet, he estimated, from woodpile to train. Marginal for a pistol at night. But he had a dozen bullets to spend.

He practiced zeroing in the sight by training it on the drunken Arab, still weaving back and forth along the platform.

Abruptly the drunk stopped. The sledge drivers lifted their heads. Bauer heard it then, too—the high, thin shrill of a distant train whistle.

Captain von Planetz walked through the train to the front car and, when no one was looking, quickly opened the forward door and slipped through to the small outside platform between the carriage and the black iron wall of the coal tender.

He buttoned his great coat against the wind and swung out onto the first rung of the steel ladder bolted to the end of the carriage. The noise and motion of the train over the track, and the billows of black smoke and sparks that swirled around him, made progress slow and dangerous.

When he reached the top rung, he was able to see over the tender and locomotive to the track ahead. Shielding his face from the wind and flying sparks from the smokestack, he could just make out a blurred pool of light glowing in the darkness about half a mile ahead.

Haparanda station.

He stepped down a rung to get behind the protection of the back wall of the tender and waited. He felt the train beginning to slow. An ear-piercing blast from the steam whistle nearly caused him to lose his hold.

When the train had slowed to a crawl, the captain stepped back up for another look.

He saw the horse-drawn sledges first, and their drivers clustered in front of them. About a dozen men. Out on the platform a solitary figure paced restlessly.

The train rolled abreast of the platform. The individual out on the platform started to walk alongside the train, keeping step with it. His movements were unsteady, like a drunk. Bauer? The captain studied the sledge drivers. Nothing suspicious there. None of them moved toward the train. He hooded his eyes and peered into the shadows around the station. No one else was visible.

The engine rolled into the shadows past the platform and braked to a stop. Von Planetz climbed down the ladder and hopped off. He jogged alongside the carriages, his eyes moving back and forth between the sledge drivers and the man on the platform.

The figure on the platform noticed him and stopped. His long coat hung open in front and his hands were plunged deep into the coat's side pockets. Odd behavior. Drunk for certain.

The engine crawled past the station house, wheezing and clanking as if exhausted from its twenty-four-hour run from the south. Behind the engine the tender lumbered past, with its high black shields, and then several freight cars. The passenger carriages creaked in last, three of them, their windows encrusted with white frost.

The door at the back of the first carriage opened. Bauer saw the conductor standing at the top of the steps, peering out at the platform. The stationmaster appeared, handed the conductor several packages, and after a short exchange of words, hurried back to the warmth of the station house.

The conductor disposed of the packages inside the carriage, then stepped cautiously down the ice-coated steps. Once on the ground, he turned and held out his hand to help down the passengers, already crowding onto the steps above him.

Bauer slowly pushed the pistol's safety lever up to the "off" position. He crouched down to line his eye up with the sight.

Grigory Zinoviev came out first, with his wife, Zina, and their son, Stepan. He headed immediately for the clutch of sledge drivers waiting by the station door and shouted at them to help with the passengers' baggage.

Fritz Platten followed, then Olga Ravich, looking far more subdued than she had been at the beginning of the journey five days ago. Next came an excited group of six or seven. They crowded eagerly in the doorway, talking animatedly. Bauer recognized them from the earlier days of the trip, but could remember the names of only three of them—George Safarov and his wife, Valentina, and Lenin's wife, Nadya.

Morozov stepped off next, his disfigured face looking white as bleached bone in the glare of the station lights.

Behind Morozov Inessa appeared. Her big fur cap and the fur-trimmed ankle-length coat, with the collar raised, hid all of her but the upper half of her face. Seeing her made Bauer anxious. She, too, appeared subdued, but whether from the fatigue of the journey or more profound causes, he could only wonder.

Following her with his eyes, he momentarily lost track of the other passengers still emerging from the train. He refocused his attention on the doorway of the carriage just in time to see Lenin materialize.

He carried a small satchel. His collar was pulled up around his neck and his cap down low over his forehead. The conductor walked away from him to help one of the women carry her bags over to the sledges, leaving him isolated in the doorway.

The perfect target.

The captain stopped and retreated several steps until he was standing between the second and third carriages. He could see the man on the platform better now. He looked Arab or Mongol. Bauer in another disguise?

A door on the second carriage opened and the conductor

stepped down, handed a package to the stationmaster, said something to him, and then turned to help the passengers down.

The captain's eyes swept frantically about, from the sledge drivers to the drunk, to the shadows around and beyond the station and the train. He wished the lighting were better. He wished it were daylight. *Bauer should be here. Where was he? Please, God, don't let him surprise me now.*

He could see the passengers plainly. Zinoviev was calling the drivers over to help with the luggage. Von Planetz watched for some erratic movement, some suggestion of trouble. More passengers came off and made their way toward the sledges. Where was Lenin?

Maybe he had been wrong. Maybe Bauer planned to wait until they had moved away from the station in the sledges. But he had already waited so long. This would be the best time. Where was he?

Von Planetz moved closer to the carriage steps. No one could fire a shot without his seeing him. Except from a distance. That was possible. He had worried about that. A rifle from a distance. But he doubted Bauer had been able to get a rifle. He couldn't have concealed it.

He saw Lenin step down from the carriage.

Bauer brought the pistol sight to rest squarely on Lenin's chest. One shot, he reminded himself. And make it true.

The drunk reappeared alongside the carriage. He stepped in front of Lenin just as the Bolshevik leader took the last step onto the ground, blocking Bauer's target.

Bauer saw Lenin push his hand out and shake his head, as if to brush the drunk aside, the way one might turn away a panhandler.

The drunk was not so easily denied, however. He maintained his position in front of Lenin, blocking his path. And still blocking Bauer's aim.

Lenin shoved against his chest, but the drunk refused to let him past. Now he embraced him. One arm encircled Lenin's neck as if the drunk intended to kiss him on the cheek.

A muffled crack, no louder than a handclap.

Lenin slumped against the drunk, as if he had lost his

footing in the snow. The drunk seemed to be supporting him, holding him up. But the Russian continued to slip through his grasp toward the ground.

The drunk released him and took a step backward. Lenin, on his knees, his face down, his arms outspread in bewilderment, tilted sideways and crunched onto the snow, landing in an awkward position which he was unable to alter.

Another shot.

Bauer looked up from the slumped form of Lenin to see the drunk stagger several steps down the platform.

Two more shots, close together.

The American looked back along the platform and saw the German captain crouching beside the engine tender, pistol raised.

The drunk ran a few steps farther, swerved into the side of the carriage, pushed away from it, steadied himself momentarily, and then lost his balance. He slid down against the carriage wheels, his body squirming and twitching like that of a man attacked by bees. He started to crawl under the carriage, as if seeking protection there, and then collapsed, his body halfway across the rail.

Lenin lay flat at the foot of the carriage steps, his face buried in the snow, his arms flung out above his head. He didn't move. The German captain rushed to his side, knelt down by him to feel for a pulse in his throat, then ran toward the body of the drunk.

Bauer lowered his pistol. What was he seeing? He couldn't understand it.

Long seconds stretched out, like dying echoes, and Bauer felt his own heart racing, but the seconds boomed more slowly still. His eyes turned to the travelers gathered around the sledges. They were talking, arranging their bags and suitcases. Some had already climbed onto the sledges and found themselves seats among the piled luggage.

The shots had caused one of the horses to rear in fright, jerking the sledge it was harnessed to out of the line, spilling passengers and luggage into the snow. Another horse pawed the air with its hooves.

In the confusion someone finally broke from the crowd ran back toward Lenin.

Others followed. Several knelt down. In

circle of men obscured the fallen figure from Bauer's view. The drivers and most of the women huddled by the sledges, too stricken to move.

The tight knot around Lenin loosened, and Bauer could see him again, still in the snow, still not moving. Zinoviev, who had been kneeling over him, ran into the station to summon help. Somebody went back to the sledges to tell the others.

There was no panic. After the stunned silence that had followed the shots, an anguished murmur of voices alternately swelled and faded and then died altogether.

It's over, Bauer thought. Someone else has killed Lenin. Pressed a pistol directly against his heart and shot him. He could not possibly have failed to kill him.

Then the German captain had killed the assassin.

With bullets meant for him, Bauer knew. He pushed the pistol's safety catch back on, pocketed the weapon, and leaned his head against the stack of stovewood. He could smell the sap of the aspen, oozing from the cut ends of the still-green logs.

Lenin's dead.

It's over.

LONDON

MOST URGENT
EYES ONLY BALFOUR
FOLLOWING INFORMATION RECEIVED HERE FROM BEF
LIAISON BY TELEPHONE FROM BORDER AREA AT HAPARANDA
AT 1900 HOURS LOCAL TIME 14 APRIL. REPORT MAN SHOT
AND KILLED ON TRAIN CARRYING LENIN PARTY. ASSUME VICTIM
IS LENIN BUT POSITIVE IDENTIFICATION NOT YET AVAILABLE.
ASSASSIN ALSO KILLED. IDENTITY NOT YET KNOWN EITHER.
WILL ADVISE WHEN FURTHER INFORMATION AVAILABLE.
ESME HOWARD. STOCKHOLM
END OF DISPATCH

WASHINGTON

URGENT TOP SECRET
TO BE DECODED AT ONCE
DO NOT DISTRIBUTE
DELIVER IMMEDIATELY TO COLONEL HOUSE

MESSAGE AS FOLLOWS:

LENIN KILLED AS HE STEPPED FROM TRAIN AT
HAPARANDA—TORNIO BORDER CROSSING. INCIDENT OCCURRED
AT APPROXIMATELY 1900 HOURS LOCAL TIME. ASSASSIN SHOT
ALSO. ASSASSIN NOT REPEAT NOT BAUER. WILL KEEP
INFORMED.

BERG

END OF MESSAGE

HAPARANDA

Captain Von Planetz jammed his pistol back into his coat
pocket, grabbed the assassin's legs, and pulled him out from
under the carriage. A savage terror gripped him, squeezing
against his heart and lungs with such power that he groaned
and gasped for breath.

He had failed, God help him.

He rolled the body over and met its face. Thick black hair.
The eyes were open, black Tartar eyes, fixed like a blind
man's on some blank, invisible place.

The captain howled in anguish and clawed the face with his
hands, trying to rip off the disguise. Nothing came away. He
dug at the skin harder, raking deep furrows down across the
flesh of the cheeks. He stopped and stared at his fingers. They
were wet with blood.

He steadied his breathing. Got to hold together, he told
himself. He looked down again at his victim, willing himself
to take the time to see what was really there. The corpse was
young, unkempt. The teeth were bad, and it stank of old
sweat and cheap alcohol.

This was not Bauer. This was not the man he had pursued
across half of Europe.

Why wasn't it?

He rubbed his hands in the snow. The icy white granules
diluted the blood to a fleshy pink and then melted it away.
He dried his fingers on his trousers. He felt sick. He had
never killed a man before.

He rose unsteadily to his knees and forced himself toward
the slumped form of Lenin, obscured by a crowd of his
comrades, standing around him.

How hard they were, he thought. They treated

form of their leader with the unfeeling curiosity of onlookers at an accident. His death had not broken them, even for the moment. They seemed hardly to care. While he was choking with despair.

Bauer remained crouched behind the woodpile, watching, waiting.

A doctor arrived about half an hour after the shooting, bent down by the corpse, felt his wrist and neck, and then stood up and threw out his hands in a gesture of finality.

After the physician, a priest materialized, knelt in the snow, and began administering last rites, only to be chased off by Zinoviev.

Local police officials arrived, examined the two corpses, and retrieved the pistol from the snow that the assassin had used on his victim. They conferred at length with Zinoviev, Platten, Von Planetz, and several others. The rest of Lenin's party stayed back by the sledges, waiting.

A police ambulance arrived. It was an ancient van, and the driver had a difficult time keeping the motor running. With the help of Zinoviev, they loaded both corpses unceremoniously into the rear.

Zinoviev showed some documents to the police, and after several more lengthy conferences, the ambulance and the police officials departed.

Bauer watched the Russians climb back onto their sledges. In a few minutes they started out along the packed trail that would take them down to the frozen Torniojoki River and the bridge across to Finland.

There was no point in watching any more. Bauer straightened slowly and looked around behind him. When he was certain that no one could see him, he moved off into the darkness beyond the rear of the woodpile.

Ten minutes later he was back in the town of Haparanda. He returned to the saloon he had visited earlier and bought a bottle of vodka. Before the night was over, he intended to be too drunk to stand up.

It had all been too quick and too easy, he thought, gulping down the first raw mouthful. Lenin suddenly dead and pushed into the back of an old police van. It had all been just too damned easy. But why should he feel cheated?

Bauer's head swam with little out-of-place memories, rough-edged images that didn't quite fit into the picture of the events of the past week. They scratched against his mind, and then gradually they began to fall together into a pattern.

Why had Lenin been so subdued throughout the trip? Not like a leader. And not like the man Bauer had followed to the park in Zurich.

And why had he kept himself so hidden from view?

And why had the members of the party seemed so nonchalant about his safety?

Bauer drank more vodka. Each recalled detail triggered the recollection of other little mysteries.

Who was the other man in Lenin's compartment? The one whom Bauer had been unable to identify. The same one to whom Zinoviev seemed always to be nodding deferentially.

And tonight Bauer had witnessed the inexplicable mystery of Lenin's wife, Nadya Krupskaya, sitting placidly on the horse-drawn sledge in front of the station throughout the entire drama of her husband's violent death.

And Inessa hadn't seemed to care much, either, for the man she had told him she was willing to die for. Why had she not wept openly at Lenin's side?

Bauer poured out another tumblerful of vodka and tipped it to his lips. He clenched his teeth and shivered as the alcohol trickled down his gullet. There was a remarkably simple explanation for all those mysteries. Bauer resisted it as long as he could, but it kept coming back at him, stronger each time. He knew it fit too well to be beaten down. It had to be right. It wasn't just a good explanation. It was the only explanation.

How could he have been so thoroughly bamboozled? The same simple deception he had used to get himself aboard the sealed train to kill the Bolshevik leader had been used on him.

A decoy. A double. Someone made up to look like Lenin. Because how many people in the world knew what the son of a bitch looked like anyway?

Bauer banged his fist on the table in frustration and self-loathing. Twice he had almost shot the wrong man. The fi̲ time on the train, when Inessa had disarmed his car̲ the second time here tonight, when this crazed ̲ appeared from out of nowhere and committed Bauer's folly for him.

And paid with his life.

The American refilled his glass. In a few minutes Lenin would be across the river and into Finland, he realized. And in another day Petrograd.

It looked like he was going to lose this one, after all.

Bauer raised his head and glared across at a patron sitting by himself several tables away. The man averted his gaze. Bauer picked up his glass and the bottle of vodka and strode over to his table. The other man, nursing a glass of beer, looked up at him contemptuously. Bauer plunked the vodka bottle down on the table and held out his hand.

"The name's Harry Bauer. What's yours?"

The man's neck and jaw muscles tightened instantly. He stared at Bauer's extended hand as if it were a rattlesnake. "Beg your pardon?"

Bauer pulled out a chair and sat down. He pushed the glass full of vodka across the table and pointed at it. "Drink up," he commanded.

The man looked down at the glass and then up at Bauer. "Get the hell away from me, or I'll call the manager."

Bauer drew his pistol out of his coat pocket, showed it to his companion, then slid it under the table. "It's pointed at your crotch. Who are you?"

The man's Adam's apple jumped visibly. "Berg," he replied in a thin voice.

"American?"

Berg nodded anxiously. "Now get that gun away from me."

"What's your business?"

"I'm Vice-Consul. U.S. Embassy."

Bauer pointed at the glass under Berg's nose. "Drink up, Vice-Consul."

Berg protested again. "I'm a government official," he warned pompously. "I'm under the protection of the United States flag. You'll get yourself in a great deal of trouble this way."

Bauer grinned. "You keep talking like that, Junior, and I'll shoot you just for the fun of it. Now drink that vodka down. It's good for you."

Berg looked at the glass. Under the table Bauer slapped

the pistol barrel against his leg. The vice-consul jumped in fright, picked up the glass and sipped it.

"That's not how you drink vodka," Bauer directed. He tipped up the bottom of the tumbler with his free hand, splashing the alcohol against Berg's mouth.

What didn't dribble down his chin, the vice-consul swallowed. As soon as Bauer let him, Berg banged the glass on the table, gasping and spluttering.

Bauer set the glass upright and filled it again. "Drink up," he repeated.

Berg shook his head, still choking over the burning sensation of the raw alcohol in his throat. "What the hell . . . why are you doing this?"

"I don't like to drink alone."

Bauer prodded Berg's knee roughly with the muzzle of the pistol again, and the young diplomat managed to get down the second glass.

Bauer filled it again.

Berg's eyes were watering heavily. He glanced desperately around the room, looking for someone to help him. A couple of bearded lumberjacks from a table nearby leered at him and wheezed with laughter. "You son of a bitch," he muttered.

"You were at the ferry dock in Trelleborg, looking for me. Who sent you?"

"Washington," Berg croaked.

"Who in Washington?"

"House."

"The White House?"

"Colonel House."

"Why'd he send you?"

"To report on you."

"Like McNally in Zurich?"

"I don't know."

Bauer filled the glass again.

By the time the bottle was empty, Berg was thoroughly inebriated. Bauer ordered another bottle and an extra glass for himself. He filled both and pushed one back at Berg again. The vice-consul was weeping quietly, his head sagging first one way, then the other.

"Go t' the bathroom," he mumbled, starting to get up.

Bauer kicked his feet out from under him. "Just piss in your pants."

"Gonna be sick."

"Forget it. Drink up."

The vice-consul struggled to get another tumblerful down. Bauer slipped his pistol back into his pocket. Berg was too drunk to escape.

"What else did House want you to do?"

"Turn you over," Berg mumbled.

"What?"

"Turn you over."

"To who?"

"Bolshi . . . Bolshiavikis. . . ."

"Why?"

Berg grinned maliciously, his eyes weaving and his head bobbing on his neck like a marionette's. "Let 'em kill ya."

"For what?"

"You know what."

Bauer drank some vodka himself and thought about it. "You mean you're waiting for me to kill Lenin. Then you'd tell them it was me."

Berg nodded lethargically, his eyes blinking in slow motion. "You got it. Let 'em kill ya. Serve you right. Bastard."

"Why not kill me yourself?"

Berg shook his head spastically. It looked as if it might fall off. "No, no, no. Don' do tha' kind of thing."

So it was the Huerta affair all over again, Bauer thought. Maybe that had been the plan all along. Somebody saw a way to kill two birds with one stone. Let Bauer do it, then feed him to the enemy. And everybody's happy. It was called international diplomacy.

"You can tell House for me that he's just making an ass of himself. The Bolsheviks already know."

Berg tried to bring his eyes to focus on Bauer's face. " 'Sa lie," he whispered. His head descended suddenly toward the table and met it with a heavy thud. Bauer grabbed his hair and twisted. No response. The vice-consul was dead cold unconscious.

Bauer moved his chair around and felt through Berg's pockets. He found a wallet, a revolver, a small pad and

Codebook, and several decoded cablegrams from Colonel House. He read the cables.

After a last glass of vodka, Bauer returned everything to Berg's pockets except the codebook and the pad, which he tucked into his own pocket. He paid the bill and headed for the door, leaving Berg at the table to sleep it off.

The hell with Colonel House, he decided. He was going to kill Lenin for certain now. Just to live to brag about it. But he knew he'd have to move fast.

Fritz Platten came over to the bench by the train station door, where Captain von Planetz was sitting. "We regret having had to deceive you, Captain," the Swiss said. "But you see now that it was a wise decision."

Von Planetz said nothing. The discovery that the assassin he had shot had not killed Lenin after all, but a planted double, had elevated his spirits from despair to something akin to a numb resignation. At least there was hope again for Marthe's treatment. But the fact remained, he had been badly fooled.

"Lenin asked me to extend to you his personal thanks," Platten continued, tilting his head in a slight bow. The cold weather had forced him to relinquish his pearl-gray fedora for a more practical fur cap, which he nevertheless wore tipped at a rakish angle.

The captain pulled the cigarette from his mouth. "He owes me no thanks."

"You shouldn't see it that way. After all, you did stop an assassin. Had he lived, he might have made another attempt. We are all grateful for your efforts."

Von Planetz resented the young Swiss's patronizing tone. "And what about the American, Bauer?" he challenged.

Platten smiled. "Ah, yes, the American. Our captain's magnificent obsession. I think he's probably at a hotel in Malmo by now, getting drunk. What do you think?"

Von Planetz didn't bother to reply. Platten cheerfully wished him good-bye and good luck, and hurried off to join the others, now gathering on the sledges for the trip across the river.

The captain forced himself up off the bench and paced the area in front of the station. The snowfall had finally stopped, and the temperature was dropping fast. He tucked his collar around his ears and pushed his hands into his coat pockets. The next train south didn't leave until the following morning. He would have to make some arrangement for the night.

The big stack of stovewood piled against the side of the station caught his attention. Something about it was subtly wrong, but for a few moments he wasn't sure what. Then he understood. There was a larger than normal opening near the middle of the stack. Even in the shadows it was visible— about six inches across and three feet from the bottom of the pile. The logs were stacked too neatly for it to be accidental. Someone had created it by removing a log from the pile.

It was probably nothing, of course. But the captain had built his reputation by finding something where others saw nothing.

He stepped around behind the pile. Out of the range of the station's lights, it was too dark to see anything. He crouched down, lit his cigarette lighter, and held it out at arm's length. The snow on this side of the woodpile was packed down, and a log—possibly the one pulled from the hole—lay in the snow crosswise to the stack, as if someone had been using it as a seat. Only the thinnest mantle of new snow covered the log and the area immediately around it, so whoever had been there had left very recently.

The captain sat on the log himself and bent forward to peer through the opening. He pulled his pistol from inside his coat and slid it partway into the opening. Resting his forearm on the wood, he gripped the pistol and sighted along it. It lined up perfectly with the platform—and the spot, barely ten meters away, where Lenin had stepped off the train.

He sniffed the surfaces of the logs near the hole for some telltale evidence of gunpowder, but smelled only the bark of birchwood and aspen. He moved his lighter around to explore further, but it spluttered and died, its small reservoir of benzine spent. It didn't matter. He had seen enough.

The captain hurried to catch up to the sledges, already well along the path toward the river.

Through that hole in the woodpile Bauer must have seen everything, he thought. Seen the Russian shoot down Lenin's double, seen him shoot the Russian. Seen it all. And never fired a shot himself.

The fresh dusting of snow made the path slippery, but the captain ran as fast as he dared, his mind churning to assess what he had learned. He tried to picture what else Bauer might have seen from his hiding spot behind the stack of logs.

He would have noticed—as the captain himself had noticed—the remarkable absence of hysteria among Lenin's followers to what should have been an unmitigated tragedy for them. He would have noticed, and he would have drawn the inevitable conclusion: Lenin was still alive.

And what would Bauer do now?

Von Planetz had no doubt about the answer. Bauer would continue on.

The captain caught up with the sledges near the footbridge, where a delegation of Swedish customs officials was going through the formalities of checking them out of the country. He found Lenin's lieutenant, Zinoviev, standing by the side of the last sledge, supervising the formal departure.

"Bauer is still with us," he blurted when he had caught his breath.

Zinoviev stopped what he was doing and turned to Von Planetz, his brow furrowed in irritation. "How do you know?"

The captain told him about the hiding place he had found behind the station's woodpile.

The Russian shook his head. "You're obsessed, Captain von Planetz. Absolutely obsessed."

"Are you suggesting I'm wrong?" the captain demanded, irritated himself by the Russian's thickheadedness.

Zinoviev sighed. "No. No. You're probably right. But you must give us some credit for being able to defend ourselves. You can't attach yourself to us forever, you know."

"I have my orders, Herr Zinoviev. Please let me obey them."

"What do you propose to do, then?"

"Cross to Finland with you."

"Impossible. You're a German."

"Let me borrow your dead man's passport. Our physical characteristics are a reasonable match."

Zinoviev's eyebrows widened. "He was Russian."

"I speak excellent Russian," the captain replied—in Russian.

Zinoviev grinned. "So you do." He glanced down at the captain's wrinkled uniform. "What about your costume?"

Von Planetz shrugged. "I'll buy some civilian clothes in town."

"Even so, we can't protect you. You can't cross as a member of our party. Lenin would never allow it. It would be suicidal for us if we were caught with a German officer in our midst. You have to understand that."

"I understand. What time does your train leave Tornio?"

"There's only the one. Eleven-thirty tomorrow."

"Then I'll have plenty of time to cross by myself. All I ask for is the temporary use of his papers. I'll return them to you at the train tomorrow."

Zinoviev considered it.

"That's all I ask. You need do nothing more for me. You can ignore me completely. Except to be aware that I'm still following my orders to see Lenin safely home."

Zinoviev handed the captain the dead man's passport. "His name was Gorodetsky—Sergei Mikhailovitch. Can you pronounce that properly?"

"Of course. Thank you."

A voice from the lead sledge was calling Zinoviev's name.

"That's Ilyich," he said. "I have to go."

"Warn him again about Bauer," the captain insisted.

"Yes, yes, Captain." Zinoviev waved his hand as if to dismiss him and started off toward the lead sledge.

Maybe he was obsessed. So what? It didn't matter what they thought. He had his orders. And Marthe to worry about.

SUNDAY
APRIL 15

TORNIO

At midnight the eight horse-drawn sledges bearing the Russian revolutionaries started out in single file across the mouth of the Torniojoki, guided by lanterns and the intermittent light of a three-quarter moon, breaking through torn, fleeting remnants of storm clouds. Wind gusts swirled the snow in drifts and buffeted the sleds. Huddled silently under coats and blankets, they made a curious, even pathetic sight—a quarrelsome band of exiles, exhausted from six days of travel, shaken by the murder of one of their number, and now fearing arrest and prison at the end of their journey.

By prior agreement with the German government, the officials in Haparanda had hastened their departure from Swedish soil by allowing them to cross directly to the Finnish frontier in the sledges, rather than be forced to negotiate the narrow planking of the footbridge.

Once on the Finnish side, the travelers were met not by Russian border guards, as they had expected, but by a four-man detachment of the British Expeditionary Force.

The English soldiers escorted the party into the fenced-in yard outside the Finnish customs house and locked the gate. One electric light, hanging from an iron pole streetlamp style with a corrugated reflector behind it, illuminated the yard with a desolate whiteness barely brighter than the moon. The wind agitated the fixture, clanging it against its reflector and causing its feeble flood of incandescence to veer and spin around the yard, sending ghostly shadows jumping across the snow.

An English officer appeared at the top of the customs house steps, clapped his gloved hands together for attention, and addressed the travelers in English. "Good evening. I am Lieutenant Chase, the officer in charge. All members of this party will be required to submit to a thorough examination of both their belongings and their person," he shouted, meeting the Russians' hostile stares with complacent indifference. "One of your party will please collect all passports and visas and hand them up to me."

Zinoviev, who spoke the best English, stepped to the front. "Where are the Russian border guards?" he demanded.

"Off getting drunk, no doubt," the lieutenant answered.

"We refuse to allow English soldiers to examine us," the Russian declared, in a defiant voice.

A corner of Chase's mouth crept up behind his moustache in an exaggerated smirk. "You have no say in the matter, whoever you are. If any of you refuses to cooperate, you'll be arrested. Now please collect your passports and hand them up to me."

Zinoviev discussed the matter with Lenin for several minutes. They decided they had no choice but to cooperate. Zinoviev collected the passports and turned them over to the officer.

The English lieutenant removed his gloves and shuffled through the documents with the ominous demeanor of a schoolmaster looking for evidence of mischief. He extracted the one from the stack that he was looking for and opened it. "Vladimir Ilyich Ulyanov?" he called, looking out over the collection of silent heads.

Lenin muttered a curse in Russian and then raised his hand. "I'm right here," he said.

The lieutenant studied his face, his passport, and then his face again. Lenin was clean-shaven, as part of the earlier effort to disguise himself, and he bore little obvious resemblance to his photograph. "Come up here," the lieutenant ordered. "And bring your luggage."

Lenin hesitated, then hefted his carpetbag and started up the steps.

Lieutenant Chase gestured toward Zinoviev. "Tell the rest of them that they will have to wait out here. They'll be called in one at a time. If any of them needs to relieve himself in the meantime, he can speak to one of the guards. He'll take you out back."

The British officer tucked the stack of passports under his arm and escorted Lenin into the customs house.

Bauer waited by the river, next to an abandoned fishing hut, just up from the footbridge. After an hour of searching, he had rented a horse and sleigh from a drunken logger in one of the taverns. The sleigh was a rickety buckboard mounted on wheels in the summer and runners in the winter, and the horse a shaggy-haired bay gelding of indeterminant age, but he only needed them to get him across the river to Tornio. He patted the horse on the neck and looked out across the river.

The cold moon bathed the landscape in a sharp silver twilight, and from the other side of the river he could see a ragged row of black shapes approaching, their glowing yellow lanterns bouncing and swaying over the ice. The sledges that had taken Lenin and his party across were returning.

He watched them until they reached the near bank just below him and turned southward. He climbed aboard the sleigh, wrapped the reins around his fingers, snapped them lightly across the gelding's rump, and started across the river.

Beneath the inch of new powder, the snow had formed a brittle crust from the cycle of spring melting and freezing, and the horse's hooves and the sled's metal runners broke through, making progress treacherous and slow. Bauer coaxed the animal onto the well-packed path used by the sledges, and from there on the going was better.

Halfway across, Bauer reined the horse in. If he continued on the path, it would take him to Finnish customs, at the far end of the footbridge, just to the south. He could see the lights of the customs yard clearly.

He slapped the reins and tugged on the left lead, to steer the horse off the path. The gelding fought the bit, not eager to step back into the crusty snow. Once away from the path, the animal became cooperative again, but moved forward only an awkward step at a time.

He should have held out for a dogsled and a team of huskies, he thought. Or simply walked across. He had considered that, but assumed the sleigh would be faster and safer, especially on the Finnish side, where the distance he might have to travel to intercept the train was unknown to him.

He heard a distant whinny of a horse behind him. He looked around but saw nothing. The second time he heard it, he stopped the sleigh, cupped his hands around his eyes, and carefully surveyed the Haparanda side of the river.

A black shadow emerged from the buildings that lined the riverbank and gradually took on shape as it moved out onto the ice. Another sledge, he guessed, like the ones that had ferried Lenin's party across.

But this one carried no lantern. Of course neither did he. Someone else avoiding customs?

The sledge found the same packed trail that Bauer had just abandoned, and advanced along it rapidly. The sharp crack of the driver's whip cut the frigid night air. The horse whinnied again. Bauer could hear the heavy pounding of its hooves, and the hiss of the runners, crunching and bumping over the packed snow. It was a powerful dray, he guessed, pulling the heavy sledge with apparent ease. The driver was the only one on board.

Bauer slapped the reins hard to prod the gelding forward again. The far shore looked to be only a few hundred yards away, but as his sleigh skidded and bumped toward it, it seemed to recede before him.

He glanced behind again. The sledge had gained on him. Keeping to the packed trail, it was soon running abreast of him, about two hundred feet to his right.

Bauer squinted, trying to see the driver, but the moonlight showed only a hulking dark shadow with a Russian-style fur cap.

The driver's arm shot up. Bauer heard his whip whistle and crack against the dray's hide. The big workhorse jerked in his harness and pulled powerfully to the left, into the crusty snow.

Bauer cursed out loud. He snapped the reins hard against the gelding's rump, but the poor beast was already moving as fast as it could.

The sledge slowed considerably in the crusty snow, and Bauer thought he was keeping ahead of it.

A Swedish frontier guard, he decided, acting on a tip. What would the Swedes do if they caught him? Not much, he guessed. Detain him for a few days. Why were they bothering?

The sledge was gaining on him, now.

The Finnish shore looked to be only a hundred feet away. Maybe less. It was hard to judge, because the land sloped so gradually up from the river and everything was covered with snow. How far would he chase him? All the way into Finland?

A silvery object the size of a tomato can plopped onto the seat beside him and bounced off into the snow.

A brilliant incandescence, a concussion, and the astringent stink of gelignite flooded the air in a smudged cloud.

The sleigh, as if sideswiped by a truck, flew up at the rear corner and flipped over, slamming Bauer headfirst into the snow. The gelding reared in terror and plunged forward, dragging the overturned sleigh behind him. One of the runners, twisted by the blast, hung at right angles to the carriage and sawed noisily through the crust.

Ears ringing, Bauer rolled onto his stomach, yanked the pistol from his coat pocket, and searched around frantically for a target.

The immense dray, head back and mane tossing wildly, was fifty feet away and bearing down on him like a runaway locomotive. He held his fire, waiting for the driver, still hidden behind the onrushing horse, to come into view.

Too late he realized the driver wasn't going to come into view. He tried to roll over, to propel himself out of the horse's path, but the crust refused to hold him, and he worked himself deeper into the snow.

He tried to stand to jump clear, but the leather-soled boots slipped and dropped him back on hands and knees.

No time left.

He faced toward the oncoming hooves, pulled his legs up under him, wrapped his arms around his chest, and pushed his head as deep into the snow as he could. He trusted the dray would not trample him if it could avoid it.

The sledge was another matter.

The driver obviously intended to crush him under it.

LONDON

MOST URGENT
EYES ONLY BALFOUR
BEF REPORTS FROM HAPARANDA AS FOLLOWS:
MAN KILLED NOT REPEAT NOT LENIN, ASSASSIN RUSSIAN.
HE WAS KILLED BY MEMBER OF LENIN'S PARTY.
NO SIGN OF HARRY BAUER.
ESME HOWARD. STOCKHOLM
END OF DISPATCH

Foreign Secretary Balfour dropped the cablegram from the Stockholm embassy back onto the secret service chief's desk. "How did a Russian assassin get into the picture, Sir Mansfield?"

Cumming removed his monocle and squeezed the bridge of his nose. "He must have been sent from Petrograd. Someone in the provisional government, I imagine. You did warn them about Lenin, after all. And urged them to do something."

Balfour picked up from Cumming's desk the shell casing that he used as a paperweight and turned it over to examine the lettering at the base. "That's true," he admitted. "Whom did he kill?"

"Someone in Lenin's party. We don't have a name."

"Are we sure it wasn't Lenin?"

"Yes, unfortunately. I got someone into the Haparanda police station to get a look at the corpse. It appears he was made up to look like Lenin. A decoy, no doubt. Cost the poor bugger his life."

Balfour replaced the shell casing on the desk. "And our American has disappeared off the face of the earth."

Cumming twiddled with his monocle. "I believe he's still after him."

"I find that hard to credit, Sir Mansfield."

"Lenin hasn't reached Petrograd yet. We mustn't pull Bauer out now."

"We agreed to pull him out at Tornio. The Bolsheviks shot that Russian assassin, after all, so they're obviously on the qui vive. We've exposed Bauer to enough risk already, letting him stay in from Stockholm. He's just not going to get the job done. If he shows up at Tornio, we'll detain him. BEF Tornio barracks has its orders. And they've been informed that he's traveling as Oskar Blum."

"But, Minister, we don't know Bauer's circumstances. He's survived this far, so he may be fully aware of the dangers. Our interfering in the situation now may be more dangerous than doing nothing."

Balfour pressed his fingers against his moustache and sighed deeply. "No. The truth of the matter is that the risks of killing Lenin are greater for us now than the risks of not killing him. If Bauer had done it right away, that would have been acceptable. But now we're running new risks. If Bauer is caught—and that's a real possibility—our culpability will become public. Wilson will know we've deceived him. And there's another consideration: suppose Lenin does come to power? We'll have made an enemy and forfeited any realistic chance of influencing him."

Cumming's mobile mouth stretched into a long frown. "Sometimes, Minister," he said, "I hate politics even more than war."

WASHINGTON

URGENT TOP SECRET
TO BE DECODED AT ONCE
NO DISTRIBUTION
DELIVER IMMEDIATELY TO COLONEL HOUSE
MESSAGE AS FOLLOWS:
KISS MY ASS, COLONEL
SINCERELY, HARRY BAUER
END OF MESSAGE

TORNIO

The interrogations continued through the night. One by one, each member of the party was brought in from the biting wind and cold of the customs yard, questioned at length, forced to remove his clothes, and then sent back outside.

The women were examined especially closely. Chase ordered them to undress down to their undergarments and while the other guards combed through their luggage and belongings, he searched their clothing, working his fingers through every inch of cloth, even pulling apart seams to examine the padding.

At three o'clock in the morning Inessa Armand was brought in. She removed her clothes without any argument, and handed them over to Chase with a taunt. "Are you enjoying your work, Lieutenant?"

"You're not as fat as the other women," Chase observed, letting his eyes roam boldly over her figure. He walked around behind her and immediately spotted the bulge at the small of her back. He lifted the petticoat and found the small derringer taped to her skin. He ripped it off and placed it on the table. "Take off everything," he ordered.

"I refuse."

"You're in no position to refuse anything."

"Go to hell."

"Don't waste my time," Chase warned. "I'll bring in my men and let them do it."

Inessa didn't argue further. She removed her petticoat, silk stockings, and underpants and stood there before the English officer in the nude. "Does that satisfy you?" she demanded, showing off her white, well-rounded figure without embarrassment.

Chase reddened. "Why are you carrying a revolver?" he countered.

"I had intended to shoot you with it."

"Don't be impertinent."

"You have no right to question us," she retorted. "You have no right even to be here. This is Russian territory and we're Russian citizens. I demand that you let us all go. At once."

Chase ignored her protest. "There's supposed to be a man with your party named Blum. Where is he?"

"How do you know he's in our party?"

"That's none of your business. What happened to him?"

"We left him in Stockholm."

"Why?"

"You know very well why."

The British officer raised an eyebrow in surprise.

"If you're finished pawing through my clothes, would you please give them back."

Chase threw Inessa's clothes at her. "No. I don't know why. Tell me."

Inessa quickly slipped into her undergarments. "He's your assassin, isn't he?"

"Assassin?"

"Don't look so surprised. We're well aware that you hired him to kill Lenin."

Chase scratched his chin in confusion. "My orders are to detain him."

Inessa laughed contemptuously. "What a stupid thing to say." She finished dressing and walked out. Chase kept her pistol.

The interrogations continued into dawn, and the mood of the Bolsheviks grew ugly. Exhausted, hungry, and cold, they started baiting the British soldiers openly, hurling threats and insults with increasing frequency and belligerence. At six o'clock the British stopped the questioning.

Lieutenant Chase slumped behind his desk, his chin in his hands. His eyes were bloodshot and his voice was hoarse. He felt groggy and weak. The four soldiers under his command stumbled in and assembled by the door in a loose approximation of attention.

Chase looked from face to face. "Nothing?" he said.

"No, sir, nothing," one of the privates replied.

"You sure nobody sneaked past you?"

"No, sir!" the private replied.

"What was that gunfire I heard—out on the river?"

The private scratched his head. "Drunk Russians, sir. Or drunk Finns. We didn't see them."

"What about drunk Swedes?" another soldier chimed in.

The others laughed.

Chase closed his eyes and sighed. The Russian guard detail was coming on duty at seven. He didn't dare hold Lenin and his party any longer. And there was no reason to. He pulled the stack of passports toward him and counted them. Thirty in all. He checked them against the list he had made of those he had interrogated. Names and numbers all matched.

The night had been a dismal, exhausting waste of time. No Oskar Blum, and, worse, no twelve million Swedish krona. He should have known better. Nobody got rich that easily.

Maybe the money was coming over later. Or they were taking it through at another border crossing.

Maybe Blum had it and was headed south with it.

Maybe the fat Dane, Parvus, was having delusions. Or he was simply a silk stocking full of shit.

Who the hell knew?

Lieutenant Chase separated Fritz Platten's passport from the pile. Other than the missing Oskar Blum, he was the only Swiss national with the party. He wagged the document at the private. "His Russian visa has a spelling mistake in it," he said. "Take the bastard back to our barracks and lock him up. We'll keep him for a night, then send him back to the Swedes."

He pushed the remaining stack of documents across his desk toward the private. "Get the rest of them out of here."

TORNIO

The big dray's hooves crashed into the snow around him. He felt the river ice beneath vibrate from the pounding weight.

The sledge runners, like giant knife blades, sliced parallel cuts through the crust on each side of him.

Nothing touched him.

He waited, head still buried in the snow, until all he could hear was his heart thumping in his ears. He raised his head and twisted around to see behind him.

It was Morozov. How had the bastard found him? Bauer wondered. Sheer chance? Why wasn't he with the others?

Bauer thrust his gloved hands into the snow and groped blindly for his pistol. His fingers found only broken chunks of crust.

Morozov hauled back on the reins and brought the sledge to a halt about a hundred feet away. No more time to look. Bauer pushed himself to his feet. The Russian was lighting the fuse on another tomato can.

Bauer started to run, counting the seconds in his head. The crust bit at his ankles, and the snow underneath sucked at his boots. He churned his thighs with the power of a base stealer taking off for second, but his legs seemed to move with the slow-motion futility of a nightmare.

He glanced over his shoulder in time to see Morozov lob

the can. It came at him in a shallow arc, slightly to the right. Bauer took three running steps to the left, then flung himself forward, in a headfirst slide.

He felt the snow crust breaking up around him like glass.

He heard the blast at the count of "six one-thousand." The bomb landed about twenty-five feet away, and the explosion passed harmlessly over him.

He jumped to his feet, ears ringing, and gasped to fill his lungs.

Morozov lit another one.

One one-thousand.

He balanced on the seat of the sledge, took careful aim, and released the bomb in a higher arc, like a looping fly ball to shallow center field.

Two one-thousand.

It was going to fall too close to get clear. He fought his instinct to flee and turned toward the arching cylinder, moving down at him as a silvery blur, just visible against the moon.

Three one-thousand.

He kicked desperately through the snow, stretching his arms up. He could hear the burning fuse, hissing like a snake. His hands strained outward. He let his palms cushion the impact, bringing them back toward his chest, then closed his fingers firmly around the can. It felt heavy as a cannonball.

Four one-thousand.

The distance to the sledge was about that of a throw to second base from deep center field. Morozov, hands on his hips, was perfectly outlined in the moonlight. Bauer's right hand took the can smoothly back behind him, then whipped it forward in a hard overhand delivery.

Five one-thousand.

The bomb sped toward the Russian at a low, nearly straight trajectory. He didn't move to get out of the way because he didn't see it coming.

It hit him squarely in the stomach.

Six one-thousand.

The Russian toppled backward, regained his balance for a split second, then fell headfirst off the sledge. Bauer held his breath for the explosion.

It never came.

The bomb was a dud.

Morozov was tangled in the harness. The big dray bolted forward and dragged him a few feet, but he quickly recovered and pulled himself free. He rescued the loose reins from the snow, halted the dray, and climbed back aboard the sledge.

Bauer looked around frantically. The old bay gelding was limping toward the Swedish side of the river, dragging part of its harness with it.

He heard the Russian laugh. The sound rippled like an echo across the frozen river. The sledge started after him again.

He'll think twice before throwing another bomb, Bauer thought. But he no doubt has a gun.

On the Finnish side of the river Bauer could see a big sawmill and several large icehouses. He started running toward them, hoping someone—a night watchman, anyone—might be there.

Whipping his steed furiously, Morozov closed quickly on him.

He realized he was too far from the mill and the icehouses to reach them. He began running to his left, circling back out onto the river, hoping to cost Morozov extra time turning the sledge.

For a while it worked. By constant sharp changes of direction, he was able to slow the Russian down, but the effort rapidly fatigued him, and the shoreline wasn't getting any closer. Each time he tried a dash toward the bank, Morozov was able to cut him off and force him back out onto the river.

It was hopeless. The Russian was just playing with him, wearing him down.

Lungs bursting, heart hammering, Bauer collapsed onto the snow, too exhausted to continue. Morozov brought the sledge up to within fifty feet and then stopped.

Bauer saw a small flicker of flame as Morozov lit another fuse. Having learned something from the previous throw, the terrorist held the tomato can for several seconds before releasing it, using up the time Bauer might have had to throw it back at him.

Bauer staggered to his feet and forced his legs to propel him away, to the right.

Morozov led Bauer, throwing the bomb to land ahead of

him. Bauer reversed himself the instant the Russian released the bomb, and managed to put about twenty feet between himself and the can when it went off.

The explosion knocked him on his face.

Head spinning, he forced himself up again.

He saw Morozov light another one. He had to counteract this somehow, or he'd soon be dead. He turned and headed directly toward the sledge.

He began to count.

One one-thousand.

His legs felt close to paralysis. He stumbled and fell.

Two one-thousand.

How far was the sledge? Thirty feet? Unable to stand, he crawled.

Three one-thousand.

He could see the bomb, still in Morozov's hand. The Russian was hesitating.

Four one-thousand.

Twenty feet.

Five one-thousand.

Morozov had to let go of it now.

Fifteen feet.

Six one-thousand.

Ten feet.

Bauer flopped down and rolled onto his side.

The Russian screamed a curse and threw the can off into the distance, to avoid being blown to pieces himself. The bomb traveled out far over Bauer's head and exploded nearly one hundred feet away, while still airborne.

Bauer looked back at the sledge. Even in the moonlight he could see Morozov's lopsided face. The hooves of the big dray were only a few feet from his head. He rolled over a few times to put himself out of the sledge's path.

He tried to stand, but his knees buckled. Why didn't Morozov come down and just finish him off? Bauer wondered. He didn't even need a gun. He could wring his neck like a chicken, and the American wouldn't have the strength to resist.

He heard the Russian laugh. "I've got all night!" he shouted, his thick accent barely understandable past the ringing in Bauer's ears.

Searing pain flashed across his side. He rolled over on his stomach to gain the protection of his fur coat, and pulled his hand and legs up beneath him.

Morozov's whip.

The long tapered coil of leather snapped explosively across his back, stinging the wind out of him. He gasped and tried to bury himself in the snow. Morozov tormented him at his leisure, lacerating him across the back and legs.

Bauer stood it as long as he could, then forced himself to his feet again, and staggered on.

Morozov let him go.

Fifty feet from the sledge, he remembered the cans and stopped. He was as neatly trapped within Morozov's orbit as if tied to a leash. Too far out, and Morozov would kill him with a bomb. Too close in, and he would feel the cut of the whip again—or be run over by the sledge.

The Russian intended to play with him, like a cat with a wounded mouse, extracting all the satisfaction from the cruel exercise that he could.

Bauer felt dizzy and weak. Consciousness was bleeding from him. Still he staggered on, no longer able to feel his feet beneath him.

Each time he tried to reach the riverbank, Morozov cut him off and forced him back out onto the ice.

The sawmill and the icehouses came into view again. They had moved farther north. His blind circuits were carrying him southward, away from the town. Away from the slim hope that somebody might see him and help.

The moon was near setting on the western horizon, and the river was growing darker. Bauer's feet struck an obstacle and he fell down. It was a low bank of snow, running across his path in a straight line. It was too sharply defined to be a drift.

Plowed snow, he thought. On the other side he could see bare ice, with thin shreds of last night's snow swirled across it.

He tried to follow the bank northward, hoping to draw Morozov back toward town. When dawn came, there would be people there. If he could survive until dawn.

Plowed snow.

Bauer staggered a step, fell, got up, and staggered on.

Have to lie down soon, he thought. Just lie down, and let

him finish me. He could sleep, he thought, right out here on the river. He was so tired. It didn't matter what Morozov did, he would fall down and never get up again. The spring would come soon, and when the ice melted, the water would carry him out to sea. Not such a bad way to die.

The bank of plowed snow loomed before him again. This time he let himself fall over it. On the other side, there were no crust, no drifts. The thin mantel of new snow had frozen against the surface of the ice, allowing his boots some traction.

He had never been so close to the shore. But even if he made it, where would he be? The shoreline here was empty. No sawmills, no icehouses. He looked behind him. Morozov was bringing the sledge over the bank of snow.

The plowed area seemed to extend all the way to the shore. He saw an odd intersection of lines just ahead of him. The moon was gone now, and the light was so dim he wasn't sure at first they were really there, but yes, they were. They must be. It was the only possible reason for the plowing.

Everything he had left in him would have to go into this.

He sucked in his breath, then broke into a slow trot across the plowed area toward the shore, toward that barely visible point where those two straight lines met in a right angle. He would run up as a close as he dared, as fast as he dared.

Invite death, because it was his last chance to live.

He heard Morozov's whip and the *thunk* of the dray's hooves on the cleared ice.

Pray that he'll stay true to form.

The Russian maneuvered the sledge around to Bauer's right, to force him back out toward the middle of the river.

This time Bauer kept straight.

On the ice the sledge's runners moved like skates, and Morozov was quickly past Bauer and turning in front of him to cut off his escape.

Bauer slowed and veered left in a shallow turn, his eyes on the point ahead of him where the two lines on the ice met.

He saw them clearly now. They marked the corner edges of a cut—where the ice had been removed by saw from the river, cut up into blocks, and stored in those icehouses along the riverbank. In the summer they would fill Russian iceboxes and cool the drinks of patrons at Petrograd's fanciest restaurants.

Bauer passed within a foot of the edge and curled slowly to his left, praying he wouldn't slip.

Morozov saw the cut, too, but not soon enough. The big dray, unable to turn or slow the momentum of the sledge, plummeted past the edge. Horse and sledge crashed through with an explosion of water.

Bauer let himself collapse onto the ice.

Morozov reacted instantly. As the front end of the sledge tipped into the river, he ran up toward the back, his satchel of bombs clutched in his hands. He reached the sledge's back beam, tossed his satchel out onto the ice, and flexed his legs to jump. At that instant the rear of the sledge slipped past the edge of the cut and dropped into the water.

It sank under, soaking the Russian up to his waist, then bobbed back up again, to float just under the surface.

Morozov stood balanced on the rear beam, transfixed with the horror of his predicament. The dray was swimming, smashing the thin glazing of ice that had formed over the cut, pulling the sledge farther out.

Morozov clung to the sledge as long as could, the freezing water lapping at his knees; then he plunged in and splashed his way toward the edge of the cut. He couldn't swim, but sheer desperation kept him afloat until he reached the thick, smooth wall the ice cutters had created with their big saws. Bauer knew he should get over near him, to make certain that he didn't somehow manage to climb out, but he was too exhausted to move.

The water level was about a foot below the frozen surface, and Morozov reached up repeatedly, searching for a hand-hold to pull himself up. He discarded his gloves and tried to dig into the ice with his fingers. They were too stiff with cold to do him any good, but he kept trying, bobbing up, scratching desperately on the surface, but always slipping back.

When it seemed that he was about to go under for good, he produced a knife from his boot and jabbed it into the surface of the ice a full arm's length from the edge of the cut.

Bauer watched in fascinated horror as the Russian put both hands on the shaft of the knife and with one desperate effort, pulled himself out of the freezing water.

Bauer sat up. He should get Morozov's satchel, he thought, and throw it into the water.

Too late.

He struggled to his feet and stumbled on.

At the edge of the river he found a path in the snow and followed it north toward Tornio.

He looked back once. Morozov was walking. One hand clutched the satchel, the other slapped desperately against his side, trying to fight off the effects of his wet clothes, freezing rapidly on his body.

Dawn was beginning to brighten in the east. No lights burned in any of the houses, but thin plumes of woodsmoke from the metal chimneys gave away the secret that the town was inhabited. Bauer fought the irrational desire to go up to one of the forlorn unpainted plank houses and beg them to let him in.

He used the last of his remaining strength to reach the Tornio railroad station, a steep-roofed cabin at the south end of the town's one street. He found it locked. A weatherbeaten piece of paper tacked to the door proved to be the schedule. The words were in Cyrillic, but the numbers told him what he needed to know. There was only one train, and it didn't depart until 11:30 that morning.

Lenin and his party could not yet have left Tornio.

He dug out his watch. The crystal was smashed and the hands frozen at 2:14. He guessed it to be about 5:30. The sun was over the horizon, flashing across the icy edge of the Lapland tundra in a blazing prism of colors.

He had six hours.

Behind the station he found an empty shed and decided he would have to hide there. He wedged the door shut, crawled behind a stack of wooden crates, and buried himself in a pile of sawdust.

He closed his eyes. For a brief instant he saw the image of Morozov against his eyelids, walking across the river behind him. Then he collapsed into a profound slumber.

THE TRAIN

The train for Petrograd didn't leave on time. Or anything approaching it. The bottom reversing shaft on the right side of the locomotive snapped in two, and it took six hours for the Finnish railroad to find a replacement part.

Captain von Planetz paced nervously through the old Russian third-class carriages, smoking one cigarette after another. Six days had now passed since the revolutionaries' departure from Zurich, and the ordeal was apparent on every face. To the mundane discomforts of delays, cramped sleeping arrangements, poor food, and limited toilet facilities, a new fear had been added, the captain discovered: the fear that Lenin would be killed before they reached Petrograd.

The shooting at the Haparanda station had done what the captain had been unable to do—it had finally brought home the reality of the threat they faced.

And Lenin's bodyguard, Morozov, had amplified it. He boarded the train late, acting like a madman. As Von Planetz was able to piece his story together, it seemed the American assassin had pursued him across the river in a nightlong chase. Bauer, he said, had shot at him, thrown bombs at him, beat him with a whip, and tried to drown him in an ice cut. He would have frozen to death but for the fact that he found a heated church celebrating an Easter sunrise mass. The congregation took him in, he said, fed him, and let him dry his clothes.

Bauer, he warned everyone loudly, was still on the loose.

Von Planetz lit a fresh cigarette from the burning tip of the one he had been smoking. Even discounting much of what Morozov had said, Bauer was taking on the mythical aspects of an *Ubermensch*—a remorseless, unstoppable superman, toying with Lenin and his pitiful band of disciples, before he destroyed them and all their hopes, just short of their goal.

Repairs finally complete, the train departed Tornio at 6:45 Easter Sunday evening, more than seven hours behind schedule. By that time, Morozov—along with several others in Lenin's entourage—had combed through the train several times, carriage by carriage, seat by seat, inch by inch, looking for the American.

Von Planetz watched them and wondered. He knew intuitively that they wouldn't find him.

But that didn't convince him that Bauer wasn't on board.

When the train got under way, Zinoviev called Inessa Armand into an empty compartment in the last carriage.

"You heard Morozov's story?" he asked, slipping the latch into place across the door.

"And I don't believe any of it," she replied, flopping down heavily on the unpadded wooden seat.

Zinoviev sat opposite her. "Your American friend is still after Ilyich." He watched the effect of his words on her.

Inessa fluffed a hand through her unruly hair. "Well, you've combed through the train with a microscope. Did you find him?"

"He might be waiting ahead of us. Just as he did at Haparanda."

"You believe he was in Haparanda?"

"The German captain had excellent evidence that he was there, waiting in ambush."

Inessa turned sarcastic. "When did you start taking this German captain so seriously?"

"Von Planetz also thinks you lied to him about Bauer."

Inessa sighed. "Grigory, you're being very tiresome."

"I want the truth from you," he demanded.

Inessa laughed contemptuously. "Do you really? And who are you to demand the truth from me? Have you been suddenly appointed prosecutor for some court with jurisdiction over me?"

"If you had nothing to hide, you wouldn't talk that way."

Inessa stood up to go. "Is this all you have to say to me?"

"Sit down."

"Perhaps you would like to make these charges in front of Ilyich, Grigory? Would you?"

Zinoviev slapped her across the face and knocked her back onto the seat. She gasped and brought her hands to her cheeks.

"Listen to me, you little whore," he rasped. "You've been getting away with murder ever since you got close to Ilyich. I know you have him wrapped around your little finger. There's nothing I can do about that. But I can tell you this. I intend to protect Ilyich's interests, even if he won't. I'm not going to let you sabotage everything—our whole movement—with your self-indulgence and carelessness. If I had my way you'd be off this train in a second."

Inessa took her hands from her face. "I do believe you're jealous, Grigory. You just can't stand to think that someone else might have more influence with Ilyich than you, can you?"

"You let Bauer go, didn't you? Admit it!"

She admitted it. "He saved my life. He deserved the chance."

"He's here to kill Ilyich, you stupid cow!"

"Here? Where?" she retorted. "Where is he? Who's seen him? Have you seen him? Even that obsessed German captain doesn't claim to have seen him! Are you all paranoid? Do you take Morozov's insane ravings seriously? He was probably drunk all last night. The American's gone! He wouldn't have dared follow us!"

"Why not?"

"Because I told him Ilyich knew about him, that's why. That we all knew about him. That he was outnumbered. That he'd certainly be killed. He understood. He isn't crazy."

"No, he isn't. And he made a fool of you. He should be dead. And if you hadn't manipulated Ilyich so shamelessly, he would be. We'd have sent Morozov, as I had begged him to do."

"You're a bloodthirsty man, Grigory," Inessa replied calmly. "It worries me, the things you say."

"Why did you join our cause?"

"We've all read Chernyshevsky. We've all confessed our reasons in a hundred cafés across Europe. You've heard mine many times. If you don't understand them by now, you're more obtuse than I thought."

"You don't belong with us. You have no true understanding of Marxism. You're in this for the excitement. The whole thing is just another cheap thrill for you."

"Really, Grigory, you're contemptible."

The Russian's expression turned malicious. "You fucked him, didn't you? The American."

Inessa's face burned crimson at the accusation. "Yes, I did! We did it in a church in Stockholm. On Good Friday. So what do you think of that? Does it make you jealous?"

"It just proves that you're a common whore."

"For someone who's tried repeatedly to get me into bed with him, your remarks are hard to take seriously."

"You've fucked everybody else, why not me?"

"I doubt you could satisfy me, Grigory."

This enraged Zinoviev. He brandished his fist in front of her face.

"Yes. Why don't you hit me again," she taunted. "You like to strike women, don't you, Grigory? Zina told me you beat her. Beneath your intellectual pretentions, you're just a bourgeois ruffian. Ilyich deserves better than you."

Zinoviev stood up. The woman was too brazen and clever to intimidate with words. He was more than just jealous of her influence with Lenin. It terrified him. It was dangerous. A threat to them all. Lenin worshiped her, the fool, and would hear nothing bad about her. That was why Zinoviev felt he must take matters into his own hands, even at the risk of incurring Lenin's wrath.

He opened the compartment door to leave. He turned and leveled a finger at her. "If anything happens to Ilyich," he whispered, "I'll kill you. That's a solemn promise."

The captain stood at the front of the corridor of the first carriage back from the baggage car and lit another cigarette. He had decided that the best approach was the obvious, systematic one. It was a small train—locomotive, tender, baggage van, and three carriages with a total of fifteen compartments. If Bauer was in any of them, Morozov and the others would certainly have found him. There weren't many places to hide.

Still, the captain had to satisfy himself.

The gangway to the baggage van at the front was locked, but Von Planetz managed to unhook the chain and take a quick look among the sacks of mail and boxes of freight. No one was there.

He returned to the first carriage. All five compartments were occupied by the remaining members of Lenin's party. There was no chance that Bauer was among them. But the captain paced the length of the car several times, anyway, checking each face against the mental file he had accumulated since they had first boarded the sealed train in Gottmadingen. Lenin—the real Lenin—sat in the first compartment with his wife, Zinoviev, and three others. He was talking and the others were listening. He looked older than his forty-seven years, with thinning hair, tired eyes, and a grim, irascible expression that Von Planetz found intimidating, even through the glass of the compartment door.

The second time he passed the compartment, Zinoviev came out. "Lenin asks you not to smoke," he said.

The captain let the cigarette drop to the floor. He stepped on it with his boot and walked away, annoyed. He was trying to protect the man's life, and the swine was ordering him not to smoke—and in a public train, at that.

The second carriage was filled with Russian soldiers returning from the Tornio border area. Many of them were drunk. Von Planetz pushed his way along the narrow corridor, scanning faces and wondering if Bauer was bold enough— or clever enough—to disguise himself as a Russian soldier. It seemed impossible. He didn't even speak Russian.

The captain paused in the open gangway between the second and third cars, and let the noise and the engine smoke and the chill wind whipping up around the buffers and couplings absorb him for a moment.

He decided to check the roof. He swung out to the iron ladder bolted beside the door and climbed up until his head cleared the carriage roofline. The wind whipped fiercely at his face. He shielded it with a gloved hand.

The roof was clear. He stepped back down and entered the third carriage. It was nearly empty. He searched through it diligently, and turned up a Russian Orthodox monk, an old Finnish couple on their way to Petrograd, and a party of sleeping railway workmen.

He picked out an empty compartment for himself and sat down to think.

If Bauer wasn't on the train, then he must be ahead of it. The train's long delay leaving Tornio had given him time to get farther down the line. But that was not easy, the captain thought. Getting from one town to the next in this part of the world was possible only by train, by foot, or by horse-drawn sledge.

But he'd give the American the benefit of any doubt. If it was humanly possible, Bauer could do it. With a six- to ten-hour lead, he could have traveled at least as far as the first stop.

An official came through and collected tickets, and the

train soon arrived at that first stop, a small settlement called Kemi.

The captain opened his window and watched the passengers board. He counted six Russian soldiers. He had a clear view of the side of the train from front to back, and he was sure no one else had slipped on. All six soldiers pushed into his compartment. They were young men, barely out of their teens, unshaven and unwashed. Their greatcoats and uniforms were torn and dirty, their expressions furtive and defiant.

Deserters, he guessed.

"Who are you?" one of them demanded, poking a finger at Von Planetz. "The czar's paymaster, I hope."

The others laughed.

"The government owes us back pay," another said. "A year's worth."

"They were counting on us dying first," another said. That got a bigger laugh.

"The czar's gone," Von Planetz replied, wondering if they had gotten the news.

"*Yeb tvoyu mat*," the first soldier muttered. "Fuck your mother. What other news do you have?"

The captain shrugged. The soldiers were in a mood to make trouble. He offered them cigarettes to appease them. They took them greedily. No one had matches. He handed one of them his lighter to pass around. The young Russian examined it covetously, then struck the flint several times without result. The captain had forgotten that it was out of fuel. Hastily he fished through his pockets for the matches he had been using. Instead of returning the lighter, the soldier held it out to one of his comrades. "What's this say?" he asked, tapping at a spot on the side of the brass barrel.

The other soldier moved it under the light of the compartment window and squinted at it in puzzlement. "*Slava Boygu*," he declared. "It's German."

The six soldiers stared at the captain with bug-eyed astonishment.

"It's a present from my son," Von Planetz lied, feeling his stomach tighten.

The lighter was passed from hand to hand, so that each man could see the German lettering for himself.

"He was at Gumbinnen," the captain added, pushing a

finger nervously against the bridge of his glasses. "He took it from a dead German soldier."

The words felt dirty in his mouth as he spoke them. In fact, it was the body of his own son that had been looted. A common occurrence, he had discovered, during the Russian advance into East Prussia in the opening days of the war.

"Where's your son now?" one soldier wanted to know.

The captain looked directly into the soldier's tough face. "He died at Tannenberg."

The Russian holding the lighter handed it back with a shake of his head. None of them asked him any more questions. Tannenberg had been a calamitous defeat for Russia, and none of them wished to hear more about it.

Captain von Planetz pocketed the lighter, mumbled something about the lavatory, and retreated to the next carriage, leaving their cigarettes unlit. He collapsed against the corridor wall, trembling from head to foot.

When he had recovered some composure, he searched through the remaining carriages again, on the slim hope that Bauer had jumped on just before or after the station stop, when the train was moving slowly.

He didn't find him.

PETROGRAD

The telegram arrived at 52 Shiroskaya Street, a tall stone apartment building in the Old Petersburg section of the city, early in the evening. Lenin's younger sister, Maria, brought it upstairs to the family's sixth-floor apartment. Her husband, Mark Elizarov, the director of a marine insurance company, and her older sister, Anna, who lived with them, were sitting and talking in the living room after dinner.

Maria ripped the envelope open and held it near the light. "It's from Ilyich," she cried excitedly. She handed it to her sister, who read it out loud: " 'Arriving Monday 11 P.M. Inform Pravda. Ulyanov.' "

"He sent it from Tornio," Maria exclaimed. "He's already in Finland!"

"We must hurry then," Anna declared, going to collect her coat.

Maria's husband went out in the street to find them a

droshky, Petrograd's antique version of the taxicab, and the two sisters rode to the offices of *Pravda,* the Bolshevik party newspaper, on Moika Street.

Lev Kamenev was there, with several others. Maria rushed in, waving the telegram. "He's coming!" she cried. "Tomorrow night! Do we have time to arrange a welcome?"

Kamenev read the telegram. "It's short notice," he confessed.

"We'll start at once," Anna declared.

Kamenev agreed. In fact, the Bolsheviks had been planning for Lenin's arrival for nearly a week. All that remained was to put it into motion. "And we'll make it the biggest damned reception this city has ever seen."

THE TRAIN

The engineer, a stocky Ukrainian named Anatoly, spoke no English and only a smattering of German. It didn't matter. There was little that needed to be communicated. Bauer had boarded the locomotive at gunpoint as it was pulling out of Tornio station and made his wishes understood quickly—that he planned to ride in the engine cab all the way to the end of the line: Petrograd.

The engineer's reaction had been little more than a shrug. As long as he kept out of the way, he had replied, he didn't give a damn.

The fireman, a boy in his teens who turned out to be Anatoly's son, said nothing at all. Anatoly had lost three other sons to the war, and now only Sasha was left. Sasha was deaf, which explained why he had not been drafted to fight. Father and son communicated with simple hand signals and nods and shakes of the head.

The cab was cramped. Bauer established himself on the fireman's tip-up seat and did his best to keep his legs out of the way when Sasha had to turn to the tender for coal to feed the firebox. The engine was an ancient 1880 2-6-0 Mogul type, remarkably like the old Baldwins his father took him on when he was a kid. A torrent of forgotten sensations flooded over him as he looked around the cab—the orderly maze of pipes and needle gauges and cylinders; the handles of the controls, worn shiny-smooth by years of men's hands; the blast of heat from the open firebox; the terrific cacophony of pounding pistons, hissing steam, and rumbling wheels; the heady smells of grease, water vapor, coal smoke, lubricating oil, and tallow.

He expected no trouble from these two. They would be constantly busy, riding this old iron horse on its nocturnal journey through Finland's wilderness of forests and lakes.

He watched Sasha yank back on the lever that opened the firebox doors and saw the perfect fire he had built, the bed of coals evenly glowing from front to back, side to side, the smoke so thin as to be almost invisible. The boy laid shovelsful of fresh coal on top, spreading them with practiced throws in small, overlapping crescents, damping the fire just sufficiently to smother the leaping yellow flames without killing the ruby-red glow beneath.

The engineer patted the boy on the shoulder, checked a couple of gauges by tapping them with his finger, then turned back to the small windshield that gave him his view of the track ahead.

Bauer felt an empathy for them, father and son, working in harmony in their closed little universe of the locomotive cab. Moments similar to these had been the happiest of his childhood. He felt a twinge of emotion that nearly brought him to tears. That was a bad sign. He was wearing dangerously thin, emotionally and physically.

He looked down at his pistol. When he had learned that the train would be delayed, he had returned to the river to look for it. Finding it was a matter of locating the black scar in the snow where Morozov's first bomb had exploded. Once he found that, he was able to identify the place where he had thrown himself down in front of the horse and sledge. The pistol was there, its grip sticking two inches out of the snow.

He had slept for nearly twelve hours in the shed by the Tornio station. But he still felt pain and deep exhaustion.

He no longer had any plan. He wasn't even sure why he was still in the hunt. All that fired him was an unreasonable determination.

"How far do you take her?" he asked the engineer, raising his voice to be heard over the noise.

"Seinajoki," Anatoly replied.

"How many hours?"

The driver held up all his fingers. There were only nine.

Bauer smiled. He must have been a brakeman once, he thought. Like his father. Brakemen were always losing fingers to those old link and pin couplings. His father had lost three.

A new crew would take over at Seinajoki, and it would be about fourteen more hours from there to the Russian border at Beloostrov. And an hour more to Petrograd.

Could he last that long? he wondered. Hiding in the cab, holding this pistol on a succession of crews for twenty-four hours?

MONDAY
APRIL 16

THE TRAIN

Early Monday morning the train approached Seinajoki, a logging town deep in Finland's inland wilderness. A heavy fog, caused by the melting snow, blanketed the ground, and the train moved at a crawl. Unable to read the positions or see the color of the signal arms in the mist, the engineer was reduced to feeling his way blindly along the track, listening for his wheels to pop one of the small explosive devices the trackmen laid out on the lines to warn the train if the signal ahead was at danger.

Captain von Planetz watched the ghostly landscape creep by his compartment window. He pulled the packet of cigarettes from his pocket and discovered that it was empty. Damn! His last pack. The Russian soldiers had taken them all. He tore the top off the foil-papered box to make sure that he hadn't missed one lurking in the corner, and then crumpled it up and threw it onto the floor, to join the litter of burned matches and butts.

He looked down at the empty pack again. The name of the German brand was emblazoned on it as bright and prominent as the billing on a theater marquee. He had passed around a package of German cigarettes to Russian soldiers, and they had failed to notice it, even after discovering the obscure inscription on his lighter.

He felt a damp sweat erupt under his arms. Only the most

extraordinary luck had saved him. He thought of Marthe again, and chastised himself for his lack of vigilance.

A cluster of delapidated camps and sawmills gradually slid into view alongside the tracks, and he heard the conductor in the car ahead calling out the next stop—Seinajoki.

The captain put on his coat, felt in his side pocket for his pistol, and moved to the corridor.

The instant the train stopped, he yanked open the door and dropped to the platform, a series of plank duckboards laid out in the mud and snow. He drew a deep breath to steel himself and headed for the locomotive.

He saw the crew coming out. The engineer stepped down first, swinging his small leather kit bag. The fireman followed close behind. The captain ran his eyes quickly along the roof of the cab, the tender, the baggage car, and the three carriages. He saw nobody.

The old crew huddled briefly with the new on the makeshift duckboard platform, exchanging information about the engine and the weather conditions on the run.

Adrenaline flowing, the captain slipped the pistol from his coat and climbed aboard the locomotive. He hit the footplate and swept the pistol around the cab, his finger tight against the trigger. It was a small space, barely eight feet across and five feet deep.

And it was empty.

The captain looked out the window on the far side. He saw workmen loading water from the tower into the tender's tanks. He looked in the coal bunkers. They were half-full of coal. And nothing else.

He pocketed the pistol and dropped back down to the platform. The two crews had separated. The new fireman climbed into the cab to attend to the boiler and firebox, while the new engineer walked down alongside the train, banging the rim of each wheel with a big spanner wrench, testing for cracks in the cast iron. His blows rang out like muted gongs in the morning fog.

The engineer who had just been relieved headed toward the station house. Von Planetz caught up with him near the door and slapped him on the shoulder from behind. The man spun around to see the captain's pistol just inches from his belly. He grunted and threw up his hands.

The captain spoke in sharp bursts to keep his voice from trembling. "Just answer me. Who was in the cab with you?"

"The fireman."

"Anyone else?"

The engineer narrowed his eyes. "Are you police?"

"That's right. Was there someone?"

"Yes."

"Where did he get on?"

"Tornio."

"Where did he go?"

"I don't know."

The captain pressed the pistol into the engineer's stomach. "Think. This is an emergency. Where did he go?"

"He jumped off. I don't know where. I was too busy. One minute he was behind me, the next he was gone. I intend to report it, of course. Is he an escaped prisoner?"

Von Planetz nodded. "Don't report anything. We'll take care of it."

The captain turned away and hurried back to the train, exploding with frustration. The one place no one had thought to look for him. And Bauer had been there. Now he was gone again.

The captain searched the area of the track on both sides of the carriages and the engine, and around the station, looking for footprints in the mud and snow that might show where the American had gone. But the ground was littered with dozens of footprints, and the fog cut visibility so severely that he couldn't see more than fifty feet in any direction. Bauer could be out there anywhere, laughing at him.

He climbed aboard the rear carriage and searched through the entire train again. By the time it departed Seinajocki, twenty minutes later, Captain von Planetz was back in his compartment, sitting by himself.

Was he a ghost, this Bauer? The captain was beginning to think so.

He went through the train again in his mind's eye. He had looked among the passengers, in the carriages, in the mail van, in the engine and tender. On the roofs. Even underneath, among the rods and springs of the undercarriages.

Where had he not looked?

There was nowhere he had not looked. But he had thought that before.

All day Monday the train steamed southeast through Finland. The fogs that had bedeviled its progress around Seinajoki condensed into a light rain, and the engineer was able to make up some of the lost time. They reached the Russian border town of Beloostrov at a little after seven o'clock in the evening. Petrograd was now only ten miles away.

Lenin and his fellow travelers strained to see out the carriage windows as they approached the station platform in the dark.

"There's a crowd there," Zina whispered anxiously. "It looks like a hundred people. God, more."

Inessa pressed her forehead to the glass and shielded her eyes from the compartment light.

"Don't you see them? Right by the tracks?" Zina said.

"Yes, I see them."

"Oh, God," Zina moaned. "We're going to be arrested."

"Stop it," Inessa scolded. "You've been saying that all the way from Zurich."

"They must be Cossacks," Zina persisted, her voice shaking with alarm. "Why else would there be a crowd?"

"Cossacks don't draw a crowd, Zina."

"Soldiers, then. Or police. That's just as bad."

"The crowd's here to welcome us," Inessa said, trying to reassure her. In her own mind she wasn't so sure.

The train finally stopped, and a crowd of several hundred on the platform began cheering. Many of them were workers from the nearby Sestroretsk munitions plant, rounded up by Bolshevik agitators and urged to meet Lenin's train.

A Bolshevik welcoming committee was on hand as well— old comrades Kamenev and Shlyapnikov, and Theodor Raskolnikov had driven up from Petrograd to greet him. Lenin's younger sister Maria was there, too, and longtime family friend Ludmilla Stahl.

Lenin hugged his sister and Ludmilla, and was suddenly swept off his feet by several workers and hoisted onto their shoulders. Alarmed by their boisterous enthusiasm, he begged them to put him down.

The crowd demanded a speech, and Lenin obliged. Someone found him a chair, and he climbed up on it, dressed in his new gray Chesterfield overcoat and bowler hat from Stockholm. He grinned broadly, raised his fist in the air in the characteristic revolutionary salutation, and spoke for several minutes about the need to wrest power from the landowners and the capitalists.

The conductor clanged his bell and called out for the Petrograd passengers to board the train.

Lenin broke off his speech and climbed back on board. His sister, Maria, and Kamenev and the other Bolsheviks who had traveled there to greet him, joined the party.

Back in the carriage, Zinoviev grabbed Kamenev's arm and pulled him aside. "You've just come from Petersburg," he said. "Are they going to arrest us?"

Kamenev grinned and shrugged elaborately, like a boy with a delicious secret.

"What the hell is that supposed to mean?" Zinoviev demanded.

Kamenev twisted his arm free. "You'll see, Grigory. You'll see. Just be patient."

As the train crept out of the Beloostrov station, the crowd swarmed around it, cheering and thrusting their hands through the windows.

Captain von Planetz leaned out a window and glanced up and down the row of carriages, looking for one of those hands to toss a bomb or fire a pistol, or for someone to leap from the shadows at the last minute and climb aboard.

But none of those things happened. If Bauer was not on the train and not at Beloostrov, then the chances were growing that he would not be at St. Petersburg either.

It dawned on him with something of a jolt that instead of relief, he was experiencing a deep and widening anxiety.

He sat down and extracted a cigarette from the pack he had purchased at Seinajocki and lit it. The brand was Russian and of poor quality. The tobacco was stale, loosely packed, and full of sweepings. It felt raw on the throat, and after several puffs the captain extinguished it.

He hardly looked forward to confronting this dangerous American, but there was a new consideration that had begun to worry him.

If Lenin arrived safely in St. Petersburg, then the captain should have been able to consider his mission accomplished. But General von Gontard's last orders had been very explicit. Kill Harry Bauer.

Only then would his mission be over.

The train slowed, and Bauer felt a series of minor jolts and subtle shifts of direction that told him it was hitting points—being shunted across the rows of tracks that funneled into a major railroad terminus.

Petrograd's Finland Station.

He should move now, he decided, while the carriages were still creeping through the dark train yard outside the terminal.

Bauer had spent the hours from Seinajoki in the fetal position, head bent forward, knees pulled up tight to his chest. If he had been an inch taller, he doubted he would have been able to squeeze into the space at all.

If it hadn't been for that damned German officer at Seinajoki, he would have been able to stay in the locomotive cab.

In last-minute desperation he had remembered a trick that American hoboes sometimes used when they couldn't find any other way to hop a train. They called it "riding the box." It meant hiding inside one of the train's battery boxes. Each carriage was equipped with two of them, suspended under the frame, one to a side. They held the storage batteries that powered the carriage's fans and lights. Since the mail van used the least power, one of its boxes was often empty.

One had been empty on this train, and he had squeezed in, thanks to the fog, without being seen.

The train stopped suddenly, and Bauer pushed against the bottom end of the door, swinging it out several inches to see where he was.

Almost at the platforms.

Now was the time.

He pushed the door out farther and rolled onto the ground. He fell into a slight depression between two sets of tracks and lay there for a moment, letting the cramps work out of his muscles.

The train bumped forward a few feet and then creaked slowly toward the station. The first carriage loomed alongside him. Faces peered out the lighted windows.

Bauer remained motionless, his eyes fixed on the windows as they inched past. For an instant he saw Inessa. She pressed her face close to the glass and cupped her hands over her eyes to shut out the light from the carriage. Did she sense his presence, so close below her in the dark?

She turned from the window, brushed a hand absently over her hair in a characteristic gesture, and then was gone.

The second carriage lumbered past. More faces at the windows. He wanted desperately to move now, before someone spotted him. He glanced around the dimly illuminated rail yard.

Lines of dark, empty carriages rested on adjacent tracks. Lanterns burned inside the signal tower and in several worksheds along the periphery. A yard engine was busy nearby, exhaling steam in large, whale-sized belches, as it strained to push a string of boxcars onto a siding. Just beyond the yard Bauer could see the station and its platforms, covered by a mammoth open shed. Lights blazed from the sheltered area as from a theater stage, and the platforms were jammed with thousands of people. Over the noises of the train yard their excited voices merged in a distant jumble, like the cheers from a crowded bleacher stand on a Sunday afternoon.

The last carriage inched past, and Bauer stood up. He would follow the train in to the platform, he decided, and lose himself in the throng. Lenin's progress from the train would necessarily be slow. He could push through the crowd, get close to him, and measure his opportunity.

A sudden blow sent him sprawling. He scrambled back to his feet. Arms locked around his chest from behind and crushed him in a bear hug. He rolled in the dirt and kicked and flailed to free himself. His attacker pulled him upright and switched his grip to his neck. Bauer tipped his head forward and snapped it back hard, smashing his cowlick into his assailant's chin. He followed up his split-second advantage with a swift backward jab of his elbow and a stomp of his heels.

The grip loosened and Bauer broke free and ran. He jumped two sets of tracks and ducked behind a freight car.

His assailant followed, encumbered by a leather satchel in his right hand.

Bauer jumped onto him the instant he rounded the corner of the boxcar. He dropped his satchel, and they fell to the ground again and rolled over several times. Bauer felt the hard iron edge of a rail beneath him, and then the flat wood surfaces of the track ties, protruding from their bed of crushed rock. He twisted over onto his side and strained to reach his pistol, buttoned inside his fur coat pocket.

His attacker pulled his arm away, rolled him over on his back, and closed his hands around his throat.

The face that loomed over him was the face he had expected. In the dim light he could see little more than his clenched teeth and the whites of his eyes. He reached up and got his own hands around Morozov's throat.

The Russian banged Bauer's head against the wooden tie, trying to break the American's grip. Bauer tightened his fingers into Morozov's flesh with all the force he could summon. As he squeezed, he felt the Russian's grip close ever tighter on him.

For nearly a minute they lay there, locked in a grim contest of strength. Bauer could no longer breathe. The Russian had gravity on his side. His weight shut off Bauer's windpipe. He tried to increase his own pressure on Morozov's throat, but the muscles in his arms were beginning to cramp.

From the railroad ties beneath him he felt a deep rumbling vibration. His eyes flicked to the boxcar. It rose up vertically, just behind him, a stationary black wall against the gray-purple of Petrograd's night sky. Immediately above him the car's two flat buffer heads protruded from their sockets at the corners.

The meaning of the vibration was clear. The yard engine must be backing a string of cars directly toward them.

When they coupled, their buffers would collide. The impact would jolt the entire string of cars forward several feet.

If he could push Morozov just a little farther up, and do it at the right moment, the lead boxcar's undercarriage would catch him in the back of the head as it rolled over them.

The vibration of the ties increased.

Bauer felt his strength ebbing rapidly. He relaxed his grip on the Russian's neck and let his arms fall to his side. Morozov reacted by raising up a bit, and then, throwing all his weight into his arms, rocking forward against Bauer's throat.

The American's lungs burned for air. His nostrils flared, his eyes popped wide. He willed what strength remained for one last effort to push Morozov up.

The vibration had now become an ear-filling rumble.

As Bauer was about to thrust the heel of his palms up against the Russian's chin, Morozov noticed the noise and turned his head.

The sudden image of the oncoming boxcar caused the terrorist to panic. Instead of ducking down between the rails, he rose to his feet to jump clear.

Bauer closed his eyes and let his arms fall to his sides. The sudden release of the pressure against his throat left him gasping like a beached fish.

The buffers collided.

Morozov bellowed. It was a savage scream, ripped from the depths of his soul.

The Russian's boots kicked Bauer in the stomach. The boxcars rocked to a stop.

Bauer's chest heaved in spasms as he tried to fill his starved lungs. His throat burned, and his eyes were blurred with tears.

Incredibly, the Russian was till on top on him, one foot on his stomach, the other on the rail near his arm.

Bauer pushed at the boot. It sagged away from him, as if weightless. Bauer crawled out from between the rails and rose unsteadily to his feet, clinging to the side of a boxcar for support.

Morozov moaned piteously. The sounds fell from his mouth in a wavery, froth-clotted blubber. Bauer wiped his eyes to see. The Russian was standing between the cars, his grotesque features paralyzed with shock.

In the near darkness Bauer couldn't grasp what had happened. Why was he standing there?

"Satchel," Morozov grunted. Bauer saw his arm flap loosely, indicating the direction.

He followed the motion and saw a black lump lying a few feet away. The same leather bag, with the bombs in it, that Morozov had thrown from the sledge.

Bauer glanced back at the Russian. The beam from a light

somewhere in the yard swung briefly past, and in its glare he saw Morozov's situation.

The Russian was impaled between the buffers.

The flat, round, four-inch-diameter heads had struck him in the stomach and the small of the back, and with the inertia of tons behind them, had pushed through him like a punch through paper. His coat was pulled into the wound, front and back, as if someone had used it to plug a hole.

He was beyond help. Bauer was astonished that he was still alive—and conscious.

"Satchel," Morozov whispered again. "Vodka."

Bauer stumbled over to it, picked it up, and brought it back. It seemed weighted with lead.

"Vodka," Morozov muttered. "Quick."

Bauer unstrapped the bag, fished inside for a bottle, and found it. About a pint remained. He uncorked it and handed it to the Russian.

Morozov drank it all in a single swallow and dropped the bottle down onto the track.

"Help any?"

Morozov shook his head.

"We all know," Morozov said, his voice growing deeper and slower, like an unwinding gramophone record. "You can't do it."

"It'll be easier—with you out of the way."

"They'll kill you first," he whispered. He sucked in a ragged breath and shivered violently.

"What do you care? You won't be around to see it."

The Russian's head slipped forward, then straightened up again. Sweat drenched his deformed face. The terrorist finally terrorized.

Bauer felt no sympathy for him. But neither did he savor the moment. He pulled out his pistol and pushed the safety to off. "I'm leaving. You want to shorten this?"

The Russian stared at the pistol barrel, his one good eye clouded with a pathetic resignation. "Tell them . . . I laughed at this."

"I'll tell them."

"No more vodka?"

"No."

Morozov nodded. "Go ahead then."

Bauer rested the muzzle against the Russian's temple. "You wouldn't have done as much for me, would you?"

"No," he admitted.

Death was making a mockery of Morozov's life, Bauer thought, killing him in a way that was both gruesome and humiliating. In a few years people would probably joke about it.

He pulled the trigger. Morozov's head snapped against his shoulder, then slumped to his chest. His arms dangled loose at his sides. The buffer heads prevented him from falling over, so he was left standing there, listing slightly forward and to one side, a macabre surprise for the yard man when he arrived to pin the couplings.

Bauer pocketed the pistol, started off, then hesitated next to the satchel.

He opened it again and felt around inside. Four more tomato can bombs remained, rolled up inside some clothes, along with an extra pair of shoes and a few other personal effects. Underneath, filling the entire bottom two-thirds of the case, were packed several tightly stuffed cloth bags, which, along with the bombs, accounted for the satchel's unusual weight.

Bauer threw out the clothes and shoes and buckled the satchel up. He hoisted it onto his shoulder and headed toward the light and noise of the station.

PETROGRAD

As the carriages moved into Finland Station, Captain von Planetz's heart sank. After Beloostrov he had expected a crowd here, but this was beyond his worst fears. The platform, decked with hundreds of red-and-gold arches, was packed with people along its entire length.

Many were in uniform. Most, including an honor guard, were sailors from the nearby Kronstadt barracks. A large contingent of Red Guards—young Bolsheviks wearing red armbands and pistols—occupied the key locations on the platform near the carriage doors.

Huge banners bearing revolutionary slogans flapped over the throng, obscuring much of it from view. Over the tremendous din of voices, a brass band blared.

Seconds before the train halted, the captain forced open a carriage door and jumped out into the crowd. Lenin was in the next carriage back, and he quickly pushed his way toward it. He wanted to be close by when the Bolshevik leader emerged.

The train stopped. The carriage door opened, and Lenin stepped out first. He had substituted a workman's cap for his bowler hat. He paused at the bottom step and waved uncertainly. He seemed stunned by the massive welcome.

There was a loud, echoing trumpet voluntary, and the Kronstadt barracks guard of honor presented arms.

A sustained, thunderous cheer shook the station.

A woman in the Bolshevik welcoming committee, Alexandra Kollontai, stepped forward and placed a large bouquet of red roses in Lenin's hands. He took it with an embarrassed grin and made a stiff bow.

Bolshevik Red Guards formed a protective cordon around their leader to keep the crowd back.

The military band struck up the "Internationale," the theme song of the worldwide revolutionary movement, but after a few uncertain bars it abandoned the unfamiliar tune in favor of the "Marseillaise."

The captain of the honor guard saluted, and after a moment's hesitation Lenin returned the salute. With his wife, Nadya, a step behind him, he strode past the honor guard, still not certain what was expected of him. Bonch-Bruyevich, a member of the welcoming committee, took his arm and whispered something in his ear. Lenin nodded.

Captain von Planetz hurried along behind, his eyes scanning the crowd. He wondered what had become of Morozov. He had not seen him get off the train.

At the moment he wasn't needed. Several dozen Red Guards were now grouped tightly around Lenin, and many more were prowling through the crowd, pushing people out of the way.

Lenin removed his cap, faced the honor guard, and spoke in a loud monotone: "Sailors, comrades. As I greet you, I don't know if you still have faith in all the sweet promises of the provisional government, but I do know that these sweet promises are all cruel deceptions. You're being deceived. The Russian people are being deceived. The people need peace.

The people need bread and land. And what does the government offer? War and hunger. And the land remains with the landowners. Sailors, comrades, together we must fight for a true socialist revolution, fight for the ultimate victory of the proletariat! Long live the international socialist revolution!"

The speech done, others from the local Bolshevik party rushed up to greet him, and after a brief detour into the Czar's Imperial Waiting Room to receive the welcome of the local Petrograd Soviet, Lenin was escorted out of the station, where a line of motorcars waited to whisk him and his entourage several blocks away to the Kshesinskaya Mansion. A month earlier the palace of the czar's mistress, it was now the Bolshevik party's new headquarters.

The scene in the square outside was unlike anything the captain had ever witnessed. It dwarfed even the kaiser's triumphal marches through Berlin before the war. Tens of thousands of people filled the square and the adjacent side streets. Automobile horns honked, brass bands played, torchlights flickered, and banners flapped and streamed in the night air like a thousand wings. Searchlights from nearby Peter and Paul Fortress illuminated the scene. Sharp and rigid as swords, their bold shafts of light slashed back and forth through the blackness above the city.

The crowd closed in on Lenin when he appeared outside the station doors. He reached the automobile waiting for him at the curb, but the crowd around it prevented it from moving.

After some confusion a group of Red Guards formed a wedge and cleared a path for him to an armored car, parked nearby.

Lenin climbed onto the turret and from that higher vantage stood before the throng, elation and disbelief at the sheer intimidating dimensions of his reception evident on his face. He tried to make another speech, but the words drifted out soundlessly, absorbed into the noises of the square.

After a moment he stepped down and climbed into the armored car. Its big engine revved noisily, and it pushed forward at a crawl, plowing slowly through the massed humanity. At the next street corner it stopped and Lenin mounted the turret once more. He tried to speak again, but realizing that few could hear him, he settled for a defiant shout: "Long

live the socialist revolution! Down with the compromisers!"
He raised both fists high over his head, like a victorious
fighter accepting the applause of the arena. The crowd roared
its approval.

Captain von Planetz studied the faces around him. Somewhere in that sea of anonymous humanity Bauer was watching, calculating his chances. The captain felt it. Bauer would
have noticed the Red Guards immediately, and he would
know that even if he could get close enough for a shot at
Lenin, someone would inevitably see him, and he would
never escape through this crowd alive.

So he would wait for a better chance.

The short trip from Finland Station to the party headquarters took more than an hour. At each corner along
Simbursk Street and at the Sampsonievsky Bridge the armored car stopped and Lenin climbed onto the turret to
rouse the crowd with defiant shouts and waving fists. Five,
ten, fifteen times he spoke, each time drawing wild cheers.

Finally, near midnight, the armored car reached the white
brick Kshesinskaya Mansion. On the palace lawns, and over-
flowing across the street into Alexandrovsky Park, another
huge crowd waited to hear him. He addressed them briefly,
and then, in the company of the commander of the Bolshevik
Military Committee and several pistol-wielding Red Guards,
he disappeared inside.

Captain von Planetz followed behind the armored car all
the way to the mansion and walked behind Lenin and his
protective cordon of guards through the palace's front entrance. Someone was already standing out on the second floor
balcony, haranguing the crowd below.

Guards were stationed at the entrance, but the doors were
wide open and packed with people moving in both directions.
No effort was made to screen anyone going in.

Lenin was escorted up the mansion's grand staircase to the
main reception room, where a group of Bolshevik party regu-
lars had assembled to meet him. Someone brought him a cup
of tea. The conversations were loud and animated. The captain glanced around the room, then went outside to the
hallway and began searching systematically through the rooms
on that part of the second floor. The palace had been completely looted of its furniture. In its place had been installed a

seemingly endless number of battered tables, chairs, and desks.

The captain went back to check on Lenin again. The Bolshevik leader was surrounded by a tight knot of listeners. Near the room's double doorway, and at intervals along the walls, Red Guards had stationed themselves, thumbs thrust in belts, hands resting on pistol grips. They looked cocky and undisciplined.

The captain went downstairs and made a hurried circuit of the rooms on the ground floor. Harry Bauer was not in any of them.

Keeping to the safe distance of the streets, Bauer explored the mansion and the grounds around it. It was two stories high, with two wings extending out from each end of the central structure to form a large courtyard. The crowd was concentrated entirely in the courtyard and in the park opposite it. Every window in the main part of the palace blazed with light. The two wings, however, were dark.

He noticed a servants' entrance hidden in the shadows of a stand of low evergreen shrubs at the back. It was the only unguarded door into the mansion. He approached it but found it was secured with a locked iron grille. He tried to reach his fingers through the grille to trip the spring latch on the other side, but without a heavy bar of some kind to pry the grille open, it wasn't possible.

He examined the walls and roof of the mansion. The few windows within reach of the ground were similarly protected with heavy bars. Scaling up to a second-story window or balcony was a possibility, but it would also be time-consuming and dangerous.

The only way in, he guessed, was through the front door.

Bauer withdrew one of the bombs and a box of matches from Morozov's satchel, and then shoved the satchel out of sight under the branches of an evergreen shrub.

He walked out to the narrow street that ran along the back of the mansion. Automobiles were parked bumper to bumper along the curb. Most were vintage 1910 or older, vehicles with hand-crank starters and trouble-prone gearboxes.

A short distance away he found something more to his liking. It was an American Dodge military ambulance, about a year old, with an open front seat and an electric starter. The key was not in the ignition switch. Bauer groped under the dashboard for the ignition wires and yanked them loose. He adjusted the magneto setting on the steering wheel, pulled out the choke, and touched the bare copper ends of the wires together. The ambulance's big four-cylinder engine coughed several times, then caught and smoothed out into a satisfying idle. Bauer separated the wires and tucked them back under the dash.

He walked back around to the front of the building and watched the activity in the courtyard. Another revolutionary orator had come out onto the balcony to address the crowd. He kept repeating the same phrase over and over in a lung-bursting bellow that could be heard all the way at the far end of Alexandrovsky Park. The crowd began to pick up his words. Starting underneath the balcony, the chant spread across the lawn and into the park, until the words reverberated from thousands of throats, like some tribal war cry.

Now was as good as ever, he decided. He stepped out onto the lawn, walked up behind a Red Guard standing at the back edge of the crowd, and swatted him with his open hand on the back of the head, knocking off his cap. The guard spun around. Bauer grinned and made an obscene gesture with his hand. The guard, a kid barely out of his teens, lunged at him. Bauer jumped out of his way and ran off into the dark around the back of the mansion. The guard pursued him.

Bauer ducked behind a bush. The instant the kid ran past, the American moved in behind him, threw an arm under his chin, and hit him at the base of the skull with his balled fist.

The Red Guard collapsed like a dropped puppet. Bauer picked him up, threw him over his shoulder and carried him over to the Dodge ambulance.

As quickly as he could, he stripped the guard of his cap, arm band, belt, pistol, and holster and put them on himself. He bound and gagged the boy with bandage and tape from one of the ambulance's first-aid cabinets and shoved him into the back.

Bauer removed the guard's ancient revolver from its holster and replaced it with his own automatic pistol. He trotted back around to the front of the mansion. Aping the manner of the young revolutionaries around him, he swaggered through the front door, chin out and mouth curled in a complacent smirk.

Inside, he moved rapidly through the foyer and up the grand staircase. A Red Guard at the top landing said something to him and laughed. Bauer replied with a *"Da,"* and pushed on by him. The only other expressions he knew in Russian were *"nyet," "ya lyu blyu"* ("I love you,") and *"yeb tvoyu mat"* ("fuck your mother"). He hoped they'd get him through the night.

The upstairs hallway was crowded and noisy. Bauer pulled his cap down a little farther to hide his eyes, and jostled through the crush. Through an opened set of double doors, he caught a glimpse of Zinoviev. He was in a corner, holding a private conversation with someone. He saw Olga Ravich talking to Inessa. Inessa seemed not to be listening. She kept glancing around, as if expecting something. In the center of the room stood Lenin, holding a cup of tea and gesticulating with his free hand before a group of listeners. His face was shining.

Bauer continued along the corridor to the next door and opened it. The room was an extension of the first room and just as crowded.

The secret, he kept telling himself, was to keep moving. Like a man treading water, the moment he stopped he'd sink.

The next door down opened into a small upstairs kitchen. Several women were there, washing cups and saucers and making tea and setting out plates of bread and sausage. They were chattering excitedly among themselves and paid no attention to Bauer. He walked into the service pantry. It was a long, narrow room, flanked along its entire length by counters and shelves. A woman bustled past him from the dining room, carrying a tray of dirty teacups.

He looked through the window in the swinging door. Lenin had moved to the front of the room. He was shaking hands with someone who had just stepped into the room through a pair of opened French doors. Of course, Bauer recalled. The balcony.

Lenin stepped out onto the balcony himself and raised his arms high above his head, fists clenched. Even from behind the pantry door, Bauer could hear the echoing roar of the crowd below.

A searchlight from Alexandrovsky Park settled its powerful beam on Lenin. From inside, the Bolshevik leader appeared suddenly cast in sharp silhouette, his figure outlined against the night sky with a ghostly, glowing blue-white corona.

Better than he had hoped for, Bauer thought.

He hurried back through the kitchen and out into the corridor. He looked to the right and left. Closed doors at each end. They open into the wings, he decided. He was closer to the left end, so he went in that direction.

He twisted the doorknob. It was not locked. He ducked through and closed the door. The corridor on the other side was pitch-black. Bauer fumbled under the knob for a lock but failed to find one. No matter. The wing was cold and damp from disuse. Bauer felt for the wall on his left, and started forward, using his hand to guide him. He passed by one door, then opened the second.

He stepped in and shut the door. Again he felt for a lock but found none.

The room was large and bare, with two pairs of French doors overlooking the courtyard. Light from outside filtered through gauze curtains. Bauer crossed to the pair on his left, pushed the curtains aside a few inches and looked out. Diagonally across the courtyard he could see Lenin, standing on the center balcony, bathed in the blue-white aura of the searchlight, one arm pumping forcefully in the air to punctuate his words.

He pressed downward on the doors' handles and gave them a hard yank. They were stuck. He yanked harder and they popped inward.

Bauer pulled his pistol from the borrowed holster and lay out flat on the floor so he could not be seen from below. He pushed the right half of the French door closed, then edged the left half inward about six inches.

Wide enough, he decided. He slid the pistol through the opening. He estimated the distance to be about seventy feet.

He had to kill him, not just hit him. Even though he was able to steady the pistol's butt on the floor, it would be a tough shot.

The noise of the crowd would hide the report of the pistol.

He'd aim for the head on the first shot. If he missed, he'd switch his target to the chest—and fire the whole clip, if necessary.

Captain von Planetz felt a chill of terror squeeze the back of his neck. He was standing next to Zinoviev, near the open doors to the balcony. The searchlight from the park across the street threw a brilliant swath of illumination into the room. The captain closed his eyes and turned away from the intense glare. When he opened them, seconds later, he was staring into the face of Harry Bauer.

It was framed in the pantry door window, at the back of the room. The bright light caught his features for only a moment, and then he was gone.

For a second the captain thought it was an hallucination. So preoccupied had he been with finding Bauer, he was afraid that he was beginning to see the American assassin everywhere.

He ran into the pantry. No one there. Farther back, in the kitchen, he questioned several of the women. Had a man just come in here? Yes, they said. What did he look like? He wore a Red Guard's arm band. Was he big? Yes. Did he say anything? No. Where did he go? Out that way, one replied, pointing to the door that led out to the main hall. Did anyone notice which way down the hall he turned? To the left, one woman thought, toward the south wing.

The captain ran out to the hallway and looked to the left. No one there. The door at the end, leading into the south wing, was closed. He hurried back to the reception room and pulled Zinoviev into a corner.

"Don't tell me," the Russian said sarcastically. "You just saw the American."

"Yes. He's disguised as a Red Guard."

"Where did you see him?"

"In the pantry, less than a minute ago. The women think he ran into the south wing."

"Are you armed?"

"Yes."

"Go see what you can find, then. I'll alert the guards downstairs. If he's really in the building, we've got him."

"Shouldn't you warn Lenin?"

Zinoviev glanced toward the balcony. The Bolshevik leader

was in full oratorical flight, his twangy voice already hoarse from the many speeches he had made that night. But his enthusiasm for his cause still burned in every word. He was enjoying his sudden celebrity enormously. Interrupting him for anything short of imminent peril would infuriate him—and everyone else.

"No. It's not necessary," Zinoviev replied. "I'll round up some help and join up with you in a minute. Go."

The captain strode quickly out to the hallway, turned left, and headed toward the south wing. At the door he paused. Something deep inside him hoped that it would be locked, but it wasn't. He pulled the pistol from his pocket and clicked the safety to off. After a deep breath he pushed the door open and stepped through.

The darkness on the other side unsettled him for a moment. He closed the door slowly and stood absolutely still, listening. In the distance he could hear Lenin's voice and the approving murmur of the crowd outside. In the blackness of the wing's corridor itself, he heard nothing but the pounding of his own heart.

It pained him to recognize how frightened he was. The thought of finally meeting Bauer face to face terrified him. He wasn't sure why. He had arrested and interrogated some pretty desperate criminals in his life. But of course he had always had the protective institutions of the law and the able bodies of the police and the soldiery to stand behind. Now he was far from home, pitting himself against a man who had demonstrated the ability to outwit him—and everyone else—repeatedly.

The captain stood inside the door for several minutes, afraid to throw on a light switch, afraid to move down the dark hall. A clock somewhere back in the main part of the mansion began to strike the hour. He counted the strokes: there were twelve.

If only Zinoviev would hurry with his reinforcements!

He heard a low squeaking noise in a room on the left of the corridor. Someone opening a window?

My God, he realized, that's it. Lenin's out there on the balcony. Bauer will have a clear shot at him right across the courtyard.

He bit his lip and started down the corridor, running his hand along the wall to guide him.

Harry Bauer relaxed his grip on the pistol and let his head sink to the floor. It was no damned good. Just no damned good at all.

What was the matter with him? He was letting desperation get the better of his experience and common sense. His chances of hitting Lenin with that pistol from seventy feet were just about zero.

It was nearly impossible to sight the barrel properly in the dark, even with both his arm and the pistol butt resting on the floor. And even with perfect aim, a pistol bullet fired over that distance could easily stray several feet wide of the target. And he didn't know this pistol's peculiarities—whether it fired high or low, to the left or right. And if he was lucky enough to hit Lenin, the chances of killing him with one bullet were less than even.

It was just no damned good. He would make a lot of noise and probably get himself killed instead. And going back inside for a closer shot would certainly get him killed.

He felt the tomato can of gelignite in his pocket. He had brought it along with his retreat in mind, but suddenly he had another idea.

He looked out at Lenin again. Seventy feet. Not that long a throw. Less distance than the average infield out. Just ten feet farther than the pitcher's mound to home plate. And he didn't have to throw it hard. Just a lob. And he didn't have to be that accurate. Anywhere on the balcony would do the job. And Lenin was alone out there. No one else would get hurt.

Bauer sat back on his knees and pulled the bomb and the box of matches from his pocket. The chances were a hell of a lot better than with the pistol. In fact, they were damned good. He knew he could hit that balcony a hundred throws out of a hundred.

The drawbacks were three. He'd have to open the French doors all the way and risk attracting attention from below. And he'd have to time the throw precisely. The bomb needed to explode within about a second of hitting the balcony—before it could bounce away or before someone had time to smother it or throw it clear. That meant holding the bomb until the fuse had burned nearly all the way down.

If it wasn't a dud, it would do the job.

TUESDAY
APRIL 17

PETROGRAD

Captain von Planetz came to the edge of a door molding and stopped. He felt carefully for the knob, turned it, and eased the door slowly inward.

No sound from inside. He pushed a little farther and craned his head around the edge. Light from the window illuminated the interior dimly. A solitary table stood against one wall. Nothing else. Through the window he could see Lenin out on the balcony. He was shaking his fist. The crowd roared back.

He inched along the corridor to the next door and hesitated. If Bauer was in there he should see him instantly, silhouetted against the light from the French doors. Bauer would have to turn around, and he should not be able to see the captain nearly as well.

The captain's advantage would last about a second. In that length of time he would have to kill him.

He turned the knob until the latch was clear of the striker plate. He pushed the door inward a fraction of an inch and then stopped. He heard the crowd outside again, cheering wildly.

His heart was tripping so furiously that his hands shook. His mouth felt dry and cold.

He would make far less of a target, he realized, if he was on the floor. Slowly, deliberately, he lowered himself onto his stomach and positioned his pistol out in front of him, settling the butt against the top of the threshold.

The captain waited until he heard the crowd again, then shoved hard against the base of the door. It swung inward on screeching hinges. He saw the light blazing through the French doors, but no silhouette of Bauer.

Harry Bauer crouched against the wall between the French doors and pulled a match from the box to ignite the bomb's fuse.

A sudden noise behind him.

He swung around, dropped the bomb and the matches and flattened himself out on his stomach, facing the corridor door. His hands swept the floor around him, feeling for his pistol. He couldn't find it.

An explosion of bluish flame erupted near the door's threshold. A bullet slammed into the wall inches above his head, spraying him with plaster dust.

He saw someone now, lying prone in the doorway. Another bang and spurt of fire.

Pain, hot as the slap of a branding iron, stung his left arm.

He pushed to his feet, took one leaping stride forward, and propelled himself toward the doorway in a headfirst slide.

His knee struck the pistol, knocking it loose. He heard it clatter off along the floor. He groped in the dark, caught a flailing arm and pinned it quickly behind the intruder's back.

He scrambled to his feet, pulling the man up with him. His arm burned fiercely.

"Who are you?" he demanded.

No reply. He pressed upward on the arm. "Who the hell are you?"

"Von Planetz."

"The German captain?"

"Yes."

Near the center of the room Bauer saw one of the pistols lying in the dim rectangle of light from the French doors. He pushed his captive forward until they were standing over it, then bent down, twisting Von Planetz forward in the process, and scooped it up.

He struck Von Planetz with the pistol butt just over his left ear, and felt him go limp. He dropped him to the floor and ran back to the French doors. Lenin was still out there on the balcony. In the noise no one seemed to have heard the pistol fire.

He fell to his knees and searched the floor to find the bomb and the box of matches again. He pulled the fuse on the can taut and measured it against the span of his hand. Four inches. It would burn at two seconds an inch. He cradled the bomb in the crook of his arm, pulled a match from the box and struck it. In his haste the matchstick broke. Cursing, he drew out another and scratched it more carefully across the box's striking surface. He let it flare for a second, then applied it to the fuse. The rope smoked for an instant, then turned red and began to hiss. He would throw it on the count of six. It would arch across the intervening seventy feet during the seven count. It would land in the balcony and explode on eight. If he was a second off either way, it would still work.

One one-thousand.

With his free hand he pushed the gauze curtain aside and yanked open the French doors. Lenin was working himself into a frenzied peroration, pounding a fist on the balcony rail, jabbing a finger accusingly into the night air. His neck swelled from the effort, and his face, purplish in the searchlight's glare, was twisted in an orgasm of passionate intensity.

The people packed in the courtyard and in the park beyond were screaming their approval. Their voices boomed off the sides of the Kshesinskaya Palace like waves against a rock cliff.

Two one-thousand.

Light from an overhead chandelier flooded the room. Bauer spun around. The German captain was still on the floor. Bauer blinked and squinted, trying to adjust his vision to the abrupt brightness.

What he saw in the doorway didn't make any sense.

It was Zinoviev. His expression was wild. One of his arms was wrapped tightly around Inessa Armand's throat. The other held a pistol pressed to the side of her head.

Three one-thousand.

Zinoviev was saying something to him. He could see his mouth moving, but he couldn't hear his words over the noise of the crowd outside.

Inessa's hair was disheveled. It tumbled across her forehead, partly hiding her face. Her fingers tugged at Zinoviev's arm. She seemed more humiliated and angry than frightened. There was fury in her eyes. This is your fault, Bauer, they said. See what you've done now.

Four one-thousand.

Why was Zinoviev holding her?

See what I've done now.

Captain von Planetz stirred. He sat up. His eyes darted from Zinoviev to Bauer. He saw the tomato can and its burning fuse and froze.

Five one-thousand.

In the next second Bauer did a lot of thinking. If he threw the bomb at Lenin, Zinoviev would shoot him. And possibly Inessa as well. If he threw it at Zinoviev, or if he just went on standing there for another three seconds, it would kill them all.

Where else could he throw it? Dropping it out the open French doors would kill people in the crowd below. But it seemed the only choice.

Six one-thousand.

Zinoviev yanked Inessa with him back out into the corridor and behind the relative safety of a wall.

Bauer clamped his teeth over the fuse and tried to bite it off. But the cord had burned too far down. The flame was sputtering into the hole in the top of the can, eating toward the igniter cap planted in the gelignite below.

Seven one-thousand.

Bauer bent down on the floor and clasped his mouth over the burning nub and sucked against it with all his strength, to starve the fuse of oxygen.

Eight one-thousand.

If it didn't work, he consoled himself with the thought that, unlike his last brush with death in the Mexican desert, this time there'd be no suffering. The bomb would scatter his brains and flesh against the four walls of the room before they could coordinate in a final expression of pain.

He held the suction. His face reddened and he began to feel faint.

Nine one-thousand.

He raised his eyes and saw Captain von Planetz. He was

lying flat on his stomach, his arms wrapped tight around his head.

Ten one-thousand.

The flame in the fuse would die slowly, Bauer told himself. If he took his mouth off too soon, it would flare back. He could hold his breath for about a minute, but the need to maintain a vacuum over the fuse was far more demanding. The slightest easing up might allow enough oxygen back over the fuse to reignite it.

Eleven one-thousand.

His lungs ached. The room began to spin and grow dim. He collapsed onto the floor, almost losing his grip on the can.

Twelve one-thousand.

He lost count.

On the edge of blacking out, he let the bomb fall from his mouth and released his breath in a shivering exhalation.

He was still in one piece inside his own skin.

Captain von Planetz was reaching for the loose pistol, on the floor to his left. Bauer dropped behind the German and got to it first. He snapped it up and pressed it against the captain's neck.

"Don't resist. I'll kill you."

The captain went limp. Bauer could smell the acrid odor of fear on him.

"Stand up."

Bauer transferred the pistol to the side of the captain's head and wrapped his arm around his neck from behind. He glanced out the window. The searchlight had shifted away. The balcony was dark and Lenin was no longer on it.

"Toward the door," Bauer said, nudging the captain forward. "Quick."

Zinoviev was still in the corridor, huddled against the far wall, his pistol still pressed against the mane of chestnut hair by Inessa's temple. Bauer stopped in the doorway, keeping Von Planetz in front of him.

"So your bomb was a dud," Zinoviev sneered.

Bauer shook his head.

"I'll kill her, Bauer, if you try anything."

"What'll Lenin say? She's a comrade, isn't she?"

"She's a traitor."

"Why?"

"She let you get away, didn't she?"

"It wasn't her fault." Bauer avoided Inessa's eyes.

"We know she helped you."

And now he had to help her.

"That's crazy," he protested. "She tried to kill me. It wasn't her fault I got away. But if you want to kill one of your own people, don't let me stop you."

Zinoviev laughed. "He's a good liar, don't you agree, Captain?"

Bauer felt the German's head nod slightly against his arm. It infuriated him, and he almost pulled the trigger.

"Your position is hopeless, Bauer," Zinoviev warned.

Inessa glared at him, her dark eyes burning with anger. Did she think he had betrayed her? He had not promised her anything, after all. She had not killed him in the church because she had assumed she could scare him away. She had been naïve to assume that.

"You disappoint me, Harry."

Bauer looked at her pleadingly. "Too much is at stake," he said.

"Too much what? Money?"

"There are other reasons."

"How can there be? You don't believe in anything else. You're a hired assassin."

The accusation stung him deeply. "The bastard is still alive, isn't he?" he shouted. "I haven't killed him yet, have I?"

"You still intend to. . . ."

Zinoviev tightened his arm against her throat and told her to shut up. "We're stalemated," he said. "Take your hostage and get out."

Bauer had already worked through all the permutations. Zinoviev was right. Neither of them could kill his hostage without immediately exposing himself to being shot by the other. Unless Zinoviev was bluffing. But even if he was, the result was the same.

"As long as Lenin is safe, she'll be safe," Zinoviev said.

Bauer glanced at his left arm, wrapped around Von Planetz's neck. Blood had soaked the sleeve and was dripping from his elbow onto the floor. He didn't want it to end like this. He didn't mind dying. He just wanted it to have some point. To make some sense.

"Go!" Zinoviev shouted, waving his pistol barrel. "Get away from here!"

"You go first," Bauer demanded. "Clear a path for us."

Zinoviev backed Inessa to the door, pushed it open with his shoulder, and retreated through, leaving the door open.

Bauer walked out behind Von Planetz. The center hallway was already deserted.

At the grand staircase Zinoviev maneuvered himself and Inessa around behind Bauer and the captain. "We'll stay here," he said. "The way is clear right out the front door. Get moving."

Bauer's eyes were fixed on Inessa, hoping for some last sign from her. Of forgiveness. Or understanding. Or just farewell. She was looking at him, but her expressive face was blank. She had retreated from him completely, broken off all connection with him. Her eyes were emotionless. Even the anger had drained away. She seemed buried within herself, her mind intent on some deep inner well of thought or feeling.

Suddenly she smiled at him and spoke to him in English. The words didn't fit the smile, and they spilled out so rapidly and softly that he almost didn't hear them.

"A trap below, Harry."

Bauer looked past to Zinoviev. The Russian didn't appear to have heard or understood what she had just said. "We're taking the back stairs," Bauer told him.

Zinoviev objected. "Why? You'll still have to go out the front. It's the only exit."

"We're using the back stairs." Bauer didn't wait for the Russian to agree. He pulled Von Planetz over to the door leading to the back stairwell, pushed it open, and retreated through, walking backwards.

Bauer slammed the door closed and started down the stairs, holding the pistol against the German's back.

The captain stopped on the landing and twisted his face around. "I'm no good to you as a hostage," he warned.

"Why not?"

"I'm a German. They didn't want me with them to begin

with. They're afraid I'll compromise them. They'll sacrifice me just to get to you."

The door on the second floor landing above them opened and a man came through, moving briskly. He clattered down the stairs and nearly collided with them on the landing.

Bauer felt Von Planetz stiffen in shock. He gaped past him in disbelief.

It was Lenin.

The Red Guards had cleared the front staircase for Zinoviev's trap, and Bauer had momentarily confused them by using the back stairs. And no one had had time to warn Lenin.

The man seemed in a transport of energized euphoria. This was his night, the night he had endured years of prison and exile for, the night he had been waiting for all his life. His time had come, and buoyed by the massive reception he had received, he exuded that assurance so positively that it radiated from him like light.

Just move the pistol out from behind the captain's back, Bauer thought. Lenin was scarcely three feet away from him. Point-blank range.

He had to remind himself why he was going to do this. He had made a contract. And he had never failed to carry one out. Lenin meant nothing to him personally. It was a matter of pride.

You're a hired assassin.

So much for Inessa.

Lenin put a hand on Von Planetz's shoulder in passing and said something to him in Russian.

Bauer watched him brush past.

There was the war. America was in it, and Lenin was her enemy.

Worth two divisions.

And the moment he carried out his mission, Colonel House would see to it that he never returned home alive.

So much for patriotism.

He couldn't come out a winner this time, no matter what he did. He slipped his hand over the captain's mouth and moved the pistol out from behind his back.

Lenin rushed down the steps and stopped to pull open the

door on the ground floor. He didn't look back, so he never saw Bauer's pistol trained on him.

What was left to hope for?

The door closed and Lenin was gone. The captain sagged against the wall. "God in heaven, you didn't do it," he gasped.

Bauer shoved the pistol against the captain's ribs and nudged him down the steps. At the bottom he stopped. "We can't go out the front. The perfect ambush point would be just outside the front door. So we have to go out the back. There's an outside door there. If we're lucky, they won't have thought of it yet. All we have to do is unlock it. Look out now and tell me what you see."

Von Planetz opened the door an inch. He turned back to Bauer. "Nothing. The corridor's clear."

Bauer released his grip on the captain. "We can move faster this way. But don't forget I can still shoot you. Let's go."

Bauer and Von Planetz ran down the corridor, through a pantry, and into the back service hall. Bauer found the back door and unbolted it.

They heard the approaching commotion of voices. "You going to stay here?" Bauer asked.

"You don't need me anymore."

"Neither do they. You said so yourself."

Von Planetz pushed a finger against his glasses nervously. "Yes," he admitted.

"Why are you still with them, anyway?"

"My government ordered me to kill you."

Bauer squinted at the German captain incredulously. "You don't look the type for the job. No offense."

"I didn't choose it. They were desperate to stop you."

Bauer nodded. "Well, we have no reason to hurt each other anymore, do we?"

The captain rubbed a hand hard across his face, the agony of indecision apparent in his expression.

Bauer waved his pistol impatiently. "The Bolsheviks will betray you to the provisional government. And the government will shoot you as a German spy. It's as simple as that. Now you want to go with me or not?"

Captain von Planetz nodded.

"Then let's go, for Christ's sake!"

The captain followed Bauer out the door. The American reached under the bush where he had hidden Morozov's satchel and pulled it out. "Straight this way," he directed. "As fast as you can move."

They crossed the darkened lawn, slipping on the traces of unmelted winter snow, and arrived at the back of the ambulance, gasping for breath. Bauer motioned for the captain to help him. Together they yanked open the rear door and dragged the bound and gagged Red Guard out of the back and dumped him unceremoniously onto the pavement. Bauer felt he was about to pass out. He pushed the back door closed and leaned against it. "You know how to drive?"

"Yes. Of course."

He motioned toward the driver's seat. Von Planetz climbed in. Bauer pulled himself around to the passenger side, clinging to the vehicle for support. He threw the satchel in, then crawled up onto the seat.

He looked back and saw a dozen Red Guards advancing toward them, fanning out across the lawn. He reached under the dash and found the wires he had pulled out earlier. Von Planetz adjusted the spark and yanked out the choke. Bauer touched the wires together. The engine coughed, then caught, then died.

"Pump the gas!"

Von Planetz pushed his foot down twice on the pedal. Bauer touched the wires again. The engine caught, spluttered, and then smoothed out.

Bauer heard a pistol shot and a high-pitched pinging noise as a bullet ricocheted off the front hood.

"Jesus! Get it into gear! Hurry up!"

Unfamiliar with the vehicle, the captain required a few moments to find first gear. Another bullet popped through the wall of the van, two feet behind the open cab.

Finally the captain released the clutch and the vehicle lurched from the curb to the street. He readjusted the spark and pushed the choke halfway in. The engine responded with a powerful surge.

Bauer looked back again and saw that their pursuers had stretched out along the street and threatened to surround them. "They'll try to cut us off at the corner," he shouted,

pointing to the intersection just ahead. Several Red Guards
were already running out into the roadway alongside the
vehicle, firing at it with their pistols. Bauer crouched down
below the windshield, one foot out on the running board. He
heard a crack and tinkle of glass. "There goes a headlamp,"
he muttered.

Von Planetz shoved his glasses back on his nose, jammed
the choke all the way forward and slammed the accelerator to
the floor. The Dodge bounded forward.

Bauer grabbed the frame to hold on. His arm brushed the
handle of the wagon's hand siren, mounted on the doorpost.
He gave it a hard crank. A whining wail rose above the noise
of the engine. Pedestrians scattered from the ambulance's
path.

A bullet struck the windshield. Bauer ducked from the
shower of glass, and looked back up. The captain was still at
the wheel, clutching it like a life preserver. The windshield
had vanished. Von Planetz pushed the one remaining piece,
jutting up from a corner, out of his way.

They were nearing the intersection.

Bauer squeezed into the space between the seat and
the floor, facing sideways out the open door, giving him
the protection of the front hood and a 180-degree view
on the passenger side.

The captain swerved once, to the protesting squeal of the
front tires, then steadied again.

The ambulance hit the intersection at sixty miles an hour.
Red Guards, crouching on the street on both sides, fired
wildly as they shot past. Bauer glanced at the captain. His
lips were drawn back over his teeth in fierce determination.

"Hold on!" he yelled.

Von Planetz spun the wheel hard to his left, throwing the
van into a skidding turn. It bounced and swayed over the
rough cobblestones and nearly flipped over. Bauer clutched
the doorpost to keep the centrifugal force from tossing him
out into the street.

The ambulance accelerated out of the turn and headed
across the Trinity Bridge.

Von Planetz jumped on the brake. Through the empty
windshield frame Bauer saw the problem. An armored car
was blocking the middle of the bridge.

"We're an ambulance!" Bauer shouted. "They'll let us pass!"

The captain didn't think so. "Not when they see who's chasing us."

Bauer looked behind them. The entrance onto the bridge behind them was now swarming with Red Guards. "We'll have to risk it. We can't go back."

The captain threw the Dodge into gear again and started forward.

Bauer opened Morozov's satchel and fished out the last remaining tomato can. "You have a match?"

The captain fumbled for the matchbox in his tunic and handed it across.

The ambulance clattered up the bridge, rapidly closing the distance with the armored car. A gunner was watching them from the turret, his machine gun twitching back and forth nervously in its mount.

Bauer lit the fuse. He felt suddenly lightheaded. He let go of the siren and pressed his forehead against the dashboard. The dizziness abated.

They passed the armored car traveling at about fifty miles an hour, bucking over the rough cobblestones of the bridge like a galloping horse.

The gunner in the armored car's turret, suddenly aware of the chase in progress, opened fire on the Dodge. Von Planetz cramped the wheel alternately right and left, sending the ambulance into a precarious zigzag to avoid the fire.

Bauer grabbed the doorpost, swung out onto the running board, and heaved the bomb.

Seconds later a blast of orange smoke belched straight up out of the armored car's turret, like a chimney fire. Two figures ran from the side doors, smacking at the flames on their clothes.

The captain accelerated across the bridge and exited onto the wide plaza of the Champs de Mars and turned right, leaving their pursuers far behind. The square, in dramatic contrast to Finland Station and the Kshesinskaya Mansion, was deserted. They drove past the massive Winter Palace and Admiralty building, and turned right again. This took them across a smaller bridge onto Vasilyevsky Island. Von Planetz followed the embankment for a couple of blocks, turned left into a narrow, unlit side street, and pulled the ambulance over to the curb.

The captain turned off the ignition and collapsed against the steering wheel.

Bauer leaned toward him. "You okay?"

Von Planetz raised his head and grinned weakly. His forehead was damp with sweat. "I've never done anything like that before."

"Don't tell me," Bauer said. "That was the best driving I've ever seen."

The captain beamed with pleasure.

Bauer braced his hands on the dash. His left arm was wet all the way to his fingertips.

"You're losing a lot of blood," Von Planetz said. "There must be something in the back. Let me look."

The American didn't argue. After the exertion of the last few minutes he felt too weak to move. The captain slid back the door and climbed into the back of the ambulance. He bumped around, lit some matches, and finally emerged with a roll of cotton dressing and a bottle of antiseptic solution.

Bauer removed his pistol and holster, then struggled out of his coat and shirt and sat quietly while the German officer dressed the wound.

"It's not so bad," the captain said, wiping away the blood. "A flesh wound. A few centimeters deep. It should stop bleeding if you keep the arm elevated. And still."

"I guess I'm lucky you weren't a better shot."

Von Planetz didn't reply. He made a sling out of the bandage material and tied it behind Bauer's neck. "Put your arm through it," he said.

Bauer winced and slipped his forearm through the sling and adjusted it. "Thanks. I'll be okay. Just tired, that's all."

The captain slid back into the driver's seat and pulled the package of Russian cigarettes from his pocket. He offered one to Bauer. The American waved it away. "You didn't see any brandy while you were back there, did you?"

Von Planetz shook his head. "Sorry."

"What time is it?"

The Captain looked at his wristwatch. "Near three."

"It's been a long night."

Von Planetz agreed.

"When did you first get onto me?"

The captain pushed his glasses against his nose. "Zurich," he answered.

Bauer whistled softly. "Jesus! That soon. How did you find out?"

Von Planetz told him about the American consul, McNally. "I persuaded my friend Steiner of the Zurich police to arrest you. But you slipped away. After that I was never entirely sure that you were real. That disguise of yours was ingenious. Really very clever."

"But you figured it out."

Von Planetz shrugged modestly. "Eventually. But not before giving you plenty of time to carry out your mission. I couldn't understand why you waited so long. Why did you?"

Bauer told him about the cane, his all-night wait in the ceiling of the lavatory, and his discovery of Inessa's sabotage.

"You'd only have killed his double, in any case."

"True." Bauer craned his head around. "You sure you didn't see some brandy back there?"

Von Planetz looked again and found a bottle of Kentucky bourbon. Bauer tried to open it with his free hand but couldn't manage it. The captain took it from him, broke the seal, popped the cork, and handed the bottle back to Bauer. The American took a long drink, then offered it to the German.

Von Planetz tasted it cautiously. "How did you get across the border?" he asked.

Bauer told him of the chase with Morozov out on the river ice. "What about you?"

"False passport. What happened to Morozov?"

"I killed him. At his request."

Von Planetz opened his mouth to ask Bauer what he meant, then changed his mind. He struck a match against the dashboard and lit the cigarette he had been holding in his hand.

"What did Lenin say to you, by the way?" Bauer wanted to know. "Back there on the stairs?"

Von Planetz grinned. "He said . . . 'Don't obstruct the stairway, comrades.'"

Bauer laughed out loud. The bourbon and the loss of blood were making him giddy. "That's something to tell our grandchildren."

The captain puffed on the cigarette and exhaled the smoke through the broken windshield. "You didn't kill him. Why?"

Bauer took another drink from the bottle, then reached through the windshield and placed it carefully on the ambulance hood. "I don't know," he said.

The captain looked at him. "To protect the woman? Miss Armand?"

"Zinoviev may not like her. But he'd never kill her."

"Why are you so sure?"

"Lenin's in love with her. Did you know that?"

"No."

"Well, he is. And Zinoviev knows it. She can do whatever she damn pleases and get away with it."

Von Planetz told Bauer about his interrogation of Inessa. "I myself was very intimidated by her. I felt I was in the presence of someone like a great stage actress—so much beauty and charm, and she knew how to use it."

Bauer nodded.

The captain reached out on the hood and retrieved the bottle of bourbon. "Then why didn't you kill him? You went to so much trouble for nothing."

Bauer pressed a hand against his forehead. It felt warm. "I could have killed him. That was enough."

"I don't believe you."

"You tell me why, then."

"Because you are also in love with Miss Armand."

"No."

"You didn't want to destroy all her hopes. Even if you disagreed with them."

Bauer rested his head against the seat back and let a long silence pass. "I'm sorry we're on different sides, Captain," he said.

"You're drunk, Herr Bauer."

"So are you, Herr Captain."

Bauer stuck his head out the window. Streaks of gray had begun to lighten the sky above the warehouses. "I've gotta take a piss," he mumbled.

He stepped unsteadily off the running board, clutching the doorpost for support, then felt his way around toward the back of the ambulance and unbuttoned his fly.

When he returned to the front, the German captain was pointing his pistol at him.

"I'm sorry, Herr Bauer," he said. "There's no other way."

He looked sorry, Bauer thought, trying to button the last button on the top of his fly. He seemed on the verge of tears. "What do you mean?"

"I have to kill you."

"Hey, come on. . . ."

"My wife needs medical help. My government has promised it in return for this. She'll die otherwise."

Bauer sat down on the running board. "You don't have to shoot me, for Chrissake. We'll work something out."

"I don't see how."

"Why not? Just *tell* them you shot me." He pointed to his sling. "In fact, you did. How will they know I'm not dead?"

Von Planetz shook his head.

"How are you going to prove to them you killed me? You going to lug my corpse all the way back to Berlin? Or just cut off my ears?"

"I'll take your papers. Your identification."

"What identification? I came as Blum. And I threw his stuff away back in Stockholm."

The captain pushed at his glasses in agitation and wiped his forehead with his palm. "I can't let Marthe die. She's all I have."

"We can work out something, you and I. I'll tell you how."

Over the bottle of bourbon the two men argued out the details.

Later the captain stared out at the gloomy stretch of alleyway that was beginning to materialize before them in the predawn. "Where are we?".

"I thought you knew, the way you were driving."

"I've never been here in my life."

Bauer pressed his fingers against the edges of his moustache. Through the open windshield a cold breeze blew against his face. "Wherever we are, we'd better start thinking about getting out."

The stub of Von Planetz's cigarette was burning his fingers. He flicked it out the window. "We have to find the docks. They can't be far."

"Why the docks?"

"It's the only way out. You can't drive out, because it's through the war zone. The train takes too long. You have to go all the way back through Finland again. So the only way is by ship."

"Ship? From here?"

"From right here. The Neva River sits at the mouth of the Gulf of Finland. That issues right into the Baltic. Stockholm is about seven hundred kilometers, straight west of here. There is supposed to be a Swedish icebreaker in port at this moment. I verified that in Haparanda. I don't know when it sails, but my plan was to seek asylum from the ship's captain and just wait on board until they could take me to Sweden."

"How do you know they'll take you?"

Captain von Planetz shrugged. "I don't."

"We'll go together. Stockholm would suit me just fine."

"How do you know they'll take you?"

Bauer laughed. "They'll take both of us, because I'll make it worth their while." Bauer patted Morozov's satchel, still wedged between the seats. He hadn't counted, but he had seen enough to know that the cloth bags at the bottom contained twelve million Swedish krona—the rough equivalent of two and a half million dollars.

Bauer picked up the bottle of bourbon from the hood and tipped it up against the faint light reddening the eastern sky. About an inch remained. He had started to offer a toast to their safe journey home, when a profound lightheadedness overcame him. The bottle slipped from his grasp and he collapsed against the dashboard, unconscious.

Captain von Planetz drove the ambulance to the docks and found the Swedish icebreaker. With the help of two crew members, he carried Bauer on board.

The icebreaker reached Stockholm a week later.

As part of his pact with Captain Von Planetz, Harry Bauer remained in Sweden until many years after the war, living under an alias.

He also obtained for the captain a persuasive set of personal documents—including a staged photograph of himself lying in a pool of blood with his eyes closed and his mouth open—to take to the captain's commanding officer in Berlin as proof of his death.

And he made certain that the same bogus information was discretely leaked to the American and English embassies in Stockholm, so that it would find its way to the appropriate parties.

It did.

FRIDAY
JULY 21, 1961

Director Dulles watched his public affairs officer, Jim Adams, place the plastic reel on the big Nagra recorder and thread the slender strand of electromagnetic tape through the heads and onto the pickup reel.

The director pulled his pipe from his jacket pocket, stuck it absently in his mouth, and stared at the other items arranged on the desk in front of him—Bauer's passports, Zimmermann's letter to Lenin, and the innocent-looking notebook that had kept him up most of the night.

Harry Bauer's story had disturbed him in ways he had not anticipated.

A rogue agent, a misfit who wouldn't take orders. The enemy of authority, a man who ignored channels, who wouldn't respect the chain of command, who sneered at rank and discipline. He had taken on the bureaucracy of four countries— Germany, Russia, England, and the United States—and single-handedly made asses and fools of them all.

And from the evidence, they had richly deserved it.

All his professional life he had been part of that bureaucracy. Its ritual and its methods had nurtured him. Men like Harry Bauer were anathema to that system. They represented the path of chaos and anarchy, the simplistic romance of the rugged individual against the impersonal machinations of governments and nations.

Dulles couldn't decide whether he felt sorry for Bauer—or whether he envied him.

An acrid drop of nicotine from the pipe's stem spilled onto the director's tongue, causing him to gag. He removed the pipe to clean it.

On the matter of Lenin, the director happened to have a little secret of his own. It was a minor matter, but it was something he had had guilty twinges about thousands of times during his long career in intelligence. He wanted suddenly to tell Adams about it.

"Did you know that Lenin called our legation in Bern the Sunday before he left for Russia," he said, looking over at his deputy. "I took the call. He told me it was crucial that he speak with someone there right away. He was quite insistent."

Adams glanced up from the tape deck in surprise. "What did he want?"

Dulles inserted the slender wire stalk of the pipe cleaner through the well-gnawed mouthpiece of his pipe, jerked it back and forth a few times, withdrew it, examined the collection of brownish-yellow tar collected on the fabric, then tossed the cleaner into the wastebasket under his desk. "To my everlasting regret, I never found out. It was late Sunday, and I was the only one on duty. I had a date with a girl I knew, Helene Herzog. I was damned if I was going to break it to listen to the problems of some Russian exile. I told him to call back the following morning. Of course by then he was already on his way to Petersburg. I was twenty-four. Naïve and arrogant. I can tell you I never turned down an offer like that again."

Dulles rubbed the bowl of the pipe between his cheek and the side of his nose to oil the wood. "I think I know now what he wanted," he said. "This letter from Zimmermann to Lenin that Bauer saved all these years. That's the key. Bauer must have found it in Morozov's satchel, along with that enormous cache of Swedish krona. Like the money, Lenin didn't dare risk having the letter discovered—and probably confiscated—at the Finland border. So he entrusted it to his bodyguard to smuggle across."

Dulles twisted the stem and mouthpiece of his pipe together again, and stuck it back in his mouth. "That letter would have compromised him utterly," he continued, the words coming out between clenched teeth. "It was written proof that he had made a deal with Zimmermann, and proof that Zimmermann had asked him to try to mislead the Americans about his intentions. I think that's what he must have had in mind to tell us at the legation. Since I rebuffed him, he did the next best thing—got off that cable directly to President Wilson, promising to continue the war against Germany if he should come to power. A classic example of disinformation, I suppose."

Adams depressed the PLAY button on the Nagra. The two men watched the tape begin to unwind slowly from one reel and stream through the playback head onto the take-up.

"But why didn't Bauer kill him?" Adams demanded rhetorically. "He had never failed on a mission before. Just in terms of pride alone, he should have killed him. He had gone to such lengths, and then he just backed off. I don't understand it."

Dulles pulled the pipe out of his mouth. "That's because you're looking at it from the advantage of hindsight. It's easy to see the consequences now. But it must have looked very different to Bauer then. For one thing, he had the satisfaction of knowing that Lenin lived only because he let him live. For a man like Bauer, that would have been important. In his own eyes, his mission was a success. And he didn't give two hoots for anyone else's opinion."

The tape continued to turn, but nothing came from the speaker but a sterile magnetic hiss. Adams turned up the volume. The hiss grew louder.

"And suddenly he had all that money," Dulles continued. "He knew it was Zimmermann's down payment on the revolution, and he must have supposed that its disappearance would not only cripple Lenin's efforts, but open a rift between the two men. Suspicion was high on both sides to begin with. The missing money might well have sabotaged the arrangement. In a way, I'm surprised it didn't."

"Well, then Bauer was simply a short-sighted egotist," Adams declared. "He didn't give a damn about the Allied cause or Russia's fate—or anything else. He was out for himself."

"That's not quite true," Dulles replied. He selected one of the passports from the pile in front of him and slid it across the desk toward Adams. "Did you notice this?"

Adams looked over at the document.

"It's a Swedish passport, made out in the name of a Karl Gustaffson, but with Bauer's photograph. This must have been the identity he lived under in Sweden after the war. There are only two visa stamps in it. One shows him entering the Soviet Union on April 23, 1921. The other shows him leaving on October 26, the same year."

Adams studied the visa stamps. "What's their significance?"

"Can't you guess?"

Adams scratched his chin thoughtfully. "No. I'm afraid I can't."

"He went to find Inessa Armand. I suspect she's the real reason he didn't kill Lenin. Even if he didn't believe Zinoviev's threat—which was sheer bluff, I'm sure—he must have come to see that Lenin's death would break her heart. And he couldn't bear to break her heart. He despised Lenin and what he stood for, but he envied Inessa's ability to believe in something outside herself. It must have been that quality in her that drew him to her. She had hope, and he envied that. She believed in something. He didn't. But if he destroyed Lenin, he would destroy her, too—along with the one hope in life he did have—seeing her again. She was more important to him than any country or cause."

Adams shook his head dismissively. "He was a fool. He hardly knew her."

Dulles chuckled at the grim irony of it all. "History turns on trivial chance as often as on momentous tides," he said.

He gazed across his large office at the tripod with the map of Cuba on it, covered with a heavy black cloth to hide the secret celluloid overlays with their markings of the units and the landing site for the abortive invasion of that island that had taken place two months earlier.

The Agency was still reeling from the fiasco. Trivial chance, indeed. Had Bauer killed Lenin there would never have been a Bay of Pigs. And Allen Dulles, career intelligence officer and director of the CIA for eight years, would not have been forced into an early retirement by a President eager to shift the blame away from himself. But the decisions had been made. After a discreet interval—a couple more months, probably—he would be let out to pasture, under a cloud that would stay with him to his grave.

"What happened to the Armand woman?" Adams asked.

"She died that same year in the Caucasus. Typhus. Bauer must have stayed with her until the end. He came back to the United States late in 1921 and started using his own name again. Harding was President, and the government had either forgotten about him or had the good sense to leave him alone."

The tape continued running silently for nearly half an hour. Disgusted, Adams clicked the machine off. "Looks like somebody forgot to press the record button. Sorry to waste so much time, sir."

"How much tape is left?"

Adams glanced at the reels and shrugged. "Another fifteen minutes?"

Dulles nodded. "Leave it there. I'll check it later."

"I promised to return these things to his widow," Adams reminded him, gesturing toward the items on the director's desk.

Dulles tickled his moustache with the edge of his finger and thought about it. "The tape and the passports, all right. But not the letter or the notebook."

He despised himself even as his mouth formed the words. He was going to cheat Harry Bauer out of his small place in history so that the places of those more important in the scale of things would not be diminished. It was an act of sabotage against the truth, but knowing the right secrets to keep—and then keeping them—was part of his franchise. Probably the most important part. Bauer wouldn't have liked it, but he would certainly have understood.

"They could still do harm," he said, standing up behind his desk to indicate that the meeting was over. "I'll take them home."

Adams left and the director turned on the recorder again, determined to let the tape run all the way to the end.

Some minutes later his patience was rewarded. The hissing was replaced by a low-pitched hum, and then the sharp scraping noises of someone setting up a microphone. A few faint whispers were followed by a low, garbled voice and the rattle of a bed's headboard.

The director turned up the volume.

Abruptly a voice boomed out at him. It was so astonishingly loud that it distorted the speaker's sound and made the director jump.

There was only one word. A cry from the heart, reaching out across the space of decades:

"INESSA!"

ACKNOWLEDGMENTS

I have drawn upon many written sources to create this novel, but one book in particular, *The Sealed Train* by Michael Pearson (Putnam, New York, 1975), was of special value. This excellent account of Lenin's journey from Zurich to Petrograd, drawn largely from original sources in German and Russian, provided me with an accurate timetable of events and a detailed background against which to set my narrative.

Other sources include: *Churchill, the Last Lion* by William Manchester (Little Brown, Boston, 1983); *Black Night, White Snow,* by Harrison E. Salisbury (Doubleday, Garden City, NY, 1977); *The Life and Death of Lenin* by Robert Payne (Simon and Schuster, New York, 1964); *America Enters the World* by Page Smith (McGraw-Hill, 1985); *Her Majesty's Secret Service* by Christopher Andrew (Viking Penguin Inc., New York, 1986); *The Code-Breakers* by David Kahn (Macmillan, New York, 1967); *The Zimmermann Telegram* by Barbara W. Tuchman (Viking, 1958); *To the Finland Station* by Edmund Wilson (Doubleday, Garden City, NY, 1940); *Northern Underground* by Michael Futrell (Faber and Faber, London, 1963); *Memories of Lenin* by Nadezhda K. Krupskaya (Martin Lawrence, London, 1930); *The Autobiography of a Sexually Emancipated Communist Woman* by Alexandra Kollontai (Schocken Books, New York, 1975); *Imperialism and Imperialist War (1914–1917)* by V. I. Lenin (International Publishers, New York, undated); *My Four Years in*

Germany by James W. Gerard (George H. Doran Company, New York, 1917); *The Iron Ration* by George Abel Schreiner (John Murray, London, 1918); *The Red Heart of Russia* by Bessie Beatty (The Century Company, New York, 1918); *With the Armies of the Tsar* by Florence Farmborough (Stein and Day, Briarcliff Manor, NY, 1975); *The Land of Deepening Shadow, Germany-at-War* by D. Thomas Curtin (George H. Doran Company, New York, 1917); *True Adventures of the Secret Service* by Major C. E. Russell (Doubleday, Page & Company, Garden City, NY, 1924); *Railways and War before 1918* by D. Bishop and K. Davies (Blanford Press, London, 1972); *Railways in the Years of Pre-Eminence, 1905–1919* by O. S. Nock (Blandford Press, London, 1971); *Military Transport of World War I* by C. Ellis and D. Bishop (Blandford Press, London, 1970); *The Locomotives That Baldwin Built* by Fred Westing (Bonanza Books, New York, 1966); *The Lore of the Train* by C. Hamilton Ellis (Crescent Books, New York, 1977); *The Boys' Book of Locomotives* by J. R. Howden (The McClure Company, New York, 1907); *Switzerland, Handbook for Travellers* by Karl Baedeker (Charles Scribner's Sons, New York, 1913); *Bradshaw's Continental Railway Guide*, No. 804, May 1914 (Henry Blacklock & Co., London, 1914).

I want also to acknowledge the help of the Strand Bookstore, the Argosy, the Military Bookman, and The Complete Traveller Bookstore. And my special thanks to Russell Snyder, a friend and train buff, for his generous advice and assistance.

BE SURE TO READ
ALL THE BESTSELLING
SUPERTHRILLERS
BY ROBERT LUDLUM